D0199404

HARLEM MOON
BROADWAY

Other books by David Haynes

Right by My Side

Somebody Else's Mama

Heathens

Live at Five

All American Dream Dolls

FOR CHILDREN

The West Seventh Series

Retold African American Folktales

The Full Matilda

A Novel

David Haynes

Harlem Moon

Broadway Books

New York

This book is a work of fiction. Names, characters, businesses, organizations, places, events, and incidents either are the product of the author's imagination or are used fictitiously. Any resemblance to actual persons, living or dead, events, or locales is entirely coincidental.

Published by Harlem Moon, an imprint of Broadway Books, a division of Random House, Inc.

PRINTED IN THE UNITED STATES OF AMERICA

Visit our website at www.harlemmoon.com

First edition published 2004

BOOK DESIGN BY AMANDA DEWEY

Library of Congress Cataloging-in-Publication Data

Haynes, David, 1955-
The full Matilda : a novel / David Haynes.—1st ed.
p. cm.
1. African American domestics—Fiction. 2. African American families—Fiction. 3. Washington (D.C.)—Fiction. I. Title.

PS3558.A8488F85 2004
813'.54—dc22

2003068773

ISBN 0-7679-1569-0

10 9 8 7 6 5 4 3 2 1

This book is dedicated to the memory of my mother,
Edna Ruth McClennon Haynes, the single most gracious
hostess the planet Earth may ever know.

. . .

To think that the sun rose in the east—that men and women
were flexible, real, alive—that every thing was alive,
To think that you and I did not see, feel, think, nor bear our part,
To think that we are now here and bear our part.

—WALT WHITMAN, "To Think of Time"
from *Leaves of Grass*

ACKNOWLEDGMENTS

I owe a debt of gratitude to the Virginia Center for the Creative Arts, which provided space and solitude for my writing. Special thanks to Dale and Mary Clemons for inspiring tours of both the Missouri Botanical Gardens as well as their own.

The thing my father told me was, Matilda my girl, the world as we know it is passing away. Any day now our entire way of life will cease to exist. We must be prepared!

That dear, sweet man, lecturing me thus. He had absolutely no idea whom he was dealing with.

The First Thing I Have to Tell You

. . .

We Housewrights have never been famous. We have never been the sort of people whose names you find mentioned in the society pages, nor anywhere else in the newspaper, for that matter. If you must know, my father thought it tasteless the way a certain sort of person paraded his life before the public, as if that person's entire raison d'être were to be ever part of some seamy side show, part of some ongoing masked ball. In Father's mind, the higher the person's station in life, the greater the shame at said person's lack of good judgment about such matters.

It is also the case that the nature of our family business has always been about being, at the optimum, mostly invisible. If my father did his job well (and my father always did his job well), you would not notice that he had been there at all.

That being said, those who traveled certain corridors in our nation's capital did know the Housewright name. If you travel such corridors yourself, I'm sure you already understand how these things work.

Let's say you are a seasoned politician and you have only recently been elected as the junior senator from your state. Big things are expected of you as a member of our nation's most prestigious legislative body, and big things are expected as well on the social horizon. Back in your home state, you have achieved for yourself and your family a certain prominence, and, of course, you are used to the finer things that life has to offer, to a gracious standard of living. It would therefore be of critical interest to you in your newest role that your affairs at every level, both in the halls of Congress as well as in your home, be arranged in a way that stand to secure you the prominent status you fully expect to be yours.

You would soon come to discover that the rules are different in the District of Columbia. This city is unlike any other you've known. To be specific, while Washington has always been and always will be a community in love with money, having money in this town buys you almost nothing in terms of social acceptance or prestige. The things that matter on your new turf are subtler and yet more telling than the bottom line of your portfolio. It makes a difference, for example, the address of your residence. It makes a difference how and when you entertain. One would not, for instance, even consider hosting a dinner party on those evenings when certain figures of prominence are known to be doing the same. In the same vein, you would be expected to know to whom invitations must always be extended, and which others are better excluded from your lists. When seating your guests for dinner, certain individuals are never seated next to others. This ambassador prefers a particular cigar with his brandy, while that one delights in a bowl of soft mints at his fingertips; and all of this information is critical. Unfortunately, you, being new to town, would have no way of knowing such things. It would be in your best interest, therefore, to retain the services of someone who does know, someone to run your household in a way that establishes you in Washington as a man of stature and of good character. You inquire around. And were the name Housewright not the first you heard, it would come awfully high on the list of persons who might be of assistance in these matters.

We Housewrights have a long and distinguished history in service. In his later years, Grandfather Josiah ran the estate of a wealthy industrialist up along the Hudson River, in New York. He'd begun his career with the livery of a branch of that same family here in Washington, and with his employer had occasion to return to the capital a number of times over his working life. (As you know, the sort of people who require our services tend to reside in our capital city at least once in any given generation.)

And when in Maryland, travelers, there is a plantation along the Severn River I recommend that you visit. There, near the fireplace in the central hall, you will find a daguerreotype of those who, around 1845, lived and worked in the main house. The suited gentleman behind the owner, the one with the crisp white tea towel over his arm, that would be Ezekiel, Josiah Housewright's father.

My own father began his career working in the kitchen of the house his father ran. Jacob, Cyrus, JulieAnne, and Bess. Those were the Housewright siblings. My father's employers insisted the children be schooled right alongside their own, that is, up until the time theirs were sent away to preparatory academies (finishing schools for the daughters). In the evenings and on weekends, my father, my uncle, and my aunts were expected to work with their parents, taking care of all that needed taking care of in households of that magnitude. Grandfather Josiah viewed this as something like an apprenticeship for his children, assuming, as one would, that his progeny would succeed him in the family profession. From what I was told, the man was something of a martinet when it came to standards and results. I can imagine him ripping the sheets from an improperly prepared bed and insisting that whichever child were responsible for the clumsy attempt return the bedding to the ironing board before trying it again on the mattress.

JulieAnne and Bess worked with their mother up on the second floor, supplementing the domestic staff. Mending, dusting, that sort of thing. I was told that my uncle Cyrus fell in love with horses and couldn't be kept from the stables. He trained to be a groom and a driver. Father made what might seem an odd choice. He opted to work in the kitchen.

Now as you can imagine, there is nothing glamorous about kitchen work. Peeling vegetables, scrubbing burnt casseroles and roasting pans. But old Jacob was no fool. You see, at an early age, my father figured out that the best place to keep tabs on everything that went on in the household would be right there in the kitchen. The family who owned the house would drop through to visit and sample whatever delicacy the cook was preparing and to inform her as to who might be expected for supper that evening. The household staff took their meals in the kitchen, as did those who maintained the grounds. In the winter anyone who had been outside would at some point in the day steal a few moments of warmth near the stove. Almost anyone on the staff could be counted on to share the latest gossip: the fact that "Sir" had ordered that Winthrop boy not be admitted to the house again unless accompanied by that no-good father of his, and how "Herself" (the disrespectful appellation some used for the wife of the household) had pitched a royal fit over being served a tough slice of lamb.

My father would linger stealthily over his scrubbing or chopping, and he would gather all of this talk into his memory. I don't believe he ever wrote down a word. He possessed one of those minds, one of those memories, where once he had heard a man's name, he never forgot it, nor would he forget the man's preferred brand of whisky or favorite dessert. And so it was that when he was ready to secure his own position, Jacob Housewright had already trained himself to be the most diligent and attentive accessory an important man could ever hope to employ.

The gentleman of the house expects a vehicle at the ready at all times, a fresh valise in the boot for those last-minute trips. He has his business callers presented with their libation of choice as soon as they are seated in his study, whereas the lady of the house prefers to call for tea service. The lady also wishes the packages from her excursions delivered with inconspicuous haste to her quarters. You are aware that her purchases are none of your concern, although her husband appreciates a discreet heads-up as to the extent of the day's expenditures.

Knowing such things made my father, even as a young man, a much sought after commodity.

Jacob Housewright obtained his first position through something of a ruse. This was during Josiah's employer's tenure in the capital, and a business associate of the industrialist reported that his manservant had fallen ill and had been sent home to his family. Frantic, quite literally helpless, the business associate had asked the industrialist if he couldn't make loan of one of his boys as a stopgap measure. You are familiar with, of course, the old maxim about good help, and this is particularly the case with exclusive and high-quality staff. My grandfather ran a tight operation, and had not been keen on giving up a valued hand for even an hour. Father, then only seventeen, and talented eavesdropper that he was, overheard his parents discussing the request. He volunteered himself for the position.

To put it mildly, Grandfather was less than sanguine about his son's ambitions. Here, this young pup who couldn't possibly know a goblet from a tumbler thought he would march into an important man's home and assume responsibility for its efficient operation. And you should know that it has long been a Housewright doctrine that each generation's work reflects on the generation preceding it. My grandfather wasn't willing to risk the family reputation by sending someone whom he believed to be less than fully prepared into such a high-profile position. He told his son "no," and that the business associate would just need to search for help elsewhere.

Father viewed this rebuff as only a temporary setback. While always professionally reticent—and appropriately so—my father could also take bold and direct action as was needed. Scouring the neighborhood where the business associate lived, Father visited each of the service establishments where persons of this standing might trade. Laundries, haberdashers, that sort of thing. By happenstance he stumbled across a tailor who had made for this gentleman some new dress shirts, and Father bluffed at having been sent to retrieve them. Costuming himself, then, in a manservant's proper afternoon attire (white collared shirt, bow tie, dark short coat), he presented himself at the needy gentleman's home.

"I've seen to your order of shirts, sir. Shall I place them in your wardrobe?"

I can picture my father standing at that man's door, fair and handsome, back straight and tall. I see his new employer, momentarily startled, but quickly assuming that this fellow must be the replacement boy he'd been asking after. Things would have become quite frayed around the house since old Pompey had been sent back home, and while this sapling looked a little on the green side, he certainly made a nice appearance and spoke well for himself.

"Very well, then," the older man would have said. He'd needed those new shirts desperately, had forgotten where old Pompey said they were being prepared. "Have one ready for the evening, by the way, with my summer jacket. We'll be attending that garden party uptown. And bring me a brandy, if you would."

I picture my father delivering that brandy (along with a neatly folded afternoon paper, of course).

"Thank you, uh . . . what's your name?"

"Jacob, sir," he would have replied, and, expecting no further conversation from a gentleman settling in for his afternoon's consideration of the news, my father would have set about getting his new place of responsibility in an order that made sense to him.

As it happened, Father's new employer's requirements were

much less taxing than those at the house my grandfather ran. The old gentleman operated from a smaller townhouse just northwest of Dupont Circle, in an area that had begun to be populated by the embassies of minor and obscure nations. He was in Washington to help guide the meanderings of a hapless and dull-witted son who had somehow gotten himself elected to the House of Representatives. Days for my father would be generally idle, tending to the usual trivia that one sees to in a small home, and in the evenings my father would dress his employer and deliver him to his son the congressman's house, or to a party they would both be attending. This gentleman knew Washington from his own tenure in Congress, during which he had spearheaded expansion of the railroads and the acquisition of western lands. A longtime widower, he now lived comfortably on the investments that had benefited from his legislative largesse.

Too young to be comfortable visiting with the other more seasoned servants, my father would often spend these evenings positioned where he could listen unobtrusively to the conversations of the congressman and his father. He remembered to me that one almost never heard the son speaking at these affairs, that the father held forth at all times and on all matters, now and again throwing in his son's direction openings that allowed the younger man to demonstrate his sagacity either by adding to the discourse some dutifully memorized fact or by, at the very least, agreeing enthusiastically with his father's brilliance. I may or may not surprise you by revealing that this rather dunderheaded young man would go on to become one of our nation's most distinguished and beloved political figures.

You have also noted by this point the care I have taken not to reveal the names of these individuals. You may think me unnecessarily coy or mysterious, but please understand that that is not my intention. Understand that the Housewrights have always been discreet; part of that long tradition of retainers who could be counted on not to repeat their employer's business in the street, a commitment that I believe extends to the grave (and perhaps beyond, depending, of course, on what the circumstances on the other side might be). And, yes, I am aware that if you happen to be among those who have traveled in these same circles, you more than likely will recognize in these stories certain individuals by their attributes, by the thinly disguised details of their personal lives, and so be it. There are some things about which I feel compelled to have my say, and so I have had to relax my own discretion by a degree or two. Father would understand and forgive, I am sure, just as I have always tried myself to do the same.

Toward the end of his son's third term, my father's first employer told him that he had no desire to spend his final days in this "fetid swamp," and that he had therefore decided to return home, allowing his son to sink or swim as he would. The old man did everything short of kidnapping "his Jake" in order to keep him in his employ, and Father, I know, gave staying with this household serious consideration. If you've never been in service, you perhaps wouldn't understand the attachment we make to those who employ us. At the risk of indelicacy I will say that a gentleman's home assistant has the most intimate contact with the man he works for, personally handling every garment, both clean and soiled, preparing baths, administering medicine and comfort as would be required. My father knew that this failing creature both needed and depended on him. Over time, a gentleman and his retinue become something like a hand and a much-used glove, each molded to the other's peculiar geography.

Across five years Jacob had learned this man's habits and predilections, and his employer had learned how best to make use of Father's many strengths. A relationship of this quality would not be easily replaced, on either man's part.

So it was with a good deal of personal regret that Father made the choice to stay in Washington, though I'd be remiss in not reporting two other factors that weighed heavily in his decision making.

Even as the household that Grandfather Josiah ran continued to operate in the efficiently sharp manner one would expect, considering who was at the helm, it seems that the lives of my uncle and my aunts were taking turns toward the unfortunate. While my father had settled effortlessly into his life of service, the rest of Josiah's children did everything in their power to cross fate.

My father's brother, Cyrus—who had been seen curling his lip contemptuously at ordinary requests, such as that he bring up the shine on the fittings alongside the new "horseless carriage" that Father's employer had purchased—had dared speak back to the man, if you can imagine. And when our father rebuffed him for this, as he'd been requested to do and as he well should have done, my uncle threatened to run off to a horse farm in Virginia.

Rumors floated through the kitchens of the better homes in Washington that Bess and JulieAnne had been keeping time with a lowly sort of person—dark-skinned colored men of the kind employed lading granite and marble to the new buildings along the National Mall. Even had these rumors not been substantiated, you can imagine my grandfather's mortification. Here were young women who had been groomed toward a loftier ambition. Grandfather envisioned his girls sinecured as personal attendants to the wives in prominent political households. From these positions my aunts would ally with men like himself and my father and form appropriate unions with these men, thus further securing their position in fine homes. Suddenly that dream threatened to come crashing down around my grandparents' heads. Josiah knew what could happen. He had seen it happen to the offspring in too many other families. The parents would begin to notice the coarsening of a child's language, sudden and inappropriate laughter, a formerly open face now hooded and cynical and cold. And by this point it would be too late. Who would want girls with reputations like these? What respectable household would even consider the risk?

Josiah was not the sort of man to stand by idly while all his hard work came to naught. He and my grandmother hadn't invested their lives training their girls in the finer nuances of domestic affairs to see them wrestled away by the common ilk. To see a daughter tricked up in rags and living in a back-alley lean-to, taking in mending and doing lord knew what else to feed a yard full of pickininnies: Not as long as Josiah Housewright lived would such a fate befall even one of his children.

Josiah called his family together. With my grandmother, Sarah, he and the two girls shared a small suite of rooms just off the kitchen of the Tenley Park mansion of his employer. Cyrus, in charge of driving (or at least for as long as he maintained his equanimity), had for years lived above the stable-turned-garage. We might think these rooms spartan by our standards, but I can assure you that at the turn of the century, my forebears lived quite comfortably. Their proximity to the ovens assured coziness in the winter, and while such tight quarters could be uncomfortable in the sweltering Potomac summers, remember that the entire household decamped to the Adirondacks in late May (often thick with pesky black flies, but altogether more pleasant than the oppressive heat of the nation's capital).

Jacob, evidently, had entirely misunderstood the reason for the family gathering. Instead of an airing of Grandfather's grievances, Father arrived expecting a routine family meal, and along with him arrived also a young lady by the name of Alma Dickerson. (She, by the way, would be the second reason my father declined to leave Washington.) The others had already seated themselves around the small parlor in my parents' quarters. I've never seen a picture of this meeting, but I did hear the tale from my father and have often re-created the scene in my head.

Uncle Cyrus, with his short trimmed beard, would have straddled his chair backward, legs splayed wide as if seated in a saddle. His brown eyes were the bright color of new pennies.

JulieAnne was slight and delicate with my grandmother's fine chiseled features. There would have been something about her that reminded you of the heroines in the popular novels of the day. You would expect her to be demure and sickly, but she was not. She would live thirty years longer than her older brother Jacob.

Bess had the quality of the pioneer women. Big boned, big breasted, and with an imposing voice, one pictured her somewhere on a prairie, widowed and with a dozen scrappy offspring whom she would rule with an iron fist. She would be able to handle her liquor, her weapons, and anything, human or otherwise, that messed with her brood. She, in her characteristic way, would have been the one to set things in motion.

"Now that his highness has arrived with his woman, can we

get this thing under way?" She would have addressed this to her father, who then, having larger game to subdue, would swallow back his rage at his daughter's impertinence. Jacob, inhaling to protest his sister's rudeness in front of a guest, would be signaled by his father to let it rest. That their father allowed the meeting to continue in the presence of a stranger is an indication of how desperate the situation had become, at least in Josiah's mind. Despite her presence, this relatively rare opportunity to have the entire clan together—unmolested by ringing bells or the ongoing tasks of running the big house—would not go to waste.

"Your mother and I have become concerned for the future of this family." Josiah sat next to his wife, and, as he spoke, he gathered Sarah's hand into his. "We thought it time we sit together and discuss the directions in which we are headed."

Cyrus laughed. "I thought I'd head on over to Foggy Bottom for some entertainments this evening." His sisters smiled at his wit, but Josiah slammed a hand onto the arm of his chair in frustration. Josiah knew of his younger son's "entertainments." They did not include the kinds of activities that persons of quality pursued (or if they did pursue them, a young man of good breeding knew not to discuss such matters in front of his sisters and his mother).

"This is the sort of thing I mean," Josiah roared, rising from his chair and pointing a finger into Cyrus's face. "All this . . . ill-disciplined wildness. What is to become of you? Of all of you?"

"Leave him be, Papa." This would be Bess again. "So the boy blows off a little steam now and then. So what. He spends all day licking the boots of these white people. He deserves some time away."

Josiah flapped his hands to indicate she should keep her voice down. Did the loudmouthed creature want them all thrown out on the street? He turned his attention to her.

"As for you, miss, well, I can hardly repeat the things people are saying about your doings. For shame, I say."

JulieAnne looked dispassionately at a small square of nothing in the corner. A childhood of unending criticism and rebuke had taught her to hold her opinions from these people. But Bess, egged on by her brother Cyrus's sneer, seemed to relish the fray.

"I'll tell you myself what I been doing. I been stepping out. I'll tell you who with. His name is JamesLee. My JimmyLee. He's a big, good-looking, brownskin Negro man. I'm gonna bring him here to meet you all."

Grandmother spoke up. "Is that how you were taught to speak? And you'll under no circumstances bring those people anywhere near this home."

"Why can't my JimmyLee come here? He brought that one in." Bess popped her chin in Alma's direction. Alma squirmed quietly in her chair. During this unpleasantness she had been giving her consideration to the pair of lovely new high-button shoes that swaddled her feet and to her own future. Could these really be Jacob's people? He had seemed so refined, but then one never knew. That's why they said it was a good idea to get a good look at the family before resigning oneself to joining it.

"That young man won't come here because your mother says so and I say so."

"Why? Because he a hod carrier? Because he comes from a family that barely keeps food on the table? Because he's not as yellow as this little gal he brung in?"

Alma recoiled at the insult.

"Yes, you. I'm talking about you."

"Bess, come on," Jacob pleaded. When he'd discovered the intent of the evening, he'd decided to stay out of the mess, but he figured he'd best speak up about this. "Alma's done nothing. Leave her out, will you? And Mama and Papa—"

Bess faced him with the fierce look of a street fighter. "What do you know? You've been gone from here. You don't know how they do us. You don't know what Julie and Rus and me have to put up with."

"But I do so know. You do the same work that we've always done."

"Listen to your brother. He's the only one of you who has made this family proud."

Cyrus popped his hands together, offering a flat round of applause.

"Enough of this!" their father ordered. "This is getting us nowhere. Decisions have been made, and the reason you all are here is to listen. Cyrus, I will see to you in my own time and in my own way." Josiah gave him a stern look. Cyrus shook his head and mumbled something under his breath that no one understood.

"As for you girls, your mother and I have been talking. We decided that we've kept you here under our direction for too long. It's time that each of you had your own independent set of responsibilities. Something to discourage you from these little . . . explorations."

Bess rolled her eyes.

"Your mother and I have been asking around the community and we've come up with a list of promising situations that we think will suit the both of you well."

JulieAnne sniffed, still keeping her eyes in the corner, the blank view now blurred by the steady flow of tears.

"Situations!" screamed Bess. "And don't tell me to keep my voice down. Julie and I don't want any . . . situations." She breathed deep with rage. "Apparently some of you didn't follow the news that day, but slavery's been over—"

Josiah stood up and slapped her to the ground.

Their mother lowered herself to her daughter and extended a chapped and dry hand, rubbing soft circles around her shoulders and up and down her spine. Through the thin calico she could feel the strong muscles that lined Bess's powerful and broad back.

"Oh, my honey," she whispered. "I'm so sorry. I know it's hard. It's hard for everyone. But this is what we do."

"Not me. Not me. I don't do this," Bess cried meekly, almost subdued.

"Honey. That's what there is for us."

"No."

Jacob stood over his sister and his mother, his fists clenched in rage.

"What, then? What?" he asked. "What are you going to do, Bess?"

"Jacob, don't." JulieAnne broke her silence, extended a hand to her oldest brother. He pushed it away.

"You're going to take your fortune and open a bank, I imagine? What are you going to do? Head off to one of those Negro colleges? Do you know what they teach our girls at those places? I'll give you a hint: You're already doing it."

Alma gently guided Jacob back to his seat. She had never seen this man's temper. Mild, yet ferocious. Frightening, but also in some way appealing to her.

For a moment or two the audible sobbing of JulieAnne was the only sound in the room. Josiah broke the silence.

"I'll tell you what she's going to do. Tomorrow morning, Bess and her sister will visit some of the households where we've heard they are looking for a good girl or two. You'll look things over. Talk with some of the women on staff. People who know about these things assure me that these are fine homes you'll have to choose from. The work will be hard. As you already know. But you'll be taken care of.

"That's it, then. You'll head out tomorrow and I'm sure that we'll find for both girls an amiable match. I will get you girls situated if it's the last thing I do."

Bess made a scoffing sound.

"What was that, miss?"

Bess was still sitting in her mother's arms, but her tears had stopped. She smiled a bitter smile and shook her head.

"I'm not going," she said.

"I beg your pardon?"

Bess stood, faced her father, and pulled her shoulders back. She turned her palms out in a way that indicated her resolve. Something—her calm, her countenance, her flat fierce eyes—said clearly to her papa that his balled fist would do him no good. The already-fading handprint rouging her left cheek would be the last thing that he would leave anywhere on her person. Which left for Josiah only a quavering finger and a shopworn speech.

"I'm in charge of this house, young lady. You are only

eighteen years old, and if I spend some of the great goodwill I've earned in this city to arrange for you an acceptable situation, then you will take it and appreciate it.

"Nineteen. It's 1905. I'm nineteen, Papa. JulieAnne is twenty-one. And I'm not going into service."

Josiah sat down hard in his favorite rocker. My father told me this was the first time that his father had seemed old to him.

"Very well," my grandfather said. He pinched his lips together in resolution. "If you don't want to work, then I don't know what's to become of you."

"Josiah, no," my grandmother gasped.

But Bess, she was unfazed. "I don't know either."

I imagine that no one moved for a moment or two. Father would have looked back between his own father and his sister, would have seen them staring each other down, would have been mesmerized by the determination set on each face. He may, in fact, have told me that this is what he did, but this is one of those instances in which his stories and my imagination become too intertwined. He told me that he always wondered if at that moment there might have been something that he could have said or done to make things come out differently, but that was him talking very late in his life.

"Julie," Bess said, and beckoned her sister to rise and follow.

"Mama," JulieAnne sobbed.

"Josiah, please," my grandmother begged.

Bess supported her sister out the door. JulieAnne kept her eye on her mother, but her younger sister did not look back.

Cyrus backed off the chair he'd been straddling. He feigned removing a nonexistent top hat from his head, bowed deeply from the waist, a bow for royalty, one my grandfather had drilled into him at a young age. He nodded at my brother, his brown eyes rimmed with sadness, and he followed his sisters out the door.

Thus, my aunts and my uncle disappeared forever from the Housewright family.

But this is Father's story, after all, and you can see now why, despite his loyalty to his first employer, he chose to remain close to my parents. Yes, and to Alma. She would become my mother.

When I found a record of Mother's birth, I realized that on the sad night that my father brought her around to meet his family, she would have been only sixteen. Which may explain why they waited another six years to be married.

I'm sure it was also the case that my father wanted to establish himself fully in his new position before bringing a wife into the household. When the first employer left the capital, Jacob Housewright had an array of homes clamoring after his services. A justice of the Supreme Court called personally on his employer to ask after him. He sat down with Josiah and considered the range of offers. They talked about the advantages of serving with a longtime Washington family as opposed to the politicians, who came and went from the city at the whim of the voters (and in any case often brought with them from the home state their own retinue). There was always new money looking for help, though the nouveau riche have never known how to deal with quality staff. (And they tend to fill their homes with items that, while flashy, hardly merit serious care; things that quickly turn threadbare or shabby even with the most delicate attention. We'll say nothing here of the company such people may keep.) The established families were always a good choice, although within such homes, openings of the kind my father had his eye on were rare. One could spend decades in a lesser position waiting for the senior male on the staff to retire (or expire).

Think back, if you will, to our hypothetical junior senator, new in Washington, looking to make a name for himself. As it happened, right around this time, such a person did arrive in town. A younger man from the Midwest. The Senator arrived from a brief stint in the home-state governor's mansion (official residences, as you well know, retain their own staffs), and before that time had lived on his family's estates. He, therefore, for the first time in his career, had need to establish his own home. The talk in the better parlors in the District, fueled as it always was by imported cigars and fine port, was that this was a young man with legs. The smart money anticipated a long tenure for this particular legislator.

"That's your man," my grandfather told my father. "That's where you build a career and a home."

I'll spare you the details of the campaign those two mounted for the job. Let's just say that in no time at all, my father was positioned to become the most powerful majordomo in the District of Columbia.

The Full Matilda

. . .

I

1947

Luck, an extraordinarily resilient set of genes, and the fact that Martin Housewright now anchored a withering branch of an already stunted family tree meant that he hadn't had the privilege of attending all that many funerals in his twenty-five years. Therefore even if it were the case that his sister Matilda had been making a scene at their father's visitation, Martin had no reference point against which to compare her behavior. Who knew? Maybe lots of other people did what she was doing. Perhaps it was perfectly appropriate for the daughter of the deceased to stand sentinel over her father's coffin, to watch over him as if he were a display of the crown jewels in the Smithsonian. (But even those guards took breaks now and again, didn't they? There had to be rules about this sort of thing.)

What did he know? Both siblings had been too young when their mother died: Martin remembered holding his younger sister's hand in what he thought was a park but had later realized was the cemetery where their mother had been buried. He remembered the sweet scent of flowers rolling over them and wondering when would happen what always happened in such parks: that someone would lay out the checkered tablecloth and unwrap their supper, a meal that he had anticipated might contain crisp and spicy chicken and maybe even some cornbread still warm from a distant cousin's oven. Despite the fact that their world that day had been filled with the mournful sighs and outright wailing of most of the important people in their lives, somehow it had not occurred to the five-year-old that the occasion required sadness or even that their mother, killed by a speeding sedan near Washington's Lafayette Park, had left their lives forever. Alma Housewright had gone to an elegant stationer near the White House to retrieve a box of engraved invitations for the Senator's wife, Penelope Stetson Hunnicutt (a grand yet solemn woman, soon to die herself while giving birth to that family's only child). Martin had always imagined that his mother had stepped into the street and then, in that absentminded way that she had, had looked down at the box of stationery and wondered whether she'd left her handbag in the store, had turned to go back only to find the bag hanging from her elbow. He saw her then turning into the oncoming traffic, forgetting to check again for cars. He would play that picture in his head for the rest of his life; that, alongside the afternoon in the cemetery. Stoic Matilda, he recalled, had observed the proceedings at her older brother's elbow. One might have described the look on her face as haughty disdain, were haughty disdain a look usually associated with persons the age of two. "You poor, poor thing," some older auntie had sobbed—one of their mother's people from down in Virginia someplace—sweeping the child up in her arms and emoting into the toddler's freshly pressed hair. Matilda had ordered the woman to put her down at once and had insisted that now meant now. Martin remembered that clearly—his sister's bossy, aggressively fierce demeanor—just as he remembered them both standing at the hole in the ground into which had been lowered a shiny wooden box, said to contain their mother's remains. He remembered saying, "See you soon," and Matilda parroting the same thing. Or maybe she had said her own simple farewell. In either case he knew that their sentiments had been sober yet sincere and that, while frequently as they were growing up, both he and his sister had missed their mother dearly, they believed that she had been a constant presence in their lives even so, and that they would, as he'd suggested to her back then, be seeing her soon, here or someplace better. What all the fuss was about remained a mystery to each of them.

Now, over two decades hence, their father had also passed—on to that other, one hoped better, place. Martin had no reason to believe that his sister's behavior had anything to do with anything as conventional as grief. What this behavior was was . . . well, crazy. Matilda acted crazy. She'd been acting crazy for the better part of the last hour.

They had arrived at the visitation at five-thirty, as instructed by the funeral director.

"We allow a private time for the immediate family, and a chance to get you settled before the public viewing begins," the man had explained, a colored gentleman, whom Martin believed might be just younger than their father had been, a man who, like their father, had honed over the years that manner of servile grace that seemed to have disappeared just when the war ended and as the whole world changed. Returning from his own duty in a mess deep inside a battleship in the Pacific, Martin had noticed that there were fewer gentlemen of the ilk of their father and of the funeral director than there seemed to be when he was coming of age. Things had gotten coarser; life was less elegant. Mr. Gibson had a way when he spoke—when he, for example, had offered Matilda a place to rest her wrap—of leaning into those he attended ever so slightly, not enough as to where a person might feel crowded, but in a way that communicated that his offer of assistance had been most sincere and that her comfort had been indeed his only concern. How often he'd seen his father cater to the Senator with that same manner of courtly attention.

He'd sat with his sister on a settee covered in velvet brocade, in one of four or five small parlors that made up one wing of the funeral home. He'd felt awkward, sitting there. He'd wished that Matilda had been inconsolable because at least that would have given them each something to do. Instead, after they'd waited (at the respectful distance indicated by the ever-efficient Gibson) for the funeral director to open the casket and prepare the body for display (draping the polished mahogany around their father's head with beige satin, making an adjustment to the bedding that in some way moved Jacob Housewright into a more dignified pose), after they'd looked their father over and assured their minder that everything more than met their satisfaction (although who was to say what might not be satisfactory? How were the dead supposed to look? Was this where one asked for more rouge, please, or that his tie be straightened slightly? Why would one do such things? To what end?), after Gibson had excused himself, and after he and Matilda had stood looking down at their father for what seemed a respectful amount of time, they'd retreated to the sofa and waited for the rest of the evening to get on with itself.

"Looks like Daddy," he'd said, and Martin had been pleased that Matilda had not rolled her eyes. His sister didn't abide small talk—a key factor, he believed, in them having as yet to find a husband for her.

"He'd have wanted all this, I'm sure," Matilda had replied, almost as a question. She'd pulled her lips in tight and had roamed her eyes over the parlor as if inspecting on behalf of the health department. Gibson stood as the finest Negro mortuary in the city, though here and there Martin's eye, trained as it had been to navy standards—not to mention his father's own fastidious ones—spied the odd threadbare bit of carpet or the less than fully polished brass fixture. He'd known that Matilda had been keeping a running tally of these same breaches and that it was in everyone's best interest that he do the same. Should his sister decide advantage might be had from calling the funeral home to task—for any reason—Martin always benefited from at least having the facts straight before he weighed in on one side or the other. (Well, on her side; it was always a good idea to agree with his Matilda.)

Their awkward silence put him in mind of close calls back on the ship, after a particularly hot encounter, after the back-slapping postmortem and the storytelling and the beginning of the making of the myths. He'd thought about how things would be, much, much later, back down in the mess, how he'd hear the silence as the men hunched over their dinners and did not talk about what had not, but might have, happened, about how no one mentioned the fact that all of this and all of them might as easily have been miles below the sea.

"Do you think they'll come?" he'd asked his sister, hoping to break the tension. He'd always found such silences unbearable.

"Who?" Matilda replied, a taunt really. She knew very well whom he meant, but just as he opened his mouth to call her on it, she'd interrupted, "Of course they will. They'd better."

Just then would have been the moment that he might have seen it coming, the . . . whatever that behavior of hers was. She had clearly been out of sorts about something.

"Are you okay?" he'd asked.

"Me? I'm fine. My father just died, but I'm fine."

"Tildy!"

She'd shoved him in the arm to let him know she was having him on. She'd given him one of those looks of hers from which he could never predict what might follow—a sentiment dear enough to melt his heart or a dressing down worthy of the starchiest commander in the fleet.

Thus they'd passed their private visitation: he from time to time broaching some line of conversation, which his sister cut off in her ever-officious manner; she rising now and again to fuss with the drape of a curtain or with a past-its-prime lily that had better been omitted from an otherwise attractive spray. Such was the service Negroes got in this city, from each other, even. Housewright and Sons, Caterers would set a new standard: this Martin swore. On the good name and reputation of the man there in the box, he swore it. Just before six, Mr. Gibson had come in to announce that their first guests had arrived.

"Very well," Martin had said, and he remembered thinking that "very well" had been a foolish thing to say. He'd surely heard the Senator say similar things as Jacob Housewright announced his guests.

And it was just then that Matilda had arisen from the velvet brocade settee, had progressed to both smooth and to billow her full skirt, had tugged at her narrow waist, and then had strode (yes, Martin thought, that was exactly the way she'd moved, she'd strode, as if to the front of a chamber to make a speech, as if pacing off a land claim on the old frontier) to the head of her father's casket.

Martin had extended his hand and then his arm to his sister, thinking they would stand in the door of the parlor to greet those friends and loved ones who had come to pay their respects to their father.

"Sir, please," Mr. Gibson had intoned quietly, indicating the comfortable settee's designated role in the ritual.

"Oh, of course," Martin had responded, resuming his seat. "Tildy," he'd beckoned to his sister, but she was having none of it. Matilda had placed her left hand on the satin cloth, just above their father's snowy white head, clamped it there as if it were an anchor. Her other arm rested quietly at her side. Her feet, he'd noticed, had been angled out: heel-to-heel almost, the way the ballet dancers' feet had been at the performance Penelope Hunnicutt had taken them to on the National Mall. And could that be the Mona Lisa's smile on his sister's lips?

"Miss?" Gibson proffered. "Generally the bereaved receives the public—"

His sister swept her arm from the funeral director's reach and swiveled her head in his direction. She'd fixed him with the same expression Martin imagined she reserved for mashers in the movie theater.

"This bereaved," she'd said, "is fine just where she is."

"As you wish, Miss Housewright."

Gibson had backed away, hands clasped, head bowed ever so slightly. Then and only then had he betrayed to Martin the tiniest of slips in his professional mien. And perhaps only the son of Jacob Housewright, someone who'd been raised under the watchful eye of the absolute master of discretion, would detect such a lapse. In turning to leave, he'd caught Martin's eye. With a flicker of a lid and the whisper of an eyebrow, his telescoped message to Martin had been loud and clear: Get up and do something about this woman.

But what was to be done? Martin had tried talking to her. He'd been quite direct, actually.

Martin had approached his sister just after John and Esther Santee had backed away from the bier. The couple had lingered for what seemed like twenty minutes next to their father's coffin. The Santees lived-in with some neighbors of Senator Hunnicutt over on Westmoreland Place. They'd stood there next to his sister, reassuring her that her father had been quite a man, quite a man, indeed.

"How kind," his sister had enthused, almost too solicitously, he thought. Jacob Housewright, while always cordial, did not exactly encourage friendship from this sort of person. He'd said that, while maintaining a respectable enough home, it was common knowledge in the professional community that the Santees toted—that they removed chickens, whole hams, and sacks of sugar from their employer's pantry. Big as life they did this. Stuffed them into paper sacks beneath their dirty uniforms and hauled them out the back door on their days off. They gave the whole race a bad name, and their late father had the good sense to draw the line with this ilk, to let them know their place. He'd have been cordial, of course, but certainly not warm. Here, he observed, Matilda acted as if the Santees had been Jacob Housewright's closest associates.

Martin waited until there was a lull to approach his sister, until all present had either found a seat in the parlor or were gathered in knots of quiet conversation.

"What do you think you're doing?" he'd asked.

"I'm greeting our guests," she'd hissed through her Mona Lisa lips. She'd said it to him as if she thought he were a moron on his way to a long stay at the state mental hospital.

"These people are not our guests. That"—he pointed to their father—"is not some new . . . gadget you're showing off at the World's Fair."

Referring to his father as a "that" had set him a-tremble. His sister was by all evidence undaunted by his snappishness.

"You want to start something, Marty?" she'd sneered. She'd used an old diminutive, and he knew she had him. Playing big brother to this woman was like organizing a chorus of songbirds: impossible and certainly entirely pointless. More than four years younger and still she'd run the show, from the time she learned to talk until he'd signed up for the service in 1942. And now, still, since he'd returned home. Matilda knew how to push his buttons. She knew which names to call and when. She collected transgressions and misdemeanors and had an uncanny sense of which ones to turn in immediately for points with their father and which ones to set aside for an even larger blackmail premium down the line. It was almost as if she'd been born knowing such things—and this skill was bad enough—but the primary thing about Matilda which he could neither escape nor abide was the fact that, somehow, for some unearthly, ungodly reason, the woman had always been right. About everything, it seemed. Always. She'd chosen his course work in high school—and had an uncanny way of knowing which classes to avoid and which teachers might help him grow and thrive. She'd told him to break up with Ernestine Curtis before he left for the Navy, told him she was cheap and unreliable. (As predicted, the conniving shrew went on to marry one of the fellows from the new neighborhood, even before Martin finished basic training.) Matilda had even been the one who told him to enlist in the first place, told him that he'd learn a good trade (he did), would come home safe and sound (he did), and be, all in all, the better for it (for the most part he felt that, yes, he was). Right on all counts, damn her.

And, damn their father, too. He'd been clear in his last charge to his only son.

"You take care of my Queenie," he'd ordered. (Yes, the man called the creature "Queenie"!) "I want her settled and married. I want you to promise me now that you'll watch over my baby girl."

"Yes, sir," he'd said, as if he meant it—and he imagined he probably did at the time. What did he have to back up that promise? How was he going to take care of this impetuous yet willful woman? That strong, straight-back thing there standing guard over their father's earthly remains. Like those songbirds, here was a woman who had no desire for organization from the likes of him, thank you very much, and had every intention of singing whatever song she pleased, despite whatever he or their father wanted.

He did owe her—them, both her and the man in the casket—at least one more chance for her to choose to make less a spectacle of herself.

"I was just thinking, Tildy, that you'd be—"

"My daddy's dead." She'd cut him with her eyes in a way that let him in on the irony of the statement and to let him know that she wouldn't be the least bit hesitant to turn her stoicism into hysteria—entirely for his benefit, to be sure. "I'm not in the best of moods, as I'm sure you can imagine. I suggest you step away from me right this second. Should you choose not to, you'll be one very sorry little sailor."

"My daddy, too," he'd started to protest, but he'd swallowed it instead and had moved off toward the parlor door.

"Little sailor" his behind. Who did she think she was? A woman who looked like Olive Oyl, for heaven's sake. A woman who he'd be lucky to find a man to have dinner with, let alone live out her existence in the wake of. Let her call him one more name. Just let her try. He'd fix her and he'd fix her good.

Fat chance, and he knew it. That's what made it worse. Matilda Housewright was the one who did the fixing. Fixing things, for better or for worse: More or less that seemed to be her primary role here on earth.

He'd spent the past hour moving around the parlor greeting the mourners. (If "Queenie" didn't have to spend the evening on that couch, then, dammit, neither did he!) Despite his pique, he thought to himself how pleased he was at the turnout, how pleased the old man would have been, as well. Professional colleagues, such as the Santees, and Paul Taylor, who'd taken over as the Senator's driver those last few years. There was Montgomery, his father's counterpart, the Senator's aide-de-camp, holding things together in the halls of Congress much the same way his father held them together on the home front.

"Young Housewright," Montgomery greeted him.

"You remembered me. I'm amazed—it's been so long." Martin hadn't seen this man since they'd all come back to the home state eight years earlier.

"I never forget a face—that's why they pay me. How've you been? Last time I saw your father, he told me you were overseas. How was it?"

"Worse for some, I imagine." Martin found himself wondering if Montgomery was being so friendly because he was genuinely glad to see him or if he was just glad to find one recognizable face in a room full of colored folks. It was hard to say with whites. Some were just as friendly as his own people were, and some would just as soon he and those like him disappeared off the face of this earth. Who could understand the rules? In another setting—on a busy street downtown or outside one of his clubs—Montgomery might as soon cut him dead. Down at the market, Martin had recently passed a man he'd served beside for almost a year and a half—a white man. There, deep below deck, they'd worked well as a team, had developed a friendly benign banter, had shared news of home as if their families had been longtime friends. "Stevens," he'd called. "It's me: Housewright." Stevens, tumbling along between two friends, had looked Martin up and down as if he had been covered in grease. "Something I can do for you, boy," he'd sneered, a toothpick dancing against his thin lips. "Sorry, sir," Martin had mumbled. "I'd mistaken you for someone else."

Montgomery guided Martin toward the front of the parlor. "Shall we?" he'd asked—and Martin again thrilled at this man's gift for making people comfortable. He'd reminded himself to remember all these little tricks once the business got up and running.

"You remember my sister, Miss Matilda Housewright?"

"How good of you to come, Mr. Montgomery." Matilda extended a hand and curtseyed.

"Here's Daddy," she said.

Martin stifled a laugh. Of the three of them, he wasn't sure exactly who she felt needed that clarification.

"Oh my," Montgomery snuffled, sucking in air, almost as if he were in shock. "Well, there he is indeed. My, my." His lips trembled as he blew out a breath. He fished a handkerchief from the pocket of his suit coat and dabbed at his eyes with the linen. "My, my."

"Sir?" Martin placed a hand on the man's arm. He wasn't sure of Montgomery's exact age. He knew he was younger than the Senator, who was somewhat younger than his father had been. It was hard to tell with older white men. Some of them aged young, he'd noticed, wrinkled and grayed early in their forties. Montgomery had been one of those. Some, like the Senator, despite his infamous shock of white hair, maintained a youthful energy and vigor that betrayed their advanced years.

Montgomery accepted Martin's arm, almost leaned into him with his grief. "My, my. The three of us were quite a team. Did you know that, young Housewright?"

"I was aware of that, sir. And the name is Martin."

"Of course it is. Martin. We'd come by the house, Martin, late, after adjournment. The Senator, Ambassador Walton, some of the other old boys. Old Jake here had everything laid out for us. 'How are you, Jake?' we'd ask him. He'd tell us, and then we'd hear Martin this and Martin that. You were all he talked about. I hope you know that."

Martin owned as how he did. Matilda stewed, he could tell. She'd exact her pound of flesh before the evening was out. As if the fact that this sad old political operative remembered a father's pride in his only son ought to be debited in anyone's column.

Not one to be ignored, Matilda stepped forward and slightly in front of her brother. "Martin is opening a catering business. Housewright and Sons, Caterers. 'Making your house the right house for any occasion.' I thought of the slogan. Martin cooked for the admiral on his battleship, isn't that right, Martin?"

Martin cringed. "Tildy, this isn't—"

"And Sons," Montgomery interrupted. "And how many sons would that be, a young man like you?"

"None yet, sir, but I'm hoping." Hoping his fiancée would show herself up soon so that maybe she could help out a little with the developing situation. Where could that woman be? And why would he expect that Evie had any experience with sisters making spectacles of themselves at wakes?

"Well, sons or no sons, I'm sure you know how my business runs. The wife and I have need for a caterer quite often. If you're anything like your daddy—"

"Oh, he is. You can count on it." Matilda flourished a business card from a pocket hidden there somewhere in her dress's full skirt.

"Fine. Really fine. I've got a big luncheon coming up within the month, as a matter of fact. I will be in touch. You can count on it." Montgomery touched the handkerchief to his eyes again. "Y'all are good people. I mean that, you know. Good people. Your daddy there . . ." He gave Martin one of the hearty slaps on the shoulder that Martin remembered as being standard greetings back there in Washington. The old man sniffled and then shambled his way toward the parlor entrance. He turned back to the two of them back there at the coffin. "A luncheon. About seventy-five, I believe. You got your daddy's chicken recipe? The one with the wine sauce?"

"Sir, I believe I do." Martin was pinching his sister on the arm. She was gouging him in the back of the shin with her heel.

"We'll be in touch." Both siblings waved and the white man left the room.

"Can I speak to you in private?" Martin said between his teeth.

"There is no privacy here. And my father—"

"And if you say 'your father died' to me one more time—"

"You'll what, swabbie?"

"Honestly, Matilda. Hustling that old man up for business right there next to our father's dead body. Had the coffin not been open I'd have expected he'd have been in there spinning like a wagon wheel."

"He's dead. That's—"

"Will you keep your voice down, please?"

"Dead. That's all I've been saying. All night. My . . . our father. And if the dead have any interest in us at all, it would certainly be that we prosper even despite our vale of tears."

"A wake, Matilda. And where did these come from?" Having eyed the opening of the hidden pocket, he fished in and extracted one of what he figured would now be his business cards. Heaven knows he'd never seen them before.

"A *visitation*. Not a funeral. And I took the liberty. Attractive, are they not? Attractive and yet simple."

Martin had to admit that the cards were just that. Still, there were principles involved. Housewright and Sons had not been called Housewright and Sister. There was a reason for that. Lines needed to be drawn, and he was about to draw them.

"I believe, as the founder of—"

"Father always said that when dealing with *this* caliber of business"—she swirled her hands in the area that had moments before been occupied by Montgomery—"the message one wishes to send is one of simple elegance. Save the vulgarity for the likes of her." She pointed to the entrance of the parlor, where Martin's fiancée had just entered.

"Darling," Evie called, and Martin made to go greet her but found himself pulled back into place by his sister.

"Tell me the heathen didn't wear *that* to pay respects to our father."

Martin had been in bar fights on several continents. He thought for a minute about breaking his sister's arm.

"Let me greet my woman," he seethed.

"You'd think this was a third-rate burlesque house. Tell Sally Rand she forgot her fans."

Martin thought Evie looked fine. Stunning, as always. The full, round figure, soft yet somehow still solid. Lips like red ripe plums. (And, yes, maybe these weren't the thoughts one should have had at his father's visitation.)

"Why did she even bother?" The question oozed from his sister's tight lips.

"My fiancée has every right . . . Tildy, for the love of God. She's going to be your sister-in-law. She loved Daddy, and he was crazy about her. You know that."

Evie's family had lived in the Woodlawn Avenue Tudor next to the home that the Housewrights moved into after they'd relocated from the Senator's carriage house in Washington. Evie had fallen under their father's charms almost at once, had spent long afternoons being regaled with his stories of the imperial city and the grand parties he oversaw.

"Martin! She came here to taunt me. She never could—"

"No, Matilda! Now, you behave yourself. I mean it." He wrenched free, leaving his sister pale and shaken.

"Good to see you, sugar," he whispered to his intended, kissing her cheek, thinking some smooth charm might be needed just then, forgetting for the moment that this particular occasion required neither charm nor insouciance. Evie held him and patted him on the back.

"How you holding up, baby?" she inquired, should he have needed any further reminder of his role in these proceedings. He assured her that he was fine, casting an eye surreptitiously in his sister's direction.

"She's a little shaky." Matilda had resumed position next to their father, looking around the room as if offering invitations to the mourners to come up for a chat. A poorly trained circus chimp could recognize that she was pretending not to notice her future sister-in-law.

"Poor thing." Evie sighed. "This has got to be rough. She was crazy about that man."

Martin concurred.

"I'll go talk to her," Evie said, and was out of his reach before Martin could dissuade her.

He'd started to call after her, started to say "Maybe you shouldn't," but stopped himself. Evie's perception that he overprotected his baby sister stood as the chief tension in their impending marriage. He also remembered what his father had told him before he headed off to the Navy.

"Grown women are very dangerous animals," Jacob had advised. "Whatever you do, you don't want to find yourself in the middle of their business."

Matilda had set her face into a grim parody of itself. She looked off to a rear corner of the parlor as if there were something extraordinarily interesting going on there (there wasn't), as if Duke Ellington himself had strolled in, as if to catch the eye of her lover.

Evie stopped at Jacob Housewright's coffin, dipped at the knee, and then crossed herself. She transferred a kiss from her lips to their father's forehead. Martin watched his sister suppress a cringe.

"He looks good," Evie said to his sister, just as he approached.

"Yes, he does," Martin answered for his sister. Evie clasped his hand. She was being very patient with Matilda, but then she always had been. In all the time since the Housewrights had moved next door to her, Evie had always returned Matilda's enmity with benign tolerance. Matilda's hatred had been immediate. Practically the same age as the young woman who occupied the largest house on the block, Matilda had taken one look at Evie's voluptuous sixteen-year-old self, her perfectly marcelled hair and the sharp outfits she'd picked up on her family's travels, and had decided that her new neighbor was the devil's spawn.

"You will be civil to our guests, young lady. That is not a request." Their father had so ordered his daughter after Matilda had interrupted his tea with Evie. This on a rainy afternoon just before Pearl Harbor.

"If she's gonna sit around here so much, she could pick up a dishcloth now and then." That was what Matilda had said, and then she'd slapped one of her father's pristine tea towels on the table and said, "They look like this, in case you were wondering." Martin had been tinkering with the radio that his father kept tuned to the news in Europe. He'd whistled as his sister stormed from the room, and his father had given him a quick evil eye, after which he had resumed conversation with the beautiful young neighbor, only a brief apology for the interruption. One, after all, did not draw attention to such behavior (and charmed as Evie had always been concerning everything about their daddy, it was doubtful she even noticed the outburst). Matilda's inevitable dressing-down had come later that evening, over supper. Delivered in his usual cool diction, and coming, as it did, long after whatever it was that had set his sister off had already simmered away, she'd been completely caught off guard and could only mumble a shame-faced "Yes, sir." Their father had been the only one who could set his sister in her place. Even Evie knew this.

"Remember the stories he used to tell us, Tildy?" she asked, staring lovingly at the old man. She dabbed at her mascara with a delicate piece of lace.

His sister looked down just past her feet. Martin noticed that she was visibly shaking. The casket wobbled, if ever so slightly, from the vibration emanating from her anchored left hand.

"Come on, sis," he said, as she collapsed in his arms and he led her to the settee.

Matilda had sobbed against her brother's shoulder for a good twenty minutes, it seemed. Evie had hovered around to help but had quickly taken the hint and let them be. She apparently had much more experience with such events than either Martin or Matilda. She worked the room almost as well as Gibson himself—Martin had overheard her asking another neighbor from the block to give the family "a few minutes, please." Her elegant and placid manner communicated to the mourners that compassion was in order rather than alarm.

"Feeling better?" Martin asked. He felt his sister's breath coming even now, heard the sobbing cease.

"I'm fine," Matilda sniffed, at last pulling herself upright. She straightened her spine, swallowed hard, worried at the creamy lace now wrapped tight around one of her fists.

"Don't think this means anything, because it doesn't." Never one to wear much on her face, the only damage thereabouts appeared to be some puffiness around the eyes.

"I'm sorry she upset you," Martin offered.

"Evie? The day I shed one tear over the likes of her . . ."

"But she triggered it."

"I triggered it. I did."

"May I ask why?"

He watched his sister lower her head down to her hands—an expression of exhaustion, he thought, rather than grief. "All right," she said. "All right, big brother." Matilda looked him square in the eye, almost daring him to balk. "If you're sure."

"Of course I'm sure," he said, though he wasn't really. Something in her manner had indeed gone off, but what was there to be done? "We're all we've got, after all," he reassured her, and that thought sent a shiver of ice through his midsection.

Matilda looked from him to Evie and back again.

"I don't know . . . what's to become of me."

Had that last part been a question? Martin couldn't be sure. "I don't know what you mean. What's to become of you? Why, you'll go on, of course. We'll both go on. That's what we do."

"You're smarter than that, Marty. This isn't sentimental mourning nonsense. It's just as good a time as any to talk about the hard bit, that's all. You know what I mean. Don't you? Don't you?" The second prompt intended to get him to meet her eye.

"All right, Matilda. All right." He bit at a thumbnail, as was his habit when nervous. (Stop that! he hectored himself. Gentlemen who cater elegant evenings do not pick at their extremities. But he could not stop.) He examined the nail as if something had caught his eye. Playing for time. That's what this was about. "All right. What Daddy said was—"

"Father is dead."

"All *right*, Matilda." Though he tried to suppress the exasperation in his voice, he could not.

"I just mean . . . I mean he's dead. That's all. He's dead."

"It's okay. I understand."

"What did Father say? To you, I mean. I know what he said to me. What did he say to you, Martin?"

He observed Evie still working the room hard. She had retrieved the guest book from the lobby and was making the rounds with it. She circulated cups of coffee. The parlor now held mostly old friends of their father's, sitting watch. Martin felt as if he and Matilda were on display, there on the settee, but a second pass revealed that all these old-timers seemed absorbed in their own private thoughts, as was his sister—who seemed not to know or care where they were or who might be noticing their private conversation.

"Tell me what he said."

"He said I should look after you."

"You! Look after me?"

"Good one, huh?" Martin chuckled.

"If you say so." Matilda examined her handkerchief and her brother felt chagrined.

"Look after me how?"

Martin thought for a moment. "The house. That's yours. You knew that."

"Yes. And yours."

"So there'll . . . so you'll always have a place."

"Yes."

"I said I'd make sure there were never any problems in that regard, and I will. You never need to concern yourself there."

"Go on."

"He said . . . He asked if I . . . He wanted to make sure you found a good husband."

"And you'll be taking care of that also, I assume?"

"Oh, Matilda." Martin looked away from his sister. He could feel his face heating up with shame.

"I didn't mean to offend your delicate sensibilities, big brother."

"Dammit, Tildy! Did you ever think that if maybe you just tried—?"

"Tried what?"

Martin turned away from his sister. She pulled on the sleeve of his jacket.

"Tried what, Martin? Look at me. Turn around and look at me."

Matilda stood before her brother. She turned around, her black skirt flaring slightly around her calves.

"See."

Her tiny waist. Her almost flat chest. The limp hair, roped into a bun atop the plain face. Their father's face. Handsome on him, it had been.

"You can stop looking now." She sat and offered her brother her handkerchief. It was his turn to release the tears.

"I didn't . . ." he sobbed.

"No, I know you didn't ask for the job." She gave his knee a brotherly squeeze. "Promise me something, Martin."

He nodded.

"Promise me that, regardless of how this all turns out—this . . . whatever it's going to be . . . Promise me that this is the last time we'll have this particular conversation. Agreed?"

Once again he nodded.

"You're a good sailor, Marty." She saluted, gave her brother's knee a second conspiratorial squeeze, and stood smoothing her skirt again.

"Back to work, I guess," she sighed. She nodded her head at Evie. "Go tell Josephine Baker to give it a rest," Matilda said, and resumed her place at the coffin.

They received guests for another hour or so. The folks on odd shifts straggled in late, as did those who had stopped at their own homes to feed the kids or to water the lawn. Martin was amazed at how many people their father had come to know in the few years that they had lived here.

He approached his sister. She was busy fussing with the pleated beige drape that billowed from the opening of their father's casket.

"Are you supposed to mess with that?"

"Beige was never his color. I'm thinking a royal purple. Or a crimson maybe. Probably too late to ask to have this ripped out."

"Gibson says the show's closing in ten minutes or so. I invited folks over for coffee."

Matilda crossed her arms and turned to face her brother. "Tell Gibson the *show* stays open until *he* gets here. Tell him if it's about the money, I'll make him whole."

"Tildy, it's awfully late. I'd think if he were coming—"

"He's coming. He is. Tell Gibson to hold his horses. Go. Tell him."

As was always the case, Matilda was right. Just at eight, he arrived. The Senator tottered into the parlor supported on the arm of his only child, Walton Hunnicutt Jr. (Had it been the case that the people all stood up when he arrived or had they all already been up making ready to leave? Martin hadn't noticed.)

"Where is he?" the Senator bellowed. "Where's my Jake?"

"Easy, sir," Martin said. He took the opposite side of the old man from the junior Hunnicutt. "He's right here. Take your time."

The two younger men led the feeble older one to the front of the parlor. Martin then shook the hand of his young friend, Walter Jr. It would be nice to catch up a bit, but tonight was the wrong time to do so. Martin had to swallow his shock at seeing the Senator so visibly frail for the first time, but it would be expected: he was what? Eighty-two? Eighty-five?

As they approached the casket, Matilda stepped away from her regular perch. She backed away toward the settee, stood facing them, hands demurely clasped at her waist, her face set with what Martin couldn't decipher—something between self-satisfaction and red raw rage.

"I don't know how this happened," the old man quavered. "I don't know how we got to be so damn old. How'd this happen, Jake?"

"Jake looks good, doesn't he, Father?" the younger Hunnicutt said.

Martin recognized the look in the Senator's eyes, that mixture of fondness and nostalgia and loss. The Senator sighed and smiled and laughed and reached for his friend's hand. A tear or two leaked down from beneath the still-white mess of hair riding the top of his head like a coxcomb. They dribbled across an ancient cheek and onto the lapel of their father's suit.

Martin couldn't be sure, but he thought he heard his sister mumble the words, "Enough. Enough."

Matilda strode (again, strode) to the casket. Reaching inside toward a hidden hinge, she jigged a lever of some kind and, after struggling a bit, lowered the lid over their father. Beige satin continued to leak over the side of the coffin like excess frosting from a cake dish.

"Sorry to say, that's all for this evening. Senator. Mr. Hunnicutt. Good to see you both again. Alas, you know how it is with these Negro funeral homes. We've been asked, I'm afraid, to quit the premises by . . ." She consulted a nonexistent wristwatch. "Why, I declare, it's already past eight as it is. We are so pleased, aren't we, Martin, that you all were able to stop by. So pleased to visit with you again, even under such sorrowful circumstances. Let's do it again, shall we? And let's not make it so long!

"Well, good night it is, then."

With that Matilda strode up the aisle and out of the parlor.

Evie shrugged and indicated with her eyes that she would go after her.

The Senator leaned over to Martin and chuckled. "That sister of yours. That Matilda. She's a pistol." He slapped Martin's back.

"Yes, Senator. She's something all right."

II

It wasn't so much that he had imagined his father would live forever, rather that Martin Housewright had always remembered feeling as if there was something timeless about the old man. Jacob Housewright had always seemed to Martin to be the sort of person who belonged to no particular era, neither to the present nor to the past. One could imagine him in a toga or in chain mail or in revolutionary breeches. Crowning whatever costume would be that same face, eyes that never missed a detail, mouth frozen in a benignly neutral line, signaling nothing in particular other than perhaps whatever the viewer needed to perceive at the moment. At the same time, his father had never appeared to be at home anywhere. He moved through the rooms of this house like a visitor, or, better, like the caretaker he had spent his life being to other people's rooms. As Matilda handed him another box or envelope or file containing their father's accumulations, it became even more apparent to Martin—how ephemeral and inconsequential and temporary it all seemed.

Matilda had been back and forth between hard-nosed pragmatism and sentimentality all day, the pragmatic side of her more often than not winning out.

"His belongings won't go away on their own," she hectored, handing him another shoebox from the closet. Apparently he hadn't been demonstrating quite enough zeal these past few minutes. He assumed they were going about this in the right way, but how would someone know about something like this? A person only had the responsibility of closing up his father's affairs once, and it ought be done properly. Surely there was a manual out there that covered the basics. The Navy had manuals for everything: packing a trunk, loading a weapon—they even had one, he had been amused to discover, giving advice on how not to pick up diseases in the brothels that lined the streets in the various ports of call the ships frequented. Here, Matilda flitted around their father's bedroom as if she herself had written the definitive guide on the subject. She had ordered her brother out of bed an hour earlier than his usual Saturday rising time and sent him to the basement to retrieve some packing cartons.

"We do it now or it never gets done, and that's a fact. That woman, the diplomat's widow, two houses down from our place on R Street: Remember when the Senator had to send Daddy down there to deal with *that* mess. The husband had been dead since the Great War and that wife of his had never touched a thing. You can't imagine the mess. What was she thinking? Suits fell right off hangers—on my honor, they did. What once had been perfectly good wool suits. Imagine! The poor soul, sitting in that house for decades with those moldering things. I'm still itching from the moth eggs. And we certainly don't want that."

"We most certainly do not." Martin was pretty sure that moth eggs didn't cause itching, but didn't see much point in starting that debate.

Matilda had much more vivid memories of Washington than he did, or at least it was Martin's impression that she did. She would call the names of obscure members of the House from the West, congressmen who she insisted had settled with their families just one street over and whose children had been frequent playmates of Senator Hunnicutt's son. She knew—or claimed to know—which route their father had taken to deliver fresh shirts to the Senator in his office. Chappy and Mr. Pickles: so were named their Georgetown neighbor's cats—at least according to his sister they were.

Martin wasn't even sure that the Senator's house had been on R Street, though he vaguely recalled the street having some initial for a name. It may well have been any of the other twenty-five letters for all he could say. He did not remember any cats.

These had never been the kind of details Martin retained. The right temperature for roasting a chicken. He could tell you that. How to hold mashed potatoes warm for supper. He could tell you that, as well. But all these little notations Matilda retained about that house back east—a house he had grown up in, after all—Martin had chosen to let go of. Perhaps it was because it hadn't ever really been their home after all; perhaps, like his father, he was destined himself to become one of those men who was never really at home anywhere. There was one thing for sure: he would never be like Matilda. The woman held on to people and places and things as if they were holy. Behind him, she noisily shuffled some metal coat hangers across the rod; she sounded like a person ripping through her own wardrobe, choosing the right outfit for an engagement. He imagined she'd hang on to half the man's old things. He'd take bets on it.

"Someone is disengaged from his task," she scolded.

"That would be me, I imagine." His nonchalance mixed with a healthy portion of routine morning sluggishness. He'd always hated mornings. Had finagled in every way he could to work swing shift on the boat, planned when his catering business took off to never take a job that started much before noon.

Matilda slung a sheaf of string-bound envelopes toward his head. With the Montgomery luncheon on the horizon (Old Montgomery actually came through. Who'd have believed it! And promised lot's more business besides, should this first job be a success.), Martin had more on his mind than his father's loose ends, but Matilda's obsessions held sway, as they often did.

"Make sure you look at every scrap of paper. Let's go. The sooner you finish, the sooner you can meet up with your fancy woman," she'd chided him.

"Yes, ma'am," he saluted. He and Evie had a standing Saturday night date. Tonight they'd be catching some music in a club he'd heard about over on Sarah Street.

He had planted himself on the bed and was sorting through stacks of envelopes, mostly containing utility receipts for the last half dozen years or so that they'd lived here on Woodlawn. One couldn't be too careful. These old guys who'd toughed it through the hard years before the last war had a way of stashing cash away in the oddest places. (Anywhere but the bank, after all.) Matilda had sworn she knew their father's entire repertoire of secret hiding places, but Martin had already twice had the satisfaction of waving recovered twenty-dollar bills in his sister's face. Even so, something about the tawdry bound piles of yellowed paper darkened his mood. Perhaps it was that such casual record keeping belied the elegant and detailed ledgers that his father had kept while running the Senator's house all those years. Each entry for each expense had been entered just-so in his father's careful hand, down and across the regulation columns of the custom-bound leather volumes. Every expense accounted for—be it seedlings for the formal gardens or two dollars and eighty-five cents in gasoline for the car—down to the last penny, and not one cross-out on any of those pages.

Yet these ragtag bundles of envelopes and receipts, corners clipped in some indecipherable code, chicken-scratched notes across ripped flaps and on expired coupons: this was how the great man managed his own affairs. Some things just didn't make sense.

"Do you want this?" Matilda swirled a fairly new-looking herringbone jacket in her brother's face.

"Sugar, that jacket's too small by half. You know my size." He patted his ample paunch.

"That would mean you don't want it?"

"Yes. That means 'no.' No, I don't want that jacket and"—he rose from the bed and picked his way across the various piles that were rising on the floor—"and I don't want this [another jacket] or this [a tweed vest] or this [a cardigan] or any of these either." He swept his hand across the bulk of the clothes in the closet.

Matilda face fell into a pout. "Well," she whined. She tossed the jacket onto a pile on the bed. "You should want to have something." Her eyes scanned the sorted clothing, searching, he was sure, for the gem he had overlooked, the one item that would be perfect for her brother's wardrobe. Earlier that morning she had explained to him some organizational scheme to the various stacks that gathered on the round braided rug covering the maple-planked floor in his father's bedroom. He had neglected to retain the information.

Rags. He did remember that one of the piles had been called "rags." Maybe she'd find him a keepsake in the rag pile.

She lifted a beaten-up old gray sweater that had been draped on the ladder-back chair that their father kept at his desk. "We should have this old soldier framed," she suggested, caressing it as if it were a daughter's ample tresses. Grease stains on front panels disguised its true pale tone. One button had fallen off; another nested in a hole stretched wider than the button itself. The garment had been their father's preferred attire when moving the papers around on his desk or for sitting by the radio listening to Basie and his other favorite bands. Martin pointed to the rag pile. Matilda bit her lip, petted the sweater, and started for the rag pile. She then gently returned the sweater to the back of the chair. Crossing to the closet, she changed her mind again, snatched the sweater from the spindles, and tossed it to the rags.

"Good girl," he praised—that would be one for the manual—and before she could snipe at his limp praise, he quoted back at her a string of her own homilies, aphorisms that had to do with hay and bitter pills, hot irons and happier tomorrows. She held her tongue, pointed at the mounting piles of paper, and snapped her fingers—an action that had him thinking he'd have preferred the tongue-lashing after all. She mounted a step stool and wrestled a clutch of hatboxes from the top shelf.

"Some of these may have been Mama's, don't you think?"

He shrugged. Who knew what their father might have held on to from those days? Would he have brought their mother's old hats from Washington? She'd been long dead when they moved here.

Matilda latched open the matte black box and removed the swaddling from a stylish homburg. She spun it in his direction, calling, "Catch!"

"Now we're talking," Martin exclaimed, sitting up and donning the sharp, putty-colored hat.

Matilda looked him over. "You're not a hat man," she concluded.

"Am now," he replied, settling back into his sorting. Evie will die when she sees me in this, he thought—also thinking that a crisp-looking, old-time hat like this one might be just the statement he needed to be making around town.

"Well, looky here," Matilda said, sliding a yardstick from the closet shelf. "We can always use one of these," she added, spinning the stick like a majorette. "Never know what treasures you might find."

"Let me know if you find a chafing dish up in there somewhere. Or a commercial oven. And some cooks. And my good mind, which I seem to have misplaced somewhere." He glanced up from his own piles to see if his sister had taken the hint.

She cleared her throat. He knew his sister. The rasping indicated that she'd heard him but had no desire to converse. She dusted the shelf where the hats had been stored. Maybe not now, but he did need to talk with her. This "Housewright and Sons" thing had been eating away at him for days now, and he needed his sister's ear. They needed to get some things straight.

Matilda pushed the step stool deeper into the closet, reached up, and made what Martin heard as a rather disgusting gruntlike noise from a place way back in her throat.

"Here's the good stuff," she announced, hauling down a green strongbox. "Daddy told me to be sure and find this." The saying of which set off a pang of resentment in her brother. Daddy hadn't told him about finding any strongbox or about finding anything else, for that matter.

"Spread some of those *Lifes*," she said, pointing to stack of magazines on the floor. "She's a heavy old thing." Matilda lowered the burden onto the face of some actress he didn't recognize but whom he bet Evie would assure him was all the rage. Martin steadied the box as she lowered it to the bed, thinking, Damn, it must weigh fifty pounds.

"I guess we're each other's witnesses. Are you ready?"

Martin scoffed. "Tildy, I trust you. You know that."

(Earlier, when he had complained to her that he really did have better things to do than dig through their father's meager belongings, she'd told him that she knew of too many families torn apart because one member or another raided the family jewels after the funeral, and she insisted that she would touch not one item were he not present as well. "You read *King Lear*," she'd continued. (Actually, he had not. Matilda had read it to him once while he dozed.) "Siblings fighting over birthright: ever and always an ugly story, across the march of time." He had told her to do them both a favor and to haul the lot of it out to the ash can.

"What do you suppose is in here?" he asked.

"Papers? Birth certificates? Daddy didn't say."

"Did he say anything about a key?"

Matilda shook her head and fussed with the latch. It didn't yield.

"It's here somewhere, wouldn't you think?" Martin rose from the bed and slung open a dresser drawer.

"It's not in there," Matilda said flatly.

"Or there. Or there." Before Martin's fingers even had made contact with whichever handle he'd thought to try next, she'd cut him off with her curt interference. She had that look about her, Martin observed, that she got when working on a puzzle: eyes cast off to one side, lower lip bit in concentration.

Abruptly, she charged out the door and down the steps to the first floor. Moments later she came back clutching a brace of keys in her fist. She pitched the cluster in her brother's direction.

"It has to be one of those."

"These are—"

"From the Senator's, yes. It's one of those. I know it is. Try all the little ones."

The fourth of the tiny keys he tried released the hasp.

"Yup. I've always wondered what that one fit. Never could match it."

"Daddy let you handle the Senator's keys? Daddy never let me touch this ring."

She snatched the key ring from his grasp. "Look here: Front door. Westmoreland garage. R Street garage. R Street liquor pantry. And this one"—she flourished a rather ordinary nickel-plated key—"opens a door on the Hill, the doing of which could get us both time in the federal penitentiary." From the expression on her face, Martin had to assume his sister was fully serious about that, although with Matilda there was just no telling.

"You ready?" he asked her.

"Fire at will."

The top of the box had been layered over with ration coupons.

Matilda sifted through the issues for tires and sugar and coffee and meat.

"I wouldn't imagine—" Martin started.

"Only as emergency bathroom tissue, I'm afraid."

"I guess you all didn't use too many of these," he said. Martin himself had only heard tell of the shortages at home, the sacrifices paid to make sure those like himself who had gone away to protect the country at least got to fight on a full stomach.

"I don't know that we used any. The Senator . . . well, you know."

Martin nodded. Hadn't it always paid to have connections?

Matilda sorted the coupons into her "trash" pile, carefully piecing through them should some treasure appear. "A waste," she'd whispered as they filtered to the floor. "Imagine what some would have done for just a few of those."

A dozen or so innocuous articles about the Senator and Mrs. Hunnicutt comprised the next layer—fluff from the society page and some stories of the "Senator Dedicates Park" variety that Montgomery had placed in the local papers so the good folks back home would remember their man in Washington. Then came a layer of official papers: birth and death certificates and what Martin told his sister were someone's military benefit papers. (Certainly not their father's. He had never served.) At the bottom of the box nested dozens and dozens of neatly wrapped bundles of bills. Fives and ones, mostly, it appeared.

"And so!" His sister chortled, covering her mouth as if she were embarrassed.

"Good Lord, Daddy. There must be thousands here."

"Oh, at least. Martin!" His sister shrieked, and the two of them burst out laughing.

"Tildy, you don't suppose . . ." Martin didn't finish the sentence. One didn't say such things about one's father, after all.

"Don't be silly." Matilda seemed reticent about reaching into the bundles of cash—odd for a woman who only moments earlier had been enthusiastically fishing through the man's underwear drawer.

"But you have to wonder, don't you? Where it came from. This much of it."

"There's no wonder. It's just money. He saved it. For us. This is what he wanted to make sure I found."

In front of them lay bundled more cash than either of them had seen in their entire lives. Martin picked up and fingered through a bound sheaf.

"Feel." He extended the stack toward his sister. "As soft as tissue, most of it. Like it's been passed through a million hands." Matilda ran several bills between her thumb and forefinger.

"Dirty, surely," she whispered, her nose turning under with revulsion.

Martin began absentmindedly sorting through the stacks. What at first appeared placed at random had been packed in some kind of pattern, he could tell. He was mesmerized; his mind jumped from one impulse to the next.

Tildy seemed to be muttering something about security and savings, but he couldn't really take her nonsense in at this point.

"You were so right," he said to her. "You knew there was a reason for me to be here today and you were so right." A packet of tens. A packet of ones. The ample crevices of the bills had blackened with wear.

"I was thinking that it probably isn't a good idea—"

"You see, I've been stuck, sis. Big plans, big talk. Dreams. Just like a lot of these Negroes out here. But I was going to make mine come to life, I really was, and I've been thinking about how I could possibly pull together what I needed. You know what I'm saying.

"I'm doing okay down at the hotel. Fair. Lot's of folks doing worse, I guess. If they'd give me a chance in the kitchen, I'd fly, I know I would, but, hey, all that's . . . well, that's somebody else's dream now." He patted the side of the box and laughed.

In front of him his sister's mouth moved, but he could attend to her.

"Housewright and Sons. I guess I imagined I'd be working my way there slowly. Save a little here for a commercial stove. Maybe cater a picnic for some of the churches. I'd do it for free at first. To spread the word, you know. Then pick up a few jobs a year for the first couple of years. Build a reputation. Then right out of the blue I got this Montgomery job. Just like that. And I'm thinking it's too soon, you know. I'm not ready. It's the big time already. I was thinking, What about a kitchen? I couldn't even afford to buy chicken, let alone a place to cook it."

Matilda said something about fine kitchens and then something about something else.

"It's all falling into place, Tildy. Don't you see?"

He looked at his sister. She was opening and closing her right hand, as if she were doing warm-up exercises for the piano. She stood, stared out the back window into their father's garden.

He heard her say something such as how she guessed she did see—hand opening and then hand closed—and then it was his father's voice in his head. The distinguished gravel, the broadened mid-Atlantic-coast velvet, the diction of an aristocrat. Back there behind this house, it had been, the old man in that raggedy sweater, trembling despite the summer heat, finger in Martin's face, ordering Martin to see after his sister. Martin parted his lips to speak, but Matilda put a finger to her own lips to stop him.

"I'll have to get out there and get into those tiger lilies before too long. They need thinning something awful." She gathered from the bed the collection of official papers that she had retrieved from the box, straightened their edges, and laid them neatly on her father's desk. From the ring of keys she spun the one to the strongbox, locked it, walked around the bed, and forced the key into her brother's palm.

"If you lose that, I'm sure you can crack that hasp. It doesn't appear all that strong to me."

He went to speak again, but no words came.

"Tomorrow. Tomorrow you get with your buddy Ralph. Find a rundown restaurant or diner someplace that's closed down. Check up on the landing and over in Mill Valley. Also down on the South Side. Some place fairly central. Find some place cheap. No more than fifty a month. You hear me?"

Martin nodded. Her benign expression set him off kilter.

"Ralph knows about these things. His daddy had that shoe repair, remember?"

"I remember."

"Paint and board over the front of the place so that it looks respectable but not affluent. No sign out front. Not yet. Make sure there's some ventilation. Make sure it's secure. You can handle that."

Not a question, but he nodded anyway.

"Daddy had a place that supplied him for the Senator's big parties. You know: extra chairs, tents if we were using the lawn. I'm sure they remember him there."

"Tildy, this isn't . . . You don't have to . . ."

"I'd appreciate it if you'd get that out of my way. There's a mess here and the day's getting away."

Martin went to embrace her from behind, but she shooed him away. He picked up the box and his father's hat, although he wasn't sure where to go with them.

III

Often over the next week Martin felt as though he were swimming in molasses. For some reason, making decisions now paralyzed him in a way doing so never had in the past; often, sitting at a salvaged gray metal desk that Matilda had uncovered from somewhere, he would stare at the range of tasks sorted across a green felt blotter and feel frozen in place. Scout produce vendors. Test the chicken recipe.

Where was Tommaso when you needed him? A ruddy, square-shouldered Italian, Tommaso ran the enlisted men's mess as if he were the conductor of a great orchestra, preferring grand sweeping motions of his meaty arms over verbal commands. He clapped his hands and spun his arms in front of his torso to indicate that time was of the essence. Tornadic whirling of his index fingers above his head meant "Serve this chow *now!*"

Once Martin had found himself face-to-face with bins of raw onion. Tommaso had pointed at him and four others, made a sweeping motion toward the vegetables, and then made a chopping motion with his hands. Martin had dug in, working with the diligent care his father had taught him. "Like this, boy," Tommaso had said, and had somehow taken Martin's hands into his own, along with a knife and an onion, and demonstrated a more vigorous technique—knife scissoring up and down, wedges of sweet white onion propelled forward by the knuckles. "Got it?" Tommaso barked, seeming at the same time both proud and annoyed.

Back there, in the ship, you did what you were told, when you were told to do it. If you didn't know how to do it, there was someone nearby there to show you how. Here, well, Martin figured he'd gotten what he'd wished for. *He* was the Tommaso here.

Well, fine, he decided. I'll follow my heart. I'll start with the menu.

He'd been thinking about desserts—maybe something decadent, a Lady Baltimore cake with figs and raisins. Maybe a charlotte russe—he'd make his own ladyfingers.

Or maybe it would be better to go with an easy and elegant dessert, such as lemon tarts, but he had to figure how that would square with his goal to pull out all the stops. He intended to serve his first client a meal that this city would never forget.

He spied there—just behind the shelves he and Ralph had painted last night—an off-color spot where apparently Ralph had neglected to fully cover over the dull green walls with the crisp white he'd selected. He imagined this was also how it would be from now on—him noticing the way others hadn't quite done what he wanted or at the very least not the way he would have done it himself. And what should a person do anyway? Should he speak to Ralph about a few missed strokes of a paintbrush, or should he save his chit for a really big problem? Was it his place to speak to Ralph at all—another grown man? An equal? A friend?

Matilda had been right; Ralph did know his buildings. They had toured empty properties and Ralph had pointed out the things Martin should be careful of: dodgy wiring, stained plaster or spotting on wooden floors that might indicate potential water damage. He had reassured Martin of Matilda's wisdom in steering him toward less desirable retail districts.

When they came across the old shirt factory, Ralph felt they'd found the right home.

"I'm not sure," Martin had responded. "The price seems a little high. Tildy says—"

"Why don't you let me deal with Miss Matilda?" Ralph had offered, along with a teasing wiggle of the eyebrows.

Martin scoffed. "Think you're a tough guy, huh?"

"I'll sweet-talk her. You'll see."

At that moment Martin had felt a surge of something—energy? Excitement? Fear?

"Ralph. You wouldn't be interested in my baby sister, now, would you?" He played it as a joke, but inside of him that surge had begun to billow.

"Matilda? She's not my type. But every gal likes a little sweet talk now and again."

Martin had been surprised how defensive he'd felt. "What's wrong with her?" he'd asked.

"I don't mean no disrespect. She's . . ." Ralph searched the shirt factory with his eyes as if an answer might appear on one of the dusty old shelves. "She's . . . I like a little more . . . body on my ladies. You know?"

Martin had rolled his eyes. At least the man was honest. Ralph was a fellow who appreciated a woman with some flesh on her bones. Still, here was a decent Negro man. Surely Matilda could attract to herself someone like this.

"Okay, let's say other than that," he persisted. "Let's say you didn't know me and you ran into her on the street or up at the club. Would you . . . talk to her?"

"This is your sister we're talking about. And Miss Matilda ain't one of them sit-up-in-the-clubs kind of gals."

Odd, Martin thought, to have a younger sister that people referred to as a "Miss." As if she were his mother or some elderly aunt.

They'd continued their tour around the rest of the small factory floor with its middle-aged Jewish owner. He'd been nice to them, at least: some of the landlords wouldn't even open the door seeing two colored men outside.

"You fellows talk it over," he'd suggested, leaving Martin and Ralph in what must have been at one time his office.

Instead, Martin wondered, "What do you think? Do you know anybody? An evening out would do her a world of good." He shrugged as if his ideas were less a concern than they were.

"What does she say about that?"

"You know her. She's shy. She holds back."

"Holds back? Matilda? Your sister is right up front from what I can tell."

"On a lot of things. But when it comes to . . . you know . . . men. She's backward. And anyway, I promised my daddy I'd look after her."

"Miss Matilda is a decent, smart lady. A lot of guys go for that."

"Do you go for that? For a decent and smart lady?"

"Absolutely. Decent and smart. As long as she's got a nice big behind on her, absolutely, yes."

Martin sighed. It was futile. There apparently was nothing to be done.

"Gentlemen," the landlord had called from the doorway. "A decision, maybe?" He was the first all day who hadn't called them "boys."

Martin sucked his teeth, looked around the high ceilings again. "I really should—"

"Act like you know what you doing, is what you really should. You in business now. Businesspeople move. They don't hesitate, and they don't check with their baby sisters."

Martin had rubbed his hands together, nodded his head, and walked over to negotiate with his new landlord.

When they had shown her the place, Martin hadn't cared for the way Matilda's mouth twisted to one side as she looked it over. In his entire life he'd never known that expression not to be followed by a critical remark of some kind. Ralph had given her the grand tour.

"You sign off on this dump?" she'd asked him

"Actually, Matilda, since I'm the one whose name—" Martin started, but Ralph cut him off.

"Ah, shucks now, Miss Matilda. Let's wait until you've had the full tour."

"There's more!" She had thrown her hand to her mouth in mock horror.

Ralph extended his arm. "Allow me to escort you to the future site of our freezer safes. We're talking walk-ins, if you believe that."

"We. Am I to understand, brother of mine, that this charming gentleman has agreed to join our little enterprise?" Just as promised, his best friend had mounted the big offensive, and his sister had responded with what was apparently her own version of flirting back.

"Ralph has agreed to help me get the business set up and to help with the odd event here and there. Is there a problem with that?"

Matilda had flashed him a look that told him he was treading on thin ice with her. "Mr. Ralph here certainly has his admirable qualities, despite his occasional"—she swept her head around the room—"lapses of judgment. So, no, brother dear, there is no problem on my part."

"Now, Miss Matilda. You find me one problem with this place and I will call that old Jew personally and break the lease."

Matilda had reached out and jangled a shelf. "Well, this is loose, for one thing."

Leave it to his sister to have found the one wobbly shelf in the entire building.

"That's fixable. Come on, Tildy. You're mad because I went over your imaginary budget. You're mad because you didn't pick it out yourself."

Matilda spun toward her brother and Martin recoiled on reflex. Her eyes blazed at him and then softened to what to an outsider might appear to be sugar and pie.

"We'll ask Mr. Ralph. Mr. Ralph, is this the face of an angry woman?"

"Why, shucks no, Miss Matilda. You look right good enough to eat."

"Now you hush!" his sister cooed, as she and Ralph strolled away. She'd caught Martin's eye as she passed, signaling him clearly that sometime soon there would be hell to pay.

In the end, she'd relented—in her own way. To her credit, she'd been over here scrubbing and hefting and raising her rollers with everyone else. And the place looked pretty good—if he didn't say so himself.

He headed for the door—he simply could not ponder the mess on his desk one minute more—figuring he'd drop in at home for a while. (Damn! Walking by the sloppily painted wall, he retrieved the brush and paint can from the room they'd designated for cleaning supplies and retouched the wall himself. Dabbing the paint on the wall, he felt the oddest mixture of frustration and relief. He repainted the whole section while he was at it. So what if it would all be hidden by industrial containers of spices—it was the principle that counted.)

Arriving home, he found his sister ensconced at the kitchen table with their father's address file, giving the full Matilda to the linen supply place.

"Oh, my good gracious, Carl." (*My good gracious!* Who did this woman think she was?) "Why, you are a regular Jack Benny, you are, with your little stories. Every bit as funny—just as

Daddy always said. But, Carl, I just don't think we can go a dollar a dozen on those napkins. What with us just starting out and everything. But I do want to thank you for your time and . . . What's that? . . . How much? . . . Carl! You'd be willing to do that for me? . . . Well bless your heart. Now these are the hemmed and banded ones that Daddy liked, I just want to make sure we're clear on that. The white ones, correct? . . . Bless your heart. Now you be sure and say hello to that lovely wife of yours, Rita, was it." Matilda wrote the correct name on the card and arranged a time to drop off the payment and pick up the linen.

"There's one born every minute," she said, hanging up the phone. "Daddy used to pay a dollar ten back in the capital."

"You think 'Carl' knows he was talking to a colored woman?"

"Since I'm fairly certain he knew our father was a colored man, and since he clearly understood he was talking to our father's daughter, yes, I think he knew. He didn't seem to care, if that's what you're asking."

"No colored companies we can deal with?"

"No. Not for what we need. Not until we start one."

"Because a lot of these supply places don't like to deal—"

Matilda put up her hand to block her brother's speech. "It's business. We're in business now. I gave the man a fair price and he accepted my offer."

"But a lot of them say that their other customers—"

"He can take his linens out back and boil them in bleach when we're done with them. Why would I care? Genovese stocks good quality. They're dependable. I got a decent price."

"Even though Montgomery's club probably has is own linen."

"Do you know that for sure?" Before he could answer, "And even if they do, we always brought our own linen. Why? Because a lot of these places, even if they do have their own, you can't count on it being fresh or not stained or cheap-looking. No one wants a less than pristine napkin on her lap. I've ordered linen that I guarantee you will be spotless and crisply pressed."

"But Tildy, twenty-sev—"

"Cost of doing business, big brother. Housewright Maxim #4: Tabletop is not one of the places we cut costs. Let's see what else." She rifled through a legal pad there by the phone. "Now, these folks I called over in the West End will supply uniforms—I asked for the semiformal for the men, you know, the short-waisted coat with the satin stripe up the outseam. Regular uniforms for the girls. By the way: I saved one of Daddy's old tuxes for you. I know it doesn't fit, but you never know, maybe some of the help will make use of it. Anyway, the supplier has got to have the exact count and the sizes by Friday, latest. My guy there, Vic, says these one-time rentals will costs us, but he'll deal on a standing contract or the outright sale of a decent used set, though I think the wear and tear would eat us alive. Vic doesn't advise new until we've got a stable staff and until we know whether most of our trade will be formal or semi or what have you, and he advises having the staff buy their own—advice I agree with, for the record. Again, he'll deal, if we've got the volume. Your decision. Now, apparently, there isn't one available set of restaurant-quality stemware in this city, but I've got an angle on the next shipment. Be ready to pounce. And I found a lady over in Cahokia who—"

"Tildy! Slow down. I can't take all this in."

"Here." She extended the legal pad in his direction. "It's all written down for you."

"I mean, it's too much. It's all happening too fast. All of it."

"Come. Sit down. Time's a-wasting." Matilda led her brother to the couch. "What do you need explained?"

"You don't understand." Martin drew his breath in, let it seep out. "My idea was to kind of sneak up on this thing, don't you see. A little at time. You know, fry the chicken and bake the pies for the ladies' auxiliary dinner at church. Do some sandwiches and cakes for a few birthday parties. Do you know what I mean? Slap up a few placards. Let the word trickle out."

"Actually, I don't understand, and, no, I don't know what you mean."

Martin was taken aback by his sister's rebuff.

"You're being silly. You're just scared. Things will be fine. Everything's coming together, you'll see."

"Matilda, you have a way of just barreling right on through, don't you? As long as you're happy. As long as it suits you. Well, what if *I* wanted to negotiate with the uniform place? What if I wanted . . . I don't know, blue tablecloths, or pink?"

"Blue linen for a luncheon? Well, there's an interesting thought. Actually the tablecloths are white. An eggshell tone, really. But if big brother wants blue, I can call around. There's plenty for everyone to do, is there not?"

And there it was: the ghost of a thought that he'd been waiting to surface. The question that had lingered near the corners of his consciousness for weeks: Yes, there was plenty to do, but what exactly did that have to do with his sister? After all was said and done, what was supposed to happen to Matilda? He had some responsibility to this woman—even if his father had not said so. But was he to just absorb her into his own dreams, into his own business? Was she just to be a permanent adjunct to his everyday life—for the rest of his life?

Reading his thoughts—as he believed she often did—his sister said, "A person might as well make herself useful. Don't you think?"

"Sure. Of course. But I guess I'd hate for you to think that you had to do all of this. I'd hate for you to feel beholden, because you are not, Matilda. I want you to tell me something honestly. Is this really what you want to be doing with your time?"

His sister, uncharacteristically, shrugged. Then she nodded.

"If you're sure then. But do me a favor: don't get too far ahead of me. I can't captain this ship if I don't know what the crew is up to."

"Aye, aye," Matilda said, although Martin couldn't tell if she did so sincerely or just to mock him. What he did know was that she wasn't trying to be cute. For the most part, cute was one of the things his sister did not do.

Matilda and Evie's initial confrontation had come over chicken. Not how to prepare their father's version of coq au vin—Martin and Matilda had eaten the dish and watched their father supervise the ingredients enough times over the years that there would be no disagreement there—but over how to get the chicken ready to be cooked. As would be expected, Martin had taken the role of cook, and he had assigned the women supplemental roles in ingredients preparation and storage. Should all go to plan, the profit from the luncheon should support the hiring of some regular kitchen help. (Martin had a couple of good fellows from down at the hotel in mind. All their father's nest egg had gone into outfitting the business and to the acquisition of the raw ingredients for the meal.)

Matilda had been assigned mushrooms, and it all might have come out differently in the long run had she kept her attention over the sink; had she focused on a vigorous scrub for each of the white fungi just as their father had taught them; had she split them, rinsed them, and set them to drain in the colander as was the Housewright way. Looking back, Martin realized that he knew his sister too well to believe that anything of the kind would happen.

Evie he had asked to attend to the chicken. He had not considered this a difficult job, and, indeed it was not. She'd been asked to assemble a fairly standard gathering of parts (already quartered and sectioned earlier in the afternoon by himself and Ralph, in a bloody butchering session that neither woman had been privy to), standard clusters organized so as to have pieces that cooked at approximately the same rate in the same groupings. She was to roll them in flour, to lightly coat them, and then deliver them to Martin's stove when requested. There, in hot oil, he would sear the pieces to a quick golden brown. He had contemplated a number of other tasks for his fiancée, including washing and slicing the mushrooms, but she had balked at all the time her hands would have to spend under cold water—something it would never occur to his sister to complain about—and Evie also didn't have the patience or precision to fill the crisp pastry shells with the hot lemon curd. She'd have made them a mess. His intended's chosen chore, while messy in its own right, required no precision—a little more or less flour didn't hurt a thing—and it gave her an opportunity to scoot by on a regular basis and make off-color remarks to Martin, banter that he happened to enjoy immensely. ("I've got those breasts you were asking about, Captain." "Plump and luscious, just the way I like them." Across the room his sister would snort in disgust.)

Everything sailed along smoothly. Martin had created just the sort of machine he imagined. Four pans of chicken sizzled at various levels of doneness. As one batch would finish, he'd freshen the oil, return it to temperature, and signal Evie for the next lot. The pastry shells that Ralph was filling had turned out flawlessly. Only one batch had overbrowned—not bad for a first time out. Martin had even considered using the darker shells—they were not that bad, but with Montgomery he took no chances. After worrying about it for the entire weekend, he had decided on the lemon tarts after all, even though they were sinfully easy to prepare and did not provide the platform to demonstrate the panache of the master pastry chef he had become at Tommaso's hands. While he'd prefer to be doing something requiring stiff buttercream and a deft hand with the pastry bag, Matilda had persuaded him otherwise, reminding him that fresh citrus had been a rarity during the war and that the guests might relish the tang of real lemons. ("Besides. It's early summer—use your head. It's fruit or sherbet. Were you born in an alley somewhere?")

All that remained for the morning was to tear apart the greens for the salad, prepare the egg noodles and the fresh peas, and reheat the chicken. It was all so perfect.

And then.

"May I ask what you're doing?"

It was his sister's voice he heard, and Martin thought, Good Lord.

"Getting rid of some of this nasty fat, honey. I can't stand too much fat on a piece of chicken. No lawdy."

Martin could tell by Evie's voice that she had as yet to pick up on the intensity of his sister's challenge.

"That fat would be what contains all the flavor. Martin, are you aware of what's going on back here?"

Martin busied himself at the stove. Too bad, he thought. Things had been going so well. Something had to give. Didn't it always?

Were he Tommaso, he'd wheel around and make a chopping motion at his neck to indicate the depth of his dissatisfaction with the parties at fault. With his spatula he would order the malcontents to neutral corners. After the meal, the sorry pair of them would put an extra polish on the silver for the officers' mess. That would show them who's the boss.

Alas, he was not Tommaso, and Housewright and Sons was not a ship. Even more, these were women—much tougher waters to negotiate, he was quickly coming to learn. He decided that what he would do was offer them each something and hope for the best.

Without turning from his chicken parts he'd said, "These pieces are looking just fine, Matilda. Nothing to worry about at all."

Then, after he'd heard his sister click back across the room, he'd added, "Old girl's right about the taste, though. Nothing like chicken fat to flavor a dish."

That stilled the water. Martin was pleased, although for the rest of the evening, he noted, there were no more saucy remarks from his fiancée. There was also, he heard, a sharper-sounding snap as his sister sliced each of the mushrooms in half.

After they'd finished, he left Matilda off first and then accompanied Evie to her parents' place.

"I'm taking a day off tomorrow to help with the luncheon," Evie announced.

"You don't have to do that. I've some young folks from the church lined up to serve. Ralph and I can handle the kitchen. Matilda can keep things moving out front."

"Yeah, but I want to be there for the big day. Our first catering job. I'm awfully excited."

As they stood on the porch, Evie snuggled into his side. A flush of something warm swept over him, something that felt to him the same as being spun on a thrill ride at a traveling carnival. He slid away from Evie—he told himself he was doing so to get a better look at his woman, but he also knew some of this had something to do with control, some fear he had of the feelings he got when he got to close to her.

Just look at her, he thought. Something else, she is, so different from all the women he'd known. The few he'd thought about back in Washington, a few scalawags he'd had the bad judgment to hook up with during his navy time—harsh and trashy things of the kind one often found near any place where men in uniform congregated.

So different from his sister. Soft, where Matilda was solid, easy where the other was hard. One might believe that rather than being different kinds of women, his sister and his intended were different species. He ran his gaze up and down Evie's body. This was something he knew that she liked, even though now and again she would pop her head up in mock indignation and ask him exactly what he thought he was looking at. "All them damn curves" is what he never replied to her. "The broad, rolling part down there and that rather plump area up top."

"This," he wanted to tell his sister, "is what a woman looks like. This is what she is, this is how she acts, this is what she does."

He wondered whether anyone had ever eyed Matilda in this way. No one that he knew of had done so. He wondered what such a person would see if they did.

Evie caressed his shoulder, dropped her eyes to address him in a way he saw as both playful and serious.

"I thought you despised the catering business," he said.

"I thought I did, too. But when I watched you and Ralph tonight . . . Baby, you just came to life in that kitchen."

"I told you. This is the life for me. I had a ball tonight."

"Me, too. Except for the dirty looks from your sister, that is."

Martin couldn't tell if Evie was truly hurt or just teasing. Whichever, he knew there would be little gained from an explanation. And what could he say in any case?

"That's our Tildy. You know she doesn't mean anything by it." That was the best he could muster, but it did nothing to assuage his woman.

"I think she does. I think she hates me. She's hated me since you all moved to town."

Though he knew that to be true, Martin chose to dissemble. "Matilda is just nervous about tomorrow, that's all. She's worked real hard, and she wants everything to come out right. Wait till things settle down. I'll take both you girls out for a little celebration. Then we'll all be friends again."

Evie snorted. "You'd think it was her damn business," she mumbled.

"Pardon?"

"You heard me."

Martin wasn't sure he liked what he thought he'd just heard "My baby sister must have really got under your skin."

Evie looked away. "A little. If you really want to know. That sister of yours can be so rude, the way she gets right in front of your face and starts in on you about something. But that's not the point."

"What would be the point, then?"

Evie walked to the other side of the porch. "Martin, where I work there is one person in charge. When the colonel says something, then that's the way it is. You were in the Navy. You served under that . . . what's his name?"

"Tommaso."

"Tommaso, right. So you know what I'm saying."

"I still don't see your point."

"Martin, I've watched you all real close these past few weeks, getting ready to open up this business. I've been real quiet. I've held my piece, but I have been paying attention. To everything. Do you want to know the truth? Your sister thinks that she is Housewright and Sons."

Martin scoffed to cover his true response, and then looked away.

"She does. Martin! Matilda makes all the decisions. Shake your head all you want to, but she does. Your sister makes all the decisions. And you let her. You do. Who decided on noodles instead of rice? Who chose the colors for the tables? Who?"

Martin rubbed his chin and sighed. Evie stood over him waiting for an answer.

"My sister is a very competent woman," he said.

"I didn't say she wasn't. I happen to like pink napkins, myself."

"Well, then."

Evie dropped herself down next to Martin. "It's not about pink napkins. You're right." Within the year this woman would be his wife, but Martin still had a hard time looking her in the eye. He just couldn't be sure yet. He trusted her, he thought, but what if . . . Martin didn't even know enough about this sort of thing to know what to be careful of. All he knew was that there was some risk here—something that had to do with holding some of yourself in abeyance, saving something just in case, and he also knew that somehow if they caught your gaze, these women, that would be that. That would be the game.

Evie continued on about his sister.

"I like Matilda. I do. I really do. I'm glad we're going to be family. I'm happy that someone like her will be our children's auntie."

Martin smiled the way he did whenever he imagined their family. Sometimes when they got carried away he and Evie would talk about twelve children, just like the family in *Cheaper by the Dozen*.

"If you want to know the truth, Martin, it's you that's the problem," Evie said, squeezing his hand.

"Me?"

"It's making you crazy. I know it is. I can feel it."

"She's made me crazy since the first time she scowled at me from her crib. What else is new?"

"Not she. It. It makes you crazy how strong your sister is. And one of these days—sooner than later, I bet—you'll have had enough of it."

She stood next to Martin and rubbed him on his back.

"Pick me up in the morning around nine-thirty, okay?" she said. She let herself in the house and closed the door without waiting for his reply. He stayed planted there on her front porch, fascinated that the empty space there beside him where Evie had been still felt alive to him.

IV

Martin dreamed fiasco. Of dry white meat, of limp lettuce, of gray flaccid peas. Inept waiters stumbled over each other's clumsy feet. A chain reaction of tripping, like a ballet almost, meringue flying, hot coffee spilled in laps. The big payoff: a face full of lemon custard for their host and benefactor. There was his sister's face, then, looming, ghostly, floating into the nightmare directly from hell, it seemed, dour mug set in smug self-righteousness. "I told you so's" dripping from her lips like venom.

Martin awoke sweating and he remembered, he thought, that in the dream his hand had been drawn back and his mouth had been open and some words had been set to be said, but he couldn't call them up, not even on a bet. He sat wrapped in his soaked sheets, throat strained, if only slightly so.

It will be fine, he assured himself.

When he stopped his car at the service entrance to the Rivermen's Club, Matilda was already waiting at the door, wringing her hands as if he and Evie and Ralph were an ambulance crew and she were the one who knew where the bodies were.

"Hurry with those trays," she started, even before the first of them had emerged from the car. "It's not good to be seen hauling food from the street. People get ideas. And as long as we're on the subject, I've got a lead on a used panel truck. Low miles, fairly new tires—at least three of them are. We could all chip in, I suppose."

"Morning to you to, Miss Matilda," Ralph greeted her, his always warm voice a relief to Martin against his sister's already abysmal jabbering.

"Ralph! You are looking positively cheflike."

Ralph blew a one-fingered kiss to his sister. He and Martin had both dressed in their chef's whites.

"Grab the lettuce before it wilts," Matilda ordered. "Surprised to see you this morning, Evie. Government holiday?"

"Just tell me what I can do, please."

"Can you say, 'More coffee, miss?' I'm afraid those . . . children . . . my brother hired have yet to arrive."

"That's because, Matilda, I asked them to come at eleven, just as I suggested you do, as well. And if you'll check your watch, it's just past ten. And, as long as we're on the subject, good morning!"

"No need to shout. As if an hour were enough to continue

grooming that motley lot. If that dark girl he hired learns her left from her right, I swear I will personally donate the money for her charm school lessons—which are sorely needed, might I add." She grabbed the box of linens. "I'll dress the tables. Come along, Evie. You might as well make yourself useful."

His fiancée directed a look toward Martin that could have denoted bemusement or stifled rage. He wasn't entirely sure. He and Ralph loaded trays onto a rolling rack and hauled them upstairs on the service elevator.

Ralph wrenched the gate aside when the elevator reached five, the floor where the banquet room was located. Martin recognized the sallow-faced cigar smoker waiting for them as a Mr. Grubb, the facilities manager of the Rivermen's Club, an unpleasant troll of man whom he had had to deal with once before—the time that he had met Montgomery to finalize the arrangements for the luncheon.

"You boys are working that noon job, I reckon. Bring all that on over to the kitchen. The caterer will be here directly to tell y'all what to do next."

"This here is the caterers," Ralph said, nodding in Martin's direction.

Grubb harrumphed. It had been less than a week since Montgomery had presented Martin to this man and told him explicitly what his role was. Martin was sure that the troll remembered who he was.

"Them gals in the dining room with you all? Ordinarily we don't allow a lady in the building without a gentleman accompanying her. Not unless they's pouring coffee."

"Yes, sir. They're here to help us set up." Martin tried to remember how his father would handle cretins such as this one. (*Be pleasant. Be brief. Keep your cool. He's not worth losing your business over.*)

"That one gal. The skinny one. She got a mouth on her. You better remind her of her place, you hear me?"

"I'll do that. Would the kitchen be available for us?" Seeing the troll's eyebrows rise, Martin added the requisite "Sir."

"Y'all come on let me point out a few things."

Martin indicated with his head that Ralph should do the honors. "I'll go speak to those *gals* for you, *sir*." Martin moved off toward the dining area before Grubb could protest. He'd already had the tour once, had already had his own patience tried as this Grubb condescendingly walked him around the kitchen, named each of the common appliances, and demonstrated the controls on a garden-variety industrial stove. Ralph, he knew, would have more equanimity about it, at least more than Martin had this morning—would be less likely to insult the old windbag by telling him exactly what he could do with his officious manner, his snide comments, and his innuendos.

More and more Martin found himself unable to tolerate the treatment he received from the likes of Grubb. Here, a man who was clearly less well educated; a man who more than likely rarely left this building, let alone traveled beyond the city limits; someone who certainly had never lived in homes as decent as the Housewrights had, felt he had the God-given right to speak to another human being in such a fashion. It was unfathomable.

When Martin had joined the Navy, it had been his hope that somehow his service might change all this. And, when he'd been overseas with all those other millions of men, all fighting for the same cause, he had believed with all his heart that when they returned home, they would be owed a debt. He believed that it would be impossible for him to be looked down on again.

And, yet, still.

What he wanted to do was to charge back into that kitchen and make sure that this Grubb understood that he was dealing with a veteran, and it was thanks to the sacrifices of the likes of Martin that the likes of him got to stand outside the steam room of the Rivermen's Club and pass out fresh towels—that and whatever other menial tasks they lined up for him on a given day. But Martin knew where such an attempted dressing down would lead. Grubb had the better of them, and unless they wished to disappoint Montgomery and, worse, be left on the sidewalk with a car full of spoiling food on their hands, he'd have to swallow it down. Again.

Better to go rein in his sister, he decided.

To his memory not one detail of the Rivermen's Club had changed from the last time he'd seen it, which had been before the war. The Senator, who remained one of the core members—as was any white man of status in the city—had been the frequent sponsor of events in this location, and Martin's father had often been in charge of the details. The same heavy gold-moiré draperies obscured the windows, draperies so rigid-looking they appeared to be weighted with lead shot. Around the walls, arrayed in the same rank he recalled, the stiffly formal portraits of the founders of the club, the nineteenth-century shipping barons who had been responsible for the city's first flourish of prosperity.

Matilda and Evie stood at the bar, sorting the linens by function into several stacks.

"You ladies need anything?" he asked.

"We're fine," his sister answered. "I was just showing Evie the proper way to fold a luncheon napkin."

"And I was just sharing with Matilda that I've folded quite a few napkins by my own self over the years."

Change the subject, Martin strategized. "Are these tables spaced properly? Is there enough room to serve?"

Matilda disengaged from her rival and focused on her brother. "I think we're in pretty good shape. But I didn't want to dress them until you had a look. Is there to be a head table?"

"Montgomery says there's no formal presentation, and there's no guest of honor. They're to sit where they choose. He'll fill in the late arrivals himself. Enough seats?"

"Seven rounds of eight. Just what we asked for. There will be a few extra places, but that's always better than not enough. Now, we do have these few mismatched chairs—the captain's chairs, there at number five. Do you think we could have that dreadful little man rustle us up some more of the others?"

Martin told his sister that he didn't think that was a good idea. "That dreadful little man, as you refer to him, said you were short with him just now."

"How clever. You made a pun. Perhaps I was. I don't recall. Times like these, who attends to the likes of him?"

"Matilda, today of all days I need you—"

"Marvelous! The flowers have arrived. Right on time."

"Tildy! Flowers! I didn't authorize—"

His sister signaled for him to zip closed his lip. "Set them over on the bar, young man, where my assistant is standing." Then she whispered, "Do you have a quarter to tip him?"

Martin fished the coin from his pants and handed it to the deliveryman.

"And before you say one more word"—she put a finger to his lips to stop his protest—"not one more word. I got a deal. A real deal."

Evie unwrapped one of the arrangements: carnations and pale pink roses tucked into an effusive bundle of baby's breath.

"They *are* nice," Evie offered.

"See," Matilda gloated. "And you'd be surprised what the promise of regular business does to the price of a spray. That, and just a snippet of guilt I larded in over those horrifyingly limp lilies at our father's funeral."

"You went back to that old crook. You're shameless."

"I was heartbroken. He was full of remorse. And these centerpieces were practically free. Come, Evie. Stop your dawdling. Let's get these tables dressed before the Little Rascals arrive." Matilda snapped a skirt across the nearest table and landed it almost square in the center.

"Just like that," she said to Evie. "I'll follow behind with the napkins."

Evie shrugged and grinned at Martin, and then nodded toward the kitchen to let him know that she could tough it out with his sister and that he best see to his preparations in the kitchen.

Blessedly, the troll was nowhere in sight. He and Ralph had the kitchen to themselves. Ralph set a large metal bowl on the prep table.

"Chicken's in the oven—slow oven, like you said. Tarts are in the icebox. Water's on for the noodles and peas. Your choice: whip the cream or break up the greens."

"Too early for the cream. Whipped cream settles. You want to whip the cream as close to dessert service as you can manage: *after* you serve the entrée—the Housewright way. You should try to remember things like that."

"I should, should I?"

"You never know when you might end up owning part of a catering business."

"If I had me the money to own something, not so sure it would be a business like this."

"You're a natural."

"I'm good at a lot of things." Ralph shrugged.

"So you don't want to talk about coming into the business with me?"

Ralph sorted the salad greens into a large colander. "Don't need to talk about it. I figure you'll take care of me."

Martin nodded.

(To Martin's credit, that unspoken promise was kept as long as the two men were partners, which would be for the rest of their working lives.)

His servers (all but one of the young women, who had forgotten she had a class to attend at Stowe) arrived ahead of schedule. This ought to have put Matilda at ease, except upon changing into their uniforms, it was discovered that the boys' pants were the wrong size. In every case, the trousers measured several inches too long.

"What hath God wrought." Matilda sighed.

She fished through the linen box and drew forth a chain of safety pins. "Scout's motto," she saluted, and she tossed the pins to Evie. "You pin while I talk."

"Now pay attention everyone. We've got to review and practice. Is this everybody? Martin, there were eight? I'm only seeing seven."

"We'll be fine, Tildy."

An even deeper sigh from his sister, who, to her credit, regained her poise. That was his Tildy: stiff upper lip for the troops, always. "This will have to do, indeed. Let's begin, shall we? Who can remind us which side we serve from?"

And Martin listened as his sister drilled her charges on the basics of luncheon service. Across the room he could almost feel the delight she radiated at the young people's proficiency—thrilled, she was, with both their knowledge as well as with her own skill as their master. My, what a good teacher couldn't accomplish with a well-honed lesson or two. What Martin knew that Matilda didn't was that Darius, the tall handsome one with the complexion like burnished oak, had met with the group in the church's basement the night before and had called on his experience as a waiter in a rival midtown club to instruct his colleagues. No wonder they did so well placing and retrieving Matilda's "practice" dishes. She had weighted the cups with tap water and the plates with various discards from the pantry. His servers handled each item almost as if they had been born to service. Martin would try to remember to slip Darius an extra few bucks in his pay.

"We're doing splendidly," Matilda enthused. "I couldn't be more pleased. Now come and sit. All of you." She beckoned them the way Martin remembered his first teachers would call the little ones together to read them a story.

She gathered her troops at the table nearest the pantry for their final marching orders. Behind him, in the kitchen, noodles were draining; the salad plates with the greens and their garnish—a fan of crisp cucumber—all cooled in one of the iceboxes. The peas had been shelled and were ready to be popped into their bath of simmering seasoned water, if only for just a second. These times would always be the hard part for Martin, this time when there was nothing else to do but wait. He'd learned well from Tommaso this lesson, to build these few minutes of downtime into every operation. To give everyone time to stop and catch his breath before the real action started. Even so, and even though it was never the case, he would never not imagine that there was something left undone, that it was wrong—bad and ill-advised—to stand around looking idle. Just in front of him, he watched his sister take a stance in front of her pupils, clapping her hands once, crisply, to signal the beginning of a new set of remarks.

"Today you will be serving guests of a Mr. Montgomery, a prominent political figure here in the city. Mr. Montgomery's guests are coming because he is interested in having them join him in supporting a cause that is dear to his heart. The nature of that cause is of no concern to any of you. I tell you only so that you'll know that the men—and I believe a few women, as well—that you will be serving today are influential, mostly very well to do, and therefore used to a certain level of service. Because they will be, almost without exception, gentlemen and ladies of a certain upbringing, you needn't expect that they will challenge you on your inappropriate behavior—should there be any, and I'm not anticipating that there will be—but you can be assured that my brother and I will hear about it, which won't be pleasant for anyone concerned."

Ah, Matilda, queen of the veiled threats. As if there were one thing she could hold over the heads of such a disparate and hastily assembled lot.

"The guests will gather in one of the rooms downstairs and will have conducted their business before they enter the dining room. Which means that our service begins as soon as they are all are seated. I will point out Mr. Montgomery to you. Just so you will know who he is. He is the one in whose employ we are, so you may find him making requests of you that others do not make. You are to report those requests to us at once and we will respond to them as quickly as we can. Is that understood?"

Martin heard the thin round of "yes, ma'ams."

"Now. You are all young men and women. You've been around some, I know, and you understand the way things are. Your parents have explained certain things, as well. Some of these things, it goes without saying, none of us likes, not I any more than any of you. But, I would be remiss were I not explicit and direct about a few issues."

The fidgeting Martin had noticed earlier had stopped. He observed the waiters eyeing each other discreetly, eyebrows raised, throats quietly cleared.

"We are here to serve." His sister paused. Martin didn't know if the pause was for effect or simply to underline the matter of fact.

"When serving, your eyes belong where you are walking, on the place you are serving, and on the condition of the table. Nowhere else. We do not look them in the eye. Is that clear?"

Martin heard no response. Something in his own chest tightened.

"If they speak to you—and it is highly unlikely that will happen—it is not to engage you in conversation; it will be to ask you to fill their coffee cup, to bring them a fresh napkin, to clear their space, something of that nature. It is not an invitation to make eye contact or to engage them in conversation. Your response will always be 'Yes, sir' or 'Yes, ma'am.' Clear?"

Again, no response that Martin heard. He wanted to step into this to . . . well, he didn't know quite what he wanted to do. He'd frozen again. He watched. Powerless. Pained.

"If there is a complaint, your response will be 'I apologize, sir. I'll take care of that right away, sir.' This is the case even if the problem is not of your doing. We can avoid much of that sort of thing if we keep the goblets topped up with water and the coffee service moving. You needn't concern yourselves with compliments. They will be directed to Mr. Montgomery."

As she spoke, his sister paced back and forth in a small path, holding herself within some invisible bounds the same way an animal too long in the same enclosure did. She was calm, serene, confident, almost smug. As she reached one end of her path, her body swiveled mechanically, in parts: torso, then head, then legs, the turns timed, he thought, for the greatest dramatic effect.

"Though I don't anticipate such a thing, one of Mr. Montgomery's guests may feel moved to speak to you directly. It has happened occasionally. He may speak to you about something other than the meal, that is. You may be asked your name, for example, or if you've worked here long. That sort of thing. You (she pointed to the tall one) would say, 'Darius, sir.' 'Not long, sir.' That is all that is required or expected of you. No one here is really interested in anything else you might have to say."

Yes, that's correct, part of Martin thought, and then another part of him said, "No, this is all wrong," but even that part of him knew that it wasn't all wrong. It was the truth, but he couldn't even imagine how he knew that was so, why his sister would know, how and why she was able to stand there and say such things as if she were giving out advice on the latest fashions or on the charms of a Hollywood film.

"One last thing," she said, executing her three-part pivot there at the end of her prescribed path. "As you know, they are not all . . . you may find some of the guests here to be, frankly, rude. You may be called names you don't care for. You young women, you may have a gentleman speak to you in ways that can only be described as . . . indelicate. A hand may be misplaced. We do not hear these things. We do not notice. Do you understand that? We are here to serve. That is all. That's what we're paid to do. Have I made myself clear?"

With that, his sister pivoted on her heels one last time and stalked toward the pantry.

"Show time, Admiral," she said, saluting him, her face illuminated with pride at a job well done.

The servers sat crestfallen, shamed, staring at their feet. The guests would begin filtering in within minutes. Martin had to act. He peeled himself away from the doorjamb.

"You all look terrific," he said, and they did, if it mattered. He walked among them nodding and smiling confidently, the way he remembered Tommaso had done back on the ship. He put a hand on each one, said things such as "Let me know if you need anything" and "You're gonna to do a great job, I know." And while he might not have washed away his sister's words, they did seem to brighten up.

"Stand in a line and let me look you over," he said, and he used a tone that he hoped implied he was only half serious. He teased a tiny girl named Polly about getting lost amid these giants.

"When I was on the ship, the one thing we agreed on was teamwork. We're a team. I'm proud to have you on board. I hope this is just the first of many successful events you'll work with me." The staff smiled at each other, though after Matilda's performance who could blame any one of them for disappearing forever.

Montgomery's head appeared around the door frame. He caught Martin's eye, Martin signaled him to usher in his guests.

"Come." Martin signaled to his troops. "Come on." He herded them as if they were his own baby chicks, found himself using that same beckoning gesture his sister had only a short time earlier. "You all wait right here. In this pantry. This space is yours. All yours. We'll set out the rolls and butter and the dressing as soon as we get about half of them seated.

"You look great. You're going to do fine." One or two of them were outright shaking, but he knew most of that would cease once they got to work.

"Remember," he said, whispering, the room filling up, loading each server with baskets of rolls and pitchers of water and iced tea. "Remember they are just people. Just like you and me."

He waved them off to their rounds and turned to find his sister giving him the evil eye.

Clockwork.

That's how service of the salad and entrée had gone, or at least from Martin's limited perspective. He had only had a few chances to peek out front, between the frenzy of charging the chilled dishes with salad greens and plating the chicken. What a kick! What timing! What a team they made. Ralph dealing the dinner plates like so many playing cards. Martin, a wizard with the ladles and tongs. As fast as the servers returned from the dining room empty-handed, Ralph waited ready to load the warmed plates of hot food.

All cylinders fired in tandem, just like a fine engine.

The few times he'd been able to sneak into the pantry, he'd found things in the dining room had been just as he'd hoped. The guests did what they were there to do—visited and savored their meals. The staff served—efficient, unobtrusive, surprisingly skilled.

"Going okay?" he'd asked Matilda. She'd been standing there in the pantry, worrying at a service towel, delivering wordless and yet clear orders to the staff, to his wonder in much the same way Tommaso had done. Thrusting a water pitcher to Darius, she'd raised three fingers, swept them to the left, and off he'd trotted to refill a water glass for an elderly gentleman with tufts of gray hair sticking off the side of his bald head.

"It's going," she'd said. "Remind me to have a word about posture. Especially with the girls."

"They look fine, Tildy. I'm sure no one's noticed a little slouch now and then."

"*I* noticed." She'd spun one of the servers around with a fresh napkin for one of the guests who had lost his beneath the table.

Martin headed back to the kitchen to help whip the cream. Ralph had retrieved the bowls from the freezer and started working half the liquid.

"I assume it's time, Captain?" he asked.

Overzealous as always, Martin wanted to say, but he remembered what Tommaso's philosophy toward such situations had been: Reward the initiative, but toss in a mild rebuke of some kind.

"I guess it's time whether I think so or not." He shrugged. "I'll catch up." He poured the remaining containers into the cold metal bowls and got to work.

Ralph beat with an aggressive stroke: Martin noticed the cream in the other bowl coming together already.

"Damn," he said. "I should hire you out to the dairy." He switched bowls with his friend, not wanting to serve his guests butter. "I'll season this batch."

He added the vanilla and just a dusting of powdered sugar, loaded the pastry bags, and retrieved the tarts from the icebox.

"Let's get this done," he ordered. "Evie, I need you over here."

Evie had been over at the dish sink trying to figure out what on earth to do with the dinner plates. Dirty dishes had been trickling in, but that trickle would soon become a flood. The sink already brimmed over with salad plates. Martin had no desire to see his woman up to her elbows in dishwater, and he'd told her to just let the china pile up. Unfortunately they'd run out of places to pile—next time, top of the list: remember to hire someone just to handle the dishes.

"I don't mind the sink. I really don't," Evie cooed, though Martin could tell by the way she dried her hands that she really did mind and that he'd earned big points just for ending that hell. He pointed her to the tray full of pastries.

"Ralph's going to swirl each of these tarts with whipped cream. I want you to place a mint leaf on each one. Just so," he demonstrated.

"Let's go," Matilda hectored, bustling into the kitchen, and in her wake, a clutch of staff, laden with dirty plates.

"What am I supposed to do with these?" she screamed. Martin

and Ralph and Evie looked up from the dessert. Evie moved to set aside her garnishing, but Martin placed a hand on her arm, signaling her to stay still.

"Place them on the floor. There by the sink."

"Absurd," she seethed. And then to the servers: "Keep moving. Those people don't care to linger in front of soiled dishes and chicken bones." She stormed back into the pantry.

The three of them worked silently, but Martin felt the tension. They each sensed, he could tell, that something was about to happen, and feared—knew—that all it would take would be the right word, or the wrong one, to set it off. Now and again one of them would exclaim at a particularly lovely swirl of cream or at the way that the perfect sprig of mint brought the whole dish together. Ralph and Martin placed the desserts on trays for delivery to the guests. Evie went over to attempt to make some order of the mountains forming on the floor near the sink.

"That's almost the last of them," Matilda said, helping Darius with an awkward load. "What a mess. This wouldn't have happened if you'd—"

"If I'd what?" Evie rose from the piles of dishes, staring at her future sister-in-law as if the woman had just slapped her. "This wouldn't have happened if I'd what?"

"Tildy! Take the dessert trays to the pantry. We'll serve the tarts now. Please."

"No!" his sister said, still faced off with Evie.

"Pardon? Matilda, the desserts . . . Never mind. Ralph . . ." Martin, just as Tommaso would have done, swirled his hands over the trays and pointed to the pantry.

Matilda turned from Evie, keeping one eye on her as if she were a wild boar. "Put those down," she said to Ralph. "It's too soon." She placed herself in the pantry door. "They're just doing a round of coffee. After it's all served, then we'll—"

Martin got in his sister's face. "Get the hell out of my way."

Matilda opened her mouth to speak, but Martin clamped a hand around her arm and dragged her across the room to the service entrance. He could see both Ralph and Evie with their hands raised in protest. And maybe they had spoken, but all that he heard was his sister whimpering in pain. And maybe he had gripped her arm too severely, but he didn't care. He pushed her up against the door and released her.

"You stay out of my way," he ordered.

Matilda rubbed at her arm, stared at her feet.

Martin pointed at the tarts and nodded his head at Evie and Ralph. "Before the cream separates," he said quietly, and began scrubbing at the pyramid of salad plates stacked in the sink.

He ran the hot water until his hands could endure no more, until it felt almost as if the top layer of skin were peeling away. He savored the way that plunging his fingers into the steamy bath caused, ironically, something like a chill, and also the way that removing them from the water felt such a relief. Doing the dishes always reminded him of the time back in high school, back in Washington, when the Senator had hosted a party for the ambassador from France. Thurester, one of the girls who sometimes helped in the kitchen, had come up sick, and his father had been desperate, had come to Martin and insisted he help. He remembered how, as he filled the pantry with shiny clean china, he'd felt a mixture of pride and humiliation. Hadn't working alongside his father always felt something like that?

"Martin." Evie touched his arm. "She's gone." She nodded toward the last place he'd seen his sister standing.

Martin submerged another dinner plate in the sink. He said nothing.

"You should go after her."

Ralph stood just behind Evie, to hear—to judge, Martin thought—what he intended to do.

"She's a grown woman. Please, see to the pantry." He nodded to Evie. "Make sure the coffee circulates. Ralph, double check on the big urn. If it's below half, start a fresh brew."

The three of them and the seven servers worked in efficient silence the rest of the hour. Luckily, there had been no disasters, save for the spectacular shattering of a dinner plate, which had slipped from Martin's hands as he fished it from the dishwater. His fingers by then had been wrinkled and numb, and the plate's demise unfortunately coincided with another appearance by the troll, Grubb.

"Y'all be paying for my dishes, you hear me? You hear me, boy?"

Ralph answered a hearty "Yes, sir, Mister Grubb, we hear you, now." He'd used that same infantile and ignorant-sounding tone that for all his life Martin had heard colored men use at times like this. And though he was grateful to Ralph for appeasing the old man, there was a part of him that wanted to strangle his friend.

Ushering away his last guest, Montgomery breezed into the kitchen, his ebullience lightening the mood considerably.

"Bravo!" he cheered. He shook Martin's hand, pumping it up and down as if it might produce oil. "An absolute triumph, if I do say so myself."

Martin's response hardly matched his retainer's enthusiasm. "Thank you, Mr. Montgomery," he said quietly. "I'm glad Housewright and Sons met your high standards."

"Met them? Why, you should have heard those folks. They raved about the food. A couple of these gals will be calling you all for their bridge club and things. I hope it's okay, I got some cards from your sister. Where is she? I wanted to let her know how well you all did."

"Matilda had another engagement."

"Well, you let her know for me, will you? And look what else." Montgomery flourished from his coat pocket a wad of bills. "These tips are for the boys out front. Folks were real pleased with the service, me included. Pass these along for me, will you?"

"Actually, sir . . ." Martin signaled his head server, who was busy helping Evie stuff soiled linen into bags. "Mr. Montgomery, this is the head of my service staff. Mr. Darius Walker." Martin nodded to make sure Darius understood he should extend his hand. Montgomery, while indicating to Martin that it was not standard protocol to take the young man's hand, extended his own like the professional he was.

"Excellent work, there, you." He pressed the money into the young man's hand. "Make sure the other boys get their share."

Montgomery then handed Martin a check. "Your daddy'd be real proud of you right now."

"Thank you, sir," Martin said, as Montgomery excused himself, saying he'd be back to them real soon—about a thirty-fifth wedding anniversary party he was throwing.

"Your daddy'd be real proud," Montgomery said again, on his way out. It seemed he'd directed it to everyone in the room, as if Ralph and Evie and Darius and the others had all sprung from the loins of Jacob Housewright, majordomo extraordinaire. Jacob Housewright, of the spotless white jackets and the always pleasant demeanor. Jacob Housewright, a man who, although almost always there in the corner of the room just waiting to respond to your every need, seemed at the same time to be invisible, seemed not to be there at all. Jacob Housewright, a man who never disappointed the Senator once in all those years of service.

In his hand Martin held a check for more money than he had ever been paid to do anything in his entire life. It was the first of reams of similar notes, enough money eventually to pay Darius's way through law school, to provide for himself and Evie and their two sons a home more grand than even they had the courage to dream possible, to keep Ralph in a similar style, and to keep Ralph as well, each season for the next half century, in the new Cadillac of his choice.

Fifty years from now, his grandson, another Jacob Housewright, would be press-ganged by Martin's son to work a banquet in a room very much like this one (it would actually be the same room, but Martin would not recall that at the time). Jacob Housewright, that future Jacob Housewright, would be earning the money to pay for some amazing music gadget about which Martin at the time would decide he was too old to understand either its function or operation. That night in the distant future, Martin would be there in the pantry, much the same as his sister had been on this day, reminding his grandson to stand up straight, to not scowl, please—wishing that that son of his had done something about whatever it was that sprouted from his grandson's head like a fountain of golden ash.

The customers would all be colored. They would not notice his grandson's hair at all. Montgomery would have been dead for a quarter century—Matilda would have to remind Martin what the man's name had been.

Until he died Martin would remember that someone or the other had told him that his father would have been proud of him. And despite the fact that even on that day of that first banquet, the number of people who knew Jacob Housewright—who had ever known his father and his work—had dwindled to a precious few, Martin Housewright would spend rest of his life waiting for someone to say those words to him again.

V

To Martin, observing his sister from the kitchen of their late father's house, Matilda resembled some kind of exotic but drab bird—one of the gangly long-legged things that would sometimes strafe the deck of the ship as it passed near some South Sea island. Perched on the center bench in the bay window in the breakfast room of their father's house, Matilda stared out at their father's garden, an image of serenity, of benign idleness. Before her, on the table where Jacob Housewright had had his morning coffee, lay strewn an array of seed and garden catalogs. Their father had treasured the rectangle of flowers and bushes and trellises and brick that sat behind his home like some bejeweled postage stamp. Martin noticed for the first time how much the garden had come to resemble the one behind the Senator's house back in Washington. He'd forgotten so much from those days, but he did remember the winding brick path and the cozy, pale-yellow carriage house that the three of them had shared. The cottage at the back of the Senator's property had always seemed to him as if it belonged in one of those fairy tales set deep in the middle of an enchanted forest, its low-ceilinged grace, its exposed beams, the pale-pink paint that covered every interior surface; how back there with his sister and their father—when their father wasn't off seeing to the Senator—it almost seemed like the Housewrights had been sent away and abandoned on some wonder-filled and magical island.

"He almost got it looking the same," Martin said.

"The clematis aren't right. There on the trellises. I'm pulling them out and replacing them with maybe a climbing rose. Maybe wisteria. Roses are so much fuss, but I really haven't made up my mind yet."

Martin tried to gauge Matilda's mood. She betrayed nothing: she may have spent the entire day here, placid, calm, examining their father's garden. Her composure shamed him, somehow.

He sat on the window seat beside her—behind her, really. Her shoulders twisted slightly more toward the window, just enough for him to get the message. He reached toward her back, to touch her, to soothe her—if it were soothing she needed; he didn't know—then he pulled his hand back. He hung his head.

"I'm sorry, Tildy. I really am."

She said nothing.

"It got really crazy there for a while. Didn't it? Nothing like a lunch service to get the blood flowing. And the temper, I guess."

Still nothing from his sister.

"But, boy, Montgomery was pleased. Really pleased. We were

a hit. Housewright and Sons are lined up for at least two more engagements."

Martin watched his sister's back for signs of her breathing, a sense of where she was and how she felt. He rubbed at the still-puckered tips of his fingers, bleached almost white by heat and soap.

"Just look at these hands. Girl, that dishwater . . ."

Matilda twisted forward, stood, and straightened her dress. She reached for the catalogs on the glass and wrought-iron table. She fussed them into a neat stack.

"Say what you came to say, Martin."

He opened his mouth, a bit stunned. "I was. Am."

"Save us both from your equivocation, please. Get to the point." Matilda stood before her brother like a girl sent to the headmistress, arms clasped demurely before her, waiting to hear both her sin as well as her sentence.

"I came here to apologize. And I just did. And since you're clearly still in some kind of a state . . ." Martin grabbed his father's homburg from the table. He'd taken to wearing the hat often. Over his life it would become something of a trademark.

"I've got some business to talk over with Ralph. You and I—"

"Will complete our conversation right this minute, thank you very much." She stepped in front of her brother. "I'll trouble you to finish what you came to say. About the business. Go ahead and say it."

"I don't know what you mean."

"Please." She challenged him to meet her eye. Martin stumbled back to the bench, reaching behind him. He tried to pretend it had been his intention to sit there all along. Matilda remained in her penitent pose.

"It doesn't have to be this way," he said. "But you've left me—"

"I've left you? I'm leaving you? What exactly am I leaving you to do?"

"Matilda. You never make things easy."

"Why should I?"

"Because that's what people do. That's why. But, no, not Matilda Housewright. Not you. You just wear people out."

"*People* would mean you, I suppose. For the record, just what is it that's worn you out this time?"

"Everything. Your bossiness. Your imperiousness. The fact that no one can do anything right except for you."

"Finally, to the good part. Well, isn't this fun?"

"You go to hell." Martin pushed past his sister and headed for the front door.

"Father would never allow—"

"And you can shut your damn mouth about our father, Matilda." He spun around as if he wasn't sure whether he was coming or going. He sighed, waved his hand in his sister's face. "I don't want to do this with you. Not today. Not tomorrow and certainly not for the rest of my life."

"So this is the part where I'm supposed to beg you to tell me what I did wrong. What if I skip right to the part where I tell you I'm sorry and that it will never happen again?"

"Do you really think it's that simple? Jesus, you'd think this was some kind of a game."

"You're the one playing, big brother. I'm still waiting for you to tell me what you came to tell me."

"All right, fine. I don't want you in my business. There. Satisfied?"

"If you are." Matilda turned and fled into the kitchen.

Martin sat at the bottom of the steps that led to the sleeping rooms.

So that was that.

Somehow he'd expected the words to come harder. There should have been constriction in his throat, a few lightning bolts perhaps. The next step was to open the door and move on. Instead, he decided to check on her. She was his responsibility, after all. Daddy said so.

Matilda hung over the sink, pressing into an old iron skillet with a scouring pad. Her back was shaking. He believed she had been crying.

"This is not fair," he said. "You wanted it, and you got it, and now you're making me—"

She wheeled toward him. "Making you? Again, *making* you. Mercy!" She slammed the skillet in the sink.

Martin held out his arms beckoning her toward an embrace.

"No!" she screamed, sobbing into a handkerchief. "You promised me . . . I won't . . ."

"I did promise. And I—"

"I will not talk about this." Matilda looked at the tiled floor and twisted at the steel wool in her hands.

"I am simply unable to be in business with you," Martin said. "It's not good for me and it's not good for you."

"Why isn't it good for me?" Martin heard a plaint in his sister's voice that he hadn't heard since childhood, a deeply seared memory from a time that their father had denied her a trip to the segregated department store the Senator's son was always bragging about being taken to.

"You knew what I came here to say," Martin said softly. "I find your reaction somewhat disingenuous."

"Maybe I didn't think you had it in you, Marty. Forgive me." She wiped her nose one last time and tossed the remains of the scouring pad in the trash. In an instant she'd gone from the naughty girl anticipating her dressing-down, to the chastised and chagrined opponent in a long bitter feud. And it was then, just then, in that moment, that he recognized the main difference between them: the fact that he had never once underestimated her.

"You and I could take over the world, big brother."

"I'm aware of that."

"There's so much that I know."

"I'll learn those things. I'm not incapable."

"I didn't say you were. It's just that . . . well, we're a good team."

"No, Matilda. No, we are not a good team. You are a brilliant and a . . . capable woman. But there is no *we* when you're around. There's no me."

Matilda shrugged

"I've got some business with Ralph. Like I said." Martin again headed for the door.

"If you would just let me—"

"Please." The word rolled forth like a wail from a drowning sailor, from some place deep inside Martin, a place he'd wished he did not own. His sister shook and cowered as if he'd made to grab her again. He reached out to her and again she rebuffed him.

"Okay," she said. "Okay, fine. I heard you."

Martin nodded and backed away.

"Should . . . I save you some supper, then?"

"Don't bother. I'll get something."

"It's no bother," she said. She pasted on what she imagined must have been a welcoming half smile, a bitter and pained expression that always broke Martin's heart whenever it visited him in his dreams, as it had done often over the years.

"I'll see you later, Tildy."

A week or so later, he retrieved from his bedroom his few meager belongings. All during the packing Matilda stayed perched in her usual spot overlooking their father's garden. They exchanged pleasantries but nothing much more, really.

On his way out the door, Martin opened his wallet and removed a check written on the new business account he and Ralph had opened with the money from the Montgomery luncheon. He placed it on a console in the foyer, tucking the corner beneath a vase that the Senator had given their father. It was her money, too, after all, and he would never not feel that way.

For the rest of their lives, for the rest of the century and beyond, the house on Woodlawn Avenue would stay in the family. Martin, he never slept there again; and as for his sister, as for Matilda, she almost never went anywhere else.

The Second Thing I Have to Tell You

. . .

The truth about men of prominence is that they are just like you and me. When you grow up as part of the household of someone like the Senator, you live behind the curtain, as it were. Out front, in the places where these people put themselves on display, everything is designed to make them look grand and important and larger than life. Back here, they are as ordinary as toast. You are all familiar with the one-leg-at-a-time method they use for dressing themselves. In addition, they are full of as many quirks and foibles as the rest of us, and for the most part their personal hygiene is no better and, often enough, much worse than the person sitting next to you on the bus. (More often worse, in fact, than you might care to imagine.) If it weren't for their often-unwieldy egos and the massive amounts of self-confidence that accompany such vanity, you couldn't tell them from the average Joe on the street. Since Americans are, for the most part, populists at heart, the images that the rich and influential promulgate must be delicately shaped in a way that transmits to "the people" a message assuring them that, despite appearances, it's "just plain folks here." Thus, those of us behind the curtain swim in an odd sea of paradox, where while we watch these great men attest to how they are just like you and me, at the same time we know that they don't believe this in the slightest. We know that there is no one more in awe of the greatness of a great man than that great man himself. The final irony for us is that as the people who know the high regard that these people have for themselves, we who have lived in their midst also know just how pedestrian they truly can be.

Lest you get the wrong idea, I happen to like the idea of these larger-than-life figures that move above the common fray. I think we need them. I think that when an ordinary person views a man such as the Senator, and particularly in the way that an ordinary person would most likely view someone of the Senator's stature—which is from a distance and projected in such a fashion so as to best preserve the most regal image possible—the ordinary person is somehow uplifted. He gets a glimpse of the caliber of man that it is possible to be in this world and believes that maybe, just maybe, he could do great things with his own life; and should you believe this view elitist, imagine the alternative. Imagine living in a world in which the most emulated individuals were criminals and deviants. Do we really want the people on the bottom of our society aping the coarse and ignominious lives of the lesser among their peers? Some might. I would not.

So the Housewrights have always taken pride in their role in giving the people they worked with every opportunity to forward their most positive image. My earliest memory in life is of toddling along behind my mother as she prepared the Senator's wife's dressing room for the morning's ablutions. The Senator's wife, an early riser, appreciated finding her bath already drawn and her clothes laid out for the day before she unfurled herself from her canopy bed. Before we climbed to the living quarters on the second floor of the Senator's home, Mother made me practice walking "with cat's feet," as she described it, with only the lightest of footfalls near the tips of my tiny white shoes. The rules in all such households were clear: children living on the premises had best be invisible. So my mother played this game with me to make sure I did nothing to disturb the family, none of whom had risen yet. It must have been the case that I'd had a restless night or perhaps had awakened from a bad dream. Perhaps my father had already left the carriage house to tend to some business and my mother thought rather than leaving me to cry all alone, she would dress me and bring me along on her morning rounds. Whatever the case, I remember her playfully caressing my body with a white bath towel she was arranging within easy reach of the tub. I remember that towel seeming larger than my whole body and that being hugged with it had been like being wrapped in a garment of feathers. The cottony tufts of the towel had smelled so sweet I wanted to put the whole thing in my mouth and chew it like gum.

My brother has never believed that I remember this morning. I may have been perhaps twenty months old at the time. But I do remember it. I know that it wasn't a dream, and I know that this is the reason I have always believed that the people who say babies don't remember what happens to them just don't know what they are talking about. (I try to always remember to be pleasant to the little ones myself. If it happens to be my face that haunts their dreams in the future, I want those dreams to be sweet ones.)

Mother died not long after this, and maybe that is another reason why my memory of her and of that early morning is so strong, the reason perhaps I've held on to it with such tenacity. After Mother left us, my brother had charge of me, at least until he started school. After that, by the time I'd turned three, I spent my day sequestered in one or another discreet alcove of the working quarters of the house, entertained, in passing, by the small staff who served under my father's direction. This one would stop and toss me in the air and the next one would sing me a song or sneak me a delicious treat of some kind. I loved them all—the cooks, the drivers, the maids, the gardeners—and I thought of them as my family, really, and I guess, in fact, they were. It speaks to my father's importance in that household that as a widower with two young children, he was allowed both to remain in his position and to keep us under his care.

My father, oh, my daddy! The magic of those moments when he would happen past whichever nook would be my designated kingdom for the day. Often I was set up in the small larder off the maid's quarters, a room that, because it was mostly used for the extra storage one needed when hosting a large party, was often vacant and never saw a lot of traffic. As often as he could, when he had a free moment from his duties at the Senator's side, Father would steal away to find me.

"How's my Queenie today," he'd say, gathering me up into his arms. He'd spin me around. He'd ask me about how I was spending my time, and I'd tell him what my bears and dollies had been up to (usually one or the other had been hosting an afternoon tea for the gang) and I'd ask him about his day, and he'd tell me who was in the house that particular afternoon. Time was precious and he'd often combine our little visits with his supervision duties, carrying me in his arms as he asked after the luncheon menu or of the status of the summer draperies. Of course, I'd love to retain the illusion that Father couldn't abide separation from his precious child for one more instant, but I know that wasn't entirely the case. As you can imagine, the mild rebukes my father delivered (over a slovenly table setting or the disheveled condition of a cupboard) must have seemed much less persnickety when the offender considered the armful of heaven that would be wrapped around him like a new mink stole. A long believer that bad medicine went down easier with a little sugar, Father wasn't above using his daughter to further his mission of heading the best-run house in the District of Columbia.

I think that for the most part I behaved myself. I'd settle myself in with my toys and other amusements. I've never had a problem keeping busy. Though I don't know that this was true, I imagine that my father slipped an extra quarter or two per week to one of the kitchen staff for watching me out of the corner of her eye. If I needed anything I would go to Cook. I would tell her that I wanted to lie down or that I needed to use the bathroom, and she would take care of it. Sometimes I did sneak away, looking for my daddy. I always wanted to know where he was or what he was up to at the moment, to know what could possibly be so important that it kept him away from me for so long. My father fussed at the staff about my escapes, and I know that my behavior sometimes frustrated him, but looking back now, from the standpoint of one who knows just how hard they all worked, surely he was being a bit unfair in his anger toward those workers. I couldn't have been easy for any of them having a small child underfoot all day.

So, yes, of course, I would go exploring. Even as a young girl I'd begun refining the skills I'd inherited from my father, the uncanny ability to identify those places in a house from which a girl could observe and listen without being detected herself. In any fine old home there are crawl spaces and passageways that seem to have been built just for this purpose, and, in fact, some of them were. Off a formal dining room, for instance, an architect who understood his client's way of living always included a pantry of some kind where the servers could follow the course of the meal in an unobtrusive way, steps from the table should the slightest need arise. Even though the hostess would be provided with a bell at her place setting for the purpose of summoning help, in your better homes one wouldn't expect such bells to be needed.

Back then, when I was that young girl stealing around after her father, times for many Americans were good. It was the period some now refer to as the Roaring Twenties, and when Congress would recess, on many days the parlor of the Georgetown house would be filled with the Senator's colleagues and their cronies and hangers-on. The Senator's house became something of a clubhouse for a certain influential set in our nation's capital. Many of them were junior legislators, thirsty for the attention of a senior colleague such as the Senator, but the circle also extended to a mixture of old Washington operatives and a rotating cast of young lions from the industrial world who thought it worth their while to drop through Washington and bend a few ears. As you can imagine, the talk would have been all business and finance and money, and even as a tiny thing who couldn't begin to fathom the nature of their discourse, I sensed these men's exuberance over the fact that they were already rich and were getting richer by the minute.

And even if I could have understood, I wouldn't have much cared. My goal simply had been to find my father and keep an eye on him when he was working. I'm sure I believed that to be my job.

Father favored black jackets for working around the house, though sometimes, to entertain in the garden, for example, he would choose a white one. Now and again, the Senator's wife would get a notion in her head that the time had come to reoutfit her staff in the manner she'd observed at one or another ambassador's residence. Our creator endows few with all the graces, and, to her credit, this poor woman made up in gentleness what she lacked in common sense. Chagrined, to be sure, Father would sometimes find his shoulders laden with epaulets or braiding, but these little excursions into bad taste never lasted more than a day or two. Over his years with her, Father developed a repertoire of delicate stratagems designed to allow the dear woman to reconsider her poor judgment. More often than not he'd be calling for the return of his basic black jacket even before his staff had finished freshening it up.

Regardless of the angle of my perch, I could always pick him out: by the crisp pleat of his trouser or the sparkle of his shoes. Just watching those shoes could provide you with an entire education in the ways of a true professional. For your edification, may I offer these Housewright maxims?

- Select shoes with laces. A slip-on shoe denotes a casual tone one would not care to communicate.
- Take care that the laces themselves have crisp, trimmed ends. Nothing marks a man slovenly more than a frayed shoelace.
- For our purposes, shoes come in only one color: black.
- Polish. Nothing else need be said.

Watching my father's feet was rather like watching the work of a fine dancer or an athlete.

Ever so sure-footed, I don't believe I ever once observed a shoe as much as slide across the Senator's carpets, neither did one hear those shoes step or stomp or make any other sort of noise at all. It was almost as if my father moved through those rooms suspended from strings.

His work seemed a complete mystery to me. I didn't know what he did in those front rooms all day amid the cigar smoke and the bombast of all those loud men. Even on the days when I would observe him from a lair that gave me a broader view of the way he moved through space, I couldn't figure out what his purpose was. I remember thinking that my father's job must be something like what the bees did out in the gardens. The men sat posed and pretty—as did the flowers that surrounded us in almost every season—except in this case the men were the ones who buzzed. Father flitted between them, and I always had the sense that it was his flitting that somehow provided the energy in the room.

I would prefer not to tell you this next part, but in all fairness, I'm afraid I must. I'm afraid I must tell you about the time one of my best secret hiding places was accidentally uncovered. I'm telling you this in case you get the idea that it was all sugar and sweetness back in those days, because that would be the wrong impression.

To reach my favorite observation post, you would tiptoe your way into the small washroom just off the kitchen, the one whose door stood next to the service pantry for the dining room. The staff used this bathroom, as did I, but what most people didn't pay attention to could be found on the other end of that bathroom, cut into the painted wainscoting, a little-girl-sized door. I imagine that it had been built for access to plumbing, but who knows. The rooms in old houses have more often than not served dozens of purposes in their history. What was then the maid's quarters had once been cold storage, so who knows what purpose this space served in the days before indoor plumbing. All I knew was that a little girl could easily pull the latch on this door, and once she did, on the other side of that door she could walk around without even having to stoop over. Old boxes and trunks cluttered the space in various-sized stacks, the tallest of which butted against a decorative vent. You already know the view that vent provided.

I'm amazed, looking back, at my fearlessness as I child. Even a few years beyond the day I refer to, long at best would be the odds you'd find me wallowing in the dust and spider's webs and heaven knows what else might inhabit a place like my secret lair. But back then, on any given afternoon I'd wait for just the right moment to ask Cook to use the bathroom, and once there, I would open the hidden door and climb my way up to my fusty roost, and there I'd stay until I heard her call my name. Sometimes I lingered for an hour or more, Cook, bless her heart, so busy with her own work, she'd lose track of both me and of the time.

Perhaps I'd been sleepy that afternoon. I remember only

snapping open the tiny latch, surprised again at the apple-green paint left behind on my fingers. I climbed up the way I usually did, and I observed below me the men, their fingers wrapped around sparkling glasses of golden brown liquid. Slipping behind one chair and then the next, my father moved lightly around the room, in his hands a taller yet equally sparkling crystal of that same gold.

And then I was on the floor, at the foot of one of the Senator's bookcases. Above me hovered a half dozen pair of eyes, and I was being cradled up into my father's arms and into my ear he was whispering, "It's okay, baby." Rotten lathe around the grate had given way. The grate lay on the floor under Father's immaculate shoes, and bits of plaster and dust sprinkled around us like freshly fallen snow.

From their initial startle (none of them able to imagine what could possible be landing on them from above) the men recovered, beginning with tender inquiries into the condition of the child, rising to deep-throated belly laughs over the fright an elder member of the ensemble had taken. Apparently this poor old gentleman first had jumped from his seat, spilling his drink in his lap, and then issued forth a blasphemous profanity of the nature that in those more innocent days still carried the power to shock.

"Our sweet Matilda," the Senator chuckled. "Get her cleaned up and settled in for a nap, Jake. I can manage our guests."

Lest you get too caught up in the low-comedy slapstick of a young child floating from the ceiling like some unbidden angel, let me assure you that despite his clearly sincere concern for my physical state, Father was neither pleased nor entertained by my performance.

Carrying me in his arms, he eased past the staff, huddled in the pantry where they'd been lurking in order to discover what the commotion had been. They knew better than to show their faces in any room my father had command of.

"Who had charge of the baby?" he demanded to know, his clipped words barely masking his true rage. I began to shake, more frightened by the tone in his voice than by my accident.

Cook collected me from his arms. "You and me talk after I settle her in for a nap."

Father harrumphed, and as Cook carried me to the maid's quarters where I had my nap, I could hear him giving his orders for the cleaning and repair of the front room.

Later that evening would be the only time he and I spoke of the incident. Now and then over the ensuing years the Senator would tease me about the exploit. Like many persons of wealth and position, the Senator held his possessions and the people around him with an easier and more tolerant regard. (This is both a good and bad thing, as you may come to understand.) Perhaps it had been his extensive travels, during which he had met many different kinds of people, that allowed him to maintain such equanimity. Broken fixtures! He could buy ten more houses—tomorrow, if he wished—already owned several others, to be sure.

As for my father, his standards were altogether a different matter. In regard to his response, I remember his exact words: "When will you learn?"

And that would be all would he say. Beginning that evening and for a long time hence I would have my first extended lesson in the power of Housewright silence. If a certain strong-willed young lady was unable to control her own behavior, then he wasn't about to waste his time dealing with her.

I know what you're thinking. How harsh. How cruel. A father, a responsible adult. The child's only parent. How could he withdraw his affections from her? What a monster he must have been. And perhaps in the world you live in, you would judge him so. But take a look at the situation from my father's standpoint. He'd finally earned himself the position he'd trained his whole life to shoulder. He was appreciated and held in high esteem by his employer and his employer's friends. He had the respect of a small and dedicated staff. Something such as this, something such as his own daughter disrupting a gathering of his employer's closest associates with her antics. These sorts of goings-on ended the careers of lesser men. And maybe it had been the case that on this particular occasion, no harm had been done. The employer had a good laugh, as had all of the guests. And maybe it had been the case that the Senator's wife had long been thinking of having the vestigial grate removed, and maybe it had also been true that later that same evening the Senator had gone out of his way to ask after the little girl and to assure Jake that he need not worry about it and that he fully understood how these things happened. Even so.

What if it had been otherwise? What then? These were not trivial concerns.

People lost their homes over foolish behavior. People lost their lives. Families were separated, parents castigated. Entire ways of life came to an end.

To be direct, in the world into which I was born, there wasn't the luxury to raise a child with a liberal hand. Too much was at stake. It just might be the case that a firm hand on the backside and a sharp rebuke would be the difference between security and instability, maybe between life and death.

So, while I was a miserable little girl for longer than I care to remember, I won't begrudge my father the punishment he selected for me, and I hope you do not judge him too harshly. He did what he needed to do, and, for what it's worth, I learned my lesson about disrupting the Senator's household.

Soon enough things returned to normal, and I was Father's Queenie again. The new cook, Eva, had a wonderful way with children, though I wasn't to stay under her attention for too long.

About this time, the Senator's wife gave birth to what would be their only child. For that unfortunate family, life took one of those turns that demonstrates the eternal truth that money and power are no bulwark against tragedy. The poor woman died in childbirth, but blessedly she left behind a healthy baby boy. Father arranged a nanny to see after the boy, and so it was that from then until I began my formal schooling, the Senator's baby and I were cosseted under the same watchful eye. Nanny let me play at being the mommy when I wanted to, but frankly, it wasn't much fun. The Senator and his wife had produced an offspring of an almost astoundingly dull and docile nature. Baby contented himself with placidly watching Nanny fold diapers and me practice writing my numbers. Now and again he'd fuss a little, which would let us know it was time to change his diaper or give him a bottle. Sometimes I'd hold him while he drank his milk. He'd look at me with his flat little eyes. To me it was pretty much the same thing as pretending to feed my baby dolls. You may be as puzzled as I have always been about this paradoxical thing that happens often in prominent families. How often it seems the case that a lackluster generation arrives in the wake of a stellar one.

How often it seems that the children of men such as the Senator prove, at best, disappointing when compared to their predecessors. Sadly, too often, they come to no good end. You know the ilk: third-rate businessmen who always have about them an aura of scandal. Daughters of unfortunate visage amass multiple marriages as well as corresponding divorces from men of questionable lineage—the sorts of men her father wouldn't allow even to collect his garbage. As for the Senator's boy, one imagines things might have turned out much worse than they did, motherless child that he was. He falls into the "disappointing" category: no real calumny or disgrace. Instead he became one of those disturbingly bland men one finds pictured on the society page of the newspaper, trussed up in a tuxedo next to his blond wife and her designer finery. In addition to attending charity balls, he is known to frequent country club lounges and to dabble in creative hobbies, such as writing "poems" and playing blues guitar.

As an older child, I lived two lives. One at school and with friends doing ordinary girl-child things, and one at home as the daughter of the majordomo of a Senator. And while there was nothing particularly wrong with my life outside the home, I much preferred the residential side of my world. Just as some students fall in love with music or paintings, I fell in love with the domestic life. I have always loved all the little details that go into making a house a home. There is the mechanical side of things: knowing which rooms are due for paint, which filters need changing, what must be done to the raised garden of annuals in the fall so that they will be in full glory the following summer. There is the logistical side, the budgetary side, the human relations side. I've said nothing of the culinary. There is a reason that in less politically sensitive times we referred to these as the domestic "arts."

Once Father discovered I would be easier accommodated than dismissed, he began to make a place for me in the house after school. One afternoon, not quite exasperated but close to it, he showed me the finer points on double checking the crystal for spots and fingerprints. Regardless of how conscientious Maid had been, Father made a point of always reviewing her table settings. He had his own collection of chamois and retired linen serviettes used solely for the purpose of adding that final buff to a drinking goblet. (Soon he would gift me with my own starter set.)

I had the sense sometimes that some of the other staff resented me. I don't know if they coveted the attention, and they certainly couldn't have been jealous of the pay. I received none. I will admit going through a phase where I pretended to be my father's second-in-command, and I even issued an order or two, but you can be sure that the man quickly reined in such hauteur. In any case, a house the size of the Senator's generated enough work to keep all of us out of each other's hair, and in order to learn as much as I could, I made myself available to whoever would mentor an eager student.

It goes without saying that I preferred Father's instruction best, and though he spent most afternoons in the front rooms with the Senator and his guests (and many others on the Hill in the Senator's offices there), on those precious days he remained "in the back," as he called it, recording expenditures in the ledger he kept on a small desk in the kitchen, or consulting with a florist over centerpieces for a banquet, I would be his shadow. I became an expected presence at Father's side when he worked behind the stairs. Once he became convinced I knew the difference between hemstitching and embroidery, he'd consult me on place settings and the like. There's an odd subtlety to the rules about such things. Were I to attempt to explain when the use of monogrammed tableware would be vulgar, you'd think me peculiarly fastidious, but at my father's side, the making of such decisions became second nature.

Father's tolerance of my presence extended only so far as the door to the front rooms of the house. When the Senator appeared, I was to disappear. At some point on a slow Washington afternoon, the pantry door swung open and the Senator yelled, "Jake! I need to see you," and my father went running. I knew better than to follow.

Being master of the domain, occasionally the Senator blustered his way back to us. In many ways this was Father's worst nightmare.

"If you see him coming, Queenie, this is what I want you to do." Father demonstrated. He dropped his hands to his sides, becoming a small and narrow sapling. Without appearing to move, he backed his way into the dimmest corner of the room.

"You don't move a muscle, you understand?"

I nodded.

"If he does spot you—and he won't—you bow your head and say, 'Good afternoon, sir.' Understand?"

I nodded again. I appreciated these lessons in invisibility. I had wondered all those years how it was done.

In that house I only had to use it once or twice that I recall.

Just after I turned twelve, Father scheduled an inventory of the dry goods, and I volunteered to help. You would be surprised how much flour and oats (and, in a Southern kitchen, cornmeal and grits) a small household consumes, not to mention the low-quantity items one keeps on hand should the need arise to throw together a nutbread or an exotic pastry. I was counting tins of baking powder and boxes of soda, when:

"Jake! I been calling you. What's all this in here? (The man had never been in the closet where we stored the dry goods!) Never mind. Say, listen, we got a problem brewing."

"Yes, sir." Father said. I had melted into the shelves as instructed. My father attempted to steer the conversation out into the hallway, but the Senator paid him no mind.

"That fellow, that one fellow from up in New York. New young congressman. We had him in here to tea last week. (Tea was the euphemism we used in our house to refer to those afternoons where the whisky flowed free and a good cigar waited at every fingertip.) What's his name?" The Senator snapped his fingers trying to call up the memory. Father filled in the blank.

"That's the one. Evidently our new young friend is stirring up trouble in committee. Something about the Negroes and voting. I think that me and this . . . What did you say his name was?"

Father repeated it. (I shall not.)

"I think me and him need to have a little visit. What do you say?"

"Another tea, sir?"

"A special one. You get my meaning, Jake?"

"Yes, sir."

"Thursday."

"Yes, sir."

"Handle it," the Senator said, waving his arm around like stirring a pot.

"Just look at all this," he added, making ready to leave, again noticing the provisions he didn't know he owned. Unfortunately he also noticed me, frozen in front of a dozen glass jars of sugar.

"Matilda! Why look at you, girl. Growing like a weed. You gonna have to lock this one up, Jake, you know that?" He came over and pinched my cheek. I reddened.

"Yes, sir. I know you're right about that, sir."

Father and I stood there frozen for a moment or two after the Senator left. We heard him out in the kitchen making loud comments at the staff. He didn't seem to know any of their names.

Then Father waved me on my way, almost as if I'd done something wrong. I started to protest, but he said, "Go! Help Eva with the salads. Go on."

It would be a few years yet before I fully understood what set Father into that mood. I knew that it had something to do with the Senator, and I also knew that that is why he always tried to make me disappear whenever his employer appeared.

I never heard another word about "tea" with the young congressman, but an odd thing happened that week, on that Thursday of which the Senator spoke. Father gave the entire staff the day off. He gave each one bus fare and money to catch a show over on U Street. From somewhere he rustled up an Irish couple for the afternoon. He even had one of them standing his own station, while he, from many of my old hiding places, discreetly gave hand signals. I had been told to stay in the carriage house, but you know me. I had to have at least one eyeful, and I did.

"You do what you have to do." That was my father's biggest lesson to me. Housewright Maxim #1. And yes, I know, it sounds like that worn-out military credo—"Ours is not to reason why . . ."—but I think that analysis misses the point.

Although on the surface it might seem otherwise, our lives have almost nothing to do with blind obedience. The blindly obedient do not think. We do. What our lives are about is easing the way, smoothing things over; we are a kind of social Vaseline.

I think of us as being like the kindly saint who offered Jesus a cup of water during his torment on the cross. Considering the circumstances, such a gesture might seem trivial, but even in the most trying of times, it's the little things that count.

We Don't Want to Change the World

. . .

I

1963

David Housewright's earliest memory of his aunt Matilda began with his father, very early on a midsummer morning, lowering him over the short wrought-iron gate that separated her front lawn from the sidewalk, and of his father then encouraging him to run up and ring his auntie's doorbell. There had been something about the light that morning. David remembered that on the way down to Matilda's, the predawn sky had announced morning with fiery pink radiance, clouds the color of cantaloupe and cotton candy.

The sky had blazed and flared for what felt like an hour and then had faded back into a deep purple, the band of blue on the horizon announcing the true morning. David remembered the amber glow of that first light just as his father set him down inside the gate.

"A false dawn!" Matilda had crowed, ushering him inside the warm house.

He sometimes wondered if he had imagined the false dawn, and sometimes when he would find himself awake in the early morning he would go to the window and wait for another. It never came, and, for him, that flaming golden morning remained one of his peak experiences—the ripe-to-perfection peach, the first sight of his true love—a moment that served as a defining moment in his short life.

As, for that matter, had been his being delivered to Matilda's in the first place. His daddy didn't want him to be here. He knew that. He had listened to his parents' whispers.

"The thought of my boy alone with that woman."

"But Martin, she adores him. She's after me constantly about this. What am I supposed to say? She thinks it's me keeping him away."

David had been seven that first time. He knew all those words he had heard whispered. There were some things he didn't know. Such as who was Matilda anyway? She was his aunt, they said, and that meant she was his father's sister, but she wasn't around like the other relatives, like his uncle Ralph who was an uncle but not really an uncle.

But that morning he had not been afraid. Not really. The sky was bright and wild. He knew Matilda. She came over for holidays. She was quiet. Nice. She would look at him all the time she was there.

"Here," his father had said, lowering him over the gate. "Give her this. Remember what I told you. Be polite. Behave. You let me know if she—" he had started to say, but his mother had told his father they had to hurry. They were going to a convention. David was going to be a big boy and stay with his auntie.

"Well, come on in," Matilda's said. "Let me get a look at you."

David held out the envelope.

"That would go here," she told him, lifting a vase by the front door. He set the envelope down and she set the vase back on top of it.

"What could be better," she asked, "than an early start to a perfect day?"

"I don't know what could be better," he replied, and then she laughed and told him to follow her.

She was tall, Matilda. He bet she was the tallest person he knew. She was all straight lines.

"This is our garden," she announced. They were on the other side of the house now. "In the summer when it's early like this, that's the best time to get our work done. Let me introduce you."

Matilda told him the names of all the things growing in the yard. Everything had pretty names like music. He couldn't remember any of them.

"One of the first things we do in the morning is visit our petunias and remove the flowers that are no longer lively. Like this one, you see?" Matilda had plucked and then shown him a wilted purple trumpet. He spied another one on a plant nearer to him.

"And like this one, too, right?"

"Splendid!" she said, and they then worked in earnest on the small bed of purple and white flowers.

"The Senator preferred pansies over petunias. He was impractical in many ways. Father and I would seed and then set out the annuals we knew to thrive in the Washington climate. Altogether more tropical than you would find here."

Matilda had lots of stories about Washington. The capital. David hadn't known any of the people in these stories, but that was okay. Her father, she told him that morning, had been an important man there.

"In his way," she added.

"Your grandfather was very intelligent. Did you know that, David?"

David did not know that. He knew his other grandpa, Grandpa Bill. Grandpa Bill lived retired in Tennessee. They went there sometimes in the summer.

"Father understood the importance of having a plan, of understanding where you want to go. Let's take these dead ones to the mulch pile. We can get started on some edging, I think. Before the sun gets too high."

There was always something to do at Matilda's, but you took it slow. That was nice. There was trimming and edging and pruning and raking. Inside there were plants to be watered and turned.

David learned that a very slightly oiled rag on the legs of the dining room table made the wood happy. The girl who did the dusting at home did not know this, he figured. He also learned that a young gentleman with his eyes on a professional career could never start early enough. Matilda said that.

"She did, did she?" That's what his father had said down at the kitchen. He'd taken David down there after the convention. He and Uncle Ralph were making pans of potato salad for a church picnic. David was helping. He got money for that. "And what else did she have to say for herself?"

David was up to his elbows in warm water. He was scrubbing the eyes and nasty parts off of potatoes. They were making "skin-on" potato salad. "Matilda says that the morning is the shank of the day. She also says that in the next decade doors may open wide for the Negro in America."

"Telling fortunes, is she?" David's father grabbed David's hands and a potato and pushed the vegetable brush harder. "Like this," he ordered, breathing over David's shoulder, muscling his wrists back and forth.

"You can tell the old girl that Martin said that change is what change does. Tell her I said that."

David's fingers wrinkled and the potatoes made them raw.

The next Saturday, David placed the envelope under the vase, and then he followed Matilda upstairs. They were airing out the linens. Matilda told David that even clean linens got musty if stacked together for too long. She handed him a pile of pillowcases.

"I've been in correspondence," she told him, "with a cousin of ours. A fascinating individual who has made his way in the legal profession. A Josiah Johnson, my father's sister's son. He suggests great potential ahead for the bright Negro child."

And since he didn't know what it meant anyway, and since now seemed as good a time as any, he delivered his message.

"Change is as change does. Daddy told me to tell you that."

Matilda moved her head back, the same way people did when the monsters jumped up at the movies. She smiled and folded open and sniffed a large cream-colored sheet.

"He's a font of wisdom, that brother of mine. You can tell Martin that Matilda said that a legacy is a gift often lost on the literal minded."

"And you can tell my sister that a bird in the hand isn't any of her business."

He'd carried that message back to Matilda a week later.

"People make their own choices in life, David, as will you." Matilda poured them a cup of tea. "You just have to come to terms with that."

David had turned thirteen by then. Cranky about many things. Life at home had been turned upside down by an obnoxious and treacherous little person whom his parents referred to as "Master Roderick" Housewright. Those people were too old for a kid his age. Everybody knew that.

He'd spent the morning at the new kitchen running tomatoes through a food mill, pulverizing garlic, grating lemon zest while simultaneously opening up the skin on his knuckles.

"Here."

"This way."

"Smaller."

These were the usual things his father said to him.

And, then, dropping him off here, he had grabbed David's arm as he exited the car. His father had this thing he did with his customers where he would wink at them and point his finger as if it were a pistol.

He said to David, "I do appreciate your taking the old girl off my hands." He handed David the envelope.

Another thing to be cranky about. A brother and sister who mostly talked through silly messages ferried back and forth by him. What was up with that?

Matilda was still talking about the little one.

"Evie waited a long time for your little brother," she said. "He's a precious angel, from what I hear."

"The precious angel whines all day. Eat and whine and break other people's stuff. That's what kids do."

"It's hard to be around these grouchy boys," Matilda agreed. "Believe me. I know." She finished off her tea and pushed her chair back. "Come up here," she ordered, and David followed her up to a room on the second floor.

"I haven't moved a thing in here for years. Since your grandfather passed, in fact. We can freshen this up. What's your pleasure?" she asked.

"Me? How should I know?"

"You? Well, you ought to know. It's your room now."

David had always slept in the small guest room across the hall. Two other bedrooms flanked the corridor, as well. One was Matilda's, and the other she called "Martin's old room," though David had never seen his father set foot in the place, nor did the room seem to hold any sense of who his father might have been. It held neither banners nor any loose ends of collections or hobbies that his father might have pursued. The room mainly served as a catchall for things Matilda could neither figure a better place for nor quite bring herself to dispose of. "Take these to Martin's old room," he would often be ordered, and then be handed a bundle of last year's *Ebony* magazines or a roll of Christmas wrap. "Anywhere in there would be fine." David would stack the old pile on top of an existing one, or he would shove things around with his foot until enough room opened up to start a new tower. Should his father ever decide to stay here, it would take him a week to uncover the bed. Thankfully "Father's room" was in much better shape.

"This is going to be mine?" David couldn't believe his good luck.

"You sleep here often enough—as the grocery bills can attest. I figure you're pretty tired by now of that horsehair mattress in the guest room."

(Horsehair! He'd been sleeping on horsehair!)

"I bet Father had that nasty old thing since they shot Lincoln. Tell me, David: Did you ever find yourself scratching? In funny places? You get my meaning?" She nodded toward the guest room. "Well, those days are over, my friend," she cheered, sounding like a commercial. "Trigger is on her way to that great roundup in the sky, and we are fixing you up a new room."

David sat on the mattress in his grandfather's room and tested it by bouncing up and down just a bit.

"We bought it right after the war, and then Father got so he couldn't climb the steps. We set him up a bed down in the parlor. There toward the end. We made sure he was comfortable."

David admired the flat-out way that his auntie would tell him stories like that one, the way she neither stared off into space like some sort of zombie nor treated him as if he might crumble apart at a sad tale. He'd made up his mind he would ask her today about her relationship with her brother. It was weird. It made him crazy sometimes. All his father would talk about was chop and dice and wash. But Matilda would talk. He bet she would.

"I figure we'll paint and put some fresh paper below the wainscoting. What color were you thinking? Blue? Yes? On the stick there."

The stick lay astride a couple of gallons of paint already waiting patiently in a box on the floor. Sky blue, he would call the color—if the sky that day were one of those perfect ones where there weren't any clouds and when the sun was high in the sky. Auntie's blue was the one you saw down along the edges or if you looked up through the trees.

"Blue would be perfect," he told his auntie.

"No time like the present." Matilda started spreading drop cloths and he packed the knickknacks off the furniture. He picked up and examined a photo in a frame. His grandfather posed in front of what looked like the Capitol Building with a white man with a big grin splashed across his face.

"Father and the Senator. Did I never show you this?"

David shook his head.

"He was a decent enough man, the Senator. He treated us fairly, you would say." She set the picture on top of the rest of the gewgaws. "If you like that picture, you can set it out again. It's up to you."

She reminded him of her "secret" tricks for a mess-free job. "Don't overcharge your brush. You want enough paint for no more than a square foot. And keep turning your brush. Anticipate the drips. Change directions. Change sides."

She retrieved a step stool from Martin's old room, pivoted forth the steps, and began to climb.

"You should let me do that," he told her.

"Why?" she responded, laughing, really. And then when he didn't say anything she continued, "Because I'm a fragile old harridan who you're afraid might break a hip? Let me ask you a question: How old do you think I am?"

David bit his lip and thought about it. "You're—"

Matilda put a finger to his lips. "Let me give you a bit of advice. If a lady—any lady—asks you that question, ever: change the subject. Let's just say I'm younger than that father of yours and we'll leave it at that."

Matilda climbed up the ladder leaving David to wonder what it was about her that made her seem the family elder.

He watched her edge a flawless strip of blue against the white crown molding, leaning across far enough at the limit of her brush to make him audibly gasp. She released a self-satisfied "Ah!" at her accomplishment, came back to center, and repeated the stunt in the opposite direction.

"You may help me down now, if you wish." She smiled from her high perch. David extended his hand. His auntie, he thought, overacted her dainty descent from the ladder—to mock him, perhaps—but let her have her fun. One of these days she might really need him and she may as well get used to being helped while it was still a game to her.

"Such a gentleman," she sighed, curtseying, handing him her brush. She ordered him to finish up his section posthaste and meet her in the kitchen for lunch.

Downstairs the table had been set with a simple sandwich and lightly dressed green salad. Iced tea, of course. They'd talked about the march on Washington.

"Wouldn't it have been something to be there?" David had become mesmerized by the words of Dr. King.

"I'm not so sure. The District can be abysmal in the summer."

"I keep reading that speech, Auntie. It said something to me."

"And you have dreams of your own, of course."

"Of course."

"A fleet of catering vans. A chicken in every pot."

David ignored her teasing and ate his lunch. When in a few years, at University High School, David would first encounter the word "Spartan," it would be these lunches that came to his mind. Chewing, his mouth full of tuna, he thought that his father would more than likely have loaded up the bowl with pickle relish and then thrown in another stalk of celery to extend the filling. In truth, David found Matilda's simple meals a relief; delighted often in the way she pleased herself with an ordinary bowl of tomato soup and a simple bacon sandwich. He lived entirely too much within a world where a lot of unnecessary fuss was often made over that selfsame soup. Martin Housewright would sprinkle each crock with homemade Parmesan croutons, garnish them with bitter herbs, and write the word "bisque" on the menu board. Rich people would pay per serving the same price his auntie paid for a half dozen cans.

"And what would be the latest report from the cheese and crackers rackets?"

"Your brother said that loose lips sink ships."

Matilda, much to his surprise, pasted a wry smile on her face. "Did he, now? Well you can tell my brother that—"

"I'm not telling your brother anything."

"I beg your pardon? David Housewright, you know my position on insolence."

David wiped his mouth with his linen, swallowed, sat up straight. "I didn't mean to be disrespectful."

"I would hope not. Certainly not after I—"

"What I meant was," he interrupted, fully aware of his further breach of etiquette, "I meant that there's a phone here and when you have something to say to your brother, maybe you should pick it up and tell him yourself."

The look his aunt gave him was genuinely scary. Piercing. Pulsing somehow.

Matilda cleared both their plates. (He still had a bite of sandwich left on his.) She placed a shortbread lemon bar in front of him; the plate made a pointed snapping noise when it met the table. As they nibbled their desserts and sipped tea, Matilda prepared herself to speak but did not. She'd straightened her back and moistened her lips ever so slightly as she always had done before one of her pronouncements, but no words had come.

Later, after the "reading hour," she asked him to join her in the garden.

"What I imagine is that you have a lot of questions—"

"Like for starters why you don't get along with my dad."

"I'll thank you to not interrupt me *ever* again. You walk a short tether as it is. My relationship with your father is complex and, frankly, none of your concern. You have a brother now, so you'll know one day the truth of which I speak. I apologize if our verbal banter that you have been party to has caused you discomfort. That was never my intention, nor your father's. I've enjoyed it over these years, for what that's worth, as has Martin, I'm sure. But that's over—as you desire. One last thing: it would be vain of you to imagine your father and I have communicated only through you. And, now, you may respond with questions or comments that I shall feel free to entertain or to ignore at my discretion."

He'd been saving them up for past few years now, questions he'd had about the Housewrights and their ways. Leave it to Matilda to make them all suddenly moot or irrelevant or off limits. And how incredible to be able to do so in a way that made sense to him.

He, too, had in fact enjoyed the playful tug-of-war he'd been the anchor of. And now he'd killed it with his big mouth, but then everything had its day. Dr. King said a new one was on its way. Might as well start with a clean state.

One thing for posterity: what could it hurt to ask?

"So which one of you won, do you think? You or your brother?"

At first Matilda appeared not to understand the question. And then, when she did, her expression made it clear he had gotten, as his mother Evie would say, "too big for his britches" this time.

And so be it, David thought. Long ago he'd figured out more about their game than he bet they thought he did. Matilda turned to head in and begin supper preparations.

David had one more round in him.

"I mean, for what it's worth," he said to her back, "I am still thinking about going into the catering business."

Matilda froze. Back in his direction she spun, but slowly, almost as if she were one of those mechanical elves in the Christmas windows downtown. What to make of that face? Some ill-matched combination of sweet and evil. She stepped back toward him and caressed his cheek.

"Oh, David. Sweetheart. Now you're just being childish."

II

1967

Steadying the vase, David called upstairs to Matilda. "Time to go, Auntie!"

"Come up here, please."

He sighed. It had been smart to leave this extra time before the presentation.

In her bedroom he found Matilda standing by her mirror, fretting, her thin frame draped in a simple, flowered frock.

"What does one wear to these pep rallies?"

"You look fine, Auntie. It's a speech, not a football game." David splayed himself across Matilda's bedspread, the nubs of raised cotton palpable even beneath his work shirt. Matilda gave him a dirty look, and he knew that she both minded and didn't mind.

He noticed a rolled-up tarp outside the bedroom door.

"Why is that up here?"

"That?" Matilda moved in front of it as if to make it disappear. (Fat chance, he thought, with her skinny self.) "I was doing something with it, I guess. It's on its way downstairs. You know that old thing. It gets heavy on you."

He hopped from the bed. "We've spoken about this," he reminded her. "No heavy stuff up and down those basement stairs. Finish dressing while I move that monster."

The canvas wasn't heavy as much as it was bulky and awkward. David had to turn the bundle sideways to clear the door frame leading down the basement steps. It seemed like they went through this every other week. Matilda would drag the tarp up the steps whenever she was painting or refinishing something. He'd haul it back, ordering her to let the thing stay put. Recently he'd brought over for her a dozen of those cheap plastic throws, the kind she could just bundle up and toss in the garbage when she finished, but you could never tell this woman a thing. She had to have *her* tarp: it was like a fetish, almost as if she thought paint wouldn't stick to plaster without it. He hoped she hadn't been trying to touch up that bathroom ceiling again. He told her he'd get to it, and he meant to, but since he'd started with the Party, things had been busy. And then there was that Patty.

In the basement corner he noticed the push mower, partially disassembled, and a file that she'd obviously been using to sharpen the blades.

In the time he'd been downstairs she'd changed to a tailored pantsuit and straightened the bedspread, which he mussed again.

"What you want to mess with that antique wreck for? What if

you cut yourself? What if you were laying down their bleeding for days on end? What then?"

"Melodrama doesn't become you, David. I've maintained that machine for twenty years without your good counsel."

"I'm buying you a power mower and throwing that old—"

"You touch my mower and—" She grabbed him by an earlobe and moved him to a chair.

"Pushing that contraption around, as hot as it gets and at your—"

"Stop your blathering and remind me why I agreed to go to this . . . thing."

"Because I'm your nephew and you love me. And you should stick with the dress. It's pretty on you."

"It's about 'pretty,' then, is it? Fashion models and go-go dancers? I'll remind you I'm a woman who prefers a quiet evening at home."

"What's that about anyway, Auntie? Why you always shut up in here?"

Matilda scoffed and stepped into her dressing room to change again. She stepped out in a different dress. Beige, simpler, but the same straight cut.

"You're a nosy boy, David Housewright. Did it ever occur to you that the normal thing was to stay home and that the abnormal thing was to run around town like a crazy person?" Matilda gathered her braid to begin spinning it around the back of her head.

"Leave it down," David said, popping up off the bed again. He laid the twisted hair over her shoulder. "Clip it at the back. Maybe put it up in a bun."

Matilda retrieved an antique silver clip from a jewelry box and David clasped it into place.

"Nice," he said. She blushed and demurred. He couldn't believe how much younger she looked with her hair down. She looked, in fact, not that different from many of the girls at the U. Peasant dresses, long braided hair.

Matilda took one more pass in front of the mirror. She sighed, rolled her eyes, and headed for the stairs.

"Will we have the pleasure of your parents' company this evening?" She gathered her things into a surprisingly stylish small bag she caught him staring at. "Spiegel," she said. "I can order you one since you like it so much.

"Time's a-wasting," she said. He offered his arm, which she took. He escorted her down the front walk. How long he'd been coming here and this would be their first excursion. He sensed an ever so slight hesitation as she stepped through the wrought-iron gate, an almost undetectable lurch in her step, the way people stopped sometimes at the bottom of escalators. But lightning did not strike. Swarms of wasps did not descend. She was out.

"For the record and since you asked," David told her, turning left onto Forest Hills, "I did ask my parents—both of them. This is an important speech tonight from Ahmed. I thought they should hear it."

"I take it they declined your invitation."

"Mother, as if I'd asked her to a mud wrestling match, your brother with a little less grace."

Matilda stifled a chuckle. "Good old Marty," she said under her breath.

"It's not so funny when you live with him every day."

"I've had that privilege." She peered out the windshield as if the entire city were new to her. Maybe it was.

"I hope you know where you're going," she said. David patted her hand. Sometimes she allowed that sort of thing.

"Do you know what he said to me? He said, 'I'm not paying all my hard-earned money so you can prance around there like some beatnik. And if you don't cut that mess off your head, I will.'"

"That's a pretty good impression, David. You should consider going on the stage. Maybe you should sit down and talk with the man."

David didn't know whom she thought she was kidding. Talk to the man. In the Martin Housewright universe, Martin Housewright talked; everyone else listened.

"Everything I do infuriates him. He's got more buttons than a dress shirt."

"No need to remind me about buttons, David. I was present for the installation. And, who knows? Martin could be right about some things. Take this hair, for instance. This . . . bush . . . thing."

"Afro, Auntie. We've been over this. It's not a bush; it's called an Afro. Say the word with me." Jesus, 80 percent of this crowd tonight would have Afros. She needed to get with the program. "Don't you ever look at those *Ebony*s you get? It's what we're wearing these days."

"Afro, Afro, Afro. Satisfied? My father always—"

"Please, no Father stories tonight."

Matilda coughed pointedly to remind him that interruption was never tolerated. David raised a hand from the steering wheel in surrender.

"My father always said that a neat and ordered coiffure was the mark of a gentleman. I leave that for your consideration."

"And for your consideration, Auntie, I will tell you that this is what African hair looks like."

"Does it, now? All sculpted into a neat ball like that. If I got off the plane tomorrow, in, say . . . Ouagadougou, this is what I'd see? Hair like yours?"

David gave a halfhearted nod. He wasn't sure that's exactly what she'd see, but it was probably true. Ahmed had said pretty much that. What he'd said was that Afros and dashikis were a direct link to the homeland.

"Ahmed says—"

"Mercy, not this Ahmed again."

Matilda had forced an argument last Saturday about David's mentor, Ahmed El Rachim, the leader of the local Party.

"This is a brilliant man, Aunt Matilda. I've already told you that."

"I guess we shall see soon enough. Ahmed. What sort of name would that be?"

"An African name. Of course."

"Well, I have to say, David Housewright. Your intellectual laziness stuns me sometimes." Matilda sneered at him. "You keep throwing Africa in my face, as if Africa were the name of some large country. Like France. Or Spain. Which Africa would we be referring to here? The teaming savannas of Kenya? The deserts of Rhodesia? Whence Ahmed? Which country's principal export would be bushy hair?"

"You enjoy this, don't you? Showing people up."

"It isn't your plan to whine your way through law school, I hope. I'll certainly not apologize for being a woman who thirsts for knowledge. And I also must say while I have the floor: Five-odd decades on earth and I have honestly never heard such a name until you mentioned it to me. It sounds like the noise a camel would make. Ahmed! Egyptian, perhaps?"

Alas, this was where his father's buttons came from. Part of him wanted to laugh and part of him wanted to strangle her. Another part figured he could use the practice. Some of those brothers in the Party could hold their own with her in the rhetoric department.

Well, maybe, almost.

"Ahmed challenges all truly righteous blacks to throw off the yoke of slavery and embrace their roots." Or something like that, the man said. David found that sometimes some of the sayings got jumbled up when he tried to repeat them. Rather than a silver tongue, his own was something more like stale spaghetti—all twisted into knots and a little on the sticky side.

"I have no idea what you just said, David. None. Ahmed. Do you suppose his name used to be Kenny? Or Phil? He couldn't possibly have been born with that name, could he?"

"Ahmed reminds us that our names are the names that the masters gave us. Many in the Party prefer to adopt new ones, ones more in keeping with our heritage."

"Oh, David. You aren't thinking of changing your name? David is so beautiful. It means 'beloved.' Did you know that?"

Actually, he hadn't known that. Until his involvement with the Party he hadn't given his name much thought.

"I don't care what it means," he told her. "I only know it's not an African name and therefore not what I would have been called had we not been kidnapped and brought to this hellhole."

"Really, David? Are you positive about that?"

"Sure. Of course I'm sure." Another lesson from the Matilda Housewright School of Verbal Warfare: Always be ready with your facts. At least he hoped he was.

"*David* is a biblical name," Matilda said. "Old Testament. Which makes it a Semitic name. A Jewish name. There aren't Jews in Africa?"

"We're talking about black Africa."

"There aren't black African Jews?"

"Fine. I give up. Whatever. You win."

Matilda sat back. David noted that her face took on the look it always did—false contrition that barely masked her smug self-satisfaction. He wanted to tell her that she was as bad as her brother, but had no desire to revisit that conversation, didn't wish to hear her gloat again about the many times she had bested Martin when they were young.

Sometimes he believed that Matilda gave David the verbal lickings that she didn't get to give to her true target—her brother. Sometimes he thought her goal might be nobler, that she was challenging him, making him ready to take on the real bullies of the world, but if that were so, why hadn't it worked? Why did he so often feel both at the mercy of everyone he met and so completely unprepared and surprised by how vicious and self-serving most of the world seemed to be? You couldn't win in this world. Brothers got you 'cause you were too bougie, the sisters 'cause you didn't have cash. His father worked him on one side; his auntie worked him on the other.

"Ahmed! Ahmed! Ahmed!" she coughed. He saw her over there trying not to laugh. He took the freeway exit for the university.

Maybe she was just a bully. Sometimes he thought that that

was exactly the case: that his auntie was simply a mean and mean-spirited woman who stood fully ready to humiliate whomever stepped through her door. And she'd hurt them for no good reason, too—simply because that was her nature and because it felt so good to do so. Maybe that's what comes from being alone too long. Maybe the sadness wells into a pool of viciousness and rage. Maybe kind words and benign chatter wear away to nothing after years of pain and loneliness.

He pulled into the auditorium parking lot.

He didn't really believe that. He didn't see Matilda as a bitter and lonely person. Yes, she was alone most of the time, but he had never known her to be pained about it or self-pitying.

If he thought about it, he wouldn't want her any other way than the way she was. He had never harbored fantasies of a sweetness-and-lace-type auntie—a moon-faced doll, full of loving platitudes and homespun homilies. There was a good heart over there in that seat. This he knew more than he knew anything else. He knew—had known since he was first dropped over her fence—that she would only push as hard as she knew he could resist, would give as much as he needed and as often as he needed it, and would take on the biggest dragon in the forest on his behalf. She'd no doubt win, too—of that he was sure—and would display the severed bloody dragon's head in her garden as the prize it truly was.

"What else do I need to know about this Ahmed before the big show?" she asked, and he knew she had decided that he'd had enough of her antics for one day. He went around to open her car door.

"I'll tell you this: Ahmed is really in the people's corner.

That's for sure. All the black kids here love him. He encourages us to stay focused, to get the best education we can squeeze out. Despite the way they treat us."

"They treat you bad here." Not a question, more a comment from his aunt. "The amount of money we pay those people . . ."

"I've done all right. But some of the other brothers really get trounced. Ahmed helps. He talks to some of the most racist professors. He's set up a tutoring program."

"You've had need of that?"

"Actually, I am the math tutor. Some folks don't have much on the ball in that area. Kind of unbelievable that they got into college in the first place, if you ask me. But I help. Ahmed says it's really important to stay connected to the people. To our people. To the ones who really need us. We talk a lot, Ahmed and me."

"I. Ahmed and I. Use the subject pronoun. Redundant subject."

David figured that sometimes the woman just couldn't resist. He ignored her.

"We're going to change things around this town. The people will rise up."

"*We* would be this Party you keep referring to."

"Exactly. We're in all the big cities, you know. Ahmed's our local chairman."

"This Party would be like some sort of club."

"It's a political party. Like the Democrats, only we're a people's party. We're interested in social justice, in helping the poor and those who the system tries to crush."

Matilda shook her head. "The world's already come farther

than I thought I'd ever see. A civil rights bill. And voter rights. When I was a little girl, colored folks couldn't even get a soda at a lunch counter in downtown DC. Less than a mile from the Capitol."

"Who wants a damn Coca-Cola?"

"Language!"

"A glass of soda water—which the waitress probably spit in—that's not what this is about anymore. Did you know that most of our people live in substandard housing? Many black children don't even get one decent meal a day. No, Auntie. A Coca-Cola is not justice."

"But a cold drink is something. It's something more than your grandfather had."

"I guess so. But Ahmed reminds us—"

Matilda sputtered her lips. "Ahmed! Ahmed says a lot of things, evidently. I hope someone's listening beside you."

"There are a lot of us, Aunt Matilda."

"He sounds dangerous to me, this Ahmed. Every generation, Negroes get in line behind one of these revolutionary fools. For all the good it does. I never trusted them myself."

"Blacks, Auntie. Get with it: This is 1967. And he's not a fool. He's intelligent and personable. You'll like him."

"I wouldn't bet my paycheck on that."

"I would. Shall we go in?"

"In for a dime, in for a dollar, I guess. I'm sure I'll be the only person here who remembers the Second World War." She giggled, a little too nervously.

Folks of all sorts had gathered for the speech. Black Muslims in their bow ties and chadors. A cluster of women in white rubber-soled shoes, fresh from a shift at the hospital. Some dudes who looked like they just jumped off the street huddled in the corners of the auditorium (typical, he thought).

Closer to the stage, along the aisle, clustered a group of sisters he recognized from the Party. There was Patty in the middle of them, done up real nice in her hip-hugger jeans and a purple top that let her belly button peep through. David grinned in her direction.

"So that's the type you go for," Matilda whispered.

David nodded.

"She bends over in those pants, and I'm phoning the vice squad."

David ignored his aunt's teasing. "Do you have a place you'd rather sit?"

Matilda gave the room the once-over. "Near an exit. In case this mob gets unruly."

"Woman, please."

David did sense the crowd making her nervous, and though he wanted to go make the scene with Patty and her friends—well, with Patty—he instead found them some seats. The location, although not entirely intentional on his part, did place them right by a big red exit sign.

"I believe your lady friend there is a wondering who her feller brung to the big dance." Matilda nodded her head toward the sisters.

Patty, of the tight, tight jeans, was clearly checking them out, did seem to be giving Matilda the once-over. David raised his fist in an anemic power salute. One of these days he'd get comfortable with the gesture, but the clutched, thrust fist still felt foolish to him, theatrical and affected, like the secret signal of some low-rent fraternity.

"Someone's jealous. She'll probably try to lure me into the lavatory so she and her minion can slap me around."

"Matilda. She's nice. Really. And she's real smart, too. She's going to medical school."

"Not in that little top, she's not. And believe me, before she operates on me, Miss Africa will be slapping an industrial hairnet over that bush on her head."

"Her name is Patty. And it's called an Afro. Afro, okay?"

"Afro, Afro, Afro, Afro, Afro."

David shook his head. Some people you couldn't take anywhere. To his horror, Patty started their way, but Ahmed approached the lectern at the same time.

"Later," Patty mouthed.

"She said 'later,' " Matilda repeated, just as the audience quieted down. "Just in case you missed it."

"Thank you, Auntie. Thank you very much."

Ahmed welcomed the crowd with the greeting he often used, "*Salaam alaikum*," though David kept forgetting what it meant.

"This is going to be in English, isn't it?" Matilda whispered.

David shushed her.

"I am encouraged to see so many of you brothers and sisters here today. It gives me great heart."

Around them, folks sat upright in their chairs, the same marginal attentiveness David noticed when his parents used to force him to services at the Third Baptist Church (a church his mother had selected less because of the fine preaching, rather because its parishioners were notorious for the lavish catered affairs they competed with each other to put on every year). Some of the women in the audience even fanned themselves, as if it were church.

"I'd like to begin this evening by saying something to my white brothers and sisters who have joined us here this evening."

A round of anemic applause circled the room. Ahmed often started off slow. This crowd would come to life as soon as he gathered his wind.

"We appreciate your interest and your support. We truly do. We are glad you turned out to hear us tonight. It shows that you are with us in spirit and that you are people of good conscience. That is appreciated. But I'm afraid that at this time, we must ask you to leave."

This time it was a gasp that circulated. David noticed some of those lethargic backs snapping to a straighter position. It had gotten interesting already.

"What—" Matilda started, but David silenced her.

"Please. We want ya'll to step to the exits please. We don't need you here tonight. This is about *our* issues and *our* concerns. Perhaps another time we can sit down together, but not tonight."

The few white people sprinkled around the room like so many lonely gulls on the beach made their way to the door. A girl with long stringy blond hair pushed her way to the exit nearest David and Matilda, tears streaming down her face.

"This is outrageous," Matilda seethed.

"Are they gone? Good. Now we can talk."

The audience broke into tumultuous applause. Matilda folded her arms sternly across her chest.

"You see, brothers and sisters, I mean no disrespect, but for far too long in this country, our people's agenda has been set from outside the community. Have you seen photos of the founders of the NAACP? Look in your history—it's the only way to learn. Look and what you'll see are white faces."

Matilda leaned over to David and said, "Ha! Many of those men were fair-skinned Negroes. Don't you dare shush me again. My father knew those men."

"Find out who are the principal contributors to the Reverend Dr. Martin Luther King's Southern Christian Leadership. It's interesting, I assure you. Well, we're not about that anymore. Brothers and sisters, it's a new day."

More tumultuous applause.

"From this day forward the movement for the liberation of black people in America will be a movement led by black people. And I don't mean these bourgeois, uppity, black-on-the-outside, white-on-the-inside, Oreo motherfuckers out here in the suburbs."

Matilda leaned toward David and whispered, "That would mean your parents, I assume. And me. And you, by the way, too."

David brushed a hand across his forehead. He'd suspected bringing his auntie here might have been a mistake, but maybe he'd imagined the wrong reason that would be so.

"But I also don't want to divide us as a people. For too long they have made that *their* stock-in-trade. It will take *all* our talents to bring about the changes in this nation that we need to move ahead as a people."

"Well, that's a relief, David. No tar and feathers for us Oreos. At least not yet."

"I have to tell you, though, it does my heart good to see that so many of you from outside the university have come to hear about the Party. I see sisters out there who I know live with hard times every day. Have to scrape and beg to feed your kids. Live in places where white folks wouldn't put their dogs. Day after day told that you are nothing, that no one wants you. Well, sisters, I'm here to say that we want you here. We need you here. We welcome you here. Welcome."

Matilda cleared her throat and indicated with her head where David should look. To his right, an obese woman, uncomfortable in a threadbare outfit, sobbed. Her clothes were made from some sort of stretchy material that once had been gay shades of pink and lavender and blue but now retained only a sad memory of their original luster.

"You brothers, just off the corner, can't find nothing to do with yourself, can't find a purpose, can't find a job, can't find a place, a home, a life. You are welcome here, as well."

More applause.

David settled into the rhythm of the speech, the way Ahmed had of beginning a sequence as if it were a car taking off from a full stop, gearing it up to the main idea he had in mind, at which point he would open the throttle, head for the crescendo, the apotheosis, blast to the climax that would leave his listeners awestruck, electrified, and often dripping with tears. And had it been only a floor show, well, that would have been plenty—more stimulation than most of these folks received in a normal year, save the tawdry pleasures of liquor and drugs. Yet it was more, David knew. This was about ideas. Here was a man with a vision for the way that the world should work. A man with a plan to bring that vision to life.

David rose to his feet with the rest of the audience. Even Matilda stood to applaud.

"He's a master rhetorician, I'll give him that. I haven't heard a speech that strong since the Senator's time. The Senator. Now, there was a man with a mouth on him. He could go on like this for days. And that's not hyperbole."

"I told you he was good."

Matilda pursed her lips in the way that meant she was withholding judgment.

"Let's congratulate him," David said, and started to the front. Matilda grabbed his arm.

"Too many," she said, shaking her head in disgust. Before he could argue, he noticed Patty working her way up the aisle.

"David!" she called. "Wasn't Ahmed something?"

Patty took his breath away. She absolutely knocked him out. Those eyes—they had no bottom. They were mirrors. That skin. Those lips. That . . . everything.

Matilda cleared her throat.

Coming back to himself, David noticed both women waiting politely for him to do his job.

"Oh. Oh, um, yeah. Matilda Housewright. This is Patty . . . uh, Patricia Jackson. Patricia, my aunt Matilda."

"Patty. Yes, of course, David's told me so much about you." Matilda bowed her head slightly. He had not so much as mentioned Patty's name to her, yet she would be too polite to say so, as she also would not—could not—reciprocate the compliment Patty had made on her dress, deferring the conversation instead toward the speech.

"That was quite a performance. Are you also an acolyte, Miss Jackson?"

"Ahmed has changed my life. I don't mean to sound like some little girl, chasing after Smokey Robinson for an autograph. But he did. He changed my definition of myself."

"And how do you define yourself, Miss Jackson? I hope I'm not being impertinent."

"Not at all," Patty replied, taking a minute to gather her

thoughts. And David realized that he had never seen Matilda take on someone outside the family. What if she took the poor girl apart? Maybe he should step in now and call a halt to this sparring match, if that's what this was to become.

"I guess it's pretty simple," Patty started. "I see my role as to serve. Here I am with the opportunity to get a good education—I'm on course with my goal of medical school. I see myself gathering my skills and my credentials and bringing them back to the community. Where they're needed. That's all, really."

"Spoken with conviction, might I add. And should the right offer to join a lucrative practice in University Hills rear its head, those principles will remain sound, no doubt."

"Auntie," David said through his teeth, but Patty's confident voice stopped him.

"To tell you the truth, Miss Housewright, I don't really know. I hope they do. I do know that I'm always going to find some way to serve my people. That's something I'd never thought much about until I met Ahmed."

"He's quite a man, evidently."

"Come and meet him," Patty said. She reached for Matilda's hand and began leading her toward the corner of the stage where Ahmed was greeting his admirers. To David's surprise, Matilda went, linking arms with Patty (something he'd been hoping to do himself; that, and other things) and holding close to her side.

"These folks will clear out soon. It's like the line of a church, you know. Tell the reverend he preached a good sermon. David tells me you've got a lovely garden."

"It's glorious just now, too. He'll be bringing you by to see it, won't he?"

"I sure hope so."

Though David could tell by their body language and dancing eyes that they were teasing, he couldn't suppress a blush.

"That patch of weeds," he said, trying to get in the spirit.

Matilda dropped her lip, feigning heartache.

"Why, David Housewright, look what you've done to your dear auntie. Miss Housewright, he's gonna bring me by as soon as we work out the details. Isn't that right, sugar?" She gave David a look that almost caused his knees to buckle.

Ahmed had a dozen or so supporters to greet before they reached him. The crowd had thinned considerably, folks rushing home to get the children in bed for school the next day. David noted the rose gold stripes that ran the length of Ahmed's robe. At a distance they had seemed regal and grand, whereas up close they seemed more feminine and precious. He'd told David he purchased all the fabric for his clothes on his regular trips to Africa. David wondered if, when he spotted the bolt of cloth stacked with the others, Ahmed had known that it would contribute to mesmerizing his audiences.

Ahmed bent from the stage to greet a man in a filling station uniform.

"Thank you for coming," he said, shaking the man's hand. He spotted David and Patty in the crowd. "Children," he called to them.

Then he noticed Matilda. "I see you've brought a visitor."

"If he thinks I'm reaching up there—" Matilda started, but Ahmed, perhaps anticipating her thoughts, lowered himself from the stage to their level.

"Matilda Housewright," she said, before David had the chance to do the honors. "I'm pleased to make your acquaintance."

"Likewise. You're David's . . ."

"Aunt. That's correct. And you are quite the skilled orator."

"Many thanks, indeed. I appreciate the compliment." Ahmed took her hand in the kind of clasp that almost looked as if he'd meant to kiss it. David noted that Ahmed was older than his aunt. He'd never thought about this. Maybe the man's ideas were not ones he usually associated with this other generation.

"I'm sure you're floating on praise at the moment. It goes to one's head, I imagine."

"It's not about me, I'm sure you understand."

"I'm sure. Tell me, Mr. . . . Ahmed: Is this your living, doing these speaking engagements?"

"I'm a full professor here at the university."

"As, of course, my nephew has informed me. Do forgive me."

"Not necessary. And my calendar, as it happens, does fill up often with engagements such as this one. Most, I assure you, with no remuneration to me, as was the case tonight."

"A noble man, indeed. Would you characterize all of your oratory as being this . . . fiery?"

"I'll accept that as a compliment, if I may. I strive always to tailor the rhetoric to the audience."

"These ideas would be your own, I presume?"

"I ride in the wake of a rich intellectual tradition."

"And a radical one, indeed. According to my nephew, a good deal of—"

"Excuse me, Aunt Matilda. Ahmed's had a long day. Others are waiting."

Both Ahmed and Matilda looked at him in ways that suggested he curb his rudeness.

"It has been a long day. Miss Housewright would perhaps consent to continuing this conversation at another time?"

"It would be my great pleasure."

"Very good. David, arrange it!" And with that, he swept up the aisle in his robe.

"Impeccable manners for a snake oil salesman," Matilda whispered to David. "Bring him to dinner next Sunday. Invite Florence Nightingale, too."

"Oh, Auntie, I don't know if this . . ."

But Matilda wasn't listening. She was off up the aisle herself, snagging Patty in her wake.

"Tell me, dear. Do aspiring physicians eat fried chicken?"

David dragged behind them, shaking his head. Like a lot of his supposedly good ideas, this one had taken an unfortunate detour.

III

"This is what you're wearing?" she asked.

David hadn't given a thought to his outfit. He wore what he always wore: jeans with some sort of T-shirt, and a collared shirt over it to keep his arms from getting cold, usually a khaki army shirt he'd bought for seventy-five cents from the thrift shop near campus. Before he could gear himself up for a lecture about fashion being a tool of capitalist exploitation, she ordered him to the dining room for inspection.

"What do you think? Now, before you say anything, I know that the formal china is a little much for a noon meal, but these chargers are so pretty with the fresh flowers. I tried to dress it down by rolling the napkins in rings, but you know how silly that looks, so I tented. If you'd prefer, we can fold them with the silver."

It wasn't the handsome plates with their black band and gold rim nor the perfect elegance of the lace tablecloth that left David speechless. It was the fact that he had seen his father set this same picture-perfect table at least a thousand times. His father, to be sure, worked with different china patterns, and did it even need to be noted that Housewright and Sons' heavy-duty glassware didn't radiate the sparkle that Matilda's crystal did, even in the intentionally modest candlelight of her dining room. But even David's less than refined eye picked up at once on the corresponding details: the buffed-to-a-sheen dinnerware, the pale-tinted virgin tapers (and the polished silver snuffer awaiting service on the sideboard), the regiment of cutlery, each setting a mirror of the next, almost as if laid out by machine.

Jesus! "It must be genetic," he said. He hoped he'd said that to himself and he also hoped that it wasn't true.

"Tents it is, then," Matilda said. "No time for gawking." She guided him by the shoulders into the kitchen and pointed him to a bowl of salad greens. "You know the drill," she said.

Damn if that weren't so. David picked through the lettuce, looking for any ribs that were either wider than a pencil or didn't flex at the touch. Housewright Maxim #17: Stalks are for horses, not for people. Greenery that didn't make the cut made a quick trip to the compost heap. It happened to be a simple job and one that David often got complimented on doing well, though a bitterness seeped into a corner of his consciousness when he remembered how he'd developed the skill. His father, upon once finding a healthy crisp rib that he had neglected to remove from a bowl of iceberg lettuce, had served David an entire salad of the watery and tasteless mess and insisted he eat it before he left the table.

"In case you're wondering, we're having the fried chicken salad with homemade mayonnaise. I know I told your girlfriend I'd fry a chicken, but I couldn't quite see myself running back and forth from the skillet to my guests. And I hate that smell in the house, don't you? This way, the food is ready to serve, the house smells fresh, and I'm not spattered with grease at the last minute. So it all works out. In case you were wondering."

"She's not my girlfriend."

"I see. I beg your pardon then."

"I mean, it's not that I don't want her to be. It's just that, as of now, she isn't. My girlfriend, that is. Yet, I mean."

"Oh, well." Matilda pressed the dinner rolls into a greased pan. They'd risen round as beige snowballs there on the counter by the stove. "She isn't . . . yet . . . but you *are* looking to catch her. Is that correct?"

"Auntie, it's not like she's a trout."

"Well, what is it you youngsters say these days?"

"I don't know that *we youngsters* say anything. People just sort of . . . hook up, you know."

"I see. Hook up. Like trout. So tell me, Captain Ahab: What's your plan?"

David scoffed. "I thought I'd club her over the head and drag her back to my cave."

"That could work," Matilda nodded. "You might want to fix yourself up a little bit first."

"Come on, Auntie. People nowadays don't care about that stuff. They like you because of who you are."

"I suppose your Ahmed told you that."

"Everybody knows that."

"These rolls ought to have risen again right on schedule, don't you think?" She covered the bread with a towel almost as if it were a baby she was putting down for a nap. She fished a thick stem from the greens David thought he had finished with.

"Make sure this piece ends up on your plate."

"You expect me to chase the girl around in a coat and tie. She'd laugh me off campus."

"Or she might surprise you. But let's assume you're right. Let's assume she finds something dashing about your little . . . hobo outfits. Did you bring her some flowers? Girls still like flowers, don't they?"

"This isn't a date," David whined, and then thought about it for a minute and added, "is it?"

"Let's hope, for your sake, that she isn't expecting it to be."

David had no idea what Patty might be expecting. It had all happened so fast. There they'd been at the rally, and then there Matilda had been organizing this . . . thing. A thing that included lunch. Wasn't there some difference between a thing and a date?

"So you're saying maybe I should run and get some flowers or something."

"What I was actually getting ready to say was 'please take that bucket of cleaning supplies to the half bath.' Don't leave any green Comet stains on the commode. On the second shelf of the icebox you will find a lovely assortment of flowers, fresh from my garden, wrapped in tissue paper and tied with a lovely velvet ribbon. You may do with them as you wish. Speaking for *our* side, I would, however, like it on the record that a lady does like to receive flowers—even if it isn't a date. Even 1960s ladies with big bushes on their heads.

"Afros, Auntie. Afros."

David shook the round cleanser box until the bowl turned the color of pistachio ice cream.

When the bell rang both David and Matilda ran to the door. He thought they both tried to play it off, tried to act as if they weren't anxious. They both giggled at their silliness.

"You haven't told me how I look," Matilda chided.

David squinted and turned his nose up as if to give her scrutiny.

Matilda scoffed. "Consider the source," she sniffed.

She actually looked fabulous, he thought, a simple pale linen pantsuit. He'd rejected it the other night, but it was the perfect outfit for this afternoon. He didn't believe he'd ever seen his auntie wearing anything quite so stylish.

Ahmed looked distinguished himself, David thought, in a dashiki that David had never seen before, a brown, black, and emerald pattern that reminded him of leaves and branches woven together by a windstorm. Patty wore a dress. A lovely dress. A really lovely dress. He'd never seen Patty in a dress. Tiny white flowers covered the navy blue dress. David had thought they were polka dots. He was glad Matilda had shamed him into at least tucking in the T-shirt.

"We'll be having our lunch as soon as the bread reheats," Matilda said, minimizing the yeast bread that she'd strategically popped in the oven when the doorbell rang. "May I offer either of you a beverage while we wait? David?"

David's throat was parched, but he knew better than to take her up on that offer. Her guests declined, as well.

"What a lovely home," Patty enthused.

"Thank you, dear. David's such a help around here. He's very handy with a tool belt, you know."

"I'm sure he is," Patty replied, and David thought he saw something pass between the two women, something in their eyes. He averted his own eyes to the crown molding he'd repainted last summer. His auntie would sell him like a low-mileage used car. He just knew it.

"How about you, are you married, Mr. . . . Ahmed? My goodness: I realize I don't know what to call you. My apologies."

"Ahmed would be just fine, and I am presently a widower. I lost my wife of twenty years last spring."

"So sorry to hear. And you must call me Matilda, of course."

"Of course. A Germanic name. Strong."

"I'm enchanted that you would know that. It had been my father's mother's name. Sarah Matilda. She was born into slavery on a farm in south-central Virginia. She saw General Lee pass by on his way to Appomattox, or so she told her son."

"The name suits you, I think."

"I've always thought so."

(Wait. What was this?)

"And what would your given name have been? If you don't mind my asking."

"Not at all. It was Kenneth. It still is Kenneth as far as the Department of Motor Vehicles is concerned."

"So Ahmed would be . . ."

"My name. My chosen name. I don't need the state to confirm my identity."

"Kenneth. Isn't that interesting, David?"

David had been trying not to stare at Patty, who had been sort of staring at him but sort of not staring—or at least that was how it looked to him. He therefore only caught the edge of a gloat in Matilda's eye.

"Pull the bread from the oven, please, David, while I get our guests situated in the dining room."

"Yes, ma'am," he said, stumbling up from his chair.

He felt nauseous. He wondered if it was something he ate, but then knew that it wasn't and then wondered if it was normal to feel this way. He opened the oven and reached for the hot rolls, and too late remembered he had no potholder. The pan clattered to the floor.

Matilda appeared at his side as if by magic. "Lucky for you they landed pan-side down, and lucky for you no one saw but me. Carry the iced tea in while I transfer these to a basket."

David removed the cold pitcher from the refrigerator.

"Try not to spill it directly in her lap."

Steady hands (though only marginally so) and years of practice facilitated his pouring a perfect round. He'd remembered to keep a clean white napkin just under the spout as he poured both to mask and to catch any drips. God, how he'd hated those long afternoons in his father's kitchen, pouring plain water into hundreds of glasses, some set deep on the counter almost out of reach, others selected for their oddly shaped rims, still others placed awkwardly behind centerpieces and others already filled with cubed ice. He'd pour and then buss the glasses from the counter so his father could check for spills. Too many dribbles on the stainless-steel serving tray meant another half hour spent aiming artful cascades into goblets intended for no customer's lips. His wrist would hurt so bad he would pack it in ice and cry.

"Your aunt is a gracious host," Patty said.

"Yes, ma'am. I mean, yes." David shook his head, hoping it would clear. "I need to remove these plates."

He lifted the charger from each setting. He could do this in his sleep, he bet. Four, forty, four hundred, four thousand. The key: remember the order of service, and keep the glasses topped up.

On cue, Matilda set the chicken salad at the guests' places. David retrieved the basket with the rolls and she followed immediately with his plate and hers.

"I think we have everything." Matilda's glance over the table was unnecessary, David knew. It was all there, and all right where it belonged, too. Individual molds of sweet butter. A tiny saltcellar within easy reach of each plate.

"I hope your iced tea isn't too sweet. I was raised in the South. A lot of people don't think of our nation's capital as being a Southern city, but I can assure you that the District of Columbia most certainly is one. In the South we drink our tea sweet. Presweetened, just as I'm serving you today. Enjoy."

"It's delicious," Patty said, taking a big swig. "I can never get mine this sweet. I always end up with a bunch of sugar spinning around in the bottom of the pitcher. What's your secret?"

"Will you tell her, David, or shall I?"

"The secret is to add the sugar right after the tea brews, when the water is still really hot."

"A man who can cook!" Patty grinned. "I'm impressed."

"It's not really cooking," David threw in, too hastily, he knew. "Hot water is more soluble than cold. It's basic chemistry. And all that."

Basic chemistry and all that. Smooth, he thought. If there's one thing he knew girls hated, it was Mr. Poindexter know-it-alls.

"Chemistry's good, too," Patty said.

"David knows all about kitchen things. My brother, Martin, is a caterer and an excellent chef in his own right."

Yep, David thought, I'm a walking fount of useless kitchen trivia. He knew which sauces could be saved with vinegar and how much tarragon to add when creating béarnaise. David knew that mayonnaise was as good as an egg for making moist brownies, and that candy caramels did a great job browning up a reluctant roast. Some days he wished he could take a wire scour (fine on stainless steel but an absolute no-no on iron skillets) and scrub some of this crap from his brain.

"But David's already decided that he's more suited for life at the bar, isn't that right?"

Ahmed nodded almost as if he were David's father. "The movement needs bright young lawyers like our David."

"The movement, well, that's an interesting thought. David and I have often discussed the relative merits of corporate law."

David took a swallow of tea to move along the slightly dry chicken that had caught on that lie. (He wondered if perhaps Matilda had forgotten to slightly undercook a chicken one intended to slice for salad, and then to finish it under the broiler *after* slicing and a few hours before serving.) Well, it was a white lie, at least. They had talked about corporate law, but only as a career he should avoid at all costs. He expected Ahmed to challenge him there on the spot, but his attention seemed to be focused elsewhere.

"My dear Miss Housewright. You can't mean to tell me that you would sacrifice one of our community's most promising young talents to the greedy corporate menace, a monster which has been a prime contributor to the oppression of your own people?"

"Call me Matilda, Ahmed. I insist. And what I'm saying is that if I send my nephew into the corporate world, at least I know what I'm getting for that bargain. A good income. Respectability in the community."

"Yes, *Matilda*, and at what cost? What does it cost all these blacks we see running after Mr. Charley and doing his will? Let's say young Martin here goes to work for these detergent makers just down the road here. I would think a young man would be hard-pressed to live with himself, knowing that in addition to soap, his employer produced the toxins that were being used to deforest portions of our homeland and to drive those who depend on the trees for their livelihood into the cities to work for almost nothing in sweatshops that it just so happens are also controlled by that same corporation."

"I would think our young man would garner enough power within the soap company to hire other like-minded individuals until they numbered enough to change the corporation's policies. That's what I'd think."

"Matilda, you are a lovely hostess, but I'm afraid you are terribly naive about the corporate world."

"Miss Jackson, how is your salad?"

Patty, mouth full, nodded enthusiastically.

"Lovely. And confirm for me, Miss Jackson, that I have, in fact, just been egregiously patronized at my own table."

"My humblest apologies, mademoiselle. Though I must reiterate my strong belief that the capitalist system is most pernicious and evil. Your fantasy of changing the system from within is, I'm afraid, just that: a naive fantasy."

"What then, Ahmed, would your so-called movement be offering as an alternative? Where is *your* city on the hill?"

"I'm talking about a true government of the people. I'm talking about those who do the work, profiting from the work. I'm talking about economic and social justice for all."

Matilda sputtered. "Communists. I thought they shipped the lot of you to Russia ten years ago."

"Red-baiting is unbecoming to so charming a host. Clearly the Party shares some of the ideology of the Marxist. We draw much more from the example of our great African leaders. Lumumba."

"I believe Mr. Lumumba has ascended to a higher plane."

"At the hands of your government, Miss Housewright."

"Yours as well, sir. And what is it we ought to have learned from the dearly departed?"

"The watchword is self-determination for African people throughout the diaspora. This, quite simply, is our goal."

"And why should my nephew choose to work toward this goal?"

David stood and quietly pushed back his chair. "I've already chosen," he said. "Shall I set up coffee here or in the parlor?"

"The parlor, I think. We'll have our dessert there, as well."

David prepared the sink to receive the dinnerware. (Very hot water, soft detergent. Do it first. Wipe, rinse, dry, return to closet. Maxim #8: One does not risk fine china in a working kitchen.) Patty backed through the swinging door, her hands a little too full of a little too casually stacked china. David restrained himself from shouting "Careful!"

"Can you believe this conversation?" Patty asked. "It's amazing. An actual debate, for once."

"That's Matilda."

"You're lucky to have someone like her."

"I'm glad you said that. I really am. I was so worried that folks from the Party would take one look at all this—this house, this china, her. I was sure they'd throw me out with the rest of the white folks."

"Oh, come on, David." Patty put her arm around him and then reached for a plate to dry. David hung on to the sink to keep from crashing into it. "You take some of those brothers too seriously. You do. All their big talk about *authenticity* and *representing*."

"But Ahmed also talks about this being a people's movement."

"Your aunt is people, too. And you. And me. I'm not moving to the projects and changing the way I speak and neither should you. Each according to his means, David. That means that you and I put in what we have to give. A doctor and a lawyer. That's a pretty big contribution."

"What about this?" David pointed to her Afro and then his.

"Honey, this is about cute. Cute on me and cute on you, too."

"You really think so?" David said, and then turned around because he thought he'd been too "aw shucks" in a Cowardly Lion kind of way. Patty swatted him with the towel.

"These are the plates for cake?"

"This would be my aunt Matilda's famous pineapple cake with the burnt-sugar frosting."

"Is there a knife?"

"Watch this," David prompted. He retrieved a bowl of ice water and a metal spatula from the freezer. He pulled the spatula through the cake twice, dipping it in the ice water between strokes and dividing the cake into fourths. "And I'll split each of these." He did so and drew forth a perfect wedge and centered it on the plate.

"Just amazing," exclaimed Patty.

"Cut as much wedding cake as I have in my life and you can do this in your sleep. Unfortunately, producing a perfect slice of pineapple cake and getting a 180 on your LSATs doesn't earn you many points on the street."

Patty filled the creamer and checked the level of the sugar bowl. Damn, David thought, the girl has potential. He'd have to keep her hidden from his father, for sure.

"There are all kinds of ways to earn your stripes."

"Which is why I'm going to that sit-in tomorrow."

"You discuss that with Ahmed?"

"He knows. He says it's my call."

"Chaining yourself to the mayor's fence. Seems penny ante to me."

"Got to start somewhere. I've said 'no' to pretty much everything else."

"Okay."

"Okay?"

"Okay, I'll go. I've got a chemistry final Tuesday, but I'm ready. I'll go. You think your auntie will be impressed if I pour the coffee?"

She's already impressed, David thought, but he kept the words to himself.

"It's been my experience," Matilda was saying when they entered with the dessert, "that men—older men—are always finding opportunities for young men, such as my nephew, to put their lives on the line for a cause dear to the older men's hearts. And I mean all kinds of men, be it the man my father worked for in Washington, or his successors there now, or even someone such as yourself."

"I'm a historian, Matilda. We could spend hours, you and I, reciting examples of this phenomenon, from the recent as well as from the distant past. Many of those causes we'd deem trivial, others we'd describe as noble. Let's say I were to ask David to, for example, to assassinate President Johnson because I believed that by doing so he would change the lives of black Americans for the better. Would that make me an evil man?"

Matilda scoffed. "A foolish question and an even more foolish example. I don't respond to hypotheticals. Here's an actual case: a charismatic man of extraordinary intelligence uses his intellect and charm to manipulate young people into joining his cause. Ask me my opinion of that."

"That's unfair, Miss Housewright," Patty protested. "David and I make our own choices, don't we, David?"

David concurred. He kind of liked the "we" part of that sentence.

"As a teacher, Matilda, am I not obligated to use my persuasive skills and to leverage my influence with the next generation toward making the world a better place?"

"Or your version of a better place."

"For your information, Miss Housewright, I don't believe everything Ahmed says is the gospel truth." So Patty had a haughty side, too. David liked this about her. He liked pretty much everything about her so far.

Ahmed put his hand to his heart, feigning pain at the revelation.

"Sorry, Ahmed, but I don't. I do believe that empowering

poor people is a good thing. I believe that collective action has the power to change the world. Which is no different than Christ or Gandhi or Martin Luther King. As for the armed revolution part, you can count me out."

"I'm so glad this young woman brought up the 'R' word. Tell me about your armed revolution, Ahmed."

"It's largely rhetorical, if you must know. But I fear we've reached the point that I don't see any other choice. When a people's needs go so long unaddressed, when the available means to access the system don't work, and when nonviolent action fails, I raise the question with my students as to which course of action remains."

"Madness!" Matilda raged. "And if an impressionable teenager happens to move from rhetoric to action, what then? Completely irresponsible. I can't imagine where a clearly intelligent man would come by such nonsense."

"We could begin with our own Declaration of Independence. Read it again at your leisure. But let me emphasize again that I raise these questions rhetorically only. You might be surprised to learn that a not-insignificant number of young people come to my office in advocacy of the status quo. A position you would support, Matilda?"

"I'm a pragmatist, Ahmed. I have always believed in doing what works. Do it well. Do it right. Take advantage of the opportunities that happen your way."

"I sense common ground," Ahmed said, extending his cup for more coffee. As Matilda poured, David believed he could see something pass between them. He didn't know what. His legs were covered in gooseflesh. He was as high as he ever had been.

"I imagine we agree on quite a few things," Matilda offered.

"You understand the primary goal as self-determination. Mine is and has always been posterity."

"My good woman: Every general worth his salt knows the difference between his elite troops and his cannon fodder."

Matilda raised her coffee cup as if to offer a toast. "I knew we understood each other. David, Ahmed tells me you're to be engaged in a little public theatrical."

"It was my choice, Aunt Matilda."

"These young people are so defensive. I swear, Ahmed, I can't imagine how you have the patience to work with them. I'll show you my garden while the children clear the dishes."

David could see from the look she gave Patty that she would just as soon that particular child not handle her dishes at all—a little too rough on the stacking for Housewright standards. A lesson was in order. Many, many lessons, he hoped.

Later, at the front door, as Patty and Ahmed said their goodbyes, David remembered the bouquet in the refrigerator.

"Hang on," he called.

"I got these. For you. 'Cause girls like flowers and all."

Matilda kicked him hard in the ankle.

"So sweet." Patty leaned forward and kissed him on the cheek. Between the kiss and the ankle, David leaned on Matilda to stay upright.

"Well, you made out pretty well there," Matilda said, closing the front door.

He didn't say so, but David believed that old Matilda had done pretty well herself.

IV

Just before his mother woke him to tell him Matilda had called, David had been dreaming of lavender icing. Vats of lavender icing. Buttercream. Someone's anniversary cake. Here is how you frost a cake. Hold the spatula level. Apply slight pressure. Allow the icing to spread in front of the blade. No pushing. No dragging. David had known this since before he could tie his own shoes. He thinks lavender is a bad idea. Precious. Hard to decorate around. Blue dyes taste metallic. David scrapes open a crumbly wound in the side of the cake. His father patches it shut. Glowers. "How big is this cake, anyway?" Golden brown sheets stretch before him like a highway. He takes a mouthful of frosting. Buttery and sweet and smooth and then it multiplies on his tongue and he cannot swallow it fast enough. The contents of his stomach rise to his throat.

He called back Matilda, giving her the one last chance she'd insisted upon to convince him to change his mind—which she had not—and then he headed over to school to pick up Patty. She lived in one of the older dorms on the south edge of campus. He could drive there in his sleep, he believed. He'd come by dozens of times, futilely hoping to catch sight of her.

She waited for him on one of the benches lining the walkway to the dorm. They commenced the kind of mid-distance sign language more established couples use to communicate across crowded rooms: He threw his hands up in a way that questioned whether she had everything she needed. She waved her arms about to demonstrate how unencumbered she was. The nonverbals, already solid: That was a good sign.

"I'm all set for passive resistance," she announced. "If the pigs snatch me up, they can't go through my purse. Oh, and look." She unwrapped the bandanna covering her Afro, revealing that her hair had been plaited down tight to her head the way black mothers did to their grade school daughters. "You like? I'm not having them mothafuckers drag me by my hair."

Head smooth as a cue ball and she'd still be beautiful to him.

"Do they do that sort of thing?" he asked. Strange, he hadn't bothered imagining this could get nasty.

"Jeanette, that dark sister, her cousin was down in Selma and she told me they snatched a bald spot out the back of the girl's head." Patty talked about the incident in the same animated tone folks used to describe who got shot on the block or which slutty girl had slept with which fraternity brother. David could feel her excitement about the rally. She had about her the manic energy of a child going off to a parade or a carnival. He asked her if she were nervous.

She shrugged. "Not really. You ever played a softball game against a team who you really hate their guts? That's how I feel. I feel like I'm getting ready to kick me some ass."

"Except in this case, you've got the ass and they've got the foot."

He couldn't believe he just said that.

Patty shook her head. "Whatever happens, happens. I just know that I'm gonna give as good as I get."

"And you don't worry that someone or something will get out of control?"

"Nah! I'm talking smack. Ain't nothing gonna happen. This one's routine."

"Like a trip to the dentist."

"Something like that. More like a little play, maybe, and everybody has their parts. The mayor, he plays the evil mayor, and his role is to keep the people down. We play the part of the people, and we come in and demand our rights. The police come in and play the part of putting everything back to normal. If we're lucky the reporters do their part and let everybody know what it is they're supposed to care about. Then, with any luck, a bunch more people will start hassling the evil mayor and he changes his mind and becomes the good mayor. And we, the people, move on to our next target."

God, David thought, that is just so damn cute, the way she said that. He'd chain himself to the Empire State Building as long as she was chained up beside him.

Later, in his cell, after he'd called Matilda to come bail him out, he'd tried to remember that speech and the sound of her voice, soft but resonant, calm and sure and pleasant and warm. How he'd wanted to reach over and hug the girl and how he wished he could tamp down the part of him that would not let him touch her. He knew that she liked him. She'd snuggled up close to him in the car, had held his hand as they approached the group. Why couldn't he make his move? (And which move, after all, was he supposed to make?)

Sometimes, at the fraternity house or down where the Party met, he'd listen to the brothers talk about their conquests and how they'd got all up inside this one or had another one begging for more. Back in high school he'd even tried to get in on the locker room prattle, but he didn't have the temperament for it. He could never quite find the moment to put his prerehearsed fantasy in the mix, had never mastered the mixture of insouciance and raunchiness that might earn him either a pat on the back or a request for further detail.

He knew one thing: he wasn't treating this girl like that crowd treated the skuzzy women they bragged about. That's not what he wanted. At the same time he had to wonder, what if she wanted something like that? What if she expected him to pull the car over, throw her over the backseat, and show her what a real man could do? What if she got tired of waiting for him to . . . do something? When they had approached the staging area for the sit-in, he squeezed her hand extra tight to signal . . . something, some message along the lines of "Wait for me, I'm figuring this out as fast as I can."

The protest had gone as she predicted, though more a farce to David's eye than a play. They gathered, a dozen or so scruffy-looking black folks, at a small park down the block from the mayor's house. Cheap-looking handcuffs were distributed along with instructions on their use. One of his father's minor kitchen knives could slice through the chain. They agreed that this would be a silent protest, no chanting, no slogans, and no profanity of any kind. A stout sister named Selena had agreed to remain unchained so that she could distribute the one-page broadside with their demands. (Shouldn't I read those first? David had thought. In case I get asked any questions.) The reporters had already been in place before they left the park.

"Scowl," Patty had advised. "They like it when we scowl."

The only (literally) sticky point had been the mayor's big Doberman, who, shortly after they'd locked themselves down, had tired of running up and down the fence snarling and baring his teeth, and for some reason had decided it was much more fun to lick slobber through the fence onto David's hands.

"It's for the people, brother," Patty had encouraged.

The cop who popped his cuffs helped David to his feet. He was a young guy who kept checking his watch and yawning.

"Walk or drag, buddy?" the cop asked.

"Huh?" David asked. He had been surprised at the pleasant sweetness of his voice.

"To the freak wagon. Walk or drag?"

"Oh . . . um . . . drag, I guess." David decided there on the spot that drag had a more authentic look about it (though the balls of his feet vibrated and hurt like hell, and he'd left a little more of his Converses back on the sidewalk than a person usually cared to see).

The men were dumped into a holding cell alongside a handful of drunks drying out from their Saturday night tear. Everyone looked bored and lethargic, and the room smelled of urine and sweat. David busied himself reading the unimaginative graffiti scratched into the drab gray paint. After a while he sat on a wooden bench, rested his head on the wall, and closed his eyes.

"Housewright!" a guard with a clipboard called. David stood.

"You're sprung."

David accepted the halfhearted handshakes of the brothers in the cell. A few anemic power fists thrust in salute.

Matilda was waiting for him in the reception area. David smiled sheepishly. Trouble was coming.

"Seen Patty?" he asked.

Matilda spun on her heels, expecting him, he knew, to follow. She stopped abruptly and David plowed into her back.

"Go tell that . . . *man* to call me a cab. Please."

Even though it was his first experience with the police, David was pretty sure one didn't demand the desk sergeant do anything. He fished a coin from his pocket and made the call himself. He asked for a ride back to where he'd parked for the rally.

"How much was the bail?" David asked.

Matilda did not respond.

"I'll pay you back. I forgot my checkbook this morning, is all. I'm good for it."

Matilda transferred herself from the cab to David's car, still stewing, still silent.

"Papers were there," he told her. "Took lots of photos. Hope they got my good side."

Nothing.

Matilda opened her door before the car stopped. She slammed it behind her and stalked up to her front door. David trotted along behind her, feeling like a naughty puppy following a little boy to school.

She spun on him as soon as he closed the door.

"Give me one reason I shouldn't pick up that phone and call my brother right this minute."

David thought.

"Ten. Nine. Eight.

"Um . . . because . . ."

"Seven. Six."

"Because I don't want you to."

"I asked for a good reason. Go on. Pick it up and dial your number. I warned you this morning."

"Can't we talk about it at least?"

"You want to talk about it? Fine. Here's how I see it: I managed to live half a century and in all that time I never set foot in one of those places. Until today."

"Technically speaking—" David started, but Matilda made one of those noises—some sort of a mixture of a hiss and a raspberry and snort. It was the sound she made to indicate that whatever he had to say she wasn't the least bit interested in hearing.

"I walk in there and they have the nerve to look at me like I'm . . . dirt. Like I'm nothing. Like some common . . . streetwalker. Do you think I enjoyed that? Do you?"

David said, "No, ma'am," although it was clear to him that no one was listening to his reply.

"And you're right about one thing. I'm leaving Martin Housewright to you. You tell your father whatever you like about your little escapade, and leave me out of it. I expect every penny of my money in my hands by the time the sun sets tomorrow or I swear I'll find you and take it out in flesh."

"Don't get biblical, Auntie."

"Of all the humiliating experiences."

"You weren't the one with a dog sniffing you."

"David! I don't want to know! Not right now. I'm too upset. That would be Ahmed at the door. See him in, please."

"You called Ahmed?"

"You bet I did. See him in. Now!"

David answered the bell and Ahmed gave him a soul shake.

"Congratulations, young brother. You're a member of the family now."

"You're encouraging this? I invited you over here to talk some sense into the boy."

"Miss Housewright! Lovely as always. May I come—"

"Hold the charisma, Sidney Poitier. We've got a crisis brewing here. A little over twenty-four hours ago, you sat in that chair and promised me you'd look out for my nephew. This afternoon, where do I find myself but at the courthouse, posting bail like some two-bit lawyer. Explain yourself."

What was this? Promises? What was she going on about?

"David was aware of the risk involved in today's action—which, I must say, was minimal."

"Do you read the papers, Ahmed? I mean the real paper, not those bleed-through fish wrappers you radicals circulate. Do you know what happens to our men in jail? A man your age! Of course you do. I'm not having it. Do you understand me? If I have to personally shut down your little coalition of thugs, I will do so."

"Aunt Matilda!"

Ahmed hushed David by waving a hand.

"I share your concern, but I do want you to understand I would never send our David into any place I felt was in the least bit risky."

"Thanks a lot." David's voice dripped with sarcasm.

"In Africa, David, we respect our elders. Be careful with your tone."

"My father was a great admirer of Ida B. Wells. I don't want you to think I'm speaking against social consciousness, Ahmed, because that is not my intention."

"Of course not."

"I felt that you and I had reached consensus on the notion that each individual added his own gifts and talents. Miss Wells's gift was language. That is what she gave. My nephew's life course has been set for him. I'll not tolerate deviation."

"Miss Housewright. I apologize for the anxiety you've been caused today. I must tell you that we had people stationed at every conceivable location where something might go awry, if it helps you to know that. In the park, in the booking room. Right there in the jail cell. Our children were watched every step of the way. There was never a chance that harm would come to them. You must believe me."

"You mean that whole thing was a sham today?" David felt the air leave his lungs, felt his whole body slump.

"They're mostly shams, David. It's theater. You've been told this. You were asked to play a part and you played it. You played it well."

"And I would as soon this particular member of the anarchy playhouse gave his last performance today, thank you very much." Matilda relaxed into her charming mode. That meant that any moment now David would be up making coffee and fetching baked goods from the pantry.

"As you wish, Matilda. David has earned his stripes. It's on to bigger things."

These words spun around David faster than his father's

kitchen crew. "Could we stop just a minute here? What do you mean 'sham' and what do you mean my life course is planned? Who do you think you are?" He shook his head. He couldn't look at either of them. Had everyone in the world suddenly lost their minds?

"We've forgotten our manners, I'm afraid. Our guest might enjoy a cordial at this hour. David, if you wouldn't mind . . ."

David lowered his head. He pushed a stack of books from an end table. He walked from the parlor.

"David Housewright, you come back here this instant. I demand—

"Control your temper, young man."

Slamming his way out, he'd wanted to yell something tough such as "kiss my ass" or "go to hell," but once again the words got stuck, mostly, he figured, because he'd never yelled those sorts of things at people he knew, and he wasn't quite sure how big a fit was called for in a situation such as this one.

V

David called up in his head the list of all the parts of the city his mother had asked him to avoid and then aimed his car in the direction of the ones she'd demonized the most. Long after the rest of the world had packed itself away for the day, many of these worn-out and desolate districts pulsed with life, a fact that had always amazed him. Roll down the window even at this late hour and one caught the buzz of alcohol-fueled conversation from the street corner punctuated by the roar of laughter or of voices raised in anger. Now and then the sound of a pistol cracked the night air.

He rolled through the neighborhoods unseen, it seemed, by anyone save the pathetic hookers working The Stroll, hefty, dark girls in ill-suited blond wigs and too-tight clothing designed to extrude the excess flesh—tube tops surrounded with what could be the exploded filling on a cream cheese wonton. They repulsed him, these girls, their audacity, the brazen way their come-ons made assumptions about who he was and why he had gone there. The women shared the streets with deacons coming home from watch meeting and with bent-over wandering old souls who one wondered if they had a home at all. In the very worst neighborhood, women off late shift at the state hospital hustled along the young ones they'd retrieved from the baby-sitter. Ancient insomniacs peered from behind curtains and what might have been the same knot of men gathered beneath the yellow glare of every other streetlamp.

What did it matter to these people that he had chained himself to the mayor's fence? What did it matter to anyone? Let's assume the mayor relented and found a few more dollars for child nutrition. So what? Would that cluster of kids—in the streets and out tonight way later than any reasonable curfew would allow—eat a decent breakfast in the morning? What power had he to fix any of this? What power did he have at all?

Matilda. Ahmed. Martin Housewright. Those were the people with the power. What couldn't they do to the world if they tried?

What was David but their toy?

He parked in front of Patty's dorm and waited for the first early-morning signs of life. As the sun set the red bricks afire, the building came into sharper contrast, and now and then the door discharged some ambitious young thing off for her morning jog. No sign of Patty. He fought sleep, but eventually gave over, awaking sometime later to a tapping on the window of his car.

"Everyone's worried about you. Matilda's been on the phone twice already this morning."

How lovely you look in this light, he thought. The sun, which had already made his car a stifling trap, illuminated her hair, made his eyes dance with the colors of a river delta: warm browns and rich deep reds. Here and there flecks of gold.

He told her he had been driving around. He asked her to get some coffee. She agreed.

They didn't talk. He found he hadn't wanted to—found it soothing instead just sitting there with her.

Patty told him that they would never do anything to hurt him.

He shrugged. He asked permission to ask her a question, which she gave.

"Did you know the demonstration was fake?"

She told him that he was wrong about that—called upon her own presence as proof.

"Ahmed said that there were all these people working behind the scene. Guards. Clerks. Reporters. He said it was all planned, right down to who would get arrested and how much bail would be paid. Fake? Or not?"

Patty sighed. Shook her head. "That's . . . how these things are done. They don't just happen, David. People make them happen. People like you and me. They set goals. They think about contingencies. That has nothing to do with fake."

He dropped his eyes to his coffee mug. "Why don't I know that?"

"That's one of the things I like best about you, David Housewright. You're innocent. You don't look at the world with the same jaundiced eye as the rest of us out here."

"Innocent, as in naive, as in inexperienced, as in—"

She grabbed his hand, led him from the booth, led him back to campus, to her room. Where later, in the gathering midmorning heat, naked under her thin blanket, she had convinced him to go make up with his aunt.

"She thinks she owns me," he complained.

"And what would be wrong with letting her think that?" She kissed him on the forehead.

The flowers David took to Matilda were the hothouse kind, not like the climate-tested captives that toiled through the seasons in her own garden; instead ravishingly fragile exotics whose short-lived glory mocked the hardy endurance of their cousins in the rectangular yard behind the house.

"You said a lady likes flowers," he said, handing her the bouquet.

"So we do. Even from naughty boys who don't call their aunts for days."

"Been busy." He suppressed a blush. When he and Patty moved in together would be soon enough for her to find out what it was that had been keeping him busy.

David retrieved from the attic an old copper smoking stand that had materialized in one of Matilda's recent dreams as the perfect plant stand.

They sorted through the empty Ball jars from last season's preserves, organizing them by size and discarding the rare one with a chipped lip.

They turned the compost—a nasty job. David could never understand why she kept the pile of filth in the first place.

Matilda wanted the dresser in her bedroom moved slightly to the right in order to center it more directly in relation to the floral still-life she had moved there from "Martin's room." He scoured the downstairs commode. Again.

They discussed law school. Matilda told David she had yet to be convinced about this Berkeley thing—wasn't that where that Davis woman was, that Angela, that one with the bush on her head? Ahmed, Matilda said, had promised to bring her some articles about various law schools, and the ones he had been thinking of for his most promising students, and, yes, Berkeley was on his list, though Matilda intended to withhold judgment. California, somehow, did not seem like a Housewright sort of place.

David reminded her that the word was "Afro"—wouldn't she please say that with him, couldn't she please discard "bush" in the same bin with "Negro" and "colored"—reminding her again that he didn't intend to have this same conversation with her for the rest of his life.

David teased her as to the amount of space on her calendar that a certain professor more and more had begun to fill.

Together they transferred a row of hostas from the side of the house to along a back fence by the alley. Matilda told David that California was absolutely out of the question: how could she get along with her nephew so far away?

On a rainy April evening in the emergency room of the city medical center a child died because some people didn't believe poor people deserved medical care after dark. David had not told Matilda about the sit-in at the hospital.

David carried out Chinese food for his and Matilda's supper.

Six brothers, a few picket signs, and a couple of hours from his day: What was there to discuss? It was routine.

Six brothers. A few picket signs. Everything had been planned, right down to a sack full of sandwiches waiting in a Party member's car. It was routine. Who expected a hysterical ward supervisor, traumatized by a year in the ER, to overreact to a small group of protesters? Who expected an inexperienced cop with a new gun, poor judgment, an itchy trigger finger, a pathological fear of young black men?

David had found the rhythm of walking in circles hypnotic. He'd forgotten where he was and had been thinking about that desk in Matilda's parlor, the one with the hammered brass pulls. So when the bullet shattered his skull he had not been thinking about the romantic dinner he had planned with Patty, or about his parents whom he hoped would see this on TV. He had been thinking instead about Matilda. Not about how she would collapse on the floor when her brother broke the news of her nephew's death, but instead about how they would next Saturday morning be moving that heavy old desk to a place where there was more direct sun, and how most likely the next thing she would say to him would be "Come on, David. Get on the other end of this thing and lift."

Here's Something Else

. . .

You might imagine it would be difficult maintaining a normal family life, living, as we Housewrights did, set down into the heart of another family's dominion, but actually our lives were remarkably ordinary in many respects. As a matter of fact, because of our circumstance, the way we conducted our lives would most certainly feel more familiar to you than had you a glimpse into many other households of the period. You are no doubt aware that our contemporary notions of traditional home life, however humble, are soundly rooted in the customs and manners of grand and prominent homes such as the one my father oversaw: the way an elegant sitting room should be appointed; the order of service at a meal; the style in which one addresses one's elders and betters. This was second nature to us even then. This is how we lived.

There are advantages to existing in the shadow of luxury. To cite only one example, the Housewrights ate what the Hunnicutts ate—as would have been the case in all the better homes in our area. When the Senator wanted chicken with dumplings, the Housewrights had chicken and dumplings. And when Himself wanted liver and onions, after my father served the man he would then delight in heaping upon his own plate and then upon Martin's a hearty, steaming helping of the same (savoring between them my always-rejected portion of that vile concoction. I'd make do on soda crackers and milk, thank you very much, before the likes of liver crossed my palate).

There was beef and pork and lamb, and we would serve wild game when Father or the Senator got word of someone around town with a brace of hens or a haunch of venison. Located where it is, Washington has always had outstanding fish and seafood. Thus, we were privileged, my brother and I, to have been able to sample as children delicacies and delights that many in the world are never are able to.

(Alas, against the peril of seeming overly romantic about life behind the stairs, I feel that I should be clear about one thing: We Housewrights rarely ate from the loin side of the bone. Jacob Housewright was no fool. You'd best be certain that under his supervision, the finest cut of whatever was prepared in that kitchen ended up elegantly presented to the man at the head of the table in the dining room of the main house, a table from which neither I nor my brother consumed one morsel, not ever. We were the hired help (nor have we ever been ashamed of that role). Even so, you'll hear no complaints from me about the stews that Cook concocted from the tails and trimmings of Hunnicutt steak. Martin and I attended school with plenty of children who rarely saw meat, let alone a savory and beef-rich pot of stroganoff.

Father prepared the menus for the week, first under the supervision of Penelope Stetson Hunnicutt and then, after she had left this world, of the Senator. There was a lot he had to consider: who would be eating which meals, when there might be entertaining in the home, what was in the larder, what was in season in the market. As the Senator had been known to leave someone else's dinner table in a huff—should he, for example, gain political advantage by doing so—the kitchen needed always to be prepared to serve a light lunch or supper.

Under Father's system, menu preparation was a Monday task. Over the weekend, stocks invariably diminished, particularly of anything perishable. The Senator always partook of a substantial Sunday afternoon supper: one kind of roast or another with multiple side dishes as a supplement. More often than not on Mondays, even before he awoke my brother and me, Father had been over in the pantries and storerooms and iceboxes, counting jars of beans and tins of fruit, pulling through bins of potatoes to see what had sprouted or turned pulpy from neglect. As I grew older, I came to understand that all his poking about had been, for the most part, superfluous. Cook—whoever was Cook at the time—knew precisely what was needed to keep that kitchen running. On Monday, before nine, each person on the staff handed Father a list of requisitions. He could have slept in, frankly, but that was the nature of the man: he needed account of every grain of rice that crossed the threshold. Staples, dry goods, hardware, and specialty items he ordered by phone or by messenger. Dairy, meat, and fish arrived at the back gate—we were on the route.

Cook shopped the greengrocer him- or herself. (They tend to be finicky about such things.) All baked goods were prepared on the premises.

On Monday morning when Martin and I came into the kitchen of the big house for our breakfast, we would find our father gathering requests from his staff, compiling orders, and recording the details in the household log, a book that he maintained year after year in his meticulously fine handwriting. My brother reminded me once that when we were smaller, our mother would serve us breakfast herself back in the carriage house. I have only the vaguest memories of that, washed away as they have been, I'm sure, by more compelling recollections of the hustle and bustle of a big kitchen at work.

Planted at the heart of the great room was a solid-maple block of a table that served as both eating and prep space. A corner at the end farthest from the stove (the better to be out of the way of Cook's maelstrom) would be prepared for the two of us, and a hot bowl of oatmeal or a platter of eggs and toast would arrive almost before we untented our napkins.

These few minutes in the morning were a precious and, sadly, major part of the time we spent together as a family. Now and again, and especially when the Congress had recessed, the Senator enjoyed a quiet evening by himself, and Father would be free to sit with his own family at the supper table in the carriage house. But Walton Hunnicutt was a man who relished a lively social calendar, and it was my father who assured that the comings and goings ticked along with efficiency and grace. The Senator knew well the advantages of playing on one's own court, so it wasn't uncommon for us to host three evenings a week. If the Senate was in session late, Father would often go to the Hill himself, preparing the Senator's office for the inevitable impromptu "conferences" that were to be had when one member or another needed convincing about the merits of seeing things the Hunnicutt way. How often I remember the dear man packed off by Driver, arms laden with one of Walton Hunnicutt's newly pressed shirts and a box of fresh provisions.

So we savored, Martin and I did, those moments at the breakfast table when Father would do his best to give us at least part of his attention. While we devoured our eggs, Father would interview us about school, and the girl who worked upstairs would appear behind me as if by magic, wrapping my hair into braids. If I am being honest, more often than not Father's school questions were of the same character as his questions to the staff—"Are you sure we've ordered enough bar soap?" alternating seamlessly with "Did you collect that spelling exercise off the sideboard?"—and we, like everyone else, responded with the standard "Yes, sir," since even if one hadn't ordered enough soap or remembered to collect one's homework, it was better to say one had done so and then to cover one's tracks than to confess a shortcoming and suffer the ignominy of one of Father's lectures about the importance of responsibility and follow-through. Had the circumstances been different, our progenitor would no doubt have been a minister, one of those of the fire-and-brimstone strain, relishing his weekly opportunity to remind his sinners of their backsliding, weak-willed ways. To his credit, the man rarely raised his voice. He understood, as do many intelligent leaders, that power resides in rhetoric as opposed to volume. Who needed a bullhorn when he could shame you with a cut of his eyes?

But it wasn't all hectoring and homilies. There were quizzes, as well. Particularly on requisition day when Father had his household log at the hand.

"If Pierson's in Eastern Market has potatoes for eighteen cents a pound, and if I anticipate nine pounds of potatoes to be used this coming week, what ought I record here under outlays? Anyone?" Martin would scratch away on the cover of his notebook or on a piece of paper he had retrieved for just this purpose. I'll admit to you that it took a number of years at that kitchen table before I caught on that these questions had been directed at my brother and me. I was a quiet and intense young child, fascinated by the goings-on around me, perfectly content to watch Cook raising the yeast rolls for the luncheon, anticipating what might cause Father to remove himself from our breakfast corner and give correction. You might imagine that a young girl would recoil at the sound of her father's sterner discourse, but I rather enjoyed it, remember one morning my own waved index finger raised in solidarity with my father toward Driver, who had perhaps done something such as neglect leaving a fresh throw in the backseat for the Senator to warm his legs. And I remember, as well, Martin's hand discreetly closing that finger in his palm and signaling me with his eyes and with a slight inclination of his head that such behavior was far from prudent.

Father asked us questions about the price of eggs and the conversion of quarts to ounces. He wondered out loud—clearly for our benefit—if it made more sense, considering the relative price of butter and lard, to serve a snickerdoodle or a sugar cookie. For a long time I'm sure I babbled in reply some standard little-girl nonsense. And then, one day, and I have no recollection what made this day different from the one before it, I keyed into my father's game. Father sketched the parameters of his problems—

for example's sake, let's say again the one about the potatoes—and I blurted out the answer.

"One sixty-two," I would have said, it being a while yet until I mastered the art of decimal dollars.

"I declare! Listen to our Queenie! She beat you that time, Martin."

The priceless look my brother gave me had been filled with what I came to think of as his usual poisonous resentment. It was a look, I'm sad to report, that I became quite familiar with.

My poor, dear brother. What can I tell you? God gifted him in many ways, I believe, but had faulted him in areas we could not account for, specifically in his ability to excel in things academic. Yes, certainly he had mastered his "basic skills," as the teaching profession so charmingly refers to the building blocks of any good liberal education, but basic skill, I must admit, was about as far as it went with him. Our school years remained a constant trial for Martin, particularly the quarterly reporting period, marked as it was always by our father's near hysteria over my brother's progress slips, covered every time with notations indicating less than adequate growth, a situation that so perturbed the man that he frequently neglected to comment on my always perfect marks.

Around my twelfth birthday Martin entered high school, and he came to my room in the carriage house to find resolution.

(Good gracious: that little yellow house! How tiny it must have been, there behind the Senator's mansion, but I somehow never imagined it that way. I remember it as huge.)

The cottage sat at the end of a short spur off the main path bisecting the rear gardens. Two rooms downstairs where the stalls had been for the horses and storage for a carriage or two, and two tiny rooms upstairs, where the draymen had their quarters. (For the life of me I can't recall my father telling me if the house had already been converted when he first came to work for the Senator.) Two mullioned windows on the front. Four over four. Dormers above. Many guests to the Senator's garden parties must have imagined it a toy house of some kind—like some sort of outrageous lawn ornament or perhaps a play fort for the Hunnicutt boy. They would actually come and peer in the windows—can you imagine! Looking around past the darling curtains that I had sown for us—cream-colored cotton printed with golden irises. And—although I know this is impossible—in my mind they are bending over, these people, when they look in at us, as if it were a dollhouse. In my mind I can see their giant faces peering in at me, observing me at my chores or reading a book. It got so I would pass garden party evenings in the kitchen with Cook or snuggled into one of my secret hiding places.

Martin had found me in my room up on the second level. We had shared a room when we were little ones, but when he got older he and my father had bunked together across the hall. He had ducked slightly to pass under the door frame—the ceilings were low on the second level. He had been carrying a stack of schoolbooks. He passed me what turned out to be a history text.

"I bet you can't read *that*," he said.

I scoffed, of course, flipped open a passage at random. Something about the Peloponnesian War, I believe.

"What's it say, Miss Knows-Everything?"

And it was about halfway through my recitation about Athens and Sparta that my common sense at last overcome my common sibling competitiveness and I figured out that I was being manipulated. I slammed the book shut.

"Read it yourself," I snapped, and I went back to my own project: hand edging some pillowcases for our beds.

Martin stood there for a long time, and I could hear him inhaling and exhaling though his nose. This was atypical for him—a more likely response on his part to slam away, hurling some epithet in his wake (assuming we were out of range of Father's hearing).

"I try," he said. "I can't."

I stilled my needle. But I could not look at him. This was an uncharacteristic Housewright moment.

"I understand the words," he said, and then he told me to look, dropping himself next to me on the narrow bed. He opened his school notebook.

"I write down what the teacher says and that helps me remember. But when it's in the book . . ."

This amazed me. Me, a person who could never remember not reading! I pointed to the notebook.

"Can you read this?" I asked. It didn't make sense to me that he could write but could not read.

"Some of it. I can read most of it. Sometimes."

And then I looked more closely at the words, and I must tell you that I was shocked. He had made up his own code, some kind of private symbol language that helped him make sense of what he heard.

School people have since developed names for all of this, as well as tests and treatments and special ways of teaching. We wouldn't have known about any of that, of course. We did what we had to do. We checked to make sure that Father hadn't returned to the carriage house for any reason. We sat in that tiny bedroom and I read to Martin about Athenian democracy and the

Christian martyrs in Rome. I read the Constitutional Convention, the battle of Bull Run, and the workings of the Supreme Court, members of which had been regularly served by our father. Martin scratched away in one notebook, and then another, reading back to me his cryptically encoded interpretations of civics and philosophy. And his marks did gradually improve.

"I knew you had it in you, son," our father crowed, and Martin beamed. It made us both so proud to please the man. Father never knew the truth. Martin never told a soul.

We make do, don't we? People see the truth that it suits them to see.

"I'll pay you back, Tildy. I swear I will."

Payback: I have always imagined that it's the universe that keeps the main tally sheet. Would you agree?

We had a yardman, of course—a man we shared with another house in Georgetown, but Father saw the garden as his own special preserve, and it was there that he and I had our most private time together. It was there, a couple of years into my brother's secret project, that Father first spoke to me of his delight at Martin's newfound academic prowess.

"The boy can do great things, Queenie. We've only to interest him in the right career. What do you think? A physician? A lawyer?"

Ever so slightly I found myself shuddering there amid the azaleas at the thought of myself sequestered in some attic dormitory reading aloud case law and descriptions of human anatomy.

"You have a cousin, I hear, making his way toward law school for the upcoming term. Who could even imagine such a thing?"

These cousins: Father would mention them now and again, but it would be many years, until just before he died, in fact, that he would tell me how to reach them.

"The world seems to be turning, my girl. I never thought I'd see the day. A man these days may have doors we never dreamed of."

Father pointed at an unruly tendril of ivy that had wandered over into the pansies. I snapped it off just above an established leaf.

(Do you sit in judgment of my father and those like him? Do you flush with a thrill of shame at the thought of some woman in your family history who spent her life on her knees with a brush and a bucket of soapy water? Some Josephine? Some Maria? Some Colleen? Where did you imagine it came from, this world we have today? What did you figure it cost? Did you figure? We did what there was to do. It's important that you understand that.)

"These young men today, they don't seem to plan the way we had to in my day. A person can make a decent life, Queenie. It's possible in this world."

I looked at him there, bent over and fussing at another quadrant of coreopsis that surrounded a trickling fountain. In a way we had the best rooms on the estate, as from our windows at night we could hear the water burbling from the mouth of the dolphin and listen as it dropped and danced from one pool to the next. Now and again as Father worked he would hand me a cutting of something to be added to one of the arrangements in the big house. He straightened his back, pressed a hand into his side. He was too old, I thought, to be out there bending and squatting.

He stretched left and right, and while he did he eyed me up and down. What he saw was a thin young thing in a summer dress sprinkled head-to-toe with tiny violets.

"What does Queenie think?" he asked.

"You mean what do I want to do?" I replied. And I could tell by his expression that he hadn't meant that at all, but the diplomat inside him shifted just that fast and he prompted me to reply to the question I had believed him to ask.

It was a different time indeed. There were not fifteen varieties of laundry soap in the store. You sewed the dress with the violets or the paisley. Those were the choices. One did what one's family did, which is why perhaps I had never much imagined myself doing anything that we weren't already doing. Which I must have communicated with my eyes, I guess, or at the very least made it clear I didn't have much else to say on the matter.

"My Queenie was going to be ballerina. Do you remember that? You would dance around this garden on your toes, spinning and twirling and laughing."

And I did remember that, and I could see in my own head the beautiful dancers leaping and pirouetting in the distance on that stage on the Capital Mall and recall how I believed I would dance the dying swan myself when the music came over the radio.

"I would still oh-so-very-much like to—"

"It is ever a heartache to me the way things are in this world," Father interrupted, his forever way of both lamenting and then shutting down discussions of the evils of life in Jim Crow's Washington, D.C. It saddens me to recall his lack of imagination in such matters. That there were colored young women such as myself already tenaciously knocking down doors, this was beyond his ken. We were not those people and that was not the world he knew.

And I was an ordinary young woman. I persisted, if only a bit. I pled my case in that voice that is every daughter's birthright: a dollop of sweetness and a dollop of shame.

"But I hear that there is a school . . ." I started, but he had already turned back to his weeding and gathering. Ballet class was an extravagance. We lived in comfort, but there were always these reminders of the illusory nature of that comfort. Whatever money he managed to put away my father recorded in his own ledger, one that he called his "house book." One day there would be enough money on the bottom line to buy a place of our own. That had been his civil rights agenda. Work. Patience. Virtue. When he got weary like this I would try to keep his eye on our dream.

"When we have our own garden," I would tell him, "I would like a white wrought-iron trellis for roses, just like the one at the embassy on Mass. Ave."

"Roses are a bother, dear girl. A person could spend his whole day looking after them."

"I wouldn't mind that. I would spend all day there. For the rest of my life. Doing only this. That's what we'll do, you and I. After we get our house."

Father straightened up again and looked at me with the gleam in his eye that he got when he was being teased. Every night he ciphered in that ledger. I would watch him sometimes fingering the bolts of cloth that arrived for the Hunnicutt mansion and know that he was imagining that chintz on his own sofa and how well the thick red velvet would drape across his own French doors.

"Just think," I said, "of what a wonder the three of us would make of a place like this.

"And so we shall, Queenie. And so we shall."

It was not uncommon for the Senator to come out and greet us while we fussed with the yard. He loved his gardens, and sometimes when things were slow in town I would see him seated out there on one of the benches, surveying his kingdom, his florid face set with self-satisfaction.

"Looking good out here, Jake" would be his usual opening, and then he would proffer his notions as to how "one of the boys" might want to get a row of boxwoods over in front of those basement windows, and what did Jake think of that? Father's usual way of diverting the Senator from his often-bad notions regarding landscaping would be to divert attention elsewhere, say, to the no-longer-attractive honeysuckle strangling the back gate. We Housewrights have never been hedge-up-against-the-house sort of people.

About this time young master Hunnicutt had reached an age where it became increasingly difficult to arrange appropriate supervision—after school and in the evenings when his father had to be on the Hill or entertaining. Walton Junior no more belonged underfoot at his father's "smokers" than I did in my own father's way. In due time this problem would be solved by one of our nation's finest boarding schools, but for now, Walton Junior was still a little motherless boy who needed his daddy (and to the Senator's credit, he loved that child more than the world). He and my father had experimented with a variety of strategies to solve their child care dilemma. I have always believed it was what bonded these two men most strongly—the fact that they had both been widowers with young children to see after. When I was younger and Walton Junior was a toddler—in the days when it made sense to engage a full-time nanny—Father would give the girl a night off now and again, and then he would leave the two of us for the evening back in the carriage house, provisioning us with rolls of butcher paper and colored pencils. We were companionable back then, Walton Junior and I, but as I had become a young lady I had lost interest in that constant blather young boys tend to engage in, and he had come to see me less as an interesting slightly older friend than as one of the adults who bustled about his world and happened not to share his love for castles and dragons.

"Matilda!" the Senator cheered. "Look at you over there in that dress, looking all grown up and things."

"Senator." I nodded. I collected the balance of irises and snapdragons my father had culled and moved off toward the kitchen to arrange them in vases.

"Now, hang on a second there, girl. Your daddy and I were discussing you this very morning, weren't we, Jake?"

As I had been instructed to do, I turned back with my elbows at my side and a noncommittally pleasant smile on my face. Whatever had been discussed, it was clear to me that my father had failed to entirely make his case and that he was clearly displeased at the occasion of this conversation.

"My daughter's industry amazes me at every turn, Senator. The child never sits still for a minute. I can't imagine how she fits in everything she does."

"A whirlwind, this one here. Always has been. Let me tell you what your daddy and I had in mind." The Senator leaned over so as to catch my eye. I looked at him but I didn't look at him at the same time, my real focus being on my father. I had always been able to read Father pretty well, but on this particular afternoon I sensed only reticence and maybe a bit of fear.

"What we was thinking, your daddy and me, was that you would help us out a couple of afternoons a week, helping to look after the boy. You know, play a few games, read him a story. Like that."

Still no read from my father. I kept my own visage neutral and cool.

"And we all know little Wally thinks the world of our Matilda, ain't that right, Jake? We was thinking, your father and me, a couple of afternoons a week, and we'd make it worth your while. What do you say?" The Senator opened his hands out to make the offer, tilted his head to the side. "We got a deal, don't we?"

"Matilda is awfully busy with—"

And then I did something I'd been taught not to do since I first developed the ability to form words. I engaged the man directly in conversation.

"Worth my while in exactly what way?" I asked him, and I could see my father, who had been standing just behind the Senator, shaking his head ever so slightly.

The Senator coughed out a nasty-sounding laugh. "What's my platform, Jake? An honest wage for an honest day's work."

Rolling eyes not being in the man's repertoire, I still believe I saw my father struggling to keep his locked in place.

"We'll take care of you, girl," the Senator appended; again, the hands, again the tilted head.

"Matilda and I will discuss—"

"When exactly would my services be required?" At this interruption my father cut his eyes at me sharply. There would be consequences for my impertinence.

"Why, I happen to have me a meeting just this minute on Thomas Circle." He waved his finger as if to indicate that this appointment had just this moment popped onto his calendar.

"The representative from New York," Father added, nodding. (Honestly, between these two men, they knew where every member of Congress hung his hat and often a whole lot else that went on at those residences.)

"Come on, Jake, help me get set up for this little consultation. Wally is on up in the playroom, sugar. Go up there have some fun with him. I won't be too long."

It would be entertaining to regale you with tales of "Wally's" bratdom and my own long-suffering tolerance thereof, but, alas, I have none to tell. My dozen or so engagements as nanny-for-the-day proved uneventful and in fact quite pleasant. Walton Junior was easy to please and a perfect young gentleman, blandly sweet as a child in the same way he would be as an adult. We meet people in life with whom we seem to make no connection at all, and this would be the case with the Senator's son and me. He and my brother, by contrast, developed an enduring bond, maintaining, to my surprise, a regular correspondence across their lives. Walton Junior and I, we were like good-hearted stepsiblings, thrown together by circumstance and adopting the trappings of civility to mollify our devoted parents. We engaged in polite chitchat and treated one another with dignity and respect. Heartfelt confession, clever nicknames, and teasing banter: those just would never be our thing.

So I would go up there and we would spend our afternoons or evenings. I could even bring my schoolwork with me, as Walton Junior was one of those boys with an active fantasy world and could spend hours arraying his hundreds of infantry men (from every period in history) across the playroom carpet, staging them for one battle and then another. This is gonna be the big one, Matilda, he would tell me and I would say in reply that I imagined that it probably would be. On many evenings that would be the extent of our conversation. We were alike in that way, the Senator's son and I. We were both young people who preferred peace and quiet and the company of our own thoughts to a lot of hubbub and nonsense (making, perhaps, our lack of connection seem even more anomalous; still, it never happened). I would spend my few quiet hours with him, the Senator would hand me a dollar, and I would return to the carriage house.

And that would have been that. Except. And every story such as this one has an "except," and I imagine you may have anticipated what mine will be.

"How's everybody been up here this evening?" he'd say, popping in the door. His son and I would say, "Fine." I always had the sense that in his own way—in that same way we are all impatient with those we love—Walton Junior found his father's folksy good spirits as annoying as I did.

"We had us a time tonight, we did. Ask your daddy about it, girl. Stand on up there and spin around for me, would you?"

I wouldn't dream of prompting my father for the latest political gossip, although he more often than not passed it along freely and with relish. (The stories I could tell regarding long-standing American dynasties.)

How odd, that first time he asked, that I thought nothing of standing and displaying myself for this man. Or maybe not: children, after all, are asked to do this all the time. "Let me get a look at you!" "What a pretty dress." What can I tell you? Perhaps it was that I had just spent an evening overseeing the idyllic childhood of this man's son: toy soldiers and fairy tales and hot cocoa I'd brewed myself and delivered in cups emblazoned with circus clowns. And then there is also our obedient natures, we Housewrights. That children's game "Simon says." Always a loser, me.

And then there was that dollar bill. He would place that bill in my hand, the Senator would, and his moist pink hands would close my fingers around it.

"That one there is just for you, little lady," he'd say. A powerful message, regardless of intentions. I had never had money, you see. Can you imagine? I'd never any need of it. Our worlds were closed inside the iron-picketed walls of that compound. At school, children did not walk around with money in their pockets. It just wasn't done.

And, so, yes, that was the only time I "spun" for him, but there were other things: he would ask me about my school day or request I read a story to him and his son—innocent enough, surely, save a hand that lingered too long on my forearm or on the small of my back. These lively public men; they have a way, don't they, of chummily bringing everyone into the fold, much the same way the rich have of marking their territory.

I'm walking a fine line here indeed. The man's son was never more than a few feet away. I have never doubted for one moment the genuine affection he felt for my father. But, still. What can I say? It was what it was, and it was also something else entirely, both at the same time.

I would wish "Wally" a pleasant evening and a dollar would be pressed into my hand.

"Go on out there and tell your daddy the Senator said to sleep well." That would be his usual way of dismissing me.

It was Father who put an end to my days as family nanny to

the Hunnicutts. He'd come up to bring news to the Senator of a late-arriving telegram and found the three of us happily reading a fairy tale, comfy in front of a fire the Senator had laid, wedged like baby birds onto a small settee.

"What it this?" my father asked, entirely eschewing his standard professional mien.

"It's story time, Jake. Come on in and join us!"

You would recognize my father's expression as being one common to men who come upon their daughters, regardless of age, snuggled perhaps just a little too close to a male who is not a member of the family. And just as quickly his professional demeanor had been reapplied and he handed the Senator the missive, noting it was interesting but not urgent. To me he said, "I'll be needing you immediately, young lady. Something has come up."

Interesting how well we come to know those we see on a daily basis. Even before we had passed through the service entrance I already knew there was no emergency. I took myself to my bedroom in the carriage house, closed the door, and that, as they say, was that.

Father never reported to me whatever words he may have had with the Senator. If any. Quite soon thereafter and lasting until young Walton began to board in Maryland, a whole series of older Irish women would come by at teatime and stay through the Senator's retirement to quarters for the evening. One of them, the one who stayed the longest, a Mary, as it would have been, struck up quite the friendship with my father, uncharacteristic as that would have been in those days. They had both been raised in service, you see, had crossed paths with many of the same characters along their respective roads. They had a lot to talk about, and they would sometimes gossip late into the night, long after either Hunnicutt had need of them. Once I woke up early to the sound of whispering in the garden and saw her being ushered out the back gate at dawn, Driver waiting to deliver her to wherever she made her home. She and Father had talked all night!

As for Father and me, we never discussed my brief foray into self-employment. He had always made it clear where his boundaries lay, so I guess there wasn't much else to be said. Walton Junior and I each still had our quiet evenings, although several hundred feet apart and with increasingly different concerns. With nothing between us there'd been nothing much to lose. As for the Senator, let's just say that I certainly had learned my lesson, although it would not have been the lesson my father had in mind.

My sudden lack of availability had been explained by my hasty enrollment in that dance studio I'd heard rumor of, advantage taken, anyone who asked was informed, of an unexpected and highly sought after last-minute opening in my age group.

It is always thus the worm turns.

And turns again. Alas, I report with sadness that the rumored ballet class turned out to be yet another opportunity for young Negro ladies to gain skill in all manner of correct behavior and deportment. We were taught dining etiquette by a slovenly person who had apparently gained her own knowledge of same by eating alongside stevedores and merchant marines. Dance class had two regular components: drill in a stilted box step (paced to the off-tempo piano stylings of the "studio" owner's eight-year-old son) and incessant practice walking back and forth across the dust-speckled parlor with a dictionary on our heads.

Idle hands being the devil's workshop, a dictionary on the

head was, I guess, better than wrinkled hands in a sink full of dirty dishes—my father's threatened alternative to my dropping out prior to receiving every penny's worth of instruction he'd paid for. To this day my posture remains impeccable. You would be amazed.

Legal Tender

. . .

I

1969

"This is not about money," his father said, his voice soaked in fake solemnity. "It's about family obligation."

Sure, Marty, Roderick thought. And just who do ya think *you're* talking to? It's *always* about the money. That was, like, the main Housewright maxim.

"Basically, you're saying I should write off my tips. Just like that." Roderick snapped his fingers.

"Ask Matilda for a tip."

"Ha!" Roderick scoffed. Fat chance. The old bat would squeeze a nickel till the buffalo shit. As impossible as it sounded, Matilda Housewright was the only person on earth tighter than her brother.

"Frankly, I don't know what a fifteen-year-old needs with so much money. When I was your age . . ."

He'd heard this sad tale before, about how his father had washed the dishes and washed the Senator's car and washed the windows, and how now and then his daddy would throw a dollar in his direction and he'd have to make it last for a month. Roderick sawed away on an imaginary violin.

"Yeah, right. Tell me: Back in the olden days when you were in the Navy, didn't they have this thing called combat pay?"

A risky strategy, Roderick knew, to call on both his father's military experience as well as to complain too much about an assignment. Housewright Maxim #2: *Never* complain about a job. Money was money. If you didn't care for the work, negotiate a higher fee—which was, after all, what he'd been trying to do. For a while, after David's death, Roderick had been expected to take on his aunt for free. "Your brother never asked for a dime," his father had said, not even blinking at what Roderick knew was a transparent lie. Roderick wasn't sure what terms had been negotiated with Pops, but his brother had gotten over somehow.

"It's not like she's begging for my company. She as much as says that all I do is get in her way." This particular ploy was often a pot sweetener—pointing out the general uselessness of these visits.

"Here's my deal. Take it or leave it. Get in there and be nice, and then, maybe—just maybe—I'll let you do that birthday party."

"Deal." Roderick thrust his hand out for a shake. He'd spent six months begging his father for his own gig. "You won't be sorry. I promise."

His father stopped the car in front of his sister's house. "I better not be sorry, or a certain person will be, and you can take that guarantee to the bank." His father handed him the envelope.

Roderick gave him the thumbs-up. He started up Matilda's walk.

His father called behind him. "You behave yourself in there. I really need you to do that for me."

Roderick shrugged. You'd think it was a rock concert instead of a couple of hours with his strange old aunt.

He found Matilda in one of her usual haunts, down on her knees in her backyard garden. "Hey. What's up?"

"Hello, Roderick."

She didn't bother getting up. So much for him being there. Roderick threw himself down on one of the park benches she had along the brick path. (What sort of person kept park benches in the backyard?) He noticed that Matilda once again wore her kneepads, the ones that reminded him of the kind the boys on the junior varsity squad wore.

"Hey, you trying out for fullback, there?"

Matilda pulled herself up using the rose trellis. "These knees take a beating some days, that's for sure. If it's not too much trouble I could use some help deadheading those daffodils."

Deadhead: there was a name.

"Say, guess what old Marty told me. I get to do a birthday party on my own. How 'bout them apples?" Roderick snipped away absentmindedly with a pair of garden shears.

"Just the brown ones, please. I doubt if my brother permits you to call . . . never mind."

Deadheading flowers: another in an endless series of stupid jobs. Marty had some guys come by in a truck and do this stuff. That's what it was like with this whole Matilda scene. One weird trip to another, from one week to the next. Some days you were out here having a garden party and the next week you were upstairs sliding furniture from one room to another—as if it mattered where the furniture was in the first place, since no one sat on it but her anyway.

A bottle broke somewhere back in the alley. Roderick walked back by the fence to have a look, but he didn't see anybody around.

"It's kind of turning into a ghetto around here, ain't it? Don't you want to be moving to a retirement home or something?"

"I've always liked it right where I am."

Everything about the city gave Roderick the creeps. Ma told him it had been just a block or two over where they burned all the stores after Martin Luther King got shot. Roderick wouldn't live here, not for all the money in the world. No way. When he made his first million, it was a house out in the Chesterfield—and a pretty wife to go with it.

Matilda snatched the shears from his hand. That's usually the way it was with her stupid activities. You had to do it her way or else, but Roderick had learned a little trick. If you showed that you couldn't care less about whatever the crap was that she wanted you to mess with, she'd take over and leave you the hell alone.

"Suit yourself," he said, about the neighborhood and the pruning shears and about all of it. He followed her into the potting shed and watched her put away her tools and gloves. Then he followed her into the house.

"I'm going to enjoy a cup of tea. Would you care for some?" She filled the kettle with water and set it on the stove.

"What else you got in here?" Roderick opened the refrigerator and shook his head with disappointment. Bare, as usual, just like Old Mother Hubbard. No bones, no nothing. "I swear, Auntie, couldn't you get some soda sometime or some Hi-C? A person could die of thirst around this dump."

Matilda clattered some dishes onto a tray and Roderick turned around to see what was wrong. He didn't particularly care for that expression on her face—one of her regulars. She was like that Miss Gulch in *The Wizard of Oz*, the one who turned into a witch. He wouldn't be surprised to find that she also spent her days going up and down the block snatching house pets from innocent children. Dirty looks like that one: in his book they were worth at least another thirty-five cents per hour.

"All right, already. I'll have some tea. Jeez, you'd think there was something in here to steal." He closed the refrigerator door and went and plopped down on one of the musty old couches in her living room. That's where she always had her tea, out on her musty old couches. Maybe she'd bring out some cookies or something, so long as they weren't those stupid dry shortbread ones. Them babies could gag a corpse.

While he waited he checked out all the old junk in the room. Nothing was new here, ever. He'd seen all this old crap a hundred times before. A dusty old clock that ticked away lazily and chimed every quarter of an hour, day and night. A pair of painted Japanese ladies that he thought might be made out of the same stuff as the dishes. They always faced the same way, those Japanese ladies—at an angle toward each other, like they were having some sort of conversation. Roderick turned them back-to-back like they were having a fight. He wondered if Matilda would even notice. He'd try to remember to check next week to see if they moved back to their regular positions. He fingered the metal paperweight that she kept on her desk. It was about the only thing in the dump he liked. He liked the way it was shaped like the Capitol Building, the way it felt heavy in your hand.

Matilda set the tea tray on her butler's table. (She'd insisted last month he learn the name of the stupid thing, had insisted that it was not a coffee table, that a coffee table was the name for the brass and glass abomination [which she said like a swear word] that his parents had in their home, and that this was a butler's table. He'd had to tell her to cool her dang jets—it was like she was going to have a stroke over a stupid piece of furniture, and who's fault would that be anyway?)

Roderick held up the paperweight. "Is this worth anything? Is it gold?"

"Have some tea if you wish. There's some lemon and sugar. I know that's how you prefer it."

Roderick tasted the tea she had already poured for him and made a face. It needed sugar, all right. Lots of it. He loaded in four or five teaspoonsful and squeezed in a big squirt of lemon. That did the trick. The crap wasn't so bad if you dolled it up a little bit. It's like his father always said: a cup of sugar, a stick of butter, and a squeeze from a lemon and you could make dog shit taste good. A little cup of tea sure didn't do crap when what you needed was a big swig of Nehi grape. Drop a hundred hints and the woman still didn't get a clue.

"I would have thought someone told you it was bad manners to ask how much things cost."

"Huh? Oh, you mean that paperweight deal? I was only asking. Shoot. What? Is it real valuable and stuff and that's why you don't want to tell me?"

Matilda shook her head. (The woman was always shaking that head.)

"Your parents are well, I take it."

Roderick shrugged. "I guess." He slugged down the rest of his tea—savoring the extra sugar syrup with the dregs—then poured himself another cup.

"And things at school are going well for you?"

"The usual. It's boring."

"Well, fine." More of that head shaking.

"Say, Auntie, you know what you need in here? A big stereo with matched components, the whole works. We can put you some speakers in the corners here and get you a turntable and a receiver. Get you a couple of Marvin Gaye records. You'd like that, wouldn't you?"

"I'm pleased with the way things are. Thank you for your concern."

"Just an idea."

Bite a person's head off, will you. And it wasn't as if this dump couldn't use something to liven it up a little. He'd go crazy living here—any normal person would. It was always the same. Nothing going on, nobody here but her. He couldn't remember ever seeing anyone visit except for him.

(Back before David died, he remembered hearing his parents talking about her maybe taking up with some college professor. Then after, according to what he'd overheard his Moms say, the old girl had told Joe College to hit the road. As if something better were coming down the pike—look at her now, sitting here all alone.)

"I could use some help sorting some things in Martin's old

room. If it wouldn't be too much trouble. When you finish your tea." Matilda took the tray and her cup back to the kitchen.

One thing for sure, it was rush, rush, rush around this dump. He'd take a few minutes and finish his drink, thank you very much (stingy little drink that it was).

Upstairs, he found her in the musty old room she claimed his father had lived in—one of those pieces of information that didn't quite fit with the world the way he knew it. This room—hell, the whole house—didn't seem quite up to Martin Housewright standards. Old Marty liked everything new. He wanted his house painted the most up-to-date colors, a car that was no more than two model years old, the latest kitchen gadgets, and any new piece of stereo equipment he could find. Which is probably why he blew out of this prison in the first place.

Matilda plucked boxes from a random mound—mountain, really—which now completely covered the bed. "I'm afraid I've gotten into the bad habit of saving empty boxes from the things I buy. I take them out and then stick the packaging in here. There are boxes here for things I'm sure I don't even own anymore."

You buy things? Roderick thought, but he didn't say that out loud. That would be rude. Matilda gave him the task of breaking the boxes down and pressing them into the bottom of a larger one.

"Pull any brown corrugated cardboard that looks like this." She held up an insert that had been used to hold part of a blender in place. "These I can use in the garden."

It was a fairly mindless job. Roderick thought instead about the upcoming birthday party and how it was going to be just the first in a long series of bigger and bigger jobs. Sure, it was just a measly kid's party, but if he could pull this off, the next step was maybe a small lunch, maybe one of the regular box luncheons they had begun catering for church picnics and business meetings. That would give him the chance to show he could handle a medium-sized production. There wasn't much difference, after all, between managing a gross of roast turkey sandwiches and plating up a Thanksgiving luncheon. Yeah, buddy! This was the start of big things.

"Hey, you know I'm gonna make a bundle of money."

"Legally, one hopes."

"Pops stopped taking birthday parties. But, me, I know how to make them pay."

"Do you, now?" Matilda tugged some plastic wrapping from a plain white box. She was piling up quite a bundle of garbage. That meant she probably would be looking for him to take it downstairs or something. Always some more unnecessary crap to deal with around this dump. And they said slavery was over.

"Pops says that someone like him has to charge too much for his services, and unless the client is rich and it's a party for his wife or something, people can't afford him, and it's not really worth his time to take the job. He only agreed to do this one for an old friend of Ma's. "But, someone like me, someone just starting out, I can take a little job like this one and turn a profit on it, you know."

"Is that a fact?"

"I figure I'll load the kids up on nuts and mints and crap. I downsize the cake just a bit and jack up the price. Just a smidgen I get a deal on some cheap party favors and I'm out of there with a nice margin."

"I guess you could always use smaller scoops for the ice cream, too."

"Great idea! You're pretty good at this stuff, you know that?"

"Young man, since apparently sarcasm is wasted on you, let me ask you a question. What exactly is your goal for this party?"

(Roderick thought maybe he heard some sort of smart remark in there, but who cared. As long as he finished in this dump by the time his ma came to pick him up.)

"To make money," he said. "That simple enough?"

"I see. To make money. Even if the client isn't happy? Even if the client warns his friends to use another caterer next time? I want to make sure I understand you correctly."

"You don't, because that's not what I said." Boy, was she one for putting the words in a person's mouth. (Hadn't his father warned him about this at some point or other?) "You know the Housewright motto. One-hundred-percent customer satisfaction, guaranteed."

"I'm glad to hear that, Roderick. Your father would be pleased. And it's not like a person would want to attract a lot of this nickel-and-dime business for . . . himself. You'll make some good money on this and then move on to whatever your father lines up, am I right? Would you please set this wrapping paper in . . . in that other room over there? Thank you."

Roderick took the Christmas wrap and placed it on the bed in the room across the hall, the room where his brother used to sleep when he stayed here. David had slept in this room a lot. He seemed to like it here, although God knows why. He wondered what this stuff was about attracting nickel-and-dime business.

"What's this stuff about nickel-and-dime business? I don't get it."

"It's like you said. These little birthday jobs aren't worth much to . . . old Marty. Is that what he's going by these days?"

"That's just my pet name for him."

"I'm sure he's thrilled with that. My point is that were Martin to believe he could use a birthday party to pick up other jobs of the same kind, then he might do some things differently. That would be if he *wanted* the work, of course. I'm sure his calendar is plenty full.

"My brother would make the party a special occasion for the children. He'd also throw in something extra to impress the parents. An *amuse-gueule*, as one might call it. A lagniappe. And, it goes without saying, he'd still make a tidy profit. That is, if Martin were interested in nickel-and-dime business. Which you made clear that he wasn't. So there's not much point wasting time thinking about such things. Am I correct?"

Nickels and dimes were only a bad thing if you were big enough to turn up your nose at them, but nickels and dimes had a way of adding up pretty fast. And this whole deal about impressing the customers: well, it really wasn't anything different from what his father was always saying about reputation. "Housewright and Sons: Making your house the right house for any occasion." (Leave it to old Marty to think of a corny slogan like that one.) The "Housewright" part of the company already had a stellar reputation, but what about the "and Sons" part? Maybe it wouldn't be such a bad idea to start getting a reputation of his own around town.

"So what you're saying is that a person could maybe do something special with the cake. Maybe use real lemon rind in the filling. If it happened to be a lemon cake. Just for an example."

"That would be one kind of example. How old is the guest of honor?"

"Eight, I think. He'll be eight."

"A boy. I guess, just for example, a person might think about eight-year-old boys and the sort of things they like to do."

"Like run around and play games and that sort of thing. Maybe play capture the flag or army or something like that."

"Something like that. Assuming the parent approves of those activities, of course."

"And forget about the lemon rind in the filling. Assuming it's a lemon layer."

"Yes, assuming all of that, Roderick, and no, you don't forget about the lemon rind. The kids don't care what the cake tastes like, but the parents do."

Roderick had taken a seat on one side of the bed. He felt Matilda sit down on the other. There didn't seem to be too much box sorting going on back there.

"Okay, but if my job is mostly to bring in the cake and the sandwiches and the soda, then what's all this other stuff—"

"Who said those were your only jobs? When your father did the Ambassador's Ball last year, I believe he picked out the color scheme, he arranged for the band, he decorated the hall. All the guests had to do was get themselves to the ballroom and have a lovely evening."

"Seems like a lot of work to me."

"That it does. Which is certainly nothing you'd be interested in—you've made that perfectly clear. But let's just say a person were interested in extending himself a tiny bit. What that person might do would be to put together some themed parties, some packages. Maybe a clown theme. A sock hop theme. A picnic in the park. Charge one price for the works.

Themed parties for a price. Jeez, Roderick thought, this was making an awful lot of sense. Matching up the colors of the cake and the party favors and the napkins: he'd been doing that sort of thing since before he could pronounce the word "pastel." It would be so easy just to take it one step further. Have a circus theme. Serve peanuts and popcorn and corn dogs. Stick one of his friends in a clown suit. Maybe rent a trampoline. What could be easier?

Matilda said, "I'm just glad Martin knows what's best for the business, aren't you, Roderick?"

"Oh. Sure. I mean, like I said. It's not something he could make money on—any of these deals. I don't even know if I can. Or could. After all, Pops does all the pricing. I've never had to worry about the budget and what to charge, so I don't really don't understand all that stuff."

"All that . . . stuff? Well, that's easy enough to learn. You're pretty good at math, aren't' you?"

Roderick nodded.

"I could show you in twenty minutes. If you were interested, that is. But it does seem like a waste of time. And I certainly wouldn't want to be part of something that your father didn't approve of."

God, what did this woman think he was? A child? He was fifteen. She had no idea how much authority he had at Housewright and Sons. On busy weekends when they had a wedding and a cocktail party going at the same time, he practically ran the place by himself.

"You know, I was thinking a person just might want to do some of them themed parties you was talking about himself. A person, me, I mean. Get a little business of my own going on the side. You know. As long as old Marty is turning down the work."

"That's lovely, Roderick. I wish you the best of luck with that.

I really do." Matilda rolled up a ball of plastic and other trash that she'd pulled from the inside of the boxes. She pulled it to herself and left.

Roderick followed her down the steps.

"Now you just relax and have a seat, young man. You've been very helpful today. Keep an eye out the window for your mother. Be a shame to keep her waiting."

She bustled to the kitchen with her bundle of garbage, pointing him to a chair in her entry. Roderick followed her.

"I'm getting pretty good at cake decorating, you know."

"Are you, dear? How interesting."

Dang, didn't this woman ever stand still? Now she was digging around in a drawer he knew to be full of junk, looking for God knows what.

"Ralph showed me how to make roses. I've been practicing. Mine are better than his now."

Matilda extracted a marker from the drawer and placed it on the table. "Better watch for Evie. You know how she hates to be kept waiting. Neither of us wants to see that woman upset."

"She can honk her horn. I can hear. You know, I've been working on a couple of great punch recipes. One I really like is orange sherbet and red cream soda. Kids will really go for that, don't you think?"

"Clear cream sodas stain less dramatically, but what would I know?" She grabbed Roderick by the elbow and walked him to the front of the house.

"Some of us prefer not to have cars out front blowing their horns as if we were a drive-by brothel. It has been a pleasure, as always."

"Wait! You said you'd show me the budget stuff." How rude! Give this woman a course in manners, somebody.

"Did I say that? Senility on the rampage again. If you can imagine, there were times I was known as circumspect. Greetings to your parents."

Roderick found himself deposited on the front porch with the door closed behind him. The nerve of some people. He'd show her who he was dealing with. He'd show her he really meant business.

The following Saturday he arrived with a briefcase full of plans and designs and drawings. His father had asked him what the deal was with the satchel, and he'd told him that Matilda had asked him to help her out with a few things—which seemed to shut him up just fine. One thing he knew about his father—as long as he thought someone was helping his sister, he was pretty much satisfied. To be on the safe side, Roderick didn't resume salary negotiations. If plans played out the way he'd hoped, the few measly quarters he was losing in tips wouldn't even be worth stooping over on the sidewalk for.

Matilda met him at the door. Now that was unusual. She brandished those blasted pair of pruning shears in his face. She waved to her brother as he pulled away and handed the cutting tool to Roderick before heading toward the back of the house, to her garden.

"Time's a-wasting," she said over her shoulder.

"But . . ." Roderick held the briefcase up to her retreating back. The old crone didn't even see it.

"I have decided that I'll not endure one more week looking at these raggedy hedges. Have you ever trimmed . . . Wait. What was I thinking? Come along." She directed him to the row of hedges that flanked the back fence and completely hid the house from the alley. Only a tall wooden gate broke the row.

"You said you would—" Roderick started. Matilda snapped her own clippers in his face. Three curt clips.

"This is a very dangerous tool. It's imperative that you pay attention." She snapped the clippers again and pointed to the briefcase. "That's in my way." Roderick set his bag on one of the park benches.

"This is boxwood. Excellent choice for screening your private space from the neighbors. In England, I've heard, they are used regularly as a border for pastureland, though I have some doubts about that fact. I'm sure to your eye it looks fine, but come." She extended her hand. Roderick held back. Matilda seized a fistful of sweatshirt and pressed the side of Roderick's head right up next to the bush.

"See. See how those shoots and tendrils stick out. Looks like someone forgot to comb his hair. No offense. I was referring to the plants."

Roderick felt the ends of branches tickling his cheek, in some places pricking a bit, felt something buzzing close enough to his ear to induce a cringe. He also saw clearly the loose tendrils and branches that Matilda was referring to.

"We cut all those off. We want the surface to be flat. The top should be slightly tapered from the base here. That way all of the plant gets sun. Do you think you can handle this?"

"Of course," Roderick scoffed. He moved to the corner to begin, finding the trimming not only easy but somehow soothing. He worked his way from the top to the bottom of a hedge, angling his head to the side the way Matilda had shown him to better see the loose ends. He'd worked about half his side of the row when Matilda came by to inspect.

"Not too bad," she said, running her hand over the surface. "They're resilient, thank heavens. Make sure you collect all these trimmings. I've done mine as I go." She pointed to a paper sack near where she was working her half.

Roderick sputtered in frustration. "You didn't tell me that."

"I wouldn't think I'd have to." She snapped her clippers in his face and said one of her stupid little sayings, something about "rest for the wicked."

Roderick started to the potting shed to get something to contain his clippings, but noticed that several paper sacks were already scattered in his work area.

"Thanks for nothing," he said. He bent down and began gathering the leaves and twigs into a pile. When he rose to dispose of them he found his aunt standing over him.

"I'll thank you to never use that tone with me again."

"Fine." Roderick turned to chop at the hedge. He felt the point of something sharp in his arm. It was the tip of Matilda's sheers. "Ow!" She pressed in harder.

"Apparently you didn't hear me."

"Yes, okay, fine."

"Yes, what?"

The crazy old bat. She'd probably broken the skin or something. "Yes, I heard you. Jeez."

"Yes, what, Roderick?"

What on earth? he thought. And then he remembered. Maybe this would get her under control. "Yes, ma'am."

"As gracious as I expected." She stalked to her section. Roderick thought the snaps from her shears sounded particularly vicious. She was probably picturing him with each snip.

This must be that other Aunt Matilda he'd heard tell of. His father had told him stories of a tough and feisty person with a sharp tongue and a lot of opinions. Since he'd been coming over here, since David died, all he'd seen was someone with a sour face, someone who hardly said anything at all.

He didn't know what she had to get herself worked up over. He was the one, after all, who'd been promised one thing and then been shanghaied (once again) into lawn service.

"You promised me you'd help me with my business." He said it to the hedge, but loud enough so he was sure she could hear it.

"When you finish this half, take all these clippings to the compost. These tendrils are tender enough, they'll do fine. We'll trim the tops another time. I'll be having my tea. To be honest, I can't imagine why I'd be willing to help you with anything."

Roderick's mouth hung open. He watched Matilda navigate the brick garden path back to her door.

The witch! He ought to march in there and put her right back in her place. He'd seen his father handle these uppity women, the ones who thought that just because they wrote the check for the dinner party that somehow that made them experts on how to cook a fillet. "Madam," he'd heard his father say, "you've worked your way through the last of what little patience your small stipend entitles you to. Either leave my kitchen or your money is refunded this instant." Something cool like that, his father had said. Being just before dinner, the hag wasn't about to have the caterer walk away. These rich clients, some of them actually enjoyed his father's iron will and firm authority. It was a form of entertainment to them. Serving lunch one afternoon, he'd heard a bleached blond client with a wrinkled-up neck bragging to her friends, "That Marty is a pill, but we love him to death. He's like one of the family now." (Minutes earlier his father said she reminded him of a purple cabbage and then had proceeded to chop the one on the table in front of him into a fine slaw.)

But dealing with a cranky old aunt was different. Just his luck, he'd go in there and say the wrong thing and then his father would be all over him. No birthday parties. No nothing.

Roderick entered the living room and set his briefcase on the butler's table, next to the tea.

"That wasn't very nice, what you said to me out there," he said.

Matilda pointed at the briefcase. She gave him a look he'd seen a million times from Martin. He moved the case to the floor.

"Thank you," she said. "Pour yourself some tea if you like."

He did, loading it up with his usual sugar and lemon. "I don't even like this stuff," he said.

Matilda sighed and shook her head. "You may well be the rudest young man I have met in my entire life."

" 'Cause I set a briefcase on a table? Right."

Matilda took a sip of tea. "It is unbelievable to me that you would use that tone with your mother."

"What . . . tone? This is how people talk. She don't mind."

"No, maybe she *don't*. Unfortunately for you, I *do* mind, and because this is my house and because I choose to live in a world where civil discourse is valued, I've decided to do something about it."

"You're not the boss of me."

Matilda laughed, as if that was something funny. You could never tell with folks her age what they might laugh at.

"Bring your briefcase," she said, and began clearing a space on the dining room table, which was covered with old photos of people he'd never seen. She'd been making a scrapbook or something—another of her endless projects.

"I've been eager to see your ideas for the party—I assume you've laid them out for me. I've got a blank ledger here and some pencils. We'll do some preliminary work on the budget today. As I told you last week, it shouldn't take you long to get the hang of it.

"The volume of voice that I'm using at present is the appropriate one for the home. You will keep your own voice at this level in my presence at all times.

"My name is neither 'Hey' nor 'Say.' I'd prefer you call me Aunt Matilda. How you refer to me behind my back is between you and whatever conscience you might have.

" 'Please' and 'thank you' are expected to be standard parts of your vocabulary in my home. Have I made myself clear?"

Have a stroke already. "Is that all? Jeez."

Matilda walked behind him and gathered between two fingers a tender nugget of ear. "Since you broached the subject, I've never been crazy about this 'Jeez' word, either."

II

1976

He hoped he'd gotten everything on her list, though he had a nagging feeling there was something he'd forgotten. Loose tea, chicken breasts, five pounds of flour: the list was more or less the same each week, though there was always that one odd thing. God, she'd give him hell. Not a good thing when he needed a favor.

"You haven't left my meat sit in that hot rod in this heat, I hope."

"They're calling them roadsters these day, Aunt Matilda. I came straight from the grocery store. These birds couldn't be fresher if you strangled them with your own hands."

"Elegant thought, Roderick." She transferred the sacks to her arms and headed toward the kitchen.

"Say, you know what, Aunt Matilda? I did five gigs today. Five. We didn't even break a sweat."

"What's your father have to say about that?" she asked, unloading the groceries, her brows furled, searching, he knew, for the missing item—whatever it was.

"You know old Marty. He's got to inspect every plate. Admirable, but you can't make money that way, not these days. Need me to do anything?" he asked. She cut her eyes at him. She suspected something, he could tell.

"I know you're a busy man with advanced university training, but if you wouldn't mind—see that birdbath in the garden?" She pointed to a blue fount set in a circle of coleus and croton. "My ornamental grass has arrived for that location. I'm moving the birdbath to the crux of the walkways. Could you do that? In the interest of sparing your fine couture, I have myself thoughtfully predrained the water."

"Sure thing, doll." She swatted him as he went past. She hated that doll talk, but who could resist teasing the sweet old thing?

Roderick didn't mind the chore—though he was grossed out by the knot of earthworms that had taken up residence in the circle of dirt beneath the birdbath. The lawn ornament weighed more than he expected, though he found that if he rolled it along its base, it moved without trouble.

He didn't understand why she had never taken him up on his offer to find her a reliable handyman. It only made sense, what with all the general upkeep around an old joint like this. He'd gotten referrals to some men whom he was assured would love a regular gig like this one, and he'd even checked their references. They were good guys. But the old girl wouldn't even allow a discussion of the subject. She'd rather let the odds and ends she couldn't handle pile up and then run him to death when he had the time.

Surely she could pay back the odd favor now and then.

"Auntie, there's someone I'd like you to meet."

"Your transparent ploy to distract me from the subject of Woolite is beneath even you."

Damn: this week's bonus item. "Let me see that receipt." He was sure he'd picked up that homely bottle. She retrieved it from the old sugar bowl where she filed her register tapes.

"See, right here. It was the most expensive thing you ordered."

"And so it was. And so hand it over."

Roderick turned his hands up. "I ain't . . . I don't have your soap, Auntie dear. They must have forgotten to bag it."

"And so much for my plans for a scintillating evening. Why are you being saccharine? You're up to something, Roderick Housewright."

"Who, me?" he responded, even as his scheme evolved. Sometimes fate intervened. "Gentleman that I am, I shall return with your missing purchase in, shall we say, two hours."

"Alas, sometimes backtracking is the only way some people ever learn the value of keeping a list."

Roderick bit his lip to keep from uttering a word or two that he'd later regret. As he pulled the door closed behind him, he said, "I'm bringing somebody back with me, okay?" He trotted off down the walk before she could respond. Cowardly, he knew, but what the hell. Desperate times, desperate measures.

• • •

I feel like you're dragging me to an audition," Katie complained in the car. She fiddled with the controls of the vents that Roderick had set to blow tepid air. He switched off the fan.

"It'll be fine," he said, loading his voice with conviction, hoping his words proved to be true. Katie had rinsed from her hair the stale smell she sometimes picked up after standing too many hours in the "better dresses" section of the department store—a rude combination of popcorn, atomized cologne, and wet wool. Katie was one of those rich girls who worked because she liked having something to do. At school she'd majored in something frivolous such as English or philosophy—one of those fields indicating the idea of employment hadn't crossed her pretty little head. He'd always had this thing for impractical smart women.

"Your aunt never married?" she asked.

"She's always lived by herself, as far as I know."

He could read Katie's mind: What could be wrong with the poor woman? Why had no one ever wanted her?

Didn't every family have a branch on its tree like Matilda? Didn't each one dread the day when it became necessary to explain to the company president or to the scion's prized catch who that strange woman over in the corner was?

Katie sighed. "I still say we should run off to Las Vegas and be done with the whole thing."

Roderick had to admit that he, too, was tempted by the idea. Who knew better than he did the real complexity of staging a wedding of the kind they would be expected to have? He couldn't imagine his father standing back and enjoying someone else's prime rib and not having a comment or two about its preparation—couldn't imagine himself not doing so, as well. (He'd already made it absolutely clear to Katie that there was only one caterer in the region who came close to the Housewright standards—this after deciding it would be too tacky and too nerve-wracking to have their own staff put together the affair.) And even if they skipped the big wedding and did run away, still.

"We've got to deal with them sooner or later," he said.

"I know that. And I told you my parents are fine. I don't understand why we just don't announce our engagement party and get on with it."

Roderick would like to believe that the Cashmans were "fine," and maybe it was true. He'd spent time with his future sisters-in-law, and they had seemed fine. But both he and Katie had had been discreet with their parents, as if they secretly feared that one word of discouragement or negativity would be all it would take to end their relationship forever. He realized how tentative this made their relationship sound. Something that could be destroyed by a stray comment from a parent mustn't be worth much. But he was determined to hang on to this woman and on to the plans they'd made together. Matilda was the only person he knew who could help him through this. He pulled up in front of her house.

"Now, I'm sure I mentioned to you that sometimes my aunt has a sharp tongue."

"Great. Now I'm really relaxed."

"I'll do all the talking. Grab the Woolite."

Any displeasure she felt, Matilda buried beneath a mask of steely charm. Katy presented the bottle of detergent as if it were a bottle of wine.

"Roderick mentioned he'd be bringing visitors. Make yourself comfortable, dear. Roderick, I left something for your attention on the counter by the stove. If you would be so kind. Katherine and I will visit."

"Of course," Roderick said. He really wasn't sure he wanted to leave Katie at Matilda's mercy, but what else could he do? In the kitchen, he found a bucket with the cleaning supplies for the downstairs bathroom. Nothing came free. Katie would kill him for leaving her alone, but if he sloshed through the job, she'd only have a few minutes on her own. He kept an ear cocked just in case he had to run to her rescue. Between rinses and flushes, he caught the odd phrase. "Since college." "St. Mary's." "Lovely house." Nothing to set off any alarm bells.

He returned the cleansers and brushes to the pantry and, wiping his hands on a dish towel, noticed Matilda's tea set, polished and at the ready on the kitchen table. A kettle of water burbled quietly on the stove, next to which sat a plastic-wrapped selection of cookies. Roderick had never acquired a taste for his aunt's bitter brews, and he couldn't imagine Katie much cared for the stuff, though they had never discussed the subject of tea—and why would they have? Though a part of him wished to ignore the whole setup, he knew that his best tack at the moment was to go with the flow. He set the tea to steep, unwrapped the cookies, and made sure there were enough spoons and napkins.

"I hope you don't mind," he said to Matilda, knowing full well that it had been her intention that he serve the refreshments. Katie's face, he could see, had glazed into a benign-looking simper that he knew masked something like panic.

"Katherine here was telling me of your intentions to marry. What a delightful surprise. Odd that Martin hasn't mentioned it."

Roderick poured the thin brown liquid into each of the cups. "We're breaking the news slowly," he said. "We wanted you to be one of the first to know."

"I'm honored. And congratulations." Matilda fixed him with a look that to Katie he imagined appeared innocent enough, but that he knew was laden with portent.

"You children help yourselves to these treats," she said, and she sat back in her chair with her cup and saucer in her lap. Roderick knew what that meant. Matilda was finished being the gracious host and leading the conversation for the evening. She was leaving it up to him to entertain his guest.

"Katie works up at Northwest. In Famous & Barr."

"She mentioned that, yes."

"We've known each other for about five years."

"She mentioned that, as well."

Roderick tried a different tack. "My aunt has an amazing garden. She has a green thumb, I swear."

"I love gardens. I go to the Botanical Gardens at least once a year, usually for the rose show. I'd love to see yours."

Okay, Roderick thought. But maybe don't try so hard. He made an effort to send the message to Katie through telepathy, but that quality had yet to become one of their shared strengths.

"It's much lovelier when there's more light. You'll come again, of course."

"Of course," both he and Katie said simultaneously.

Roderick managed to maintain the inane prattle for another ten minutes or so, and then thought, Enough.

"Well, Aunt Matilda. Thanks for the tea and everything. I just wanted to stop by and have you two meet." He'd started to say something hokey about the two most important women in his life, but was pleased to have been censored by the god of common sense.

"Lovely to meet you, my dear." Matilda extended her hand.

"And you, as well," Katie replied, the simper she'd plastered on her face now drooping into something like a demonic cringe. He was getting them out of there just in time. Ten more minutes and Katie would likely be slumped over and limp with fatigue or depression. Over the course of their long life together he would never learn to identify that particular emotion in this woman.

"Need anything else, Auntie? I can stop by tomorrow afternoon. We've got kind of a slow day."

"In fact, I would like to see you tomorrow. Please do stop by."

Didn't sound good, but what choice did he have? He told her he'd look in on her around two and steered his fiancée toward the car.

"Are you okay?" he asked as they pulled away from the curb. Katie's expression had evidently frozen on her face.

"I haven't felt this way since I rushed Theta back at school."

"You get used to her," Roderick encouraged, and then wondered to himself if he ever had.

The next day Matilda met him at the door, and motioned him to his usual seat in the living room.

"Well?"

"Well, what?"

"Always one for the games, aren't you, Roderick? Too bad you aren't any good at them."

"You're the one who asked me to stop by," he said, and then

thought, Damn, she's right. He wasn't any good at her stupid games. But maybe if he continued the small talk and the buttering . . . They usual worked with her.

"Katie's really a nice girl. I hope you liked her. She sure liked you."

Matilda shook her head, not to mean, Roderick knew, that she hadn't liked his future wife, but that she found his evasions pathetic.

"She's a lovely girl. Not much of a sun worshiper, I would imagine."

So she wanted to play hardball. Fine. Roderick was game. He'd taken on distributors who would leave an old bird like this one shredded on the kitchen floor.

"Okay, fine, Matilda, she's white. I said it. Are you satisfied? Is that what you've been waiting for?"

Matilda scoffed. "I've not waited for anything. You're the one who came by here with something to tell me. Now you did. By the way, I'm not blind, and I'm not stupid, either."

"Okay, fine. I guess that means—"

"What do you want, Roderick?"

He dug around in his mind to find the words that he'd rehearsed, but found only the odd out-of-context phrase floating around, seemingly without purpose. Why had he thought he could work this crafty old thing around to seeing the logic in his plan? Were there enough hours in a year to work such magic? No. Something like that never would have happened with Matilda. So just get it on the table, and be done with it.

"I want you to host a dinner party. I want to invite her parents and mine so that we can announce our engagement. I'd like to have it here."

"Now, see, that wasn't so hard, was it? And the answer is 'no.' " Matilda got up and headed through the dining room and kitchen, on her way to her garden, retrieving her work gloves from a counter on the way out.

"Wait a minute," Roderick said, following behind. "You didn't even think about it."

"Sure I did. You asked. I considered it. I said 'no.' And I don't appreciate being hovered over when I'm pruning."

"Can I at least ask why?"

"Yes, you may. I need to see where I'm cutting."

"You know what I'm talking about."

"An ignorant old colored woman like me. How would I know something like that? Why, I'm so stupid I can't even figure out when I'm being manipulated."

"I'm not manipulating you."

"Fine, Roderick. Have a pleasant week. When you bring the groceries next Saturday, please pick up a jar of sweet relish." She snipped at green nubs sprouting off her trellised roses.

"God, you're stubborn."

"Good-bye, Roderick."

He started back toward his car, then turned and let the words slip off his tongue.

"You'd have done it for David," he said.

Matilda stood. "What did you say to me?"

Before he could answer, she removed a glove and slapped him hard across the face. She fled into the house.

Roderick felt his cheek, which burned, which stung, which felt as if were glowing, which may have been bleeding. He felt his face. His hands, he saw, came away wet, but not with blood.

Why hadn't some mad genius yet invented the machine that

could stop time and whisk you back for a second chance? Why wasn't it possible to reach back a few minutes or hours or days and suck the words back into oneself, to unsay what had been said and undo the already done? Sometimes Roderick hated himself.

He found Matilda sitting on the bed in the room his brother had slept in, wiping away the last of what appeared to have been a lot of tears. Roderick knelt at her feet.

"I'm sorry, Aunt Matilda."

She nodded. She wouldn't meet his eye. They sat quietly that way for what seemed like an hour.

"I love her. I know that's not an excuse. It's just that I'm afraid."

"What are you afraid of, Roderick?"

"That she'll . . . that they will think that we . . . aren't good enough, I guess. I'm afraid that Pops will do . . . I don't know what. I just know that I don't want to lose her."

"There. Not as hard as you imagined it would be, was it?" Matilda petted his head. "Unfortunately, you credit me with powers I don't possess."

"You do. If anyone on earth can figure out how to make this work, you can."

"I wish I could say I was flattered."

She rose and walked down the steps to the front door. Roderick followed.

"Three weeks from today for dinner," she said, not to him. "That should give them adequate notice and time for us to prepare." She held the door open to indicate Roderick should leave.

"Thanks, Aunt Matilda." Roderick bent to give her a kiss, but she spurned his advance. "I owe you. I really do."

Matilda said nothing. She closed the door and Roderick heard the dead bolt click into place.

For the engagement party, they agreed to serve a lamb roast, rolled and seasoned throughout with bits of garlic and salt, crusty brown and savory on the outside and inside pale pink to gray. Matilda had roasted it in a way that there were lots of medium- to well-done tips for those who liked it that way, and Roderick had purloined his father's secret recipe for a minty sauce, a creamy mixture of a variety of fresh herbs with just a hint of horseradish and cream. He and his aunt had tangled over which potatoes to serve. Matilda prevailed, arguing the wisdom of new red potatoes over what she called a "messy mash." Simple, fresh string beans from her garden: there had been no debate about that.

"I expect you in a coat and tie," she told Roderick the day before the event. "And you are planning to bring the girl's parents yourself. They shouldn't arrive on their own. If you haven't made—"

"I did. We talked about all this, and I did everything the way you said."

"A person can't be too careful," she said, and went back to fussing with the tablecloth, which she was allowing to "settle" on the table overnight. "I want this to go well for you. State for me, please, your exact goal for this dinner."

"Um—"

"We're way past that, Roderick."

He sometimes forgot about Matilda's directness. Since she'd

agreed to the party, this was the longest conversation they had that didn't concern produce.

"I want the first dinner the two families share to be a success. I want them to see what kind of people we are. I hope it brings us all together."

"I've done my part, then. May I offer you some advice?"

Roderick hesitated to accept the offer, but reluctantly agreed.

"I don't know these people, but I can tell you one thing for sure. That girl wasn't raised in an alley. These are decent people. I'm sure of that. They may reject their daughter's choice for a spouse, but that is between them and her."

"And me."

"No, Roderick. Not you. They will either accept you or they won't. She will either accede to her parents' wishes or she will not. There's not a thing you can say or do to change that. The same is true for Martin and Evie."

"My parents will be fine."

"Or so you hope. People have a way of surprising us all the time. I can tell you one thing. Don't expect any scenes here tomorrow, because there won't be any. The Housewrights aren't alley people, either."

Roderick knew that this would be his only chance, perhaps forever, to find out, so he asked the question.

"What do you think, Aunt Matilda? About all of this?"

"*About all of this?* You make it sound as if you were talking about a Fourth of July parade. Does it matter what I think?"

Roderick knew that she knew the honest answer to that question.

"I guess I'd still like to know."

Matilda's eyes reminded him of the steep cost of speaking one's mind with this woman—almost, though not quite, as costly as not doing so.

"Fair enough. I think you're going to have a tougher time than either of you can even imagine. And I fear for your children."

"I'm not sure why. It's the seventies. Things have changed."

"If that were so, then why all this?" She waved her hand over the table upon which she'd already begun placing miscellaneous serving implements.

"Maybe . . . just . . . I don't want to take any chances."

"And maybe your families will be the least of your worries. Why do you want to marry this girl?"

Because I can, Roderick thought to himself, and chuckled. Why did anyone choose a spouse? When he was in high school, he'd bought into all of that crap about two hearts beating as one and being head over heels and all kinds of other crap, the kind of rancid sentiment one heard on every other song Motown Records produced. But life wasn't that way—he knew that to be true. What a man needed was a partner, someone who shared his aspirations and dreams, someone who could contribute to those dreams and pull her share when needed. He needed someone who understood how the world of business worked, who wanted to get ahead herself. He needed someone who would know what to do when they finally got where they wanted to be. Katie was that person.

"She's the right one for me," he told his aunt.

"Do you love her, Roderick?"

An internal shudder marked his hesitation, shuddering both at his surprise at the question and his own vacillation in answering.

"I think so."

"You think so," she repeated, hardly masking her contempt. She gathered a collection of creamers and butter dishes to be polished later in the evening.

As predicted by Matilda, the dinner came off without a hitch. Both families were as gracious as their hostess, who when answering the door for the family donned a pleasant smile that she did not allow to lapse for one moment over the entire evening. Roderick studied that smile, wondered where he'd seen it before, why it haunted him so. He realized, then, that it was the same smile he'd seen his father employ for countless banquets: the relaxed lips, the affable confidence radiating from the white teeth, and the eyes that seemed truly interested in everything the guest had to say.

"Might I have another slice of that delicious lamb?"

"It would be my pleasure."

The absolute comity of the evening threatened to break only once, when, after they'd announced the engagement, after Roderick had watched both mothers almost but not quite hide their disappointment (ironically both betraying themselves with almost identical too-shiny eyes), and after Katie had wisely circled the table embracing both women so that their tears might run for a more appropriate reason, the fathers leaned forward to give voice to requisite fatherly cautions, however mild they might be.

"I have to say—" one or both of them began, but Matilda, as Roderick expected, anticipated their speeches and cut them off at the proverbial pass.

"Gentlemen," she said. "Surely now, on a special occasion such as this, we'll not play *Guess Who's Coming to Dinner*?" She then let loose her most charming laugh, the infectious one none dared resist.

"Show Aunt Matilda that rock," she said, loosing another round of laughs. Whatever fits were to be thrown—and Roderick expected one or two down the line, and so be it—would have to wait for another time.

"A lovely gracious woman, that aunt of yours," Jim Cashman said as Roderick drove them home. It was telling that this was the only thing he said, but his wife concurred enthusiastically. Matilda had worked her magic.

Roderick stopped by the next day with a giant bouquet of mixed-color tulips, amazing and exotic with spring long past. He found her hand polishing each piece of her silver service before storing it away in its velvet box.

"You're fantastic, Auntie," he said. He retrieved the cut-crystal vase from the breakfront for the flowers.

Matilda polished silently.

"I think it went really well last night, don't you?" he asked.

Matilda shook her head and sighed. She finished the last serving spoon. She rolled her polishing cloth and stored the lot within the buffet. She retrieved a piece of paper from beneath a bowl of fruit on her kitchen counter.

"You know the difference between you and your brother?" She dared him to respond.

"David never would have asked." She walked to the front door and opened it for her nephew.

"I've thought about that quite a lot these past few weeks, and I know that I'm right." She handed the piece of paper to Roderick.

"You should also know that I've decided not to forgive you.

Ever." She closed the door in his face and latched it with the dead bolt.

Roderick examined the piece of paper: Matilda's standard grocery list, rendered in her ever-so-elegant hand.

This week's bonus item: peaches.

III

1976

Roderick wasn't sure whether a giant conch shell was the right gift for Matilda, but he did believe his choice had been better than some of the things that Katie had suggested: beach sandals for a woman who never went to the beach. Flower-laden sarongs for a woman who didn't own a single item of clothing that wasn't traditional and tailored. The island had been a terrific place to honeymoon, and they had fun, but he wondered if they hadn't spent an inordinate amount of time shopping for this one particular gift. Who could imagine that so many tacky and horrifying things would be for sale? Napkin holders carved from coconuts and driftwood walking sticks and cheap porcelain ashtrays shaped like commodes. To be honest, he and Katie had had a great time matching families and friends with the perfect cheap trinket. Embroidered straw bags for the mothers and bottles of island rum for the old men. Only Matilda had vexed their efforts. They'd walked the market from one end to the next, had despaired of the precious time they were losing from the beach, when Roderick spotted the giant pink shells.

"What about these?" he'd asked Katie.

"They're pretty, but what would she ever do with them?"

"Sit them in front of the fireplace. Just for decoration. It goes with her colors." The shells' lively mixture of peach and cream and salmon and rose would flow right into the pastels of Matilda's living room.

"We couldn't possibly pack those," Katie had warned, and she proved right. The shells had ridden in his lap all the way back from the island, wrapped in some cotton shirts he'd purchased for himself.

He wrestled the grocery bag under his arm to counterbalance the shells that he cradled in the other arm. He managed to ring Matilda's doorbell with one of the fingers supporting the shells.

"I'm back," he announced, maneuvering across the threshold. He took the bag to the kitchen and set it on the table, began unpacking.

"Pops remembered to bring the groceries by, didn't he?" He hoped his father had been careful to get everything on the list. Old Marty got cranky when you gave him too many suggestions, had insisted on reminding him that he'd been stocking pantries since long before Roderick showed up on Earth.

"Look what I found. This imported Scottish shortbread. I

thought you might like to try it. I figured we were running low on Comet, too. Unless Pops picked up some extra. It's not like it goes bad."

Roderick noticed some liquid had accumulated in the bottom of the meat compartment of the refrigerator. Could be trouble. He pulled the tray from the shelf and ran some hot water in the sink. One needed to throw a little bleach on this sort of thing. Hot water and bleach. You couldn't beat it, and you didn't even need a maxim for that. He sure hoped that the motor wasn't going out on that old icebox. He checked the freezer and it seemed to be holding temperature just fine. No frost, and the cubes were solid and dry. Maybe she spilled something and didn't notice. Odd that old Marty hadn't attended to this mess. That one was a stickler for a hygienic workspace. Well, no harm done.

Matilda placed a towel next to the sink. Perfect for drying the bin.

"We had a great time on the island. Katie sends her best. She had some hours at the store today. You'd like it down there, Auntie. All the flowers and things. We visited this great garden. At this plantation house back up in the hills. Tour guide said slaves had cleared the local vegetation out so the master could make this garden. They had plants on sale in the market, but they said customs wouldn't let us bring them in. Who knows if we could even get them to grow out there. You could maybe. We got you these shells. What do you think? I thought we might try them in front of the fireplace. With the colors and everything."

Roderick carried the shells and placed them on the hearth. They did look good there, he thought, even though they were the only things of their kind in the room. They added a bit of character and interest. Character and interest were always good when setting a table or arranging a buffet.

"We can move them if you don't like them there."

He noticed that the roll top on her desk was askew—one side halfway down, the other side pushed a few inches higher toward the recess. He'd warned her about fussing with that old thing. Up or down, he'd said. It's only for show at this point. Apparently she'd changed her mind and wanted it up. He retrieved a rubber mallet and some light grease from the basement. He used the grease to line the track.

"Poor Kate. I knew she'd get sick of that department store, but she insisted she wanted to stay. She has no idea what she wants to do next. I offered her to come into the business, but she didn't want to. Can't say I'm sorry. She's competent and all that, but I think we'd get on each other's nerves seeing each other all day, every day. And then what about when our kids come? You know what I'm saying."

A couple of taps with the hammer did the trick. The grease did help the roll top slide, but she would have to leave the thing be. A couple of more fights and it would be kindling.

"I gotta run. Pops has got us on a private dinner way out in West County. French service, if you can believe that. He wants me on the floor—he's got a couple of new guys he's breaking in. You'll call me if you need anything? Auntie?"

IV

1980

Roderick watched Katie wander up the walk to the seminary. Well, that's a crass notion, he thought, wondering if having a wife in the divinity school might somehow give him an edge for the university food service contract. It had been a smart move, he thought, taking the housing operations people on one of the airline flights he catered. Let them see the quality he could provide in bulk service. The luncheon for the deans hadn't hurt, either.

God, there was a lot of money to be made, if a person just got out there and hustled. The university account would be the fourth major billing he'd snared in the past year and a half. Managing such a large operation might prove to be complex, but he had a line on a food service director from a small college upstate who was looking to make a lateral move. He'd have to get hooked up with a different class of vendors, too. Things ought to go fine, as long as Pops didn't get an up-close look at commodity cheese.

He hoped Matilda enjoyed the fresh raspberries. He'd ordered them flown in special for the Zoo Ball last night and had managed to set aside a small container for her. It hadn't been easy. The berries were fresh and firm and sweet, and he thought he'd pop a vessel, yelling at that crew to keep their hands out of the bowl. The shortcake had been a hit—leave it to Pops, who still had the touch with an old-fashioned pound cake. Old Marty had shown him that recipe a hundred times, but somehow when Roderick made it, it never turned out quite that luscious.

The Zoo Ball: the World Series of catering gigs. Pops' dream come true. How many years had that man fantasized about designing and serving the biggest society bash in town? But things had changed. Folks all over town were lining up to give business to capable black firms. Even if he didn't get the contract at the U, there were three other live wires on the line, including the daily catering for one of the big construction firms and the concessions at the art museum. Housewright, Incorporated, was already the second-largest food service operation in the region. A few shrewd moves and they'd be national—within the year, maybe. He'd be meeting with a New York investment banker early in the week.

Look at that nasty old gate. When was the last time he painted that thing? Back in college, maybe? Rust bloomed from every joint and seam, an explosion of red through the crackling black paint. He'd have Shirley get some paint sent over here and then tackle it next weekend. He made another note to Shirley to get a meeting with that linen supply place. They'd cut it a little close on delivering the Zoo Ball. So what if the catering arm of things was only Pops' boutique business? The events Pops put together caught the eye of the big money in town. Roderick wasn't risking looking bad over tardy tablecloths.

Maybe he'd buy that linen outfit. God knows they went through enough aprons and napkins and tablecloths and rags. He'd have to talk that over with the accounting department. Could be a nice investment and save them quite a bit in overhead. Or maybe they should start their own linen operation.

He hoped Katie remembered her vitamins. Frankly, he didn't think she needed to be working on this damn degree while pregnant, but try telling her that. It seemed most of their conversations were telling each other to slow down, him telling her she didn't need yet another graduate degree, her telling him that one more big account wasn't worth his health and to please come get some sleep. What would they call them when she finished her doctorate? Would they be Mr. and the Reverend Dr. Housewright? When did they come up with the deal that women got to be ministers?

He removed the flat of petunias from the trunk. (His Mercedes dealer would have a fit if they saw the things he hauled around in there. It hadn't been twenty-four hours since he'd had to retrieve an emergency air cargo shipment of flowers from the airport. They'd arrived packed in foul-smelling raffia.) It was a shame that hailstorm had ruined Matilda's earlier plantings. He'd had to drive to two nurseries to find the color flowers she liked. (How many afternoons back in the old days had she lectured him on the vulgarity of striped petunias?) He raked the battered stems from the ground and began staggering the new ones in the pattern that she had always specified. He remembered being in high school and how on one spring day he'd made the mistake of clustering the plants too tight.

"Plant them yourself," he'd told her. She'd rolled her eyes and sighed as to how cranky boys would be the death of her.

"Like this, if you're interested," she'd said, and had gone on to finish a row herself. Tired of sulking, he'd helped her finish the other side. Careful pinching made hers the most prolific display of petunias he'd ever seen. The same was true year after year. Sometimes he wished he could cut out his impetuous tongue.

He had to admit there was something comforting about rooting around in the soil this way. He didn't do much of this in the new place he and Katie had built out in Chesterfield. The outfit they used for the lawn did an excellent job. Katie told them what to plant where, and like magic, there it was. The owner of this particular landscape nursery had been after Roderick for a portion of his flower business, so maybe they'd gotten special service. That's how things ran in this town. He'd gotten a bargain on Katie's Lincoln because the dealer ran the livery they sometimes used for weddings. Unfortunately, even Lincolns needed routine service. He'd have to remember to get back for Katie by five when her weekend seminar ended.

He carried the empty flats to the potting shed in the backyard. Matilda saved the damn things—he couldn't imagine why. A stack of plastic trays already reached his waist.

Matilda was fussing with some knotty old wisteria vines on the trellis—would the woman ever get those the way she wanted them? They looked fine to him, lush and wild and sharp. Walking through the arch, a person swooned from the abundant flowering. He'd never seen such a proliferation of blossoms. He remembered when he was little and he'd come over here—oh, how he hated it then—and how back then the first wispy tendrils had finally climbed to the pinnacle of the arbor. He wondered what his own children would make of the gnarled branches, the cloying scent, the green-brown cave of fragrance.

A boy. He was hoping for a boy. Katie wanted girls, which would be nice, too, as long as a boy came along at some point.

He used the pitchfork to turn the compost.

He sprayed some WD-40 onto the axle of the hose caddy. The squeak must drive Matilda crazy. He'd thought about installing a lawn-watering system in the yard—had taken an estimate from his own yard service—but somehow it just didn't seem like the sort of thing Matilda would stand for. She enjoyed aiming her hose just where she wanted it, seemed to know the exact amount needed for each cluster of growth.

He checked the second floor. Good, that toilet wasn't running. He liked those old porcelain handles and knobs. They were classy—they'd come back in style real soon, you just knew it. But the plumbing up here left something to be desired. He'd changed that trap last year, and still the thing ran. It was probably haunted.

Everything in her closets seemed fine. The garden shed, the foyer, that nook back by the basement steps.

Nothing else needed doing. It was time to swing by and pick up his wife.

Matilda was sprinkling bone meal at the base of the roses.

"Okay, Aunt Matilda. I'll see you next week," he said.

"You take care of yourself," he said.

"You call me if you need anything," he said. "Anytime, okay?"

He said, "Good-bye, Auntie."

V

1985

Akron. Ashtabula. Springfield, Illinois.

"Come on, man. Get a move on. She doesn't like it when we're late."

Sacramento. Santa Fe. Salt Lake City.

"Mommy told you this morning to leave that in the drawer, didn't she? Scoot."

The problem with a lot of the smaller cities was getting there. There used to be direct service to some of them. A lot of these places never had decent airports, of course, and it made sense to drive in from the nearest big city. He'd come more and more to appreciate the quiet drives on his own, especially since the girls had come. He loved the twins, and they were sweet-natured babies, but the mewling of infants wasn't always music to the ears.

"Trust me. She won't be interested in those Transformers."

Three vice presidents and ten regional managers, and somehow he was still the only one who could put out a fire. Now that Katie had her own congregation she complained more about the travel, and Roderick couldn't blame her. It was a tough job managing three kids and a whole sanctuary full of wild Presbyterians. But when the CEO of a major metropolitan medical center signed off on a food service contract in the million-dollar range, he expected the president of Housewright Food Distribution (HFD) to be present, shaking hands and passing around the tokens of his warm esteem and eternal gratitude.

"I bet you wouldn't have any idea how this half-eaten sandwich got under your bed."

All in all he couldn't complain. If he'd written the script himself (which in many ways he had), things couldn't have gone better. The trajectory was as seamless as the flight of the space shuttle. He'd been smart. He'd hired shrewd strategists and a top-notch research staff. HFD had specialized in picking up bids from thriving institutions that had been burned by lackluster service from second-rate contractors. Such companies were a dime a dozen, it seemed, ripe for the plucking, and he'd wisely picked the cream of the crop: hospitals and prisons and universities; organizations with sound accounting practices and a healthy bottom line. Then it had only been a matter of standardizing recipes and procedures and service protocols. The rest flowed like honey on a warm stove.

"I need you to be on your very best behavior. It's really important to Daddy."

The challenge ahead: growth and choosing the best directions for that growth. He'd been looking at a couple of fledgling processors—a couple of snack-chip outfits, one producer of gourmet condiments. The board had been pushing in the direction of some up-and-coming fast food franchises and theme restaurants, but Rodcrick hadn't been too keen on that end of the business: something about the long-standing Housewright aversion to retail.

Perhaps it was time to go public. Or maybe diversification was the right tack. Hadn't he said years ago that HFD ought to pick up a string of regional bakeries? (But old Marty held that line like it was going out of style. He wasn't serving his customers not one slice of that spongy factory-made garbage, and that's all there was to it. That's how he continued to run his tiny catering division. Housewright and Sons didn't serve one loaf that hadn't been shaped either by Martin himself or by someone he'd trained. His father would most certainly have a stroke if he knew the number of commercial loaves HFD purchased for institutional clients. What he didn't know wouldn't hurt him.)

"You'll learn a lot. That's one thing I can promise you for sure."

Or he could sell it all. Every last pan and warming cart and truck and contract and all the goodwill. Keep a small kitchen in town for Pops and his trade. He could sell it all today and retire a wealthy man and sit around on his butt for the rest of his life. Why shouldn't he? Why the hell not? A lot of days he was worn down to a nub. It wasn't the hustling and negotiating and the mad deadlines and the crises. No eggs in Des Moines. Salmon stuck on the runway in Seattle. Please. Housewrights handled such crap in their sleep. Here he was, the CEO of a multi-multimillion-dollar corporation, a man with over a thousand employees, some who quaked in their boots when he walked by. Here he'd just bought the family a second vacation home, this one in Telluride, snow to complement the sand on Marco Island.

"She teases sometimes, but you'll get used to it. I did."

Here in Manhattan he can't get a taxi to stop for him—after leaving a meeting of the board of another corporation he'd been asked to direct. Here some woman in the grocery store looks at him like he's some sort of child molester because he's holding the hand of a fair-skinned child with curly blond hair. Here people sneer at him and his wife when they walk into the department store—where she used to work.

There, right there: That was the killer.

Everything he'd worked so hard for: what had it got him?

Some days he wondered why he bothered leaving his house.

"This will be a regular thing, you know. It'll be fun. I promise. Go on up and push that doorbell."

He grabbed the sack of groceries from the backseat. One thing he could say about her: she had always given him what all his money and power and success had not.

The things we do to people. Oh, Matilda.

"Aunt Matilda. Look at the surprise I brought for you."

He had tried in every way he knew how. There was only one thing he knew to do.

"This is Jacob, Auntie. Master Jacob Housewright. I thought it was about time he paid you a visit. Say hello to your aunt Matilda."

"Jacob, is it?" She extended her hand and enclosed Jake's tiny one inside it. "Well, I've sure heard a lot about you. You're about all your daddy talks about. It's about time he brought you around to see me."

"Jake just turned five, Aunt Matilda. Isn't he something?"

She rubbed his blond curls. "Funny-looking little thing, isn't he?" she said to Roderick.

Roderick swallowed. "I warned him about you."

"Did you, now? And isn't he something?" She caressed the chubby cheeks of his son.

"Here he is. He is something, isn't he? Here he is for you. He's about the best thing we got."

The Other Thing

. . .

When the business of America came to a standstill in the thirties, things turned down at the Senator's house, as well, though it would be disingenuous of me to suggest that those of us in the Georgetown mansion experienced the sacrifices that most citizens did. The Senator had resources squirreled away that he tapped into as needed, and, unlike many, he happened to have a regular job to go to, at least as long as the citizens of the home state would have him. Like everyone else, we did tighten the purse strings. An enigma that I've had a chance to observe firsthand is the way the expenses of running a house expand right along with the income of the homeowner. Similarly enigmatic is the way that for the well-to-do, being presently somewhat less rich than one once had been is infinitely more painful than the equivalent experience is for the poor. When someone such as the Senator's fortunes decrease, even if what remains would ransom a minor king, one just comes to expect histrionics of epic proportions, followed by much gnashing of teeth. While the Senator's friends threw themselves from windows in New York, the least among us planned on making the watery bean soup last yet another day. Believe me, our household survived just fine, though some corners did need to be cut.

The Senator directed Father to effect certain "reconsiderations in the operation of the household," and then laid out his guidelines for those changes, the substance of which had been that life in Georgetown would on the surface remain unchanged. He intended that his home continue to be the center of "informal consultations" in the capital, that the guests be greeted with the same standard of grace and hospitality, that his own standard of living not be noticeably lowered, and that all of this would happen within the limits of what he referred to as an "ever-so-slight decrease in household expenditures."

Father sputtered around our carriage house in exasperation upon receipt of his new budget.

"Blood from a turnip," I heard him bellow, the other parts of his sentences buried in rapid-fire and indecipherable murmurs.

"You must calm down," I pleaded, knowing that part of his frustration lay in the fact that the scaled-down budget placed a major impediment on his dream to move his family off the Senator's property and into our own home, perhaps over in the Adams Morgan area of the District. Knowing Father, he would scale back his own dream long before he made any other cuts.

"We all have faith in you," I encouraged him, as well we

should have. No one could have made the adjustments flow any smoother and with any less pain than my father.

And adjustments there were, although in keeping with the Senator's mandate, the casual observer would be aware of nothing.

We had to let go some of the staff. This had been the hardest part for Father. He knew how little the chances were that any of them would find work during those hard years; he went out of his way, in fact, to call around town to see who might need to pick up a hand, but times were just that bad. Everyone cut back. Great leaders such as my father know that sentiment has no place when tough decisions are due. Father looked around at what jobs were essential, at who was the best at doing each task, at who could be counted on to do more than one thing. If an old retainer needed to make way for a multiply talented young hand, so be it, and God be with the poor old soul—that became all of our attitudes. I'd like to believe that those among us who had to leave understood my father's position, but I know there was bitterness. There always is at such times.

Those of us who remained increased our capacity for hard work, and, yes, I count myself in this lot, for although Father never asked me directly, he knew he could always count on me to pull my weight. Martin, my brother, he protected. Father wanted more than anything else that Martin, just beginning his high school years, not be disrupted from his studies (ah, the secrets we keep), and though I sometimes resented the free ride my brother usually received, in actuality he was often more trouble than he was worth. Martin hated life in the Senator's house, and when he'd be asked to pitch in—as was necessary on rare occasions, such as when one of the now-skeleton staff fell ill—he did so grudgingly, completing each task with barely minimum effort, and always with a sour expression on his face. Slovenly work became something of a trademark for him during those years.

We cut back in other ways, as well. Cook limited the range of dinner rolls she might prepare for a special meal, savings always to be found in the choice of volume over variety. Gone were the days we'd have a fresh pastry every morning. Her expertise at overnight storage increased exponentially, as did Father's at finding clever ways of making each morning's offering seem special. (Never underestimate what can be done with a tasteful garnish and a sprinkling of confectioner's sugar.)

Slightly raveled napkins that at one time we'd have discarded to the rag bin, no questions asked, landed on a stack of mending. That became one of my chores. In the evenings, Martin and I would gather in front of the radio back in the carriage house and listen to the comedies. I read to Martin from his textbooks and he scratched in his notebooks. While he wrote I sat with a needle and a basket of fine threads, rehemming the linens with the delicate stitch that I'd been taught. To my care also fell the rest of the tableware, the long years of apprenticeship under Father's demanding chamois finally made use of.

When he was able to join us in the evenings, Father often sat in his favorite chair with his ledger open on his lap and a sharp pencil at the ready. One end of the pencil was red; the other end was blue. He'd sigh and click his tongue over the figures in the household accounts. Those ledgers always balanced, but they never came out the way he'd hoped. While his continuous quest to squeeze another penny from the budget more often than not bore fruit, and while I can assure you that the bottom line always remained in positive figures, the poor man was never satisfied.

"Aha!" he'd crow, and Martin and I would shake our heads and roll our eyes, watching him delete another percentage or two from the next day's expenses. Tomorrow there would be that many fewer walnuts in the cookie jar.

But please remember that I am not complaining. We remained warm and well fed while many others were not. Father kept aside what food he could from any big dinners to send along with the workers if they knew someone who needed it—and there was always someone in need. Raggedy old men haunted the back alleys of even the better parts of the city, asking after work or for a handout if you could spare it. Father took to avoiding the back gate. More often than he would like, beneath the dirt and stubble lay a face he remembered as having worked just down the way, in a home not much different from ours.

"That looks like old Pete out there," he'd say, sadly and to himself. He'd send me or one of the others out to the back gate with a biscuit sandwich or a quarter or a piece of fruit.

I remember around my fifteenth birthday observing my father and the Senator together and thinking, Where did these two old men come from? Father would have been nearing sixty during this period, and though neither of them had yet to show even the slightest sign of slowing down, each face bore the subtle early signs of old age. Both men had become jowly, though the Senator more so than Father. He had a good decade on my father, so one would expect those years to show. The Senator's hair had long been white—and famously so—though he'd for many years seemed youthful to me. Father's salt-and-pepper hair became more salt than pepper.

The two men had been together for thirty years, longer than either of them had been married to their wives, and just like a longtime couple, they would bicker and snap at one another. They would correct each other's memory and worry over the other one's health and whether he were eating enough, each accusing the other of becoming silly and senile. The Senator, by then a senior and much-admired figure in Washington, had grown tired of both the political and the social hubbub. He maintained a calendar of just enough events so folks would know he still remained a force due consideration, but more and more he preferred quiet evenings at home.

Many nights you'd find him and my father and Mr. Montgomery, the gentleman who served as his chief of staff in the Senate, sitting around the kitchen table, playing cards.

"Jake, you cheating again. He's cheating again, I can tell."

Father extended his wrists from his sleeves to indicate that no cards hid there. "You're just getting so you can't remember which cards have been played."

The Senator laughed his loud, gobbly laugh.

I would hang back in a shadowy pantry and watch them sometimes. Father had strictly forbidden this behavior on my part, but I'd decided that as long as I remained quiet and undetected, no harm would come from my watching. Many evenings the three of them sat at the table and turned their cards, and hardly a word would be exchanged, save an occasional "Gotcha!" or perhaps one of them petulantly accusing the other of skipping his turn to deal. Maybe over all the years they had spent together they had run out of things to talk about, but I'm not so sure.

Here were three men who spent their lives managing the machinery that made worlds run. They guided those engines seemingly without effort, through a well-placed word here or a strongly placed reprimand there. They made simple declarative statements, sans ambiguity, and they expected—entertained not a single doubt, in fact—that their word would become manifest. For men like this, it could have been that after so many years of living on the strength of your will, nothing seemed better at the end of the day than a nice quiet game of cards among old friends.

I have always envied them their companionable silence. Wouldn't it be nice to be in possession of friends such as these, friends where none felt the need to poison the room with his own personal inanities, if only as a bulwark against the awkwardness of silence? Watching them on these evenings, one could almost believe that they were just three longtime buddies, killing time and waving off the mosquitoes that always managed to find a way into that drafty kitchen. Only they (and I) would know their true history, but on these nights, none of that mattered. Sometime well before midnight, one of them, usually the Senator, would toss his cards on the pile to indicate he'd had enough of their nonsense. And that would be that until next time.

Like many young women with widowed fathers, I'd become extremely protective of mine. His early signs of aging hit me hard; I came to view almost any mundane chore as potentially overtaxing for the dear man.

"That bench is too heavy for you, Daddy," I'd cry, rushing to his rescue.

"Let me carry that tray. You'll strain yourself."

Father, as you can well imagine, had no truck with mollycoddling.

"A certain young woman, if she knows what's good for her, will see to her own affairs." He vigorously shooed me away from the service pantry he used to stage the Senator's smokers. Under no circumstances would a daughter of his be delivering drinks like some common barmaid, even if the customers did happen to include the nation's leading policy makers.

Personally, I wouldn't have minded. Those men neither impressed me nor scared me in the least. I'd scraped away the filth they'd left in our ashtrays, had been overhearing the verbal equivalent of that filth since I was a toddler. I hardly paid attention to them anymore, to be honest. To those of us behind the stairs, those men were merely the reason we had to prepare finger-sized toasted ham and cheese sandwiches or strain fresh-squeezed lemon juice into cocktail shakers. Nothing more.

Increasingly, however, in my new protective-daughter mode, I came to resent the way these men spoke to my father. It wasn't so much the crass newcomers—the sort of men who would snap their fingers and call for the "boy" to come freshen his drink. That ilk, they have always been with us, and they have long been beneath scorn to those in service, hardly worth the time to do more than perhaps spit in their drinks, opportunity permitting. It's long been a marker of quality families that they taught their children how to interact with the household staff. Those familiar with the workings of Washington know that the finger snappers of the world, while perhaps gaining in seniority, more often than not languished on the social vine. Eventually these sorts of people dragged themselves back to their home districts, their desperately lonely wives and disreputable children in tow. Here on the Potomac, not one tear would be shed in their absence.

It's hard to describe the kind of behavior that set me off back then. I guess I resented the way that certain ones among these men had of speaking to Father—as if he were a child, as if he were perhaps *their* child. And talking is the wrong word, because

I'd seen many of these men pull my father aside for a quiet word, I assume about some way he might make them more comfortable, so I knew very well the difference between speech and the behavior that set me off. Perhaps joking would be a better word for what bothered me, or maybe teasing. Whatever you would call it, I didn't care for it one bit.

These men—and especially some of the older men—adjusted their voices to a nasty-sounding tambour, a hooded and smoky kind of voice that eliminated the need for nuance or interpretation. They drew in their faces into the pouty, puckery smiles young boys applied when trying out on each other the foul language they learned from their older brothers.

"How you cutting it with them gals in the back there, Jake?"

"Why, I bet he's a pistol, that's what I bet."

"Old Jake here, I understand he's something of a handyman."

That sort of thing.

Father generally responded with a warm chortle; sometimes he'd add a "yes, indeed."

I would linger back in the pantry and stew. Just whom did they think they were talking to? What sort of a home did they believe the Senator to be running?

Don't get me wrong: I understand the way men are. More so than you may believe, I do. The business of politics is an ugly one. To get things done you need to interact with all manner of men; therefore, over the years we'd seen our share of scoundrels and buffoons pass through those front doors. In all fairness, this little bit of teasing was mild compared to some of the crudeness displayed in this house over the years, though only recently, it seemed, had it come to be directed at my father.

Granted, in some of your lesser homes, homes where the staff commits the common error of familiarity, one would expect this sort of behavior. We knew of a situation in Upper Georgetown where the headman took to calling certain guests by their first names, had been known to offer advice even on the intimate details of running a household. One heard rumors that, coincidence or otherwise, this home wanted in all other manner of standards, as in the way a spotted tablecloth makes one wonder about the cleanliness of food preparation. Over time, all but a certain second-rate kind of family declined invitations to this residence. This is what happens, you see, and thus my conundrum. Father's standards had never been more than pristine. One would not find him ever in any more than the most perfunctory conversations with the Senator's guests. He never contributed a single word to the interactions in these rooms: no clever bon mots at his employer's expense, never even a cleared throat at the sometimes provocative discussions he witnessed. So it wasn't clear to me how he had suddenly become part of the joke. Maybe it was that he had aged. Maybe there's something about an older man that invites this sort of sniggering behavior on the part of seemingly civilized men. Whatever the case, this change in the atmosphere distressed me to no end. I told Father of my concerns.

"You simply must remind the Senator that he should discourage that sort of foolish talk. It's unseemly. I've got half a mind to go in there myself and put a stop to it."

Father waved his hand to indicate he thought me the foolish one. "You'll do nothing of the kind. Step back to the kitchen, please, and tell Flora to ready the savories. I'll come back for them."

I stood there with my hands on my hips until he scooted me along, much the way a conductor signals his orchestra to stand.

I stomped down the hall, a behavior I knew he didn't care for. I had another surprise in store for him, as well.

While Cook arranged the trays of canapés, I made my way to the bathroom to check my appearance. The same little-girl-sized door still beckoned there in the wainscoting, but I'd become much too big a girl to fit it. At fifteen, I'd already grown to half a head taller than my father. I had no figure to speak of (and never would as far as that goes), but I was clearly presentable, save for the childish braids hanging in front of each shoulder. For as long as I could remember, the simple braids had hung there. In a busy household they were the simplest response to a motherless girl-child's hair. I wound the braids behind my head into the neat bun that in the future would become for me something of a trademark. From the pantry I retrieved a clean service apron. Combined with my school uniform, the fancy lace of the apron lent me a most professional mien.

"I don't know what you about to do, missy, but I know your daddy not gonna like it."

I ignored Cook and picked up the two silver trays. I set my face with a rigid but not unpleasant demeanor. Just let one of those men speak to me the wrong way. I had no idea what I would say, but I knew it would set them straight.

My father's back was turned when I emerged from the pantry with the trays. As would be expected, the men hardly acknowledged my presence. Father spun around and with his eyes flashed a warning at me, which I ignored. I handed him the other tray and set about my task.

"Sir?" I'd whisper, bending to each gentleman's place and proffering my tray of tidbits. With the other hand I'd offer a clean napkin for messy fingers.

I must have been quite full of myself that day, because when I arrived at the Senator's seat, I even met his eye, something one never did in my chosen role for the afternoon. This close I could see the network of crow's feet that radiated across his temples.

"Senator?" I whispered, presenting him the tray. (You, a man who can't even keep order in his own parlor!)

He surprised me by greeting my hard eyes with delight. He waved off the tray and rose at his place. He placed a proprietary hand on my shoulder.

"Gentlemen. We have quite a special honor this afternoon. Delivering this delightful repast we have none other than the lady of the house. Miss Matilda Housewright. Our Jake's daughter."

To my horror, I received a round of applause.

"Ma'am," many of the gentlemen murmured. A few rose partway from their seats.

"Miss Housewright, everyone," he repeated, and propelled me forward.

I didn't know what to do, so I curtsied. The men nodded their heads in return. Many had that look on their face that parents do at kindergarten pageants, that isn't-she-adorable look. Adorable had not been my intention, and I'm sure I had turned the color of ripe plums. (Ah, the trials of the fair-skinned woman!) I couldn't see it, but I just knew that the Senator was behind me winking at my father with pride. The look on Father's face said that he was.

I have no memory of doing so, but I know that I transferred my remaining canapés to my father's tray, handed him the balance of the napkins, and strode from the room. I went back to our carriage house and cried for the rest of the afternoon.

When Father came in later that evening, he placed a covered plate on the table where we only rarely shared our meals.

"Flora said you didn't eat."

I didn't respond. I waited for the explosion I felt simmering just beneath his surface. Or maybe this time he would go directly to the silent treatment.

"I have been asked to convey a message to you from the Senator."

I inhaled to steel myself for my dressing-down. Here it came: the velvet claw. Men such as my father and the Senator had a way of using the gentlest language you could imagine to reduce you to the size of a flea.

"The Senator would like you to know that he was most charmed by your appearance today in his parlor. He hopes that this afternoon portends many similar ones."

I waited for the "however." It didn't come.

"Is that it?" I asked.

"That would be it." Father set about the usual evening routines of his not-so-usual evenings off. He placed a paper by his lounge chair, moved the hassock nearby for his feet. He prepared himself a tall glass of sweet iced tea. He reached to turn on the radio. A low hum filled the room as the tubes warmed themselves. I followed all this, my mouth somewhat agape.

"So?" I asked.

"What do you want, Matilda?"

"That's all? That's all you have to say about today?"

"What I have to say is no longer an issue. Is it?" To ask that question he had stopped and looked me right in the eye.

"It is to me," I replied.

"I appreciate your solicitude, daughter, but, alas, there are others involved in the matter."

"The Senator? He's not here. I'm asking you."

"But you already know what I think. What I thought. You did what you wanted to do anyway."

"I only wanted to show those men I wasn't afraid of them. That's all."

"Those men. Who hadn't even known you existed. And now they do. So you made your point."

"And now you're angry at me. I was only trying to show you that I could help—"

Father cut me short, rising from his seat, raising his voice to a level I'd never heard. "I know what you can do. Do you think I'm blind or stupid? I had my limits. You knew what they were. No daughter of mine would be on display out front. For any reason. Ever. That was my limit. How do you think I felt seeing you out there?"

I sobbed, miserable at his rage. "I thought you'd be proud."

He reached up and gathered me up in his arms. "Of course I was, honey. You know I was. I was proud, I always am. My Queenie."

We talked some more. Father told me about "how things were." This is a speech that all parents in service give their children at some point. The essence of the speech concerns the dream they all have of a better life out there for the next generation.

I protested. "But I'm not ashamed of what we do."

"I know that. And maybe if I were my daddy, I'd feel different. But we are a dying breed, Matilda. In another generation or two, our kind of world will be gone. I'm just afraid that there's nothing here for you to aspire to."

I already knew that what he was saying was the truth. Households that had pared back during the early hard years did not seem to be staffing up now that the economy was improving. Whether it was the case that people wouldn't live in, or that families preferred more privacy, many of the newcomers relied on caterers, day maids, limousine services. Just like my father, many of the traditional retainers were gotten up in the years. When they died, that would be the end.

"For now," I said, "I'm here. So I might as well do what I can, yes?"

"I know my Queenie, and you didn't look too happy out there today."

I looked back on my embarrassment, tried to locate its source. I somehow couldn't admit to my father that I had hated being looked at by those men.

"Maybe we can just forget today," I suggested.

Father snorted a laugh. "You and I can forget it, but I'm afraid your charms have already worked their magic."

Tell him "no," I started to say, and then I remembered the way things worked between the two of them.

By now the air around us filled with the sound of horns as the radio blared a music show that Father loved to listen to. I sat at the small table across the room from him and picked at my cold supper.

I have never appreciated being boxed in. At school, when the teacher would ask if we children preferred to do our geography or a history lesson, I saw through the ruse. This was the illusion of choice. What if we'd preferred to study math at that moment or to repair to the playground for a running game?

I thought through every angle that I could, and no matter how I worked the logic, it always came back to the Senator's words and the way my father reported them to me. So that was that, then.

"Fine," I said, standing over my father's reading chair, startling him. He looked confused.

"Fine. Tell Himself that I'm generally busy in the afternoons with my studies, but I'd be happy to serve his breakfast."

I headed away to my bedroom, but turned to add one more critical detail.

"When I'm available."

Father put his hand to his brow and shook his head the way he did when Cook tried to explain why the vinegar was in the oven.

Yes, I'd serve him his meal, all right, but I didn't have to be nice about it.

Do you spot a contradiction here? Absolutely not. Being professional means being pleasant. Pleasant and nice are not the same thing.

On most mornings, the Senator took his breakfast right at seven, which meant there was plenty of time for me to serve him before I left for school. He preferred meat, either ham or bacon, and some sort of warm fruit on his tray; therefore, that's what everyone in the house ate. (In my own personal hell, the devil will serve stewed prunes.) Cook had a handy touch with quick breads, so the kitchen always had a cozy smell about it. At least there had been that blessing.

Father and the Senator went over the day's agenda before he left for the capital: the who, the what, the when, the how much, the anything and everything that concerned the house. Though he'd never admit it, my new role in the household was something of a boon to my father. He and his employer were able to have their little conference each day sans Father excusing himself to check on the biscuits. It was my misfortune that the first voice I heard every day was often that of the Senator, with all of its mid-continent, low-budget, folksy charm.

"I been getting a bad feeling off this old boy from up in Michigan, Jake. You know what I mean?"

Father responded, "It's been reported that the Speaker's wife has banned him from her residence."

"Is that a fact? Well, it's about to be some banning going on in other places if I can help it. Tell me what you hear about how he likes to spend his evenings."

This is the sort of blather I would interrupt with my platters of French toast or shirred eggs.

"I've the Senator's breakfast," I would announce, in my flattest, most noncommittal tone. Father would minutely raise his left eyebrow to signal that I walked the border of a tone that he didn't care for.

"Matilda! Morning, sweetie," the Senator cheered. "Bring them victuals on."

"I'm not your sweetie," I wanted to say.

I had practiced setting plates on the table in a way just this side of impertinent. A crisp snap, not quite a slam. That became my signature.

"Can I get you anything else?" I'd inquire.

"Oh, no thank you, honey. This'll be fine, just fine."

I'd sidle back to the kitchen and roll my eyes at Cook. Butter wouldn't have melted in my mouth.

Things would be quiet for about fifteen minutes, while he and my father talked. Then I'd hear my name yelled.

"Matilda! Coffee!"

This was before I began delivering a silver coffee service to the table. I'd bring it in right after his plate. A big believer in personal-attention service, Father hated the "self-service" nature of my innovation. Every afternoon, I polished that urn to a luster, and this seemed to assuage him to a certain extent.

In an odd change of character, my father withheld his judgment over my breakfast chores. He seemed content to allow me to fail or succeed on my own merits. One morning, feeling quite self-assured, I even delivered a cup to where he sat reviewing the upcoming day. Father reddened and then pushed the cup away with a mumbled protest. The Senator stilled his hand.

"Thank you, darling," the Senator said in his sugariest voice, and then personally filled Father's cup with the warm brew.

I curtsied and excused myself from the room.

In hindsight, even I view this as a bridge too far—my father's cup, that is. One just doesn't eat with them. I'm sorry, but that's the way it is. It's not that one wouldn't be welcomed. Though this is rare, it does happen. There are those of the he's-just-a-member-of-the-family school who when overcome by their liberal fellow feeling, can only but insist that "Rochester" join them for a meal. This has always been a mistake. No one is comfortable.

Enough said. Except as the weeks went past, I noticed Father actually relaxing with his coffee, that he and the Senator took turns refreshing each other's cups. It felt like this had been going on for decades, and even after I relinquished my morning responsibilities, even after we'd all left the District of Columbia, the tradition had taken root and would remain a part of the men's daily routine for the rest of their years together.

Soon enough I'd run through my entire repertoire of stunts. Nothing much I dared attempt got even a rise out of the two of them. What had begun for me as an annoying challenge had deteriorated into simply annoying. We became a perverse parody of a family, where each member knew the routine and did his part. I no longer even pretended a friendly greeting, even though the Senator, ever the hale fellow well met, at the very least had a cheery wave for me. Looking back, I imagine that as men who spent their lives in the company of other men, the two of them hadn't a clue what to do with a gawky female adolescent. On one of those topsy-turvy mornings when nothing went as expected, I even snatched the Senator's plate from him midbite. No mischief had been intended; in fact, it had just been one of those days.

"I'm late for my streetcar," I called, and then, realizing what I'd done, readied myself for the coming tirade at my rudeness. Instead, through the swinging door I heard gales of laughter from the old coots. Cook looked at me over her glasses the way she always did when she thought I'd lost my mind.

And then I turned sixteen.

Increasingly few in number are persons who remember the time before the endless "teenager" (a marketing invention, as long as we're on the subject, of the self-serving men in the media industries). A decade of idleness, frivolity, and profligate consumption: we couldn't have imagined such a paradise in my day! Yes, of course there was that small and privileged minority—Walton Hunnicutt Jr. as an example—who floated through their teen years, cosseted in preparatory academies and summer camps (although of the young Hunnicutt's exploits I can only attest through hearsay and gossip, as we had left the Senator's employ long before his prime teen years). The rest of us worked. Remember that in the first half of the century, an eighth-grade education was considered an accomplishment (and, for the record, in most cases would stand up well against most of the high schools here lately, and quite a few universities, as well). You became an adult when you got a job, and for a lot of young people, for example those who grew up on farms, adulthood would have arrived long before sixteen. It is known that as many as a million young people of my generation simply left home—rode the rails, following their hearts and rumor and fortune, and I can understand this, if you must know. It was hard for any of us to know what to do.

For Negroes of a certain class and of certain breeding there were expectations. (I hesitate to raise here the specter of "the talented tenth." I have always had, as did my father, problems with this notion, my own having to do with Dr. DuBois's solid faith in his percentage—and let me assure you, at least according to Father, who had occasion to debate this directly with the man, Dr. DuBois was quite rigid in his construction.) "Betterment" was the quality sought by all, a step up the ladder of miracle that is America. We were each expected to do our parts. At Dunbar High School this message was as much a part of the curriculum as were mathematics, chemistry, and Latin. Our teachers, men and women who had bettered themselves, pointed us daily toward the paths to success.

For women those paths were still fairly proscribed, and for black women in particular the roads were narrower still. Schoolmistress. Nurse. Domestic. Two jobs I had no interest in and one I was, frankly, already qualified to lead classes in. And, yes, of course there were those Negro women who were already making inroads across a spectrum of new career options, and, believe me, the more progressive of our teachers made sure we knew their names as well as the details of their struggles. These speeches were made often enough in front of my desk, directed at me, or at least that had been my impression at the time. I was the class star, which I admit with no shame or modesty. That's what I was. It was expected, clearly, that I would "blaze a new path" of some kind, to quote my teachers directly as to the expectations.

Unbeknownst to my teachers—kind and well-meaning people, all of them, and may God rest their souls—their tales of perseverance and single-mindedness had the exact opposite effect on me than they were surely intended to. I would hear, for example, the story of Dr. So-and-so, who graduated at the head of her class at X, Y, or Z medical college, how she had been made to listen to an anatomy lecture from a chair in the hallway because the professor couldn't abide her presence in his lecture hall. Or how not even the patients at the hospital clinic trusted her touch, how she gained her hands-on experience walking the back roads of the South, treating men and women who were too poor to know that her gender was an issue. Our heroes and heroines lived in dank basements, scrubbed toilets in exchange for tuition, were subject to every manner of humiliation.

"And you have been called to the challenge as well, young ladies and gentlemen, and shall most certainly rise to the occasion!" And we would stand and sing "Lift Every Voice," and a prayer would be offered and we would march from the auditorium, our spines rigid with resolve.

And, I would think to myself, Well, Matilda, maybe not. Maybe not you. I knew myself quite well, as you should have surmised by now. I was not a woman raised to live in a hovel, be spat upon, or suffer indignities of any kind. I wouldn't have it. And call me vain or spoiled if you will (although I would challenge you to locate another spoiled young woman who worked her fingers raw polishing the household silver). I'm just being realistic. I had been born at the wrong time. This was something that I had known since I was a child.

I needed another plan.

And I have already anticipated your next argument. Signing my life away to some man quite simply hadn't been an option. I am a plain woman. It's as easy as that. All the Max Factor in the world wouldn't change that. Yes, of course a few of the young men did become friendly with me, there at the high school, and there was the son of a family who lived-in up closer to Dupont Circle and who would come by the back gate and chat with me. But there's one thing about being an intelligent woman—you tend to see more quickly through the ruse. I was Matilda, the girl who could factor an equation and who had more than a passing acquaintance with Latin grammar. The Matilda who found a fresh rose on her desk or a mushy note slipped into the pages of her rhetoric book: She was another girl. We shared classes over the years. She would look at me with pity, that is, at least until the look I returned in her direction suggested she save her compassion for those who wanted it.

If I could tell you more of how I felt and what I remembered of that time, I would, but, frankly, I have put it in my past.

Mostly I recall being moody and unfocused and ill-tempered. For days I would lose myself in large and maudlin Victorian novels, imagining my own name had been Tess or Dorothea or Jane. Mr. Thackeray hadn't written one word I'd not read twice.

Breakfast remained as routine as washing one's teeth. Serving their eggs and toast (yes, Father had even come to eating with the Senator) was just something I did every morning, nothing more. Until the morning when the Senator stayed my hand after I served his plate.

"Matilda, darling, old Jake here and I wanted you to be the first to know."

I snatched my hand from his grip.

"As of January 1939, I will no longer be a member of the United States Senate." He announced that as if I were an assembled audience of radio correspondents.

I looked at my father across the table from him. He nodded along with the speech as if extreme wisdom were being uttered.

"Okay," I said, shrugging. I'd long since lost any interest in the palace intrigue that made up the usual interaction between these two. More and more over the last years, the two of them huddled in deep conversation, often joined by Mr. Montgomery. Whether the subject was the troubles in Europe or one of the Senator's colleagues' halitosis, it didn't matter. They huddled and whispered and finger-pointed and made the kinds of disgusting noises males are known to make. They reminded me of schoolboys with a not-very-dirty dirty joke.

"Yes, ma'am. I'm retiring and we are all headed back home."

That stopped me: that *we*.

"Home?" I asked.

My father cleared his throat. "We're going back to the

Senator's hometown and setting this whole operation up back there. Isn't that something?" He said that with a big smile. As if what I'd heard had been some sort of good news.

"What did you say to that?" I asked, though his previous statement had already made it clear what he'd said. His eyes suggested that I'd better remember where I was, but I couldn't care less about demeanor.

"Well," I prodded. "What did you say?"

"He said 'yes,' " the Senator said, and then laughed his broad laugh, to break the tension, I'm sure he hoped. "Hell, it was Jake's idea. He said, 'It's time for this old dog to set on the porch for a spell.' And that's what we both intend to do."

"Is that true?" I asked. "So we're leaving here. Just like that. And you weren't even going to tell me."

"Umph." The Senator smacked his lips. "Eva done knocked herself out today. Matilda, honey, get your daddy one of these corn muffins. They're mighty tasty." He fingered some crumbs from his dish.

"Get it yourself," I said. I slammed out of the dining room.

I stormed to the carriage house. I could hear my father in my wake.

"Young lady," he called, but there was little chance he'd catch me. He'd slowed down even more around this time.

"Now, see here," he said, coming in behind me. "I'll not have one moment of this—"

"Don't talk to me," I ordered. I gathered my schoolbooks and my coat and started out the door. But I was not done. I came back.

"Just tell me this: You're allowing yourself to be dragged away from the only home you've known, and you don't even care."

"Oh, Queenie. Of course I care. But everybody has to—"

"What about Martin? What's he going to do?"

"Martin's a young man. He's ready to be on his own. Honey, I *have* thought about this. I know that this is the right thing."

I stormed out the door again. Again I returned.

"What will be settled on you, then?" I asked.

He looked puzzled.

"The settlement. What do you get for uprooting yourself and your family and moving halfway across the country?"

Uncharacteristically, Father shrugged. "I get to keep doing what we've been doing. Seems like a good deal to me."

"Ha," I scoffed. "And what about your dream? What about that little house you had your eye on?"

Again, the uncharacteristic shrug. "Dreams change," he said. "When you reach our age, you begin to—"

I held up my hand and stopped him. "That man," I said, voice laced with fire, finger pointed toward the main house. "That man owes you. You get in there and you ask for what you have coming. If you don't, I will."

He did not respond, so I added one more grace note.

"I mean it," I said.

In front of me my father suddenly seemed shaken and frail. I felt bad for my petulance. I went up to him and caressed his leathery and tired old face. I'd begun noticing more and more the patches of white bristle his razor would miss.

"We'll talk after school, okay? But I really do mean it. You worked hard here for a lot of years. I think you should ask for what you deserve. Okay?"

He nodded, though I had no sense what he meant by that nod.

When I returned in the late afternoon, he sat at the table in front of his house ledger. He seemed out of place: he was almost never here in the afternoon. He looked bedraggled, the way he sometimes did when worrying over the details of an important luncheon. His fingers were smudged with graphite from the pencil, from erasing.

"I've been going over some figures," he told me. "It looks like if we maybe lower our sights, we just maybe could afford us a little old place with a couple of rooms. Things are cheaper out there, I hear. We just might do okay."

He sounded defeated, heartbroken, though I could tell he tried to mask it for me. Those figures in that book he'd gone over a thousand times in his head, every night before sleeping, I was sure. What could they possibly represent? A couple of thousand dollars he'd squirreled away in a bank? Enough, if we were very lucky, to maybe buy a three-room "shotgun" shack in the poorest enclave of the Senator's city. The walls like paper. The whole place riddled with vermin of every kind.

I knew the house he dreamed of, because I had dreamed this same house myself. We'd never need a place as large and ostentatious as the Senator's. We were not fancy people. But a nice house. Two stories, with an elegant if not too grand stairwell. On the second floor we'd have three bedrooms, one for each of us. A nice bath for all of us to share. On the main floor, a large parlor to entertain in, a dining room where you'd be proud to serve a meal. And in back, a kitchen big enough to move around inside and to prepare a proper meal, and I'd tuck off of that a small sunny nook for breakfast and for Father to read his paper. For me, I'd build a window seat, and from there I'd watch the seasons of our garden. Not as grand a garden as here in Washington, but every bit as gorgeous, every day a show.

I kissed the top of Father's head. "We'll do fine," I encouraged. I averted my eyes from his pathetic figuring.

Fine, indeed. We'd do more than fine if I had anything to do with it.

It was hard to find a time with the Senator when my father wasn't underfoot, but I waited until one day the following week when he had gone off to confer with a florist about the arrangements he'd require to celebrate the Senator's retirement.

"I need to see you," I said. I'd let myself into the man's study, something I'd never done in all my life—on fear of my life.

He beckoned me to a seat in front of his desk, but I chose to remain standing. Not a man for small talk, the Senator cut right to the heart of the matter.

"So you still got that bee in your butt about our upcoming adventure."

I stared him down. "I'll respect my father's decision. I wish others respected him as much as I do."

The Senator lowered his glasses to the desk and leaned up in his chair, pointing to me the way I imagine he did to younger legislators who were stupid enough to cross him.

"You listen here, little lady. Ain't nobody on this Earth respects that man more than I do. Anybody in this house or anybody in this whole city will tell you that's the truth."

"Then you need to give him what he wants."

He blew out his lips in exasperation. "You always was a hardheaded thing. Ever since you was a little girl. He told you, and I told you, and now I'm telling you again. This all is Jake's idea."

I smirked. They always think they know us. They always think we can't see right through them.

"My father wants a house," I said.

"And we gonna get us a house. A good house. I got some boys out there already scouting us a fine place in the West End. Plenty of room for all of us. Your daddy will love it."

"My father wants his own house."

The Senator leaned back. He bit his lower lip as if he were thinking that over.

"Jake never said—"

"He wouldn't. Not to you."

The expression on the faces of those not used to being interrupted is always priceless.

"I see," he said, and he pondered it some more. He rocked in his chair, cleared his throat a few times. Nervousness, perhaps.

"You owe him," I added. Something I imagined would further his thinking.

The Senator derided that idea with a nasal snort.

"You do," I insisted.

"Looka here. I took care of him. I took care of all of y'all. I took care of you good. So don't you come up here in my house talking about what I owe and don't owe, you hear me?"

"You owe him." I pronounced each word crisp and clear and solid. Just in case he'd missed my point.

He rose from his chair. He came around his desk and stood in front of me the way men do when squaring off for a fight. I stood my ground. He looked me up and down the length of my body and he set his face in a leer. He laughed a nasty quiet laugh.

"Houses cost," he said. He looked me up and down again.

"You owe him."

Another nasty laugh. He was close enough I could smell the afternoon cocktail on him.

"You something else, you know that?"

I did not respond.

"All right, then. Your daddy wants a house. Or so *you* say."

"A house. That *you* owe him."

Which prompted another laugh, this time a long one.

"And what, little lady, are you willing to do for the good of the order?"

I felt his hand on my hair.

The more sophisticated among you saw this coming, and as for those with delicate sensibilities, look away if you want. Sigh a little if that helps. Save your horror or outrage for others, however. Your pity, too. I don't want it. I won't be your fragile maiden. I graduated at the top of my class. I've read Virgil in the Latin. If I had to I could kill you with my bare hands. I wouldn't think twice about doing so.

This is not a story about a victim.

This is a story about how your government works.

Beneath the checks and balances, it looks a lot like everything else in life. You decide what you want, you find out the cost, you dicker a little bit. Then you make the best deal you can. If you can't make a deal, you walk away.

I did not walk away.

My father lived by a credo. He believed that if you worked hard and if you always did your best, you would be rewarded in the end.

The people who run your government suggest you read the fine print. The end is now. You take what you can and you take it whenever you can. These people: they are as unsentimental as starved wild dogs.

When you learn this lesson as a young girl listening at doors, you perhaps tend to be less romantic than your fellow Americans. Rather than cynical, I prefer to see myself as a pragmatist. As opposed to lying there "and thinking of England," I lay there trying not to wretch. His disgusting pink thing and that shrivelly paper-dry pale skin. God's cruelest joke: old age.

We made our deal. I did my service. I left. Longtime observer that I was of our nation's politics, I never doubted he'd keep his word.

My father. Oh, that dear, dear, foolish poor man. He never did figure it out, the way things worked in this country. He never appreciated the difference between being wanted and being needed. He thought they loved him.

He lived for the kind rub on the shoulder from a familiar face or for the moment that same face would turn to his boss and say, "Good old Jake!"

He disdained the unctuous, condescending "thank yous" of those who didn't understand that he was only doing his job, or the greasy dollar bills that some of the more ignorant men who visited the house would press upon him, as if he were a beggar or the bathroom attendant at some third-rate supper club downtown. Insulted, he stuffed that money away in a strongbox where he stored the family's important papers, never once deigning to spend even a penny of it. Thousands of dollar bills. Enough money for the home of his dreams.

Pride: both a glory and a sin. I guess it depends on your perspective.

In the summer of 1939, days before the invasion of Poland, moving trucks paid for by the United States Congress delivered the Housewright family to the door of a well-furnished, freshly painted house in the Senator's city. The Senator greeted us at the door and placed into my father's hands a key and a lien-free deed. His dream house, bought and paid for.

Every morning a driver came by to deliver my father to the Senator's place. Who knows what the two of them did all day long? Surely it was both more and less important than either of them imagined. Their daily meetings continued every day until my father could no longer rise from his sickbed.

Back when I crawled out of that other bed, that same one I'd watched my mother change in the predawn gloom one morning long ago, I dared the bastard to show his face at my father's funeral. Then I dared him not to.

This is what I believe: One's plan is the thing that happens; one looks back and there it was, as if it had been written in stone, but it never is. The plan is what happens. This house is what happened to me: 4973 Woodlawn.

I got this place for my father. He passed it my way, which is exactly as it should be. Out behind our home there is a garden as fine as any in America. On the interior, each room has been appointed in good taste with your every comfort in mind. Trust me: if you came here you would never want to leave—as I myself have not.

Ladies and gentlemen, this is not a gracious world. It has not been so for quite a long time. Chances are good that you have already discovered this for yourself, but court not discouragement, dear friends. There is grace to be had in this world. Real grace. The real thing. It is here for you.

If you want it badly enough . . . If you know where to look . . .

It is here. Believe me. It's the one thing I know to be true.

My Most Remarkable Boy

. . .

I

1986

Auntie Matilda had three floors. A basement, an upstairs, and a regular floor with a kitchen and a place to watch the flowers. Jake liked to climb from one floor to another floor to another. Be careful on the steps. That was one thing Auntie Matilda said. Auntie Matilda also said Jake should sit still sometimes. Auntie Matilda didn't have a television.

"Come help your auntie with these petunias."

Jake laughed. Petunias was a funny word. There was a cartoon on TV with Petunia on it. You couldn't watch that at Auntie Matilda's. Jake picked the brown curled-up flowers off their green stems. They felt crinkled and slimy, like coloring paper at school when you spit on it. Jake found a ladybug.

"Can I keep it?"

"You could. I think she would be happier living here with her friends."

Auntie Matilda touched Jake's hair. Auntie Matilda was always touching his hair. Sometimes the boys and girls at school touched his hair, too. It was okay, if they asked permission first. Jake's hair was the color of the shiny brass knobs on Auntie Matilda's doors. Jake liked brass. He put the ladybug in his pocket. He would feed her some cereal. He hoped ladybugs liked cereal. They did.

"You are my most remarkable boy," Matilda said.

Jake thought this remarkable thing must be pretty good because Matilda always smiled when she said it.

"Do you have any snails over here?" Those snail shells were something, weren't they?

"There's one or two around here, but you can only see them at special times. Like right after a summer shower."

"We could sure use some rain, right, Auntie?"

Matilda laughed. Jake liked Matilda's laugh. Matilda's laugh was like the songs the music teacher played at school where notes floated through the air like the songs of birds.

"Let's get out of this sun. More and more I hear them say that it's bad for you. Me, I've always had the good sense to wear a hat."

Jake wondered who "them" was.

"I've got a hat," he said. "Teacher says I can't wear my hat in school." Jake had five hats. He had a Cubs hat and a Cardinals hat and a Rams hat and a couple more hats that he couldn't remember. Matilda had a big old funny hat, the color of corn flakes—the kind of hat the people on the rice bags wore at

Grandpa Marty's work. Jake liked going to Grandpa Marty's work. You got food there. Some of it you didn't know what it was and it tasted funny. Grandpa Marty was Matilda's brother. Everybody knew that.

"You bring your hat next week. We don't want you to get burnt."

Auntie Matilda's face did not get burnt 'cause she had a hat. Her skin was sort of pink and sort of brown and sort of the color of cereal. Auntie Matilda was almost the same color as Jake's mom. Jake's mom was white. Everybody knew that, too. Jake wondered if Matilda's mom was also white, but he didn't ask her that. People did not talk about those things. Nice people didn't. His mom said that, and his dad said that, too. They did not talk to Jake about those things.

Jake's skin is the color of caramel corn. The kind that you get at the shopping mall, not the kind in the box.

"When your father was a little boy, do you know what his favorite food was?"

"Cheeseburgers?" Jake answered. Sometimes if you said the food that you really wanted, adults would give that to you.

"Roderick loved tuna fish sandwiches. Or maybe that was his . . . Anyway, I made a big bowl every week and it was always gone."

Jake liked tuna sandwiches, too. He liked sausage pizza and macaroni and cheese and tacos, but not the kind with the soggy shells. He would eat corn, but not creamed corn, and green beans sometimes if he had to, and broccoli if it had cheese sauce on it. Cheese sauce, not cheese. And applesauce was okay. He also liked all kinds of ice cream and chocolate cupcakes with vanilla frosting. His mom made those. He did not eat celery, grapefruit, liver, or any meat with blood coming out of it.

"You finish that and then we'll go look at pictures."

"You eat your sandwich, too." Sometimes Auntie Matilda just let her food sit. Daddy said to tell him if that happened. Daddy said Aunt Matilda had to eat more. Daddy brought the groceries and fussed at her.

Auntie Matilda took a big bite. Jake smiled to let her know she did a good thing.

"That is my father and that is the Senator." Auntie Matilda showed Jake the pictures. She kept the pictures in a big scrapbook, and she kept the scrapbook wrapped in soft cloth and hidden in a big piece of furniture in her living room. Jake had seen the pictures before, but that was okay. He didn't mind. He liked sitting on the couch and watching the big pages of the book turn. They were like a secret he and his auntie had all to themselves. Jake's mom and dad didn't have any pictures. Or maybe Jake's mom and dad had pictures and they kept them wrapped up and hidden just like Auntie Matilda did. He should go look for those pictures one of these days. That's something he should do. Sometimes Auntie Matilda fell asleep and Jake got to turn the pages himself. They were heavy. People were not in color back in the olden days.

"I get tired in the afternoon, Jacob. Some days I lie down right at this time of day."

Jake liked nap time. No more nap time since kindergarten. They just kept making it harder. That's what Jake's father said.

"We could go to the store. I got five dollars."

"You have five dollars. And why do you have five dollars?"

"Daddy gave me. Just 'cause."

Auntie Matilda rolled her eyes around in her head. Jake's mama always told him that was rude.

"Your father apparently has enough money to burn a wet mule."

"That's just what Grandpa Marty said. Mama says that Christ loves even the least among us."

And that one time, Jake's father said that Christ would love the least among us to get a job just like the rest of us, and then his mother started to say something back, but then the little girls started to fuss. Katrice and Katrina. Those were the little girls. They were okay, but they liked to break Jake's things. No one said anything because they were little girls. Jake's mom and dad had funny fights. Not real fights, but for fun. He could tell. They didn't happen much. No one was ever home, except for Helena. Helena was the au pair. Jake hated Helena. She talked funny from another country and made up rules.

"You pay attention to your mother. Katie is a smart lady."

Jake thought his mom was smart, too. And pretty. Jake's mom was white. Everybody knew that. He would like to see her more. And his dad. Everyone was busy. His dad said it was the eighties. That's the way it was.

"You hold on to your riches, Jacob. We'll go to the store another time, okay?"

Jake said okay. He didn't think they would ever go to the store. Auntie Matilda didn't go anywhere.

"We'll just sit here and be quiet for a while."

Being quiet was good. Jake liked running all around, but Jake liked being quiet sometimes, too. Jake snuggled next to Auntie Matilda. Auntie Matilda was skinny and warm. Jake liked all the quiet. No Katrice and no Katrina and no Helena and no karate class and no arts and crafts club and no Jack and Jill. A person could just sit here and take a nap. Just like back in the good old days, just like back in kindergarten.

Everything was creamy.

"You're my most remarkable boy ever."

Matilda said that sometimes. Being remarkable was a good thing. Everyone knew that.

II

1995

Do this, Jake. Don't do that, Jake. Take this class, but don't take that section. "*We*" take section two. Join this club. Them guys is lame. Stay away from kids who wear black.

You've got "potential," Jake. A mind is a terrible thing to waste. Huh? What was this potential shit? Jake had boatloads, they said. He's looking to unload, cheap. Potentially bored. Potentially crazy. Most likely to be a serial killer. Buy me a gun and then duck real quick.

Jake pictured all the lips flapping in his face the same way he imagined babies saw them—oversized heads making loud indecipherable noises. That's why babies laughed. If he thought about it that way, it was almost funny. Almost.

They hated it when you sat around and thought about things. Them: the other "they." Not the babies. Jake knew this to be true.

"What's going on in that head of yours, Jake?"

People said things like that to him.

Or, "Earth to Jake." Who came up with that great line? Jake had a score to settle with that dude.

Or, "Are you in there, Jake?" Of course he was in there. Where else would he be? People were dumb.

"He's a growing boy. Teenagers need lots of fuel." That was the sort of thing the Reverend Mom said. That's what she'd tell his dad when Jake sat on the couch eating Doritos and staring out the window. "He's just figuring out the world's problems, aren't you, Jake?"

Right, Mom. Usually he was thinking about whether there were any more Doritos in the cupboard when this bag ran out. Hopefully the nacho cheese kind and not the plain ones. Jake hated the plain ones, though even they would do in a pinch.

Jake could swear that sometimes his mind was an absolute blank. Like the white marker board before Advanced Algebra started writing on it with her blue and green pens. What was that woman's name? She had one of those names with too many consonants in it, one of those names that sounded like someone hawking up her breakfast. Jake called her Advanced Algebra. Guess what he called his World History teacher? Jake was bad with names. Maybe they were married. Excuse me, Advanced Algebra, he'd say. I don't get this equation. She'd point to a page in the book. That's what teachers did. Teachers were there to point to the right page in the book where the picture showed you the answer in living color. If you looked at the picture long enough, things became crystal clear. It always happened. Someday soon school would be on the computer. Teachers would be locked away in closets, alongside vinyl record albums and non–self-cleaning ovens. Everyone knew this.

"Whatever you do, Aunt Matilda, don't ask me what I'm going to be when I grow up."

Jake spent Saturdays helping his aunt Matilda. She was about five thousand years old and lived in the city—Crips territory, he thinks. Jake never wore red.

"I thought you were going to be a fireman."

Was she kidding? You couldn't tell with Matilda. She went off sometimes—to Happyland. That's what Jake called the place she went to. Sometimes she waltzed around the room and hummed. Sometimes she called him David. She petted his curls and called them a bush. David was an uncle or something who died a long time ago. Jake never knew him. Jake liked the whole concept of Happyland. He would like to have a Happyland of his own to go to. Maybe that's where he went when his mind went blank. Not that it was really blank. Usually there were Doritos there, or girls, or babies. Jake liked the idea of babies. Babies were nosy and smelled great. Matilda, he thought, sometimes forgot that he was not one.

"Little boys want to be firemen, Auntie. People my age are the ones who start the fires they put out." Jake was fifteen.

"You've always had interesting ideas, Jacob. Squeeze the water from the vermiculite, please. We'll repot these violets now."

Aunt Matilda was forever repotting this or trimming that. Sometimes in the summer she'd make you spend all day out there clipping and snapping and raking and hoeing. (Hoeing. There was a great word. Get me that hoe, Auntie would say. And stop your snickering!) The girls never came to do gardening. They got to go help Grandpa Marty in his kitchen, and better for them. That Katrina. Asked her to pass you the butter, she said, "I'll break a nail." "Break this," Jake said, and gave her the finger. "This is a Christian home. We'll have none of that," said the Reverend Mom. Jake stuck his arms out and hung his head like he was on the cross.

"Jake just needs a creative outlet." The Reverend Mom was always saying shit like that.

"Ever thought about opening a laundry?" Matilda said. She was a hoot sometimes—a one-liner for every situation, even for wringing hot water from this brown crap she plants her plants in. Plants are everywhere here.

"I said don't ask me about that. You promised."

"Me! I promised? My, but I'm forgetful these days. I recall as you said something about don't ask you about careers and I held my tongue. Poor Jacob. Who's making your life miserable this time?"

Everyone, that was who. Big Rod. The Reverend Mom. Advanced Algebra. Computer Science. Every other sophomore in the United States of America. What, if you didn't get in line for some fancy job by the time you were seventeen, you'd spend the rest of your life shaking a Starbucks cup outside the bus depot? (And what was wrong with that? It wasn't like people had to give you money. The only downside Jake saw was spending your day talking to "bus" people. That would be sad. Could a person shake his Starbucks cup at the Galleria? That would be better.)

And what happened to none of the above, anyway?

"You're like five thousand years old, right, Aunt Matilda?"

"Give or take a few thousand."

"What are you gonna be when you grow up?"

"A fireman. Didn't I already say that?"

Matilda should have her own show. Really. Jacob would co-host. *The Matilda and Jake Show*, right after *Regis and Kathy Lee*.

"Seriously, Jacob. It's different for women."

There's another guy on the top of Jacob's list—the different-for-women guy. Or maybe it was a girl who came up with that one. In either case, he or she had better watch his or her back. Don't use sexist pronouns. This was another rule. It was only different for girls when that gave them the edge, like when there weren't enough seats at "teen club." The Reverend Mom made Jake go to "teen club." It was her church and it wouldn't look good if her own teen didn't show up.

Jake, sit on the floor so these young ladies can have a seat.

Sit right here on my lap, honey. Slide around.

Jake came from a "Christian home" and wasn't allowed to say such things. When you sat on the floor you could see up the girls' skirts. Jake hated "teen club" anyway.

"A gentleman always needs a plan. That's what my father said. The one you're named after."

"And a lady doesn't?" All the ladies Jake knew had a plan. Jennifer Rose Shannon had plans to get inside his best friend Greg's pants. Everyone knew this. Katrina and Katrice had plans to move to California and become famous twin singer-actresses. They were ugly as posts.

"Society has always had different expectations. People talk about how much times have changed, but when you live thousands of years, as I have, you see things stay pretty much the same. Due to the fact of your gender, you are expected to support yourself and others, as well. You're expected to be responsible. And if a war comes along—and it most likely will—you'll be expected to go fight for your country. Just like your father did, Roderick. Many of you will die. So sad—all the young boys."

Sometimes Matilda called Jake "Roderick." That was okay. Jake had some names for her, too—some pet names—but Matilda wasn't a pet names kind of person. Like Big Rod or the Reverend Mom.

"I once considered joining the ballet. I was built for it, if you hadn't noticed. Tall and slender, with long legs and a strong straight back. At the time, in Washington, ballet classes did not cater to a colored clientele, so I set that dream aside. In this life one has to do such things."

"It's African American, Auntie. Know I'm saying?" Colored. That's what you did to Easter eggs.

"Or I might have been a botanist. Maybe I would have spent my life in the Amazon, searching out the exotic cousins of these beauties. Do you know, Jacob, that when I was your age, I let pass my opportunity to attend a university. Right where I grew up we had the premier colored institution in America. But here I am instead. Isn't that something?"

People were always trying to get Jake to go to some college or the other. Big Rod. The Reverend Mom. Chemistry II. Counseling. The other day Counseling had said, It's never too soon to start browsing these catalogs, my man. (My man. Everyone in America lived in a Wesley Snipes film.) You can write your own ticket . . . Then he read Jake's name off a three-by-five-inch card. Jake wrote his own ticket back to study hall.

"You could go to college now, Auntie. A mind is a terrible thing to waste, you know."

"I'll bet I could teach the course about my beauties here. Or about roses. Did you know that Christopher Columbus's crew fished roses from the sea and that's how they knew they had almost reached another shore?"

Did you know that a guy once found an entire rat inside a bottle of Coke? Or that there's this one girl who plays tennis who used to be a guy. She maybe had a singsong kind of name or maybe it was foreign. You know the one. It was on a TV movie, which is how come Jake knew. Maybe it was the actress who had the funny name.

Jake didn't know what Matilda's job had been. She retired from something, didn't she? Which tells you how interesting that was—spend most of your life doing some job, and it's so boring you don't even talk about it when you leave.

"See this violet? It could be named after me."

A Houseplant Named Matilda. A Tribe Called Quest. A Boy Named Sue.

"It's a hybrid. I created it. Notice the variegation on the leaf here, the subtle color pattern, that faint scalloping on the edge. The color of this blossom, that rich lavender. You could spend the rest of your life scouring the earth and you would never find another even remotely similar."

Greg had a cousin who had six toes on one foot and if you touched his hand on the side you could feel underneath the skin where they removed an extra finger. Jake maybe believed that was true. People were always making shit up. Tim Jamison had a third nipple. Everyone knew that. Matilda said she'd taken a nap on Eleanor Roosevelt's bed in the White House. Those beds saw a lot of action, that's for sure. Matilda's father, she said, had keys that opened secret doors in the United States capital. Sometimes Matilda said this shit like she really believed it, and sometimes you could tell she wanted to laugh. Like when she said she could make prime rib in her sleep. Jake hated prime rib. Prime rib was bloody. It was like taking a bite out of a live cow. Jake could make prime rib, too, though maybe not in his sleep. Coarse salt and a really hot oven, for starters.

"I was thinking of becoming a ski bum," he told his auntie—the same thing he said when he wanted to drive Big Rod crazy. He was kidding. It was cold in Colorado. Skiing hurt your ankles.

Matilda set the violets in the greenhouse window. Jake helped her install that window. Actually some guys with a truck installed it. The truck said Richarsdon Renovations. Jake watched. Matilda sat in the front room and sighed.

"I would have liked to have gone to the mountains myself. I've been reading lately about the mountain kingdom of Tibet. It must be an extraordinary place."

"Sara Jensen's thinking of becoming a Buddhist." Sara used a lot of words these days like "godhead" and "nirvana" and "koan." She said that since Jake already didn't eat meat, he might as well join the club.

"You surprise me, Jacob, knowing that Buddhism is associated with Tibet."

"I'm not as dumb as I look," Jake said. And World History actually talked about interesting shit now and then, like "Rock for Tibet." Jake wondered if he became a Buddhist would Sara Jensen give him some.

"To our project, shall we?"

Great. The project. A yawnfest, two thumbs down. Matilda spread her boxes of pictures and clippings on the dining room table.

"There's a story here," she said. She said that a lot. A scintillating saga of dust and mildew, narrated by the five-thousand-year-old woman. I'll write the theme song.

"I'll get us some Cokes." Jake brought Cokes from home. Matilda never had any. Matilda had tea and water and more tea and more water. Some days she had iced tea. Some days she put ice in it.

Good. No rats in this particular can.

"Did I ever tell you about this gentleman?" Matilda held up a picture of an old dude with white hair.

"Ain't that the dude on the rice box?" Jake hated plain rice but he liked fried rice, with shrimp. Shrimp wasn't really meat. Was it? It depended on whom you asked. It was one of those kinds of questions.

"We've discussed the use of the 'A' word in this house. This was my father's brother, Cyrus Housewright."

Cyrus Housewright was on a magazine picture. You could tell that. It was glossy, like the pages in *Vibe,* except it had turned yellow. Maybe it came from one of the first magazines ever or something.

"Cyrus became a lawyer, and very late in his life became one of the first Negroes in the Northeast to earn a judicial appointment."

"People of color, Auntie. Afro Americans. Where do you want me to paste Uncle Ben here?" Six scrapbooks and there was some sort of code that Jake didn't get, except that the white smaller book at the bottom of the pile was just him and his father and the dude with the *Soul Train* Afro, the one who didn't get talked about. David. That's what Jake would do! Write his own book: *Things That Don't Get Talked About*. He'd organize it by people and what they refused to talk about.

BIG ROD: If I'm so rich, why can't Jake have that new pair of Air Jordans? Also, sex and how I know it's not a good idea for you in particular.

ADVANCED ALGEBRA: Why do you need to know this?

THE REVEREND MOM: If there really is a God, then why did he allow babies to be born with their brains on the outside of their skulls? And: What's up with this Bosnia shit? (Also, see above, under "sex.")

THE GIRLS AT WEST HIGH: Giving Jake some.

KATRINA AND KATRICE: Get a bag—we're scaring small children!

"I had a letter here somewhere from his daughter, our cousin Julie. It arrived a number of years back. Let's put them together. Where did I file that?"

"We have cousins?" Chapter Six! All his life Jake never heard of any more Housewrights than Matilda, Grandpa Marty, Big Rod, and his sisters—the gruesome twosome.

"The family became estranged. You know how that goes."

Actually, Jake didn't.

"I wonder sometimes what became of these people. There was Julie and Joan Marie. And their brothers, Carl and Frank and Earl. Each of them had several children—at least according to Julie. By now there must be a couple of dozen grandchildren. Your age, I would guess, and younger."

Imagine: a room full of Housewrights. Jake had a hard enough time with the crowd on Grandma Evie's side. Let's not even talk about the Reverend Mom's clan.

"You wouldn't understand what it was like in Washington in those days. Fault lines tore through families, ripped them apart. People disappeared. Entire branches of families would just be gone."

Maybe Jake's fantasy was coming true. Back along the Housewright family tree, wise guys everywhere. He knew it. He'd always known it.

"Organized crime, right? Like the Corleones." Those were great videos. You could put those in and not have to get up for hours except to pee and change the tape. Jake could see it. His family as sort of a 1920s version of an NWA video.

"Skin color, Jacob."

Jake's stomach clutched.

"My father had fair skin. Like you and I."

Jake didn't want to hear this.

"Uncle Cyrus was dark . . . Well, no, not dark really, but darker. Like your grandmother's people."

Acorns. Weak tea. Coarse paper towels—the nonabsorbent kind in the boys' bathroom. Jake never noticed such things. The Reverend Mom said not to. Good people didn't pay attention to that, she said. Ignore those kids, they're just ignorant. God will judge. You're beautiful. One of God's creations.

"We didn't make the rules, Jacob. That's the way things were. Everyone made choices—your father included. My father, I mean. People had to make a living."

People have to make a living. People were always saying that to Jake. A boy like you can go places. So many advantages.

"They grew away from us, these people. The darker ones. It's ironic, isn't it? They're the ones who went away, and they're the ones who get Judge Housewright."

"Don't say the darker ones. Don't say that."

"Did I say that? I'm sorry. People survive, Jacob. Everything comes out all right in the end. I guess."

I can't believe your dad's black.

Your mom can't be white, brother.

Don't sit with them. Not if you want to sit with us.

"People are stupid."

Jake didn't see what the big deal was, why everything had to be such a big deal. People should just get along. Everyone said that.

No one acted that way. Not many anyway. Stupid people everywhere you went. Can I touch your hair?

"What do you want me to do? I'm not going to lie to you, Jacob. This is who we are, where we came from. Part of us are people who turned their back on others of us."

"That was dumb. This is dumb."

Jake shoved some pictures. He got some more Coke.

No rats in this can, either. Life was still good.

He went to the living room.

"May I have some of that?" Matilda had an empty glass with some ice. Sometimes Matilda had ice. "You can dissolve a nail in this. That's what I hear."

You can erase Lincoln's face off a penny, and there's a guy in Michigan somewhere who doesn't have a stomach because he drank a whole case every day. Also you could get high if you take five aspirins and chug a twelve-ounce can.

"I didn't mean to be insensitive. I went through some of the same things back in the Stone Age."

Marauding velociraptors. Seething volcanoes. Villages of racially confused Neanderthals. Or were they Cro-Magnon? You couldn't tell by looking, that's for sure. Who got to decide? Did it make a difference?

"Your father never forgave me, but then Martin was a man always sure of his convictions. I slathered his face with complexion cream."

"He's not my father. He's my grandfather. Did I tell you I decided to be a fireman?"

"Jacob. Of course. What did I say? You'll have to forgive me. I slept fitfully last night. This old brain. We'll have to order me a new one one of these days."

"That's okay. It's all right, Auntie." Jake felt bad. Don't yell at old people. Or babies. Or retarded kids. Maybe the Reverend Mom could get that added to the Ten Commandments. Amendments. That's what the world needed.

Thou shalt not deprive thy son of new Air Jordans.

Thou shalt adorn thy ugly daughters' heads with paper bags and thou shalt keep thine bags in place, and lo thou who removeth thine bags, he shall also die.

Thou shalt keep thine pantries stocked with plentiful snacks, and, yea, thine snacks shall be of the Nacho tribe.

Mixed-race boys have penises, too.

The last one needed some work.

"Promise me you won't tell the boys. Please."

The who? Oh, those boys. Grandpa Marty and Big Rod. Grandpa Marty and Big Rod were boys the same way that yogurt was food. You had to call it something. Eat some yogurt, Jake.

Please, Reverend Mom: Thou absolutely shalt not.

"We worry about you, Auntie."

Matilda waved her hand. "I'm fine. I just get tired. A couple of glasses of this poison, and I'll be fine."

This was probably true. Matilda took a slug. A couple of cold cans in the morning could carry you through an hour with Advanced Algebra, her husband, and several of the rest of her friends, too. Eat some food, the Reverend Mom ordered. As much as an invitation for a bowl of chips.

"You're a good boy, Jacob. A most remarkable boy, indeed."

"Let's finish your scrapbooks." Jake stuck his hand out. Aunt Matilda took it.

"Oh, I wish we could finish. I fear I'll never get it organized. So many pictures. So many stories."

"One page at a time." Hey, that was great! Sometimes Jake said great things. That should be the name of a new show on TV. *One Page at a Time*. The story of a normal teenager and his wacky family. Mariah Carey will star. Her wacky family. Mariah was like Jake. Everyone said that. To make him feel better. Mariah's that way, too. That's what they said. *That way*. Like six toes or a brain outside your skull.

"Maybe I can work as a scrapbook paster. I'm pretty good at this."

"Well, actually . . ." Matilda wiped at a white smear. She had eyes like a hawk. Brown eyes. Jake had brown eyes. When they weren't green. "The photo corners are self-pasting, remember."

Napoleon had hemorrhoids; when multiplying numbers with powers, add the exponents; Emily Dickinson poems can be sung to "The Yellow Rose of Texas." So much to remember. Sometimes Jake's brain hurt. So many rules to figure out.

Was shrimp meat and if it wasn't meat, what was it? Did three bags of Doritos count as three items or one in the six-items-or-less lane?

What could a person be in life if he didn't even know what he was?

"Well, what is it that you like to do, Jacob?"

Jake hadn't asked that out loud, had he?

A list of things Jake liked:

Doritos
Girls
Gangsta rap (East Coast)
Afternoon naps
Babies
Coke (rat-free)
Shrimp fried rice

"Nothing you'd get any money for." That's one thing Jake knew.

"Money isn't everything. You'll always have enough of that. You should care about the world, David. We talked about that."

Jake grabbed the white album.

"Tell me the story on this one." The one with the *Soul Train* Afro. That one was David. He wasn't David.

"Oh, yes. One time, around when your father and I first

started the catering business, we'd gone to farmer's market to buy eggs. Martin made the mistake of pulling the wrong egg from the display. If it hadn't been for me—"

"Martin's not my father." Jake held out his hand. "Come and lie down. Please, Auntie?"

"I didn't say Martin. Did I? I know that. I know these things."

"I know what you know. Come on, Auntie. Come lie down." Jake was scared. This was scary. What did you do about stuff like this? Was he asleep when they talked about this in class? What class would that have been?

"You better remember all of this, Jake. I'm forgetting it so fast myself."

She should lie down. That was the best, he thought. "Come on. We'll work on them next week. We will. I'll help you. I will."

Jake would. Jake would help. That was something he could do.

III

2000

Cats are licking him. Scratchy wet tongues across his forehead and cheeks, up and down each side of his neck.

"You owe me for another set of sheets."

Talking cats.

Matilda. Matilda's house.

Jacob doesn't know how he got here.

He remembers yesterday. Parts of it, part of a party.

Swallowed things. Inhaled things. Music. Noise. People.

They say when you start blacking out, that's when you know you're in trouble.

Blacking out. There was an expression for you. Another one of those sayings people were always saying.

(Why wasn't it "whiting out"?)

(Or maybe, in his case, graying out.)

(That was a Jake Joke.)

Jake stills Matilda's hand. Moans.

"Back in the world, are we?"

His tongue tastes of dirty ashtrays and ripe soft cheese.

"No lectures, please."

Matilda feigns innocence. His auntie! Sanctimonious! Never!

"Drink this," she orders. She supports the back of his head with a spotted old hand. Jake feels a tremor in the still-strong fingers.

The ice water irritates and soothes at the same time. The coldness trickles from the corner of his mouth and down onto his chest.

Matilda caresses his face. Jake looks away.

"I know," she says.

Jake wishes he knew. He rolls up, gets his bearings. His head falls between his knees. The head, the hair: all of it weighs a thousand pounds.

He is in the room she calls David's room. He must have at least been walking when he arrived—can't imagine the old girl carrying him up the steps.

"Is my car . . . ?"

Matilda shakes her head, not, he knows, to indicate "no," rather to stop his absurd inquiry in its tracks.

The car might be anywhere. He remembers . . . well, of yesterday he remembers nothing.

"What can I do?" Matilda asks. No pathos or impotence in her voice. Just give her a task.

"I'm sorry. I shouldn't have come."

"You can always come here. It's our home."

That both is and isn't true, he thinks.

He says, "It isn't your job."

"Someday you'll pay me back. Come on down when you're ready. Call me if you need me."

Jake rolls back on the bed, tries to remember. What yesterday was, what was the occasion, why he ended up here, again. How he'd ended up here in the same way he'd ended up here so many times in the past. No answers come. It doesn't matter anyway.

Some party he was at. What else could the answer be? Same as the last party before it—last month, last week, or yesterday.

How many times had he ended up here—that's how he should count it. Leaving out the times he'd ended up on the floor of some warehouse or in the bed of someone whose name he either didn't know or couldn't remember and whom he hadn't seen before nor since. An alley, once. The backseat of a car.

In his own house, until Katrina or Katrice (one of them or both, it didn't matter which) told him they would "no longer enable his abusing himself in this manner," several hundred dollars' worth of beads and extensions thrown noisily and dramatically over the shoulder—in the same way as the character she no doubt imitated, from a "very special" episode of whichever sitcom she had cribbed the speech from.

Showered and as shaved as he ever gets, the previous day's outfit replaced by other clothes, clean ones. He vaguely recalls these replacements belonging to him. From last time. Or the time before.

He finds Matilda down in her breakfast room.

"Dashing," she says. "Sort of Chiquita Banana meets the Sheik of Araby."

Jacob doesn't know any Chiquitas or Arabys, but figures she's referring to the towel into which he's wrapped his dreads. The towel, he decides, has soaked up enough of the moisture from his hair. He releases his locks from the pink terry cloth, feels the damp tendrils spilling over his shoulders and down the back of his neck. Matilda reaches out and fingers one of the ropes.

"Fascinating," she says. Not a criticism. She's never seen anything like this. She has told him this many times. She examines his hair as if it were an exotic blossom or some new variety of seed for the garden: gold, black, and red spun together like yarn. She does this often. Jake doesn't mind.

On the table are a variety of cold foods: fresh and dried fruit, cereal, breads and muffins, cheeses. Jake snatches off a cluster of grapes, out of habit more than anything else. He doesn't know if he's hungry or not, or if his stomach can even manage food.

"Help yourself," she encourages. "I can make you something warm if you like. Just ask."

"Thanks," he responds. The pulpy sweet grapes cloy. Part of him wants an omelet, another part would be happy never seeing another egg in his life.

I am destroying myself, he thinks.

Matilda gathers her gloves and a trowel and heads off to the garden.

Jake drops his head into his folded arms. He has been burning hard going on two months. Get up. Go party. Crash. Repeat.

"The boy's just finding his niche. You know these creative types." This is what the Reverend Mom says. "He's always been artistic," she adds, homage, no doubt, to a wild finger-painting phase back in his first decade of life. The Reverend Mom believes from the depths of her soul that all persons are good and have a purpose in God's scheme. She leaves in conspicuous places—on his bed, taped to his bathroom mirror—brochures for alternative colleges and adventure travel, treatment programs in the guise of art camp. The wide eyes of her enthusiasm betray her thinly veiled panic and fear.

"You'll be okay, honey," she says. "You just need to find your niche." She cuts her losses. She focuses on beads and braids and ballet for the girls. A long shot (in his book), but better odds than he promises.

"Niche my ass." This is what Big Rod says, but he says it in mumbles, under his breath, avoiding the eyes and ears of his son and his daughters and his wife. Jake numbs his father. He knows this is true. What, after all, does the successful businessman of the universe do with a gangly yellow thing with twisted raggedy hair and a bad attitude?

He passes his son to his father.

"The old man needs a server. Can you pitch in?" Big Rod makes these offers on the fly. Big Rod is always on the fly.

"Anything for Grandpa Marty."

Anything for Grandpa Marty.

Grandpa Marty fusses at Jake's tux and uses a leather tie to gather the dreads in a neat collection behind his back. "If I were the father . . ." he mumbles, clicking his tongue and shaking his head. This one's all starch and structure.

"Straighten your back, young man," the old man orders. "Say 'yes, sir' and 'yes, ma'am' to our guests. Keep your eyes to your business."

Jake deals out the plates of old Marty's special chicken dish and of roasted pork tenderloin and of bloody prime rib. The older "guests" eye him with fear or contempt or pity.

"You're focusing on an education, I hope," the livelier ones prompt.

"Pardon, sir?" Jake replies. One did not engage the clients' inquiries—one only asked after their comfort.

The younger "guests" flirted. The women. The men, too, sometimes. How's it going? they'd say. Nice earrings, they'd say. Jake forgot to remove his metal sometimes. Grandpa Marty didn't tolerate metal on his men.

"A little polish, a little discipline, I daresay you'd make into something halfway decent." The sort of thing Grandpa Marty said while handing him his tips.

Gee, thanks, Gramps.

Grandpa Marty had Big Rod's number dialed before Jake cleared the door, ready to lecture and hector and order his son to take the boy in hand. Jake knows this is true. Jake's been known to blow those tips before the phone got cold again.

He returns the cold cuts and milk to Matilda's refrigerator. Kitchen hygiene: a Housewright reflex. He spies green plastic lawn bags on the counter. He takes them out to his great-aunt.

"I was wondering where those got to." She snaps one open and bends to gather trimmings from the trellis.

"Let me," he offers. He can hear her bones popping as she straightens and returns to her shears.

"I've been thinking of pulling this wisteria out of here. Gnarled old thing. Just a little too woody for my taste down here at the roots."

Jacob shrugs. It looks fine to him. It has been here as long as he can remember. He stuffs another handful of trimmings into the bag. The sun feels good, as does the fresh air. Bending and raking have set his blood on the move. The Reverend Mom would have some comment about the "clearing of toxins." She'd offer something green and pulpy from her blender.

Are moving poisons better than stagnant ones?

He feels better.

So, they must be.

"One thing about this garden: there is always something to do." Matilda lowers herself gently to one of her benches. She dabs at her forehead with a handkerchief. A mild day, yet she's worked up some perspiration.

"You work too hard, Auntie."

She waves that off with her hand.

"You know you do. Fussing around in that house. Out here in this yard." Jake plops himself on the bench next to her.

He jokes, "You should take a lesson from me and live the easy life."

Matilda looks him in the eyes as if she's giving his suggestion some serious consideration.

Then she asks, "Why are you so unhappy?"

Queen of the non sequitur.

Jake feels the question like a knife in the gut. He shakes his head, shaking the question away.

"I'm okay," he says quietly.

"If you say so." She rises and heads to a stand of daylilies, begins pinching and fussing at some withered blooms. Jacob follows with the clippings bag.

"As for me," she says, "today is a good day. I remember who I am and who you are. I haven't referred to you once by your father's name or your uncle's name; at least I don't recall that I have. I remember my secret recipe for fertilizing the African violets and that I still have to mend the hem of the comforter in your room.

"My bones don't hurt so much today. My joints all seem to be pulling in the same direction, the way one prefers them to. That pain I sometimes feel in my lower spine, the one that feels like a hot burning iron, is blessedly absent. I even have a bit of an appetite.

"Tomorrow I might be calling you David. Tomorrow I just might turn on the radio expecting to hear Arthur Godfrey. It's almost certain I'll be in enough pain to send a normal woman to the insane asylum.

"You, Jacob, are the most unhappy of all my boys."

A sound emits from Jake like he's been punched in the stomach.

"If you want, you could always talk to me. You know that, don't you? Just make sure and catch me on my good days."

He nods. He doesn't feel unhappy as much as he just doesn't feel anything at all anymore. Doesn't care to. Can't. Won't.

"You were such a contented little one. All my boys were. Even your father. Happy, but ornery, that Roderick."

Jake cannot even giggle along with her.

"That Roderick. That boy, from the first day I met him he had money on the brain, your father did. That's one thing I'll say for my Roderick: he always knew what he wanted. Never one minute of doubt."

That truth spins Jake deep.

"I remember one time your father came strutting in here sporting some brand new calfskin wallet he'd just bought himself. The thing must have cost a pretty penny, even back then. Soft brown leather. A beautiful thing, if you must know. Your father spent the entire day trying to find reasons to flash that thing in my face. Tried to give me stamps, to show me pictures of his friends, to show me his new library card—any excuse to flourish it from his back pocket. Charming. Crass and pretentious. But charming all the same. I don't even think he was a teenager then."

These days men like Jake's father never touched real money. Money was electronic blips on the computer screen, assorted figures arrayed on balance sheets.

"I wonder, Jacob, seriously, do you think that all that success has made your father happy?"

"Yes," he replies. No hesitation.

"You really believe that?"

Jake had no doubt. Roderick Housewright had everything in the world he wanted and needed—got more of it as every day went by. His father, he knew, was the most satisfied man on the face of the earth. Except for one thing.

"Ask him if you don't believe me. There's only thing in the world he wants that he doesn't have."

"And that would be?" Even Matilda seems surprised that her nephew wanted for anything.

"A different son." Jake hated the self-pity he'd just heard himself utter. He'd outrun self-pity years ago. Ironic detachment, simmering rage, smug New Age enlightenment: He'd outrun all of those, too, for that matter. He'd long been southbound on the express to the sort of places where it's too dark to read the catchy nomenclature.

"I'm sure all Roderick wants is for the one he already has to be happier. That's all."

That's all, huh? It was that easy?

"Fine, then," he says. "Fine, then, Auntie. If that's all it takes, tell me then. Tell me where he can buy some of this happy and we'll run out and get a gallon right now." He drops the plastic bag and stalks off into the house.

He should go—somewhere.

There isn't anywhere. Nowhere he's wanted. Nowhere he's needed.

No way to get there if there were such a place.

Matilda eases up behind him, all whispers and soft breath.

"Have I said the wrong thing? I'll apologize if I have." She rubs lotion into her hands that have been working so hard.

"Thank you for storing away the food," she adds.

Jake shrugs.

He says, "You make *happy* sound like it was something you picked up at the mall."

"Happy's something that people choose."

"Like this chair or this one." Jake plopped himself down in the softer of the two.

"Or hot tea or iced," she said, handing him the latter.

"Or black or white," he said, bitterness dripping like the condensation on his glass. "There's a choice for you." He toasted her and then swallowed half of the cold sweet liquid.

Black or white. White or black.

He'd tried one, the other, neither, both.

Back in grade school no one cared. They were all just kids on the playground, wild and stupid and dumb. Ah, for the good old days.

Then it's high school, and now you have to pick. This table or that one. Sitting with the white kids or sitting by yourself. Hanging with the homeys or hanging yourself from the nearest light fixture.

"That Jacob, he's so cool. He's hardly like the black kids. He's almost just like us, just like a regular person."

"Hey, Jake, you know me and my friends were like listening to that song 'Back That Thing Up.' We really like that."

"Kris says you're sort of cute and everything, but, like, she thinks as far as going out and all that, people should stick to their own kind. But she likes you as a friend and all that."

Or

"You gonna sit here, you need to stop acting white and stuff. I'm serious. Why you talk like that anyway? Think you better than me?"

"Can't stand them white m.f.s. If my moms was white, I'd move her ass out."

"You nice looking and all, even if you . . . you know the way you are. But, I mean, you know, if I wanted to go out with a white boy . . ."

Or

"You know how it be. I don't hang with them other white girls. I only date the brothers. You a brother, right? You are, aren't you?"

Or

"We are so glad our Sheldon has friends of other cultures. His father and I marched in the sixties, you know."

Or

"Wow, you are so not like other guys. You're like some sort of exotic butterfly. You're not black or anything, are you?"

Or

"Dude, swallow a couple or three of these," and Jake did, and then he swallowed a couple or three more. Often he did. Sometimes, but not often enough, he could forget all the chatter and all the falseness and all of the dead ends.

Sometimes he would think, yes, this is someone who sees me for myself. Like the new girl from out west who he met at the coffee shop. A California girl. Free, open. She had seen a lot.

She liked guys who were different.

"You're an artist," she said. She liked artists. She wrote poems herself.

"Most of these suburban guys—yuck!" she said. She gagged.

She wrote poems about sunshine and about painting the Golden Gate.

They spent a Sunday in the zoo. Holding hands, eating dumb kid food that came in loud colors and stained your tongue. They stared down the people who stared at them.

"Take a picture, it'll last longer," she said.

They made up names for the animals.

Gorzinkulas.

Snaderlitches.

Retumbulas.

They watched some boys jump the turnstile and scatter wild up into the park.

"Why do they act that way?" she asked.

They?

"Dumb kids," he said.

"You don't see the other kids doing it."

Oh, *that* "they," he thinks.

"I guess they can't help it. I guess that's how they're raised," she says.

No doubt. That "they." Again.

Does she see me? he wondered. Does she know who I am?

He wants to cry. He wants to scream. He wants to jump the turnstiles himself.

Instead, he says good-bye to California.

He takes some pills. He takes more. And then he takes some more after that.

The people with the pills, they don't care about "they." They don't care about anything.

The pills are good. They cover up the pimples and hide the fat thighs and make up for the lack of breasts and social skills. They render the welts on your back from your father's belt buckle invisible.

The people with the pills don't have names. Or they do have names, but the names change and they aren't real names in the first place.

Bongboy

Juicegirl

Monk

Lid

Screed

Jake is "Marley." When he is anything.

"I'm afraid we've never had a choice," she says, breaking his reverie.

"Meaning?"

"Meaning, I think, that our lots were drawn."

Jake scoffs. He could use a hit right about now.

"We were put here. We were brought here. And here we are. What's wrong with accepting your fate?"

Jake cringes.

"But I'm different than you," he says. "Different than my father. Different than your brother."

"Maybe you only want to believe that you are."

"But everybody says—"

"Everybody isn't us. Everybody isn't you."

Jake finds himself melting into the soft chair. The air around him thickens and presses at his lungs.

Maybe she was right. Maybe the game was fixed.

"I'm drowning," he says.

"It's okay. I'm here."

"Can I stay here?"

"For as long as you need."

And so he does.

He sleeps.

They eat.

They garden.

He sleeps.

She wakes in pain. He helps if he can.

He sleeps.

They eat.

Sometimes it is he who wakes up screaming.

She comforts.

Why do you take care of me so good?

It's what we do. It's what you do if you're a Housewright.

Why?

It's what we do. It's what we've always done. And anyway, I may need you to take care of me someday.

You can count on me.

I already know that.

IV

2003

The family had a legend. It went like this:

Jake's great-aunt Matilda had a shelf in her basement where she stored the pickled remains of babies that she kidnapped from strollers outside the Fashion Bug store on the Rock Road. Supposedly the parents of the unlucky infants were too busy browsing the "Under $10, Must Go Now!" racks to have noticed the distinguished-looking, if clearly old-fashioned, grandmotherly person bending over and cooing at their precious angels. And while a person had to feel sorry for the innocent children, those bargain-hungry and neglectful mothers would roast in hell on special rotisseries designed just for them.

Everybody in Jake's family had stories about her. This one or that one; equally as horrid or bizarre or strange. Jake never understood why. He figures the primary purpose of these stories was to instill in the youngest members of the family a proper and healthy respect for their eccentric maiden aunt.

Jake remembers last Christmas, when one of his cousins on his mother's side bounced a toddler on his knee and, pointing to the old lady in the ladder-back chair, whispered in the child's ear. Jake doesn't know what he said. Maybe he said, "There's a nice old lady." Maybe he said, "Stay away from that one." All he knows is that the boy's eyes had grown wide, and for the rest of the afternoon and into the evening, the little one had walked a wide circle around the dear woman.

Jake knows that there are no pickled baby remains displayed on shelves in her basement or, for that matter, in any of the other rooms of her elegant home. Where would they come from? She leaves the house only on holidays and then only then to spend the minimally socially acceptable time sitting at Big Rod and the Reverend Mom's house.

And, anyway, she didn't believe in putting up fruit.

"Enough fine companies make a good jelly, there's no call these days to stew in one's kitchen like a scullery maid." So, there.

She said that to him. She says lots of things like that. Or used to. Not so much for a while. That makes Jake sad. No crying, he reminds himself. He promised.

Do your part, she said. I'll do mine.

Jake said, Okay.

He wonders if he should serve jelly on the tray.

Jake's Part

. . .

Jake makes the tea the Housewright way:

We start clean. Scrub, if necessary, then rinse thoroughly the kettle, the teapot, creamer, and each cup, saucer, plate, and utensil. Dry thoroughly with a lint-free cloth.

Jake checks the kettle for scale. (Discard rime-encrusted teakettles. This is not an option.)

Jake fills the kettle with distilled water. Distilled water is best. Everyone knows this. He sets the kettle over a low flame. A "soft" boil—that's all you're looking for.

While the water comes to temperature, he fills the sugar bowl. (Unless the sugar has hardened or tainted, there is no need to discard the previous contents.)

(Matilda doesn't take sugar in her tea, but that's beside the point.)

He readies the infuser. Tea bags are an abomination. From his backpack he retrieves a can of Darjeeling, direct from the importer Grandpa Marty uses. Housewrights prefer your darker teas. The dry leaves crackle as he sprinkles them from the package, and the air fills with their sweet and pungent scent.

Housewright Maxim #37: If you can't smell it, you probably won't be tasting it, either.

Jake crumbles the leaves onto a square of muslin. He folds the corners carefully and ties the pouch with a bow made from another strip of muslin. He leaves one string long enough to hang from the edge of the teapot. Care in this step avoids bitter and stubbly dregs. No one, after all, will be reading fortunes here today.

Just before the kettle whistles he removes the water from the fire. Then—and this is important—he immediately rinses the inside of the teapot with hot water. This prepares the vessel for brewing, keeps the water to temperature.

Jake places the muslin pouch in the teapot and then slowly, carefully, fills the teapot with water. He wraps the teapot in the same linen napkin he will use to serve the tea (nothing so fussy as a tea "cozy" in this family). While the tea steeps (five minutes max), he goes to check on Matilda.

"Which do you prefer?" she asks, holding up two dresses. She says the words slow so as not to slur them.

"Your father bought me this one. He liked to see me in it." Big Rod's dress shakes like she's found bugs on it, and the other one falls to the floor. She inhales sharply. She's gotten so bad. Maybe it *is* time.

He runs to assist her.

"Please," she says, pushing him away, but feebly. "I can do it. Just get our tea. Time's a-wasting."

Jake finds his way to the kitchen. He can hardly stand.

How can he be doing this?

Because this is what Housewrights do.

He tried to tell them. His father. His grandfather.

She's just old and ornery.

See what the doctor says.

She wouldn't see any doctor. She's doing this her way.

This is the way Housewrights do things.

Had he been sent that particular memo?

He isn't strong enough for this.

His watch vibrates. The time is up.

Time is almost up.

Remove the pouch from the teapot—be careful in case the pouch has opened up.

Discard the contents of the pouch. (Persons of questionable training might consider a second brew. Housewrights were not such people.)

Place the teapot on a tray. Whereupon you have already arranged wedges of lemon and a platter of scones. Marmalade and soft butter.

(Neither of you takes lemon or the cream that you retrieve from the refrigerator. But this is beside the point.)

(Neither of you will eat.) (Ditto.)

"Help me, please," Matilda slurs. She has managed to pull the dress over her head and arrange the front of it. She cannot handle the zipper.

Jake places the tea on the bed tray. He helps her finish dressing. Two of her could fit into that dress.

Matilda slides herself up onto her bed. Jake notices the sheets have been changed to her favorite linen. Pale cream. She almost shines against them. The bedding smells sweet.

"Now," she says, smiling. "We'll have our tea."

How often they have had tea this way in the afternoon. So civilized. That's what she always says. A time to sit quietly and reflect and enjoy a comforting beverage. A time for warm conversation, cozy silences.

"Why don't you pour for us?" she asks, her overture a charming counterpoint to her inability to handle the task to her own exacting standards.

"I'd love to," Jake says. It's tearing him up, but he's doing all he can to pretend that this is just another afternoon. He pours them each a cup. Three-quarters full: That's the standard.

"Lovely," she coos.

Jake bites his lower lip.

"Do me a favor, my love: I believe I've misplaced the antimacassar for the chair you're sitting in. Check that top dresser drawer, would you."

Jake opens the drawer. He doesn't know what an antimacassar is, knows that even here at her lowest there is nothing she could have possibly misplaced. His duty: to turn his back. To allow her to do what needs to be done. He listens to the delicate click of silver against porcelain, her vigorous stirring.

(Does it dissolve? Will it be bitter?)

"Perhaps not," she says, and he thinks she's read his mind. She reads minds. Everyone knows this. But, no, she only means that she has finished doing her part. Just the way they talked about it. He can turn around again.

An involuntary spasm seizes him, a gasp and a shudder. He's losing it. He promised he wouldn't.

"Jacob," she barks. Harsh. A warning.

Then, "Come and enjoy our tea." As sweet as her tea is not, that's the way she says it.

He pulls it together.

She sips, does not grimace.

"Darjeeling," she enthuses. "We Housewrights prefer a black tea."

Everyone knows this.

She relaxes her shoulders.

(Does she always do this during tea?)

(Yes, always!) (But why this hope?)

He moves to the edge of the bed, grabs her hand.

"Jacob. My best boy." She smiles. She reaches for a rope of his hair.

He will hold it together. He will. He promised.

"I should tell you this," she says. "Maybe I was wrong about something."

"That's okay."

What does it matter now?

"No, I should tell you this."

"Okay, Auntie. I'm listening."

"David. Do you remember what I said to you one time? About the choices we make in life. About happiness? Maybe I was wrong. Maybe I was altogether the wrong person to ask. I've been a coward, I think."

Jake kisses her on the cheek. She is so beautiful.

She says, "I used to believe things, but I don't know anymore. What if somewhere back in time someone got it wrong? What if lots of folks got it wrong? What if maybe all these masses of humanity made a few really bad, wrong turns? Did you ever stop to think about that?"

"Auntie," he says. "Doubting your fellow man?" He reaches to take her teacup. She can no longer hold it in her hand.

"But all in all, we've done pretty well, don't you think? Our Housewrights."

He concurs. He isn't sure always, but she has always been right before.

"Maybe, Jacob, the key word isn't '*or.*' Maybe it's all about '*and.*'" Her voice is thin. "Don't you think?"

"I do think," he says. "Great minds think alike, huh?"

She smiles.

Later, he will return the tea service to the kitchen. Everything must be cleaned just the way she likes it, each item stowed in its proper place. What kind of place did he think she was running around here, anyway? People would be coming around. One did not receive visitors to a messy home.

He will call his father first.

"Dad," he will say, and because he did not ever call his father "Dad," and because his father would hear it in his voice, Roderick will say, "Oh, Jesus," and Jake will hear him drop the phone. He will need Jake's help with all of this. This is something Jake can do.

"You tell Grandpa, okay? Okay, Dad?"

Grandpa Marty. The man who would see the beginning and end of this life. How could he bear it?

"Jake?" his father will say, but he doesn't really have anything to ask.

"It's okay, Dad. You go get Grandpa. It's okay." Jake will say this, and his father will say "okay."

Jake will arrange her room the way she would like it. He'll arrange cut flowers from her garden in crystal vases—the heavy leaded ones you can't even buy anymore. Three vases of flowers, enough to scent the air and be pretty, but not enough to be vulgar or anything. On her nightstand he'll place the hybrid violet that should bear her name.

He'll smooth the sheets so they are crisp-looking and welcoming. That is how she likes them, and he'll arrange the pillows, the comforter. He'll arrange the draperies just so. One didn't want to fade the rugs, after all.

He will go down and sit on the steps, down in front of the

front door. Now and again he will break down and bawl like a baby, but he will try to remember that he promised to be strong. He will sit there on the steps and wait for the rest of her boys to arrive.

For now, he leans in close to her.

"Yes," he says. "*And*. Never maybe. Always sure. Just the same way you taught us."

He tells her about a girl in his drawing class at the college of design. Her mother is Japanese and her father is Mexican, if you can imagine that—and they have another friend who is Swedish-Nigerian, a Norse god with dreadlocks blonder than Jake's. And there are others.

There is a whole tribe of us. We're going to do it our way from here on out.

Matilda squeezes his hand.

Can you imagine what our children will be like? I can only barely imagine it myself. They will have left all the rest of this behind. What he thinks he sees in her eyes is the hope that this might come true.

He tells her about his art classes and how he plans to be famous one day, maybe.

I think I'm pretty good. People like my stuff. I'll show you sometime.

Her eyes close. She can see the painting of herself that he will create someday, the famous one that will hang in New York City. It won't be a portrait exactly. More abstract than that. But people who walk past it will know that it is formidable.

He brushes her hair behind her ear.

He tells her what he plans to do with the garden, reminds her it's time to put in the fall annuals.

You're sure we can't have those purple mums this year? They're not so trashy, at least I don't think so. I use that color a lot in my work. That faded kind of purple. I was thinking maybe we could put them up along the front walk this year—replace the petunias for once. I know you like to keep those old petunias out there, but the ones we got this year turned leggy. Big Rod had his eye on this oak-leaf hydrangea for the back. I told him what you said about dark red leaves, but he says he thinks it will work. Maybe we should try it. I don't know. Maybe a lot of color *is* vulgar.

He keeps talking.

Jake and his auntie will talk this way for the rest of his life.

One Last Thing

. . .

There's one other thing I wanted you to know, and I promise not to take too long. I blanch at the idea of being one of those tiresome souls who goes on forever, but there's just this other small thing.

I wanted you to know that for the most part I have been a happy person.

I understand that it may often have appeared otherwise, but all the same, I was. Happy, that is.

I made my own choices, and I always did what I wanted to do. I always understood the alternatives.

And I think I made the right ones.

Or at the very least I've never chosen regret.

Back in high school we read a poem. I'm sure you are familiar with it. There was a line in the poem. "They also serve who only stand and wait." Milton, I think, but you know us Housewrights, we never were much for the great books. (Though any good household has a set on display, as I'm sure you yourself do.) Milton was blind when he wrote that poem.

In any case, that poem, or that line from that poem, the line about the people who serve, I've never given it much thought, to tell you the truth, and for the life of me I couldn't begin to tell you what exactly it's supposed to have meant. But even so, even despite my ignorance about such things, every time I heard those words repeated I always assumed they must have had something to do with me.

About the Author

David Haynes teaches creative writing at Southern Methodist University in Texas and in the Warren Wilson College MFA Program for Writers. Named one of America's best young novelists by *Granta*, Haynes has had his short stories recorded for National Public Radio's *Selected Shorts*. He is the author of several critically acclaimed novels, including *All American Dream Dolls*, *Live at Five*, and *Somebody Else's Mama*.